THE CROWD

a novel about fitting in and standing out

ALLEECE BALTS

For the original boy with hot chocolate,
with all my love

CONTENTS

The LORD is my strength and my song;
he has given me victory.

Psalm 118:14 NLT

Courage is more exhilarating than fear and in the long run it is easier.
We do not have to become heroes overnight.
Just a step at a time, meeting each thing that comes up,
seeing it is not as dreadful as it appears,
discovering we have the strength to stare it down.

Eleanor Roosevelt

PROLOGUE

The cab driver glanced in his rear view mirror as the taxi slowed to a stop. A girl of about seventeen sat hunched in the back seat. He couldn't tell if she was awake or dozing, but as the light turned green and the car accelerated, the exhaust pipe backfired and the girl jumped, tugging the headphones from her ears.

"You okay back there, kid?"

"It's Ella," the girl reiterated softly for what seemed like the hundredth time in as many miles. "I'm fine," she managed and pursed her lips together.

She looked from the back of the driver's head to her window where the trees were rushing by, but the sight made her queasy and she lowered her gaze, silently tallying the stains on the seatback in front of her.

"Is it much farther?"

"At least another hour," he replied brusquely, "but tell me if you're gonna be sick again and I'll pull over."

The driver squinted back at her through the mirror once more. The girl wore a short-brimmed newsboy cap and under the cap, trailing over her shoulder was a braid of thick, black hair. The hat obscured her eyes, but her skin appeared nearly as pale as her lace-trimmed white shirt and at the moment was tinged a delicate green.

"I'm fine," she repeated, more convincingly this time. "It's not the car. Just a nervous stomach. I wish I could get in touch with my aunt. I don't have a key, so if she isn't at home when I get there..."

Ella trailed off, staring at the single name and address printed on the creased sheet of paper in her hands. Meg Keller. 324 Hemlock Terrace, Whitfield, Vermont. She folded the page in half, rotated it, and folded it another time, again and again until the sheet was a dense, crumpled square. She dropped it on the seat next to her.

Meg Keller. Her only aunt had once been special, but was little more than a name to her now. A signature on a drawer full of old birthday cards.

Ella's stomach tightened into a knot but relaxed while her fingers traced the outline of a worn patch on the seat.

Spending a year with an absolute stranger was worth it if it meant attending the most prestigious school in the United States, she reminded herself. Worth moving away from home. *Not that it was much like home now with Mom and Mal both gone.* Worth leaving her friends her senior year. *Not that there were so many friends to leave behind.*

"I just wish I could get in touch with my aunt."

The driver's gruff voice softened. "Nothing to worry about. I'll bet she'll be waiting at the door to meet you," he reassured her, reaching toward the dashboard. "Hey, kid, do you mind if I turn this song up? It's a classic."

He looked back to see her nod, but missed the secret smile that spread across her face as a familiar voice came on the radio. Leaning back against the headrest, Ella closed her eyes to listen. She was nearly asleep when the taxi backfired again.

1. AN ARRIVAL

Meg Keller looked up sharply from her knitting. A sudden sound like a gunshot a few miles off had ripped through the sleepy afternoon silence. Gently, she shook her head and attempted to soothe her rumpled nerves before raising her knitting needles once again. Long since reformed from a wild youth, she had grown accustomed to stillness in her middle age. The town of Whitfield, nestled at the foot of a mountain in southwestern Vermont, was an ideally tranquil spot.

Meg lived at the edge of Whitfield, down a long lane that had only been paved in the last three years, and over one of the county's five quaint covered bridges. Every summer the town was overrun by tourists whose population peaked over the Fourth of July and trailed off as the August humidity set in. The first week in July, visitors began venturing from the candy shops and antique stores in town out to her quiet country lane for photographs of the historic old bridge. In vain, Meg would shut the windows and close the blinds to block out the murmur of voices and rumble of engines. But the days were growing shorter and cooler now. The tourists had flown and — although it was not yet autumn — it seemed the little town had already settled down for its proverbial long winter's nap.

The only cars to pass by the house now were those of the three neighbors on the street and the instructors at the private boarding school at the end of the lane — Whitfield's sole claim to fame — and those were seen but seldom. Meg could sit in the kitchen near the sunny window and neither see nor hear another soul for hours, especially during these lazy summer days.

As Meg rested there this particular August afternoon, she paused to massage her arthritic hands. She was a small woman, with a lean figure and surprisingly graceful limbs. Her recently greying hair was pulled back into a smooth bun, but a few wisps had escaped and were curling in the thick humidity. She tucked a loose ringlet behind her ear, and picked up the ball of green yarn resting in her lap and the wooden needles she always had close by, like a child with a favorite blanket.

A roaring engine approached the house, and a squeak from the brakes reverberated through the neighborhood. Meg hoisted herself out of the hard chair, and glancing out the window, spotted a dull yellow taxi parked in her driveway.

By the time she reached the front door, the driver was slamming the trunk shut with his elbow, a suitcase in each hand.

"Wait! What —?" she sputtered, flinging open the screen door. On the porch, she nearly tumbled over a bulging blue duffel bag.

"I'm gonna need the last fifty dollars, ma'am," barked the driver, stepping forward with the last two suitcases.

"Excuse me?"

"Round trip from Albany. The fare is two hundred fifty dollars," he added, "and that's a good rate."

"I'm sorry," Meg stammered. "I'm afraid you must have the wrong address."

"I don't think so." He pulled a crumpled half-sheet of paper from his back pocket. "Three twenty-four Hemlock Terrace. That's you, right?"

"Yes, but —"

"And you must be," he said, looking down at the sheet, "Meg Keller."

"I am. But I don't see —"

4

"Your niece already paid the two hundred, and she told me you'd pay the rest when I dropped off her bags."

"My niece?" Meg asked skeptically. "Ella? I don't understand. Where is she?"

"She said she had a meeting at that school down the way, and she'd walk here after."

"Yes, I know she's going to the school, but what are these bags?"

"Look, ma'am, I don't know. The girl only told me she was going to that school but needed her stuff left here and you'd pay the last fifty."

Meg stood rooted to the porch.

"The meter's running, ma'am."

Though her brain lingered in a cloud of confusion, Meg's legs seemed to move of their own accord and she stepped inside the house to retrieve her purse.

A short distance away, Ella peered through a high iron gate. Her face – lifted to the sprawling brick building – was slender, the nose and cheeks slightly freckled below wide eyes, which were grey with flecks of emerald that flashed to life when her emotions were heightened.

Her eyes appeared very green indeed as she took in the prospect beyond the gate. Perfectly trimmed hedges lined the school grounds. Far off, she could only just see the boarding house with a long row of windows gleaming in the fading afternoon light. Though she had studied the school's website assiduously, Ella hadn't paid much attention to the description of the boarding house. Since she wouldn't be living there, it hadn't seemed important at the time. But now a sudden curiosity gripped her and she strained her eyes to make out the building in the distance.

She was recalled from her scrutiny by a voice, and turned to see a young woman approaching her from the ivy-covered main building. She wore a short sleeve, black sweater and her pinstripe pencil skirt fell gracefully about her knees as she strode slowly along the path.

"Eleanor Parker, I presume?" the woman inquired, as she reached the gate. Her dark blonde hair lay loosely about her face, which looked fresh and youthful apart from the deep circles under her eyes.

5

"I'm Ms. Walsh. I believe you'll be a member of my World History course next week."

"Please call me Ella. Most people do," she responded, snatching the cap from her head and smoothing her own untidy skirt as she stepped through the massive gate and shook hands. "I'm so sorry. I hope you haven't been waiting for me long."

Ms. Walsh assured her of the contrary.

"I would have called to reschedule but I couldn't get through to the headmaster's office, and I didn't have another number to try. I was supposed to arrive last night," Ella explained in a rush of words, "but one of my flights got cancelled and my aunt's phone keeps going straight to voicemail. So I had to convince a taxi to make the trip for me, which was probably good because I have this thing with flying...and heights in general... And I'm...sorry for babbling," she added with a grimace. "It's been a stressful day and this place is...much bigger than I'd imagined."

"Don't mention it. I'm sure I would be giddy myself after traveling all day. Headmaster Tutwiler sends his apologies, of course. I'm afraid he had some pressing business, but I'm more than happy to introduce you to the Academy, if you'll follow me."

The young instructor started up the hill at a brisk pace and began her rapid-fire speech.

"As I'm sure you are aware, Whitfield Christian Preparatory Academy was founded in 1910 as a college preparatory school for boys. In 1972, the Academy merged with the Edna Earle Percy School for girls. Following the merger, the Academy dropped the 'Christian' portion of its title, though we do still offer religious studies and there is a nondenominational chapel on campus."

As Ella stepped over the threshold through a pair of massive double doors, she gaped at her surroundings. Light streamed through a wide window above the entry and glistened off the sleek marble flooring under her feet.

Worth it. Absolutely worth it.

The *click clack* of Ms. Walsh's high heels echoed through the corridor as she continued, "The campus consists of fifty-two classrooms, three science wings, an art gallery and sculpture garden, a state-of-the-art

6

computer lab, and a library with access to two hundred fifty thousand print and electronic volumes," she rattled off as they passed a glass trophy case spanning the length of the wall. "Athletics are emphasized as a central part of life at the Academy. In addition to a weight room and track, all students have access to our nine tennis courts, four volleyball courts, three soccer fields, and two basketball courts, when not in use by an Academy team."

Ella hoped to ask something intelligent, but only managed to inquire, "And music?"

"Certainly! We have a Fine Arts Center with special studios for chorus, art, photography, and orchestra. Also, an audio-visual recording studio was recently added to the fine arts suite. In addition to our standard courses, the curriculum offers many opportunities to participate in arts, science competitions, clubs, and foreign language. The Academy boasts of having the most sought after foreign language instructors in the country. Our faculty includes two Pulitzer Prize-winning authors, the former undersecretary for Public Diplomacy and Public Affairs, and the former ambassador to Morocco."

"That's impressive," Ella said, once again wishing she could think of a better remark. She'd felt so mature and self-assured that morning when she'd embarked on this adventure but suddenly, next to this businesslike young woman, her clothes seemed disheveled and her thoughts jumbled.

Ella glanced up from her outfit to see Ms. Walsh looking at her quizzically and wondered if she appeared as lost and vacant on the outside as she felt on the inside.

"I'm sorry," Ella laughed sheepishly. "I should probably be asking questions or something. I'm a little overwhelmed now that I'm actually seeing the Academy in person."

Ms. Walsh smiled sympathetically. Ella found her much less intimidating when she smiled.

"I understand. It is a lot to take in all at once." She looked around at the oil paintings adorning the long corridor and glanced at her watch. "I think we can skip the formal tour for now. I'm sure you're anxious to see your aunt. What's your first class?"

"Yours. World History."

"Perfect! I'll show you how to get to my classroom so you'll know where to go on your first day. I'm certain the other students will help you with the rest and you'll find the campus easy to navigate within a few days."

Trying her best not to gawk, Ella walked briskly at Ms. Walsh's side, mentally mapping her path. Later, when Ms. Walsh opened the high iron gate at the edge of the grounds, Ella thanked her enthusiastically, already excited for her first day.

Ella saw her Aunt Meg sitting in the porch swing as she approached the house. She was bent over, knitting needles working rapidly in her hands. From this distance, Ella could almost imagine the figure on the porch was her mother, the two sisters were so similar.

Ella crossed the porch in three nimble steps.

"Hi, Aunt Meg," she said with a sweet, clear voice and offered a tired smile. "I tried to call."

"Ella! You've gotten so tall!" her aunt exclaimed, standing and giving her a stiff hug. "My cell phone must have shut off. I don't get many calls, but if I'd known you were coming today, I would have made sure it was charged. I didn't expect you to visit so soon."

Ella opened her mouth to reply, but only hiccupped.

"Visit?" she finally asked, her eyes wide.

Meg's answer was cut off as a rusty truck rattled into the driveway. The old pickup door opened with a creak and a short, thin man with silver hair and a bristly grey beard crossed the lawn. He stooped with age and fatigue, but his hazel eyes were bright and sparkled behind his thick glasses.

In a low, trembling voice he said, "I daresay that's little Ellie Parker! How are you doing, doll?"

Ella grinned at the town's elderly handyman. "It's been a few years since anyone's called me 'little', Mr. Sherman. But I'm good," Ella replied, as he tousled her bangs. "I'm good."

"Well now, when Meg here invited me over, I had no idea you'd be visiting. What a treat!" he said, adjusting the suspenders holding up his loose, shabby shorts.

8

"To be honest," Meg put in, "I was only hoping you could take a look at the Buick for me." She flashed Ella a brief but sincere smile. "I didn't know you'd be here myself."

The green faded from Ella's eyes as her gaze flitted from one face to the other.

"My mom talked to you, didn't she?"

Her aunt nodded. "We spoke a few weeks ago. Your mother said everything was finalized and you'd be going to the Academy in the fall."

Another hiccup formed in Ella's chest.

"And...and staying here. Has the plan changed?" Ella faltered.

Meg's light brown eyes stared blankly at her.

In the silence, Ella's pale cheeks reddened and she felt tears coming to her eyes. "Mom said boarding at the school would be too expensive, but...but she would talk to you about living here."

Looking between the two distressed faces, Mr. Sherman cleared his throat.

"*Ahem.* Meg, I could sure use a cup of coffee before I get started on that old Buick. Maybe we could all go inside."

In an instant, Meg's aggravated expression melted away. "Well, we certainly can't get to the bottom of this here in the front yard. Ella, your things are right inside the door. We can put them in the spare room at the top of the stairs. I'll see if I can get your mom on the phone and correct this misunderstanding."

Ella simply nodded and followed her aunt inside. A haunting scent of lavender hit her as she stepped through the front door. Many years had passed since she had last been in the house, and a rush of memories came back to her with that scent. She saw a perfect picture of her father sitting at the piano in the living room, her mother standing beside the piano bench, smiling down at him.

Though her father's memory would remain the same forever, the mother of her memory was more blithe and youthful than the woman who'd kissed her goodbye earlier in the week. The lines and wrinkles marking her now had little to do with the years that had gone by. Sorrow and grief had aged her in a way time could not.

9

With a sigh, Ella shook off these heavy thoughts. She slipped the strap of her duffel bag over her shoulder and lifted the two suitcases from the floor. Maneuvering up the narrow staircase behind her aunt, Ella did her best not to scuff the walls as the ancient stairs groaned under the weight of the luggage in her arms.

When they reached the top, Meg opened the door in front of her and ushered Ella into the glaringly plain room. A soft blue and cream quilt was spread across the bed – the blue standing out sharply as the only color in the room. Four bare walls stared down at the cream carpet and white lace curtains fluttered in the window. A thin, wooden desk and chair peered shyly out of the far corner of the room.

"You must be tired," her aunt said tactfully. "I'll leave you to get settled, and there'll be a cup of tea waiting for you in the kitchen whenever you'd like to come down."

When she was alone, Ella shoved the duffel and the largest suitcase into the closet. The air within it smelled stale and she shut the door firmly. Setting the smaller suitcase gingerly on the bed, she removed her toothbrush and comb. Unpacking was useless if she wasn't going to stay.

Unconsciously, she hummed a quiet tune as she loosened her braid and combed through her tangled hair. But there was no one else there to hear it and the notes died as they hit the blank walls.

She walked to the window and as she looked out, the curtain fluttered against her cheek. She shivered and recoiled as if the touch had been the cold fingers of a ghost. Taking a calming breath, she hugged her arms to her chest and looked out again.

Although her nervous stomach would have preferred a room on the ground floor to the height of the second story, she couldn't complain about the view. The scene outside could have been a postcard picture. Carefully tended lawns surrounded the old Colonial houses. Leaves shimmered as a breeze swayed the limbs of trees lining the avenue, and vibrant flowers beamed at her from her aunt's garden. The neighborhood was the essence of peace and hominess, yet, Ella didn't feel at home. She felt homesick. Closing her eyes, she breathed out a prayer.

Dear God, help me. Coming here was a mistake. I somehow thought I'd be less alone and out of place in Whitfield with Aunt Meg than on the far side of the world, but the opposite is true.

All at once, the prospect of traveling to the war-torn Middle East with her mother was more appealing than attending her dream school and living with her aunt. Here, not only did she feel alone and out of place, she felt – with a stab of pain – unwanted. Being a stranger was one thing, but being considered an encumbrance or a nuisance was completely different.

Ella fought to remember her initial impression of the Academy, like a fairytale castle, and regain the excitement she'd felt such a short time ago. The cost of boarding there for a year would be a challenge, but not an insurmountable obstacle, if there really *had* been a misunderstanding with her aunt. Spending a perfect year at the Academy was worth sacrificing a chunk of money from her college trust fund – especially since she wasn't sure where she wanted to go or what she was going to do with the rest of her life anyway.

Ella tucked a wayward strand of hair behind her ear and pushed the vague, uncomfortable thought of the future away to focus on the present.

It's going to be worth it, she insisted half-heartedly, but couldn't suppress the growing fear she didn't belong here.

The feeling wasn't new. She hadn't managed to belong anywhere since her father died. The cancer had taken him in less than a year and their family was left reeling. In time, the others seemed to have regained their footing. Ella's older brother, Malcolm, had focused his entire being on sports. Scouts from Michigan State had taken note of his talent and Mal was kicking off his sophomore year with a hockey scholarship. Ella's mother had likewise buried herself in work, winning multiple awards for reporting and receiving a coveted journalism assignment overseas.

Still, after eight long years, Ella felt lost. It had been surprisingly easy to leave her hometown and social circle. While she had a number of friends, none were close. She had retreated into herself, quietly filling her days with school and books and above all, music. Her passion for music had been shared by her father and she felt nearest to him when they sang together. Even after his death, she sang, though more and more often in a minor key.

Despite everything, the Aunt Meg she held in her mind was constant, never changing. Her family visits to Whitfield were the happiest part of her childhood, seemingly untouched by her season of grief. The years and distance had consecrated this place to her memory.

As she turned from the window and took a seat on the bed, Ella faintly heard the sounds of water being heated in the kettle on the stove below, and the soft murmur of voices. In the kitchen, her aunt was having a different conversation.

"How can a campus that size be completely vacant? You'd think the headmaster – or *someone* – would be on call," Meg snapped, as she removed her delicate tea set from the cupboard.

"It is still summer, after all," Mr. Sherman interjected meekly.

"And what do you mean 'keep her'? She's not a stray dog that wandered off the street. There's no way Kate would ever trust me to look after Ella, and the school will be expecting her. I can't keep her."

"But don't you want to?" Mr. Sherman coaxed.

The water in the kettle was boiling furiously now. Meg lifted it from the stove just as it began to whistle, poured the steaming water deftly into her rose-print teapot, and turned back to Mr. Sherman. She held his gaze for a long time, and when she spoke again there was an ache in her voice.

"Of course I do. Of course I want her to stay with me." She raised her eyes to the ceiling, as if she could see Ella sitting forlornly in the room above and said, almost in a whisper, "Poor girl."

Mr. Sherman pulled off his thick glasses, wiping them with a napkin. "I can't believe that young woman is our little Ellie. The last time I saw her, she had pigtails and was singing like an angel at her father's knee – with a lisp, if I recall. Does she still sing?"

"I don't know. I don't know anything about her. You should have heard my heartbeat when she walked up to me. For one idiotic second, I thought it was Kate standing there on my porch."

"She looks very much like her mother," Mr. Sherman agreed. "Like both of you girls at that age."

"Except her eyes. I think her voice and her eyes came from Axel, not Kate." Meg chuckled ruefully. "It's funny, I almost didn't recognize Kate's voice when she called to tell me about Ella and the Academy. It's no wonder we misunderstood each other. Honestly, I was so flustered to find myself on the phone with her, I barely remember the conversation."

"Maybe it's not my place to say, but wouldn't having Ella here for a time help to mend that bridge?"

"It's possible," Meg said hesitantly. "But if Kate meant to send her to the Academy, I've no right to force her to stay here."

"Don't you think she'd be better off?"

"She might be. And I suppose I'll enjoy her company while she's here. But you can't honestly think *she'd* be happy here with only an old woman like me for company?"

"Take it from someone who knows," Mr. Sherman ordered with a twist of his silver beard, "you're still a spring chicken, Meg Keller."

She gave him a look of mingled gratitude and exasperation.

"I certainly feel old and worn out lately," she said, rubbing her swollen hands, "but maybe you're right."

Lifting the teapot, Meg filled a pair of cups to the brim and took a long, slow sniff of her tea.

"Still," she went on, "I'm not her mother. I'm sure Kate knows what's best."

"But –" Mr. Sherman began again.

"When Kate returns my call, I'll go by whatever she says, and that's that."

2. GIFTED

Ella was in the shower the next morning when the phone rang. Though her hair was thick with shampoo, she immediately shut off the water in order to hear the conversation. But the voices were too muffled for her to make out any words. She wrapped herself in a towel, stepped out of the shower, and quietly opened the door.

With shampoo suds stinging her eyes, Ella crouched outside the bathroom at the top of the stairs and listened in silence to the monologue below.

"…I understand… Thanks for getting back to me so quickly… Okay, well, don't let me keep you. Sounds good….Uh-huh. Bye."

Ella jumped as her aunt rounded the corner downstairs, carrying the morning paper. Meg stared up at Ella.

"It's not eavesdropping if it's about me," Ella exclaimed defensively, clutching her towel. "What did she say? Can I stay here? I promise I won't be a burden if you keep me, Aunt Meg."

"Keep you?" her aunt replied, her ears ringing with Mr. Sherman's words from the previous day.

14

"Yes. I can help around the house with dishes and laundry. Or cooking," she added. "I'm not a good cook, but my mom says you are, and I'm a fast learner."

"That was Mr. Sherman," Meg said slowly. "He found the part I need for the car and he'll be here in a few minutes to fix it."

"Oh," Ella murmured, blushing furiously at her own outburst.

"Of course I *would* keep you, Ella, if you'd like to stay here. But we'll have to be sure your mom agrees. If I haven't heard from her by Saturday, I'll try to contact someone at the Academy again. They should know what the arrangement was. And as for helping around the house, you can start by not dripping all over my hardwood floor."

"Yes, sorry!" Ella apologized hastily and stepped toward the bathroom.

Anxiously awaiting her mother's reply, she spent the better part of the morning pacing and singing quietly to herself as she straightened knickknacks in the living room. Meg, seated on the couch, looked up from her knitting needles.

"Your voice is even more beautiful than the last time I heard you sing – if that's possible."

Ella started and spun around, a little taken aback.

"Thanks," she replied, her cheeks flushing.

"You ought to consider joining our church choir while you're here."

"Are you sure? I haven't sung in public since..." She stopped. "It's been a long time. I mean, of course, I'm glad to do it. But do you really think they'd want me?"

"No doubt they'd be grateful to have you. Just something to think about. There's our annual ice cream social tonight at church, and you can audition for our choir director then if you're interested."

Ella hiccupped and moved an elephant, carved out of petrified wood, from one end of the fireplace mantle to the other. She looked at it a moment and slid it back to its original position.

Meg paused in her knitting. Living with another person would be an adjustment, if Kate agreed. This receiving blanket was supposed to be shipped out tomorrow, but she'd dropped two stitches and would have to pull out an entire row and start again.

15

"Ella," she said, more crisply than she'd intended, "would you mind checking on Mr. Sherman in the garage? I'm not sure if he'll want lunch, or if he'll be finished before then."

"Sure," Ella chirped and ambled out of the room.

The narrow garage was full. The shelves lining the walls were stacked with dusty boxes, worn out tools, and other ancient artifacts that were unrecognizable to Ella. The floor was a network of pails filled with assorted nuts, bolts, and screws.

"Mr. Sherman?" she called at the door of the garage.

A grease-smeared face emerged from the far side of an enormous, blue Buick. "Right here."

"How's it going?" Ella asked, threading her way through the maze of open floor. "Do you think you'll want lunch?"

"Most likely not. I'm nearly done. Hand me that flathead, would you?"

She glanced in the direction he had pointed and retrieved the screwdriver.

Detecting how violently his hand shook in taking it from her, Ella grimaced. She'd always considered their aged family friend an old man, but he'd deteriorated rapidly in recent years.

Mr. Sherman was not oblivious to her sudden expression of distress.

"Thanks, doll," he said cheerily, and with a wink disappeared behind the vehicle again.

"How are you doing, Mr. Sherman?" Ella asked meaningfully.

He was mute for a minute before replying. "Not bad, dolly, not bad. I had to spend a few days in the hospital this past spring and I'm in to see the doctor pretty often."

"I hate hospitals." Ella shuddered. "Even more than heights."

"Me, too. But my doctor says he's pleased with how I'm getting on, and I'm still able to help out around town and do all the things I like. I've got a young man who's been placed with me and he's a big help."

He poked his head up again on the pretense of getting a wrench, but he gave Ella a sidelong look.

"How are you doing, Ellie?"

16

A tension swelled in her chest, and she replied a little too quickly, "Fine. I'm fine. Will you be at this ice cream social tonight?"

"Afraid not." Mr. Sherman shook his head. "I have to be in court this afternoon."

"Skipped out on bail?" Ella grinned.

With a chuckle, Mr. Sherman shook his head again, then the lines of his face deepened. "Just sorting out a few legal details for this coming school year. The young man staying with me is in the foster system. It was supposed to be a short-term placement while his mother was working through rehab, but she's had a few setbacks. He's been with me a little over two years now."

Her eyebrows shot up. "Two years?"

"Might be closer to three now," Mr. Sherman mused quietly, as if to himself. "Not that I'm complaining. He's a good boy. I'll introduce you on Sunday."

"Great," Ella replied with a sudden warm glow.

A new friend.

She checked herself. Not just a new friend, her only friend here.

Dear God, please let this all be worth it.

Ella felt sharp, mortifying tears coming and said hastily, "I'm going to go see if my aunt needs any help with lunch."

"Okey-dokey. Tell her I'll be done in a jiffy and out of her hair."

Meg was mincing garlic when Ella entered the kitchen. The sweet, musky smell permeated the air and Ella filled her lungs to drive out the scent of motor oil clinging to her.

"Mr. Sherman said he'll be done in a few minutes."

"Thanks for checking on him," Meg replied, tossing the garlic into a sizzling sauté pan. She turned to ask a question over her shoulder when the phone rang in the other room.

Her eyes met Ella's for a split second before she dropped her wooden spoon on the counter.

"Watch this garlic for me," Meg requested quietly.

Ella nodded, and walked mechanically to the stove but her eyes followed her aunt out of the room. She strained her ears but failed to hear

17

Meg's voice. With soft steps, she moved to the door and opened it slowly. Still nothing.

Returning to the stove, Ella found the garlic dark brown and smoldering. With a cough, she switched the burner off as the pan began to smoke.

Ella, growing alarmed, attempted to stir the burnt remains but they stuck to the pan. Suddenly, the smoke detector in the kitchen started blaring.

Ella grabbed a nearby towel and fanned the air, with a frantic, "Help!"

"What's all the commotion?" Mr. Sherman hollered, shuffling into the kitchen.

"How do you shut it off?" she bellowed over the shrieking alarm.

"Are you trying to burn the house down?" Meg called as she rushed through the door. She grabbed an oven mitt from an open drawer, and clamped the lid on the hot pan. "You weren't kidding about your cooking skills."

Ella choked on the smoke and the lump in her throat. "Well?" she gulped.

Meg groaned, straining to open the kitchen window. A fresh breeze swept round the room and the smoke detector stopped blaring with a final earsplitting shriek.

"It wasn't your mom."

"Oh," Ella mumbled, humiliated and crestfallen.

"But I think you should unpack anyway."

Ella stared at her.

"I can convince Kate if she disagrees with me and I'll even make arrangements with the Academy if it comes to that."

"Really?"

"Really. There's more to life than an expensive education. Clearly someone has to show you how to cook properly and I doubt they'll teach you anything useful like that at a fancy institution," Meg said grimly, but the eyes that surveyed her ruined sauté pan were full of humor.

After swallowing her lunch in as few bites as she could manage, Ella rushed upstairs. She'd unpacked her laptop the night before, patiently untangling the perpetually knotted power cord. But after receiving a garbled automated reply in response to the short note she'd shot off to her mother, Ella had slammed her laptop shut in disgust.

Now, she looked through her email in a better mood, reading a light, teasing message from Malcolm asking if she had survived her flight, and outlining his class schedule at Michigan State. The message from her mom, however, was another memo in an indecipherable foreign language.

The suitcases in the closet glowered at her, but she ignored them and sat down to write each a reply. With both emails sent, Ella knew she must finish the chore ahead of her.

Initially, she'd been worried about having enough space for everything she'd brought. But after unpacking all of her jeans and sweaters, her complete works of Shakespeare, Tolkien, Twain, Austen, and Dickens, a stack of CDs nearly a foot tall, and all of her framed photographs and maps, the room still looked practically empty.

Ella finished organizing her things while the sun was still high in the sky. Dumping the contents of the final bag into an empty desk drawer, she glanced around the room.

It looked even bigger than before.

For some reason, the space — and perhaps the unpacking — made her feel utterly drained, and she slumped onto the expanse of empty floor. It had already been a long day and Ella's eyelids were heavy as she surveyed the white ceiling. The bareness stared back at her, so she turned her gaze instead to the line of pictures arranged on her desk.

It was comforting to see Malcolm's face, with his perpetually calm, blue-green eyes. She'd always secretly envied the fact that her brother had been graced with their father's mesmerizing eyes, and had also received his curly, blonde hair.

Somehow — Ella felt it was a cruel twist of fate — she'd ended up with neither. Mal had told her again and again that her eyes resembled their father's more, but she could never believe his empty reassurances, failing to see the rare emerald sparkle when she looked at her reflection in the mirror.

She stared with longing at the old family portrait. The forced smiles in their more recent photographs seemed like a lie, and the unnaturally casual poses failed to conceal the missing figure that ought to be filling the space beside her mother.

But the old portrait was different. Her father sat in the center, his hands resting lightly on his lap. Her mother stood behind him with one arm around each of her children.

Ella looked out of place. With her straight, dark hair and grey eyes, she looked as if she'd been transposed from a black and white photograph. Not only did she have the wrong color hair and eyes, but her skin was wrong, too.

Ella detested her skin, which refused to tan, but would simply burn and soon turn white again. She knew from experience that the present pink glow of her cheeks – a reward from the intense August sun – would fade within a few days.

Perhaps if she was lucky she might still have a slight trace of sun on her cheeks for the first day of school. Her lips curved lazily at the thought and her mind edged toward sleep.

Suddenly she sat up, her heart pounding.

She'd promised Aunt Meg she'd sing for the choir director tonight.

Her chest tightened in the same way it did when she found herself up high, or alone in front of a crowd. A loud hiccup burst from her lips.

She took a long, deep breath.

After her father died, a grief counselor had determined her frequent hiccups were due to a habit of repressing her feelings, and made Ella practice deep breathing techniques whenever she sensed hiccups coming on. Ella insisted hiccups were simply the result of an irritated diaphragm but in the end found it easier to go along with the psychobabble.

Now, whenever she was upset, Ella inhaled deeply and murmured "I am…" then exhaled slowly and murmured "relaxed."

She felt like an idiot when she did it, but considered that a reasonable option if it kept her off a shrink's couch. Besides, Ella had been told when she practiced her deep breathing she could do anything.

She would put that theory to the test at the church in a few hours.

"Mark, this is my niece, who I told you about," Meg announce, sauntering up to him after the ice cream social with Ella in tow. "I think she'd be perfect for the choir."

Ella had watched the choir director intently from the moment Meg had pointed him out and thought with his steely eyes and grim mouth, he looked more like a boot camp sergeant than a church cantor.

"*Hmm*, I see." He surveyed her with a cool glance. "Well, let me hear you."

Ella hesitated. "What would you like me to sing?"

"Oh, sing anything you'd like." His lips hardened into a straight line. "Sing 'Amazing Grace.' You don't need a hymnal, do you?"

"No, I know it. Do you want me to sing right here?" Ella asked, looking around at the group of people who still remained, chatting in small circles.

"Yes, please go ahead," Mark replied distractedly, as the line turned into a frown and he glanced at the screen on his phone.

Ella inhaled a deep breath and began.

Instantly, a hush fell over the room. Two young boys squabbling nearby stopped their bickering and turned to listen. The families who were headed towards the door altered their course and returned to the sanctuary with eyes bulging.

The choir director looked up from his phone with a glorious expression that had not graced his face for many years. Ella waited for him to give the word that she should stop, but he said nothing, and she continued.

All those present listened with rapt attention until she finished the hymn. If it hadn't been a casual audition of which most were eavesdropping, the audience almost certainly would have applauded and Ella was asked – with unwarranted reverence – if she would be willing to sing a solo on Sunday morning.

The next several days were filled with more pacing and distractedly rearranging Meg's possessions until Saturday afternoon, when Meg swept Ella out of the house and sent her on her way to attend choir practice at the church. Mark's introduction was glowing and she was met with a few friendly glances, but most of the group remained looking at their sheet

a took her place in the front and the accompanist began the first
e piano.

rong voice soared above all the others.

A collective shiver went through the choir as the graceful rise and fall
of Ella's vocals gave chills to those standing around her. Slowly, one voice
then another dropped off to hear the purity of her song.

Suddenly all was quiet.

"Why did you stop?" the girl beside Ella asked in an awed tone.

"No one else was singing," Ella replied shyly.

"Quite right," Mark remonstrated, shuffling the papers on his music
stand. "Let us all continue *fortissimo*."

They resumed, the rest of the choir half-singing, half-listening to the
beautiful voice in their midst.

"I think I'm going to go over it once more on my own," Ella told
Mark after he dismissed the choir.

His voice was condescending. "It was perfect."

"I have a nervous stomach." Ella swallowed. "Sometimes I get sick. If
I'm lucky, I'll just get hiccups."

The choir director looked alarmed.

"It's not so bad if I'm really prepared," Ella reassured him hastily.
"You might say over-prepared."

"In that case, take all the time you need." He turned and said over his
shoulder, "Please be sure the door is locked behind you."

After hearing the door swing shut, Ella played a few clumsy notes on
the piano. She hiccupped and her hands dropped from the black and white
keys. Closing her eyes, she began the piece a cappella. She sang through it
once very quietly. The second time, in full voice.

She had reached her crescendoing solo when she was startled by an
echoing crash.

Opening her eyes, Ella saw a figure wearing a backwards baseball cap
crouched behind the last pew. The young man in the cap stood quickly,
lifting a broom from where it had clattered to the floor.

Ella caught her breath, not only from the suddenness of his
appearance but from the boy himself. Even with his current puzzled
expression, he was handsome, with a firm, square chin and dark skin. A

large ivory tattoo, outlined in black, was visible under the sleeve of his shirt, stretched taut across his muscular bicep.

Pulling his cap from his head, he ran a hand over his short hair and across his face as if to wake himself. He stared at her but said nothing. Ella looked back at his wide, brown eyes, and every last one of her coherent thoughts wandered out of her mind.

After a long pause, the young man broke the silence.

"Who are you?" he asked, taking a step forward.

"I'm Ella Parker." She watched as he made his way to the aisle. "And you are?"

Ignoring her question, he asked, "Where did you learn to sing like that?"

"My dad taught me, I guess," Ella replied, her cheeks flushing. The boy was still advancing up the aisle, his penetrating eyes seeming to sink through her.

"Your dad sings? Like you?"

Ella sat rigidly at the piano and nodded slowly. "He used to. He had a solo career for a while, and before that he was the lead singer for Wicked Youth."

Her response had an effect. The young man stopped.

"Seriously?" he managed. "Axel Parker?" He gaped at her, his steely eyes fixed on her face. "You – you're Axel Parker's daughter?"

Ella nodded again. "Ella Parker. And you are?" she repeated.

"I'm Lucas Morales," he said, passing a rough hand over his face once more.

He looked up at her with a sudden warm smile which made Ella catch her breath a second time.

"I didn't mean to scare you. I just... Wow..." He trailed off. "Just wow sums it up, I think."

"Thanks," Ella replied bashfully to his praise. "It's nice to meet you, Lucas. I don't really know anyone my age in Whitfield."

"Yeah," he said, raising an eyebrow, "what are you doing here anyway?"

"We just finished choir practice. I'm singing a solo during the service tomorrow morning."

"I figured that from, you know, the voice." He cocked his head to the side. "Tell me what a rock star's kid is doing in Whitfield, I mean. I didn't think this place was even listed on a map."

"Oh." Ella's cheeks reddened. "I moved this last week."

"So you're new. Have you ever been to Whitfield before?"

"Yeah, my grandparents lived here – my aunt still lives in their house – so my family visited a lot when I was a little girl. But it's been a long time. The last time I came, I was seven or eight, I think. I mostly remember the park behind the middle school."

"I don't think there's a park there anymore. I hope that's not too devastating for you," he said playfully.

Ella smiled. "I feel as if the whole foundation of my childhood is crumbling."

"Hey, do you want to get a piece of pie or something? Maybe talk about these feelings?"

He flashed her a dazzling grin.

Ella hiccupped loudly. "Uh," she stammered and turned scarlet, "I don't...*um*... I'm not sure."

"Seriously though," he added quickly, "the place across the street has the best pie ever, and I could show you around the town a little. I guarantee it's changed a lot."

Ella hesitated, glancing at the broom leaning against the back pew. "Do you have to finish here?"

He shrugged. "I'll get to it. Sweeping isn't all that important in the grand scheme of things. But I would forever regret not buying Axel Parker's daughter a piece of pie."

Ella acquiesced and they walked side-by-side across the street to the Silver Spoon Cafe, blinking a little as they stepped into the gloom of the interior. The tiny restaurant was more or less as Ella remembered it, though the coffee bar had expanded and the fudge within the gleaming glass case had nearly tripled in price.

They ordered and a moment later their waitress materialized beside the table, depositing two plates of pie with a clatter.

The conversation dwindled as they ate, but after finishing their pie and small talk, Ella ordered a hot tea to go and they slowly ambled along

Main Street, Ella blowing on her steaming chai and reminiscing about all of her old favorite places.

A few had changed, but most of the storefronts appeared untouched by time. Although the old school playground was indeed gone, there was still a large squirrel nest in the crooked tree that had stood near the swings and now towered over the entrance to a McDonald's, which looked distinctly out of place amongst the stately shops and eateries.

They circled back to an old wooden bench outside the church and sat. Ella tentatively sipped her steaming tea.

"I'm surprised I haven't heard about you yet," Lucas said, slanting her a sidelong glance. "Apart from tourists, Whitfield doesn't get a lot of new people, and nothing exciting happens around here. You'll be a nice piece of gossip when word gets out."

"It's funny you said that," Ella replied with a wry face. "Right before choir practice, the director and I were talking about my dad and he told me it would be best not to publicize my family connection."

Lucas frowned. "Seriously? Why not?"

"Well, it's like you said," Ella began slowly, "my dad used to be a rock star, and he could never really shake that bad boy persona, even after he gave it all up. Most churches don't want their Sunday morning soloist to be associated with trashed hotel rooms and cocaine overdoses."

"When you put it that way..." He looked long at Ella again. "So Axel Parker gave it all up to start a family and come to Whitfield. Crazy world. I always kind of thought he died."

Ella's eyelids flickered momentarily and all at once she was a child, standing amid a mob of fans, celebrities, and media along Hollywood Boulevard. The customarily buzzing Walk of Fame had been silent that day when she stepped out of the assembly, carrying a wreath of yellow rosebuds.

Her fingers clutched and squeezed the paper cup in her hands as if she could still feel those stems she'd held as she approached the pink terrazzo star on the sidewalk – already covered with daisies, votive candles, photographs and notes.

The flash from a camera a few feet away dazzled her and she dropped the fragrant wreath. It fell with a light bounce, scattering leaves and petals on the ground. She hiccupped and scrambled after it, a cascade of thick, black hair spilling over her shoulders as she knelt.

Rising with the wreath clasped in an even tighter grip, she hurried forward, her shoes slapping against the pavement in a frantic rhythm.

She murmured apologetically to the name emblazoned on the sidewalk and bent to place the flowers over the star at her feet.

"Sorry, Dad." Ella shook her head with a grimace. She was nothing like him – able to captivate an entire room with his voice and at times simply with his presence.

She couldn't even manage to carry a memorial wreath.

Her fingers felt stiff and somehow horribly empty without the sharp thorns pinching her skin. Balling up her fists until her knuckles were white, she mumbled another apology.

"And I'm sorry about the funeral. I know you said to be brave, but that huge audience, all those strangers…"

People from all over the world, who had never met Axel Parker, but still felt like they knew him.

A mass of expectant eyes met hers as she glanced up and another hiccup erupted from her mouth. Dropping her voice along with her gaze, she whispered, "I hope you weren't disappointed. I thought maybe –"

She paused to brush a loose strand from her forehead as wind from a passing car swirled the hair around her face.

"Maybe I can sing something today instead," Ella finished quietly, crouching low enough to kiss the pavement.

A flurry of cameras flashed to capture the embrace but her lips stopped before they reached the sidewalk, hovering just above the star and moving in a song no one else heard.

Ella blinked and the memory faded, the quiet Whitfield street rematerializing before her eyes. Lucas was sitting on the bench beside her with an inquisitive expression.

"Actually, yes," replied Ella, her voice crisp and matter-of-fact, "he died a little over eight years ago."

Lucas flinched. "I'm so sorry. That was…really dumb."

Ella sighed. *Be kind*, came the mental order, delivered firmly in her father's voice.

"It's okay. Really. It was a long time ago."

"Still, I'm sorry. It would have been awesome to meet him. He was a legend. I can only imagine growing up with Axel Parker, touring across the country with Wicked Youth."

"I only know a few of those guys well," Ella cut in. "Dad left the band before I was born, and never quite fit with his old friends and fans after he started singing Christian music."

"Wait." Lucas shot up from the bench. "You're telling me Axel Parker – *the* Axel Parker – left Wicked Youth to sing gospel music? Crazy, crazy world. How did I not know that?"

"His solo career wasn't as successful as the band," Ella explained. "He was sort of an outcast in the Christian community, even after he became a Christian."

"But how did that happen? There's got to be a story there."

The clock on the church tower chimed overhead. Ella glanced up. "Does that still chime five minutes after the hour?"

Lucas nodded.

"I've got to get home. Another time, maybe?" Ella offered.

"Count on it, Songbird."

Meg was at the sink, washing a frying pan, when Ella walked in and dropped into a chair at the kitchen table.

"You're back late. Did choir practice run long?"

"Uh, not really," Ella deliberated, picking at her purple nail polish. She was suddenly self-conscious of her afternoon's activities. "I met someone at the church and we talked for a little while."

"Someone at the church? From the choir?"

"No," Ella replied slowly. "He was cleaning after choir practice."

Meg turned to look at Ella over her shoulder. "You don't mean Lucas?"

"Yes! Lucas. Do you know him?"

"I do know Lucas," she remarked somberly. "What did… Did he tell you anything about himself?"

Ella thought back. "He didn't talk about himself that much. We mostly talked about me. He's a really good listener."

"I happen to know a little about him," Meg said, swiveling her eyes to the pan in the sink.

"You do? How?"

Meg smiled ruefully. "It's a small town, Ella. Lucas lives with Mr. Sherman. The boy's mother was one of Mr. and Mrs. Sherman's foster kids growing up. She had some problems. Well, still does, I believe. I understand she went into rehab and arranged to get Lucas placed with Mr. Sherman." Meg paused. "Please be cautious, Ella. I've heard some unsavory rumors about Lucas."

"He warned me gossip spreads quickly here."

Meg pursed her lips. "That's not my point."

"Lucas seemed nice, Aunt Meg. He was friendly. And polite."

"And he's quite handsome as well," Meg added stingingly.

Ella didn't reply, but dropped her face to hide her burning cheeks.

"By the way, your mom called while you were gone."

Ella looked up sharply.

"I guess it was always the plan for you to stay here. She told me it was part of your tuition agreement with the Academy. I'm still not sure where the miscommunication came in but it's all settled now."

When Ella remained silent, Meg said more gently, "It's not my place to tell you who you can and can't be friends with. I'm not your mother and you're practically a grown woman yourself. But I do feel somewhat responsible for you while you're here with me and I hope you'll make wise choices."

Ella rolled her eyes discreetly. "I'm not one of those kids, Aunt Meg. I won't be out binge drinking or inciting a riot."

"I'm not saying that. Just be careful who you choose to open up to. I don't want to see you get hurt."

"I have to be friends with someone, Aunt Meg," Ella whispered. "I have nobody."

Meg turned back to the sink. Ella groaned.

So much for being kind.

"I didn't mean nobody, Aunt Meg," Ella insisted. "I'm sorry. Obviously, I'm really happy to –"

Her aunt interrupted, "Please don't apologize. I understand." She smiled again. "Are you ready for dinner?"

Ella wasn't hungry but forced herself to eat every bite from her plate as penance for her hurtful words, and agreed without hesitation to a nightly Bible study of Proverbs with her aunt.

That night, she slept fitfully, her thoughts full of Lucas and Aunt Meg's reproof. When she had finally put them from her mind, she remembered her solo the next day, and tossed and turned until morning.

Though tired and nervous, she managed to get through the performance without a hiccup, literal or otherwise. The church had an exceptional choir, generally acknowledged as one of the best in Vermont, but they had never heard singing like they heard that morning. It was not merely the novelty of such a slight, plain girl with such a voice. It is true, of course, that most in the audience had barely noticed her when she took her place on stage, and the rest had disregarded her almost at once. Ella faded into the background until the music began.

When the first notes of the song trickled through the air, those listening sat straighter in the pews. As Ella's strong, soprano voice soared, some people jumped as if an angel had appeared in their midst. With her song, she took them to the very gates of heaven and the congregation sat captivated.

Following the service, she was inundated with handshakes and accolades. But Ella, with her song sung and her hiccups in check, was more interested in the tall, dark boy with an ivory tattoo displayed on his arm at the outer edge of the group surrounding her. When the throng finally finished their well wishes, and the mob departed, Lucas came forward.

"Hey Songbird, that was amazing. Even better than my sneak preview."

Ella beamed. "I'm glad I met you yesterday. I won't feel so out of place at school tomorrow knowing I'll see one familiar face."

"So you're going over to Ashby High School?"

Ella's heart sank. "No, actually I'm going to Whitfield Preparatory Academy."

"Oh, that makes sense." Lucas looked disappointed but his tone remained light. "Well, that's a good school. You'll make plenty of friends there."

"Yeah, I'll be fine," Ella said, brushing it off with an attempt at self-assurance.

"Hey, I should give you my number," Lucas offered conversationally, drawing his phone from his pocket, "so you can text me and let me know how your first day goes."

"I will," Ella replied, and did her best to conceal a broad grin.

Ella would have preferred to stay all afternoon talking to Lucas but she spotted her aunt waiting for her at the door, and asked, "I'll see you next Sunday, right?"

"Definitely," Lucas replied with a warm smile.

Ella was still thinking about that hypnotizing smile later in the afternoon. Wanting to time the trip and avoid being tardy on her first day, Ella walked down the lane from Aunt Meg's house to the Academy.

She'd intended to visit the school again after her brief tour on that first day in Whitfield, but hadn't returned. For the most part, the school grounds looked exactly as they had on her first visit. But today, a babble of voices floated down the hill from beyond the boarding house, and she could only just see the figures of students, clumped together in small groups in the distance.

Standing there outside the iron gate, Ella noticed that, although subtly, the ivy-covered main building looked more imposing than she'd initially thought. A breeze swept over the sprawling lawn, swirling leaves across the ground. Ella shivered.

September seemed to have come more quickly than usual.

3. NEW

With her books stuffed in her mother's old messenger bag and her pleated skirt and collared blouse under a crisp navy blazer, Ella assumed she was ready for her first day at the Academy.

As she stepped through the high iron gate toward a mass of students milling around the lawn under the towering black walnut trees, a lanky boy called out, "Great sneakers!"

Ella glanced at her new black running shoes and kicked up a heel. "Thanks."

Those in the circle around him laughed and Ella's eyes fell to the designer stilettos the other girls wore on their delicate feet. Her face clouded slightly as she continued edging her way along the mossy cobblestone steps through the group. Though she wore the same uniform, Ella suddenly felt out of place.

Quickly pulling her ebony hair out of its windblown ponytail, she ran her fingers through it until it matched the smooth, shiny hair she saw around her as she reached the high double doors. She mouthed a short, silent prayer and tugged the heavy door open.

Shuffling inside, her shoes squeaked on the lustrous marble flooring. As Ella looked up to the lofty ceilings of the vestibule, she swallowed a gasp, momentarily trying to imagine the shiny red and blue lockers from her old high school here among the stone and brick.

"I don't think I'll ever get over this view," she remarked to the girl walking nearest her, gesturing at the ornately carved beams above them. "This building is so huge, I bet I could fit every school I've ever attended in here and still have room for an Olympic-sized swimming pool!"

The other girl raised her eyebrows in reply and quickened her steps.

Ella's feet sped up to match the pace. "Do you know where room one hundred thirty-two is?"

"No," the girl mumbled and quickly rounded a corner.

Ella stopped short and someone collided with her.

"Sorry," the boy muttered in her direction.

"Hey, could you help me find –"

"Sorry," he repeated hastily and passed her.

A little stunned, Ella wandered through the labyrinth of corridors amid the surging students. During her tour, when the main building was empty, it had been easy to find her first classroom. But now – without Ms. Walsh at her side and engulfed in a jostling, bumping sea of bodies – every corridor looked the same, yet none looked familiar.

When the long hallway she found herself in came to a dead end at a large stained-glass window, Ella turned back. She continued her exploration for another few minutes, choosing narrow side hallways at random. Just when she thought she'd found a pattern in the numbered doors along the corridor, a piercing *clang* sounded from the bell in the courtyard.

Five minutes later, a panicked Ella stumbled into her first class – World History. Despite her tardiness, Ms. Walsh offered a sympathetic look as Ella scuttled to the only open seat in the back row, and picked up the sheet of paper on the desk.

Ella carefully studied the page, a detailed syllabus, as Ms. Walsh resumed speaking. She soon settled herself and listened attentively, her hands folded lightly in her lap and her eyes following Ms. Walsh as she walked to and fro at the front of the room.

"You should bring your homework to class every day. There will be a penalty on late homework and any homework more than a week late will not receive any credit."

As it became clear they'd only be covering the syllabus, Ella took her pen and began to doodle absently on the sheet in front of her. Soon, a river of inked-in music notes ran around the page, morphing into a weeping willow near the bottom and swirling into stars toward the top. When she had run out of room on the page and feared her pen would run dry, Ella surveyed the classroom.

At first glance, the room appeared similar to many of Ella's old high school classrooms, although admittedly much larger. Where those rooms had shabby posters of the periodic table or trite messages about teamwork, this room was adorned with exquisite paintings. The piece of art covering most of the left wall of the classroom looked shockingly like the original *Washington Crossing the Delaware*.

But, that's in a museum, obviously.

After taking in the room, Ella turned her attention back to the young instructor.

"If you don't follow the instructions announced in class concerning how to organize and submit your homework," she warned, "you may not receive full, or any credit for it."

As Ms. Walsh was speaking, the thin girl in front of Ella leaned to the redhead next to her and whispered, "Have you seen Dr. Martin yet?"

The other girl shook her head almost imperceptibly, making her vibrant red curls sway slightly. "I have him next period. Why? Did Mummy make him a new sweater over the summer?"

Clapping a hand over her mouth, the thin girl stifled a giggle and ducked behind her textbook as Ms. Walsh glanced up from her notes.

Ella quietly pulled a scrap of paper from the pocket of her blazer and looked at her own schedule.

World History, Miss Amy Walsh, Room 132.
Business Calculus, Dr. Franklin Martin, Room 215.
Physical Education, Mrs. Laura Swenson, Lincoln Gymnasium.
French I, Dr. Erich Friedman, Room 102.

33

Hoping to avoid another tardy, Ella surreptitiously followed the redhead when Ms. Walsh dismissed the students from World History.

With her head held high, she attempted to stroll confidently and met every face with a gentle smile. But few met her eye and no one shared her smile. The momentary looks she received in return were disinterested glances, at best curious perusals and nothing more.

She walked a few strides behind the flowing, auburn hair to the second floor and paused, awkwardly, when the girl stopped to talk to a friend. While the two girls whispered conspiratorially, Ella pretended to admire the painting of a sailboat battling a rough sea on the wall behind her. She leaned in to study the painting more closely, all the while watching the redhead out of the corner of her eye.

Ella shifted on her feet as the minutes passed and glanced around uncomfortably. The girl and her friend still appeared deep in conversation.

Ella was about to chance finding the classroom unaided, when the red-haired girl started down the hallway again. Ella followed, feeling more inept than ever. After a few paces, she rolled her eyes and groaned as the girl stepped into their classroom – only a few feet away from where she'd been self-consciously waiting.

While the other girl turned to speak to a friend in the doorway, Ella slunk between the desks and took a seat at the back of the classroom. From there, she quietly observed her fellow students as they trickled steadily into the room.

She watched each of them closely, making mental notes on their shoes, hair, and accessories. After the fifteenth tan face framed with blonde hair stepped through the doorway, she lost interest. Pulling *To Kill a Mockingbird* from her messenger bag, she flipped to the dog-eared page. As the room around her faded gradually away, she was only vaguely aware of the hum of voices clustered near the doorway, and even less aware their conversation centered on her.

Diana Taylor flipped a ringlet of brilliant, red hair over her shoulder and observed with a lazy sigh, "That must be the new girl."

"I thought she was supposed to be pretty," Courtney Harris said with the softest of Southern drawls, glancing up through a veil of fine, blonde hair.

"Why ever would you think that?"

"Oh, someone or other saw her last week in the *village*," Courtney sneered disdainfully and emphasized the word, "and said she was attractive."

"Must have seen her from far off," remarked Julian Carter, who'd joined them in the doorway.

He crossed his thick, muscular arms over his chest and laughed loudly at his own joke. His bass snicker echoed through the room.

"I'd have been right embarrassed to look like country come to town on my first day," Courtney said smugly. She looked haughtily at her own freshly manicured nails and smoothed a pleat in her skirt, purring condescendingly, "Bless her heart."

A rumbling Southern drawl echoed hers. "Whose heart are you blessin' now, Miss Courtney?"

"Why Jack!" Courtney beamed, and took a small step closer to him. "Where've you been hidin' yourself all mornin'? How was your summer?"

"I hardly know," Jackson Montgomery replied, one corner of his mouth pulling up in a crooked grin. "It was over faster than a knife fight in a phone booth."

Diana's auburn curls bounced as she shook her head teasingly. "Honestly, Jack, I don't understand half the things you say."

Jack's grin widened, revealing a set of dimples, and he casually shrugged the strap of his leather attaché case from his shoulder. "Now, who were y'all talkin' about?"

"Oh, nobody," Courtney replied, nodding in Ella's direction. "Only the new girl."

"New girl." Under a pair of heavy eyebrows, Jack's dark blue eyes sparkled mischievously. "I reckon that's not her name."

"You never know. Parents are choosing some strange names these days," Julian replied, and suppressed a laugh.

"There's somethin' interestin' about her," Jack said, the words flowing slowly off his tongue.

Ella was bent low over her book, and Jack's gaze rested on her as he mused. She wasn't remarkably pretty, at least not in comparison to the beauties in the seats to her left and right. Her pallid complexion presented

35

a striking contrast to the bronze skin of the other girls, and her dark hair was nothing like the blonde summer highlights around her. Somehow, he thought, that wasn't why she stood out. It wasn't the rumpled appearance of her uniform, which evidently hadn't been pressed. And it wasn't her lack of jewelry either, even though the earlobes and fingers around her glittered with baubles.

"Jack, always the gentleman," Julian said with a smirk. "I suppose 'interesting' is the polite way to put it."

Jack, squinting at Ella, didn't hear his comment.

"We're readin' the same book," he murmured. To the others he said, "I've a mind to introduce myself. You can always trust a good book to recommend a person."

"What? Right now?" Courtney pouted.

"Yes, directly, if y'all will excuse me," Jack replied, and strode to the back of the classroom.

Ella unconsciously tensed as a shadow passed over her book. She looked up to see a tall boy with a lean frame and unruly dark hair. He had a hard, angular jawline, but the ghost of dimples appeared playfully on either side of his full lips.

After holding her gaze for a moment, he said in a dulcet drawl, "Excuse me, darlin', but I'm readin' that book."

"N-no," Ella stammered a little more loudly than she'd intended, blushing a delicate pink.

What followed was one of those unfortunate moments when a room grows quiet just when a bustle of activity would be most convenient. Every face in the class turned to her, mingling looks of contempt and wonder.

Ella, already flustered by her unusual morning, had never been so embarrassed. Perhaps the only person who may have been more disconcerted was Jack himself. He stood, staring blankly at the deepening flush on the girl's cheeks and the green glow in her eyes outshining the dull grey.

"No," Ella repeated in a lower tone, fixing her attention on Jack alone, and clutching the book to herself defensively. "I didn't take it. I brought this book."

Jack's puzzled eyes creased in an expression of pleasure, and he burst out in a laugh. The rest of the class ogled at this spectacle and Ella's cheeks burned a still more brilliant shade of red.

"No, I reckon you're confused," Jack chuckled, reaching for his own copy of *To Kill a Mockingbird* from his attaché case.

But the opportunity passed as Dr. Martin, attired in a lumpy orange sweater, entered the classroom and immediately began speaking. There would be no going over the syllabus here. The real work started immediately.

With a furtive look at Ella, who was clumsily rearranging her books on the desktop, Jack slipped into an empty seat two rows over. He raised the novel in her direction and hoped to catch her eye but she flipped open her notebook and started writing as speedily as she could in an effort to keep up with Dr. Martin's brisk pace.

Though she excelled in nearly every subject, math had always been Ella's weak spot, and she knew calculus would be a challenge. She had suspected foul play or at least an administrative mistake in the transmission of her school transcripts when the Academy placed her in advanced math. Had she questioned it, the oversight would have been corrected, and her future very different. But the Lord does indeed work in mysterious ways – even through typographical errors – and Ella never asked.

Determined to overcome her failing, Ella listened to Dr. Martin's droning as if it were a symphony. Perhaps if she hadn't been so engrossed in the lecture, she wouldn't have missed what Jack was doing.

The handsome boy who'd accused her of purloining his book was coughing with increasing volume. Everyone else seemed to have heard him clearing his throat. First one set of eyes, then another, glanced over at Jack. But he ignored them and continued coughing. It wasn't until Dr. Martin paused to adjust his glasses and survey the boy in the back row with a critical eye that the noise finally subsided.

In his defense, Jackson Montgomery wasn't in the habit of having to get a girl's attention. Glancing around the room at random, Jack made eye contact with no less than five girls who'd been staring at him with unconcealed admiration.

Although he was not the most handsome boy at the Academy – that distinction fell to the muscular and blonde Julian Carter – he was doubtless in the top ten and knew it. Jack acknowledged the fact without conceit or arrogance. It was simply the truth. He had good genes. And the fact that those genes had left him a not-so-small fortune didn't hurt either. His wealth alone would have easily made him the most sought after boy within the school even if he'd had a third ear protruding from the middle of his forehead.

So this pale, plain girl before him, who appeared inexplicably oblivious to him, couldn't help but arouse his curiosity. As Jack studied her appearance, the difference between her and the others became more concrete and yet somehow more intangible.

Maybe her eyes, he thought finally as Ella glanced up from her notes, still continuing to scribble furiously in her notebook. *Very fine eyes, almost like shimmering emeralds.*

Still studying her appearance, Jack heard his name.

"Mr. Montgomery," Dr. Martin said abruptly, "could you please answer the question on the board?"

"Yes, sir."

He glanced at the problem on the whiteboard and quickly wrote a few notes on the tablet in front of him.

"The instantaneous rate of change if x equals two is ten, Dr. Martin," Jack said after a few seconds.

"Very good. As you can see, the instantaneous rate of change is the same as the value of the derivative at a particular point."

Although Dr. Martin continued his explanation, Ella had stopped writing and was staring – her mouth slightly agape – at the dark-haired young man. He'd answered that question in a matter of seconds! She'd been working on the same problem since Dr. Martin had put it down on the board ten minutes ago! And – her cheeks flushed at the thought – her answer had been off by twenty-five.

Rude and good at math, Ella thought with a scowl, her dislike of him growing every minute. Suddenly the boy looked over at her. Still blushing with mortification, she quickly returned to her notes.

Jack — imagining she'd seen the novel and he'd made a good impression with his answer — flipped his textbook open with a flick of his finger and began scanning the nondescript graphs and tables with a triumphant air.

Dr. Martin's lecture ended just in time, as Ella's hand would have been hopelessly cramped if she had written another word. The moment he dismissed the class, she gathered the books spread out on the desk and grabbed her messenger bag from under her chair.

Ella found herself being swept along by the throng of students to what she only hoped would be the cafeteria. Her stomach had begun to rumble an hour earlier, but she couldn't imagine that a place like the Academy would allow eating in class. She was sure she'd imagined correctly when she reached the Main Hall accompanied by the raucous crowd.

Ella gasped in spite of herself.

The room was nearly the size of a football field with a vaulted ceiling, making the large space resemble an enormous cavern more than a lunchroom. The Hall, being at the center of the main building, was devoid of windows but was lit by glittering lamps that reflected their golden light in the polished surface of dozens of long wood tables.

The Academy students filed in noisily and ambled to the Café, a small food court at the end of the Hall, which seemed as out of place in the stately Main Hall as the McDonalds in dignified downtown Whitfield.

Ella attempted to start up a conversation with a boy in line but was once again rebuffed. After buying a turkey pita and yogurt parfait, she approached a nearby table with her tray. A small cluster of girls sat eating and talking merrily.

Setting down her tray, she pulled out the chair. "Is this seat taken?"

"Yes," one girl said quickly, "sorry."

Ella's lip almost quavered but she replied cheerily, "Oh, no problem."

She lifted her tray and walked to the other end of the long table, watching the sea of students stand in line for salads and plates of sushi and waiting as the long tables began to fill. But no one came near the end of the table where she sat, alone, focusing on deep breaths.

Although she felt utterly isolated, Ella was under more scrutiny than she could have imagined. Every student in the population had noticed her arrival that morning. One person in particular had been observing her intently from the moment she entered the Main Hall.

Jack watched her carefully arrange each item of her lunch in a perfect line on the table in front of her. He watched as she meticulously scraped the yogurt from her cup. And he watched as her sparkling eyes scanned the room for another open seat next to a friendly face, but never met a responsive glance.

"I wonder," he said, more to himself than anyone in particular, "why no one is sittin' with her?"

"Sittin' with whom?" asked Courtney, looking up.

Jack hesitated and replied sheepishly, "The new girl."

"I thought that wasn't her name," Courtney said archly, sweeping her blonde bangs from her eyes.

"I didn't have a chance to meet her." His dark eyebrows creased together in a frown. "But she was lookin' at me in Calculus. I reckoned she might come sit with us."

Julian snorted and Courtney's mouth fell open at the idea.

"Bless your heart, Jack! We'd need a larger table if every girl who looked at you tried to sit with us!"

She instinctively inched her own chair toward his protectively.

"But why is *nobody* sittin' with her?"

"I suppose everyone else is waiting for one of us to make the first approach as –" Diana paused, searching for the correct word.

"– as ambassadors of our class," Courtney finished with a smirk.

The conversation lulled momentarily as the four young students at the table concentrated on the food before them.

"How long do you think they'll wait?" Julian suddenly asked.

With an impish grin, Courtney replied, "Y'all care to find out?"

Julian and Diana laughed in agreement, Julian's bass laugh loud and booming, and Diana's light and tinkling. Jack, still lost in his own thoughts, said nothing in accord or dissent, and his silence was taken as approval by the others.

Ella escaped her uncomfortable solitude in the Main Hall the moment she finished her last bite, and left in search of her next class. The walk from the main building to the Lincoln Gymnasium was down a narrow, winding path. Warm beams from the midday sun fell soothingly on Ella's face and her mood brightened.

I am relaxed, Ella told herself. She walked slowly, breathing deep the crisp autumn air.

"Are you here on a scholarship?" asked a saccharine drawl.

Ella turned to the girl who had appeared beside her. She was without a doubt the most striking person Ella had ever seen up close. Soft, golden hair framed her face, and a pair of brilliant blue eyes set off the delicate features of her face.

"No," Ella said, frowning. "Why?"

"I just assumed, naturally," Courtney replied sweetly, dropping her eyes behind a set of fluttering eyelashes.

Ella stopped walking. "What do you mean?"

"I thought it was obvious," the girl replied with a bored sigh. "You just don't really fit in here."

"How so?"

She gave Ella a cool stare, her starry blue eyes wide. "Where to begin? You look so unkempt and, frankly impoverished. I assume you're smart, at any rate?"

Bewildered, Ella stammered, "I...yes, I think."

"Certainly eloquent," Courtney muttered with a sneer. She sauntered away, adding over her shoulder, "Welcome to the Academy, new girl."

Ella's eyes stung as she walked unsteadily forward toward the Lincoln Gymnasium.

Dear God, would every day be like this, or would it get better?

She tried to swallow the lump in her throat.

Could it possibly get worse?

With eyes painfully brimming with tears she refused to let fall, Ella scanned the horizon past the high iron fence surrounding the grounds in hopes of a glimpse of Aunt Meg's house. Even if the trees had been devoid of their brilliant leaves, she knew it was too far to see, but she looked all the same.

41

For a brief moment, Ella considered dropping her bag and bolting. She mentally calculated the minutes it would take for her to race home, mount the stairs, slam the door of her room behind her, and collapse onto her own bed. There she could cry in peace, without the risk of further humiliation. The urge to run grew stronger, building inside of her. With an effort, she forced her feet to continue on the path the remainder of the way to the Lincoln Gymnasium.

Her Physical Education class was nearly over by the time she regained her composure enough to raise her eyes from the floor. Thankfully, they did little in class and no one noticed her watery eyes. Mrs. Swenson, their instructor, simply took attendance, and the weights and measurements of the students.

As Ella waited in the line for the scale, she glanced around, searching for a noticeable disparity between herself and her classmates. Standing two places ahead was Courtney Harris, whom Ella recognized as the beautiful girl who had insulted her on the walk to class. Ella sucked in her breath and averted her eyes when Courtney turned to look in her direction. From the corner of her eye, Ella watched her toss her head prettily and beam at someone over Ella's shoulder.

Ella turned casually as if to stretch her back, and groaned to find herself sandwiched between the malicious blonde in front of her and the impolite boy from her Calculus class a few feet behind. As Jack held his place in the disorderly line, a small semicircle had formed around him, listening with rapt attention to a story from the summer he was recounting with animation.

"...by the time I finally made it out of the water and up the riverbank, there wasn't nothin' between me and the good Lord but a smile," he concluded.

The group around him erupted in riotous laughter.

"Let's hustle!" Mrs. Swenson's shrill voice shrieked over the clamor of the chattering students, "Please have your shoes untied and be ready to step on the scale!"

Ella knelt to loosen the laces of her black sneakers and, in standing, turned toward the little cluster of students and that one boy especially. He was no longer speaking but he remained at the center of the close circle.

Standing there in the middle, arms crossed over his chest, he seemed to dominate the atmosphere around the group. They all clearly admired him and the more detached he appeared, the more energetically the others sought his attention.

Even though the boy seemed somehow withdrawn – confidently indifferent to the crowd surrounding him – Ella could tell he was listening intently and she had time to study his face in detail. She couldn't deny he was handsome. His firm jaw and heavy eyebrows were tempered by an engaging smile and laughing, inky blue eyes. Without his uniform jacket, she could see the contours of his upper body and lean, muscular arms under his plain, navy t-shirt. He ran a hand through his dark hair, leaving the waves more disheveled than before, as he chuckled at another boy's anecdote.

As Ella stared at Jack, wondering what curious quality made him so irresistible to the others, Jack glanced back at her. As their eyes met for the second time, Ella flushed in embarrassment and her gaze quickly dropped to the floor. Jack rewarded the assembly around him with a dazzling grin which they took as an approval of the most recent joke, and which Ella – still intent on the polished hardwood floor – missed entirely.

"Attendance is required in this course," Mrs. Swenson was saying as Ella took her turn on the scale. "It is extremely important for you to attend class regularly. Although I may not take regular attendance, I will fail any student who I believe has had excessive absences."

Ella nodded. She waited in silence while Mrs. Swenson entered her height and weight on the clipboard and retreated to a remote corner of the gym.

She stayed there, a safe distance from the other students, until Mrs. Swenson announced, "Bring your tennis equipment tomorrow. We'll be starting drills!" and dismissed the class.

Ella discovered her French I classroom and took a seat before the bell rang, feeling proud of herself. In addition to being the easiest to find, French was the most enjoyable of Ella's courses that first day. She didn't recognize anyone from her other classes, not that it mattered since none of them would speak to her anyway, but a girl with ebony hair and velvety black eyes gave her a shy smile when Ella answered a question put to the class by Monsieur Friedman.

Their teacher, with his thick German accent, had the potential to be a most entertaining instructor and, from the syllabus, it didn't seem like the course would be too difficult, at least compared to her other classes.

As she walked through the tree-lined avenue on her way home, Ella dialed a familiar number and waited for the greeting. A friendly voice prompted her to leave a message with her name and phone number.

"Hi, Kelly. It's Ella. I was calling to see how school went for you. I had a…weird day. I miss you. Call me."

She tried another friend but reached a second recording. There was no point in calling Malcolm. He would be at hockey practice. She decided to leave her mom a voicemail just to check in, and was surprised when, after the third ring, a real voice answered.

"Hello? Ella?"

"Mom!" Ella's voice almost broke. "I can't believe you picked up! What time is it there?"

"Don't you worry about that. How was your first day?"

She sounded excited and Ella compelled herself to match her mother's tone.

"Classes were good," she said chirpily. "I think Calculus and History might be intense, but French should be interesting. And we're starting tennis in Phy Ed."

"That sounds great! It'll be fun to learn tennis! Is the school what you expected? Or did the website exaggerate?"

"No, it's all true. Marble floors and stained glass windows and everything. The place is actually bigger than I thought it would be."

"Good! I'm glad you like it!"

Ella forced a cheerful air as she said haltingly, "It's been…harder to make friends here than I imagined."

"I've been praying about that," her mom replied. "It's been a few years since you were at a new school, and it takes some effort. You're not going to make friends with headphones over your ears and your nose stuck in a book all the time, sweetheart. Did you talk to anyone?"

44

Ella hesitated while her mind ran over the students in the hallway who'd refused to help her find a classroom, the tall boy who'd practically announced to the class that she'd stolen his book, the girls in the lunchroom who'd denied her a seat, and the horrible blonde who'd flat out told her she didn't belong.

"Yes, I spoke to a few people today," she said coolly.

"Then I'm sure you'll make friends in no time."

Ella, distracted for a moment from her own troubles by a noise in the background, asked, "Mom, is that gunfire where you are?"

"No, sweetheart," was the quick reply. "I'm only going over some footage from earlier."

Ella was quiet and her mom added reassuringly, "I'm staying safe here. Really. I've seen some chilling things, but I've never been in harm's way myself and I'm just so thankful for the opportunity to get to be here reporting. It is an enormously meaningful assignment. And it's all the better knowing you're at your dream school. I'm so glad you like it," she repeated warmly.

Ella's eyes filled with tears and she said hurriedly, "Better let you go, Mom. I'm almost to Aunt Meg's."

"Okay. I love you, sweetheart."

"Love you, Mom."

Ella hung up and immediately regretted her haste.

She sat on the curb and – hiding her face in her hands – burst into tears, not caring whether any of the neighbors might see or what they would think. She'd finally spoken to her mother in person and hadn't even asked where she was or what she'd been doing. She reproached herself for being stupid and selfish.

Ella had been worrying about how her mother was faring on the other side of the world and still didn't know. Malcolm's face materialized in her mind. He may as well be on the other side of the world. It seemed like forever since she'd seen him. She was alone – more alone than she'd ever been. Although Aunt Meg was kind and helpful, Ella felt like an awkward, uninvited guest with her. Their Bible study of Proverbs helped to fill the silences at the dinner table, but the image of crying on Aunt Meg's shoulder was appalling.

She wished for a warm body to lean on and dry her tears, but knew she could find comfort in prayer.

Dear God, please...

The right words wouldn't come. She didn't really want to go to a different school. Nor did she want her mother to return home or Malcolm to leave college. She didn't even want a whole social circle, perhaps just someone to study calculus with or sit by at lunch.

She closed her eyes and silently prayed for a friend. One friend would do. After wiping her face with the heel of her hand, she slung her messenger bag across her shoulders and walked slowly home.

4. THE CROWD

Ella curled up in bed that night with a heavy feeling in her stomach. Wrapping a blanket around herself, she hugged her knees to her chest and pulled her headphones over her ears. A soft, steady guitar strummed and her fingers clutched the blanket. The air caught painfully in her lungs, the way it always did when she heard her father's familiar voice.

"This is a lullaby for Malcolm," he murmured as the track began.

Ella held her breath and snaked an arm tightly across her stomach to keep quiet. Staring at the blank wall in the darkness, her eyes grew blurry – the tears coming slowly, then in a sudden rush. She lay there late into the night, listening to her favorite song over and over again before crying herself to sleep.

Ella did not sleep soundly and had dark circles under her eyes to attest to that fact the following morning. She awoke early, as the first rays of sunshine penetrated the curtain of leaves outside her window. The house was dark and quiet, her aunt still in a deep slumber.

She spent a long time in the shower letting the hot water beat against her face, imagining that each drop landing on her cheek was melting away a freckle, and the drops that struck her closed eyelids melted away the dull grey of her iris. The moment she stepped out of the shower her perfect complexion and enchanting blue eyes would be revealed.

Wiping away the steam from the bathroom mirror, her sweet imaginings came to an end. There was no denying the white skin spotted with freckles and the grey eyes, now dry from a night of tears and rimmed in a bluish purple from her lack of sleep. Though she understood the futility of the task, she took special care of her appearance that morning.

Ella painstakingly straightened the frizz from her hair, applied a delicate pink polish to her fingernails, and a generous coating of concealer around her eyes. After slowly dressing, being careful not to wrinkle or crease any of her clothes, she kicked her new sneakers under the bed and retrieved her shiny, black church shoes. A three-inch heel of no particular label, they were still clean and not scuffed. She finished breakfast and brushed her teeth to within an inch of their lives. Checking the clock, she quickly added a touch of mascara, ran down the stairs two at a time, and out the door on her way to school.

Sadly, all of her efforts were in vain.

Ella tried tenaciously to speak to a handful of her fellow students in the hallway but received monosyllables in reply. Once again, no one spoke to her. And again, she ate alone.

That isn't to say she went unnoticed.

"You know, I actually think she could be quite pretty if she tried," a particularly chic young girl commented to the mass of friends around her at a table in the Main Hall.

The little cluster had been diligently evaluating Ella's improved hair and makeup for some period of time.

"I agree! There's something uncommon about her, isn't there? I'd never call her beautiful, but she still seems sweetly appealing in some way."

Courtney, overhearing, said with unwarranted volume to the group at her own table, "Yes, nice to see she made an effort today."

"Courtney, don't be catty!" Diana replied with a toss of her hair. "There's no reason to be jealous, just because Jack's been staring at the new girl for the last hour," she added spitefully.

"Y'all mean Miss Ella," Jack corrected. "In Calculus today, she said her name was Ella."

"And?" Courtney prompted with a raised eyebrow.

"And what?"

"And…you're staring."

It was true. Jack, who had thought Ella simply interesting the previous day, now found her downright fascinating. With an effort, he snapped back from his reverie.

"Oh, yes. I was wonderin' if she had an umbrella. It's fixin' to rain this afternoon, and she'll be walkin' home."

"Jack, you are the epitome of chivalry," Diana cooed, "but you, of all people, don't need to concern yourself with the new girl."

"Miss Ella."

"Yes, of course," she said, in a somewhat less obsequious tone. "Don't concern yourself with our dear little Cinder*ella*."

Against the counsel of his sycophant, Jack returned to his room following lunch to retrieve his sturdiest umbrella from the closet.

He caught Ella after their Physical Education class, near a large window inside the gymnasium. The raindrops had already begun to fall from the overcast sky, and she was watching as they etched chaotic paths down the window pane. Standing there motionless and silent with an otherworldly expression on her face, she gave Jack the sudden and arresting impression that she was a pale marble statue, a living work of art.

In truth, after walking to school and traversing the enormous campus, Ella was regretting her choice of shoes. She had been fine through the morning and during tennis practice, never noticing the painful blisters until she returned her athletic shoes to her gym locker and slid her feet back into her high heels. Afraid to shift her weight and rub her already aching feet, she stood still and grave, and tried to focus on the distant rolling thunder and softly falling raindrops.

"When it rains, it pours," Jack said pleasantly as he approached her. His voice was soft and low, and with Southern grace he drew out the lowliest one-syllable word into multiple melodious syllables.

Ella started slightly and glanced around the deserted gym, trying to find the intended recipient of this remark.

"I guess," she said at last, when she was finally convinced that he'd spoken to her.

"You don't live with us on campus, do you, darlin'?"

Viewing his comment as a thinly veiled insult, Ella responded defensively. "No, I don't. I live with my aunt down the road."

"Could I offer you an umbrella for your walk home?"

Her eyes flashed at his patronizing tone. But a verse from Proverbs chapter fifteen resonated in her mind in her aunt's calm voice. *A gentle answer deflects anger, but harsh words make tempers flare.*

Be kind, Ella reminded herself, struggling to swallow down what she wanted to say.

"No, thank you. I have my own," Ella replied coldly, and gave her bag a pat.

"Oh," he faltered, crestfallen.

Ella's lips curved in a polite smile before turning away, but her eyes were steely.

By the time she was dismissed from her French lesson, puddles the size of large ponds had formed on the front lawn and weathermen were now predicting scattered hail showers. Ella stood inside the towering double doors, looking out at the driving rain.

She sighed quietly to herself. She'd always loved storms – watching lightning illuminate the sky and the ethereal smell of wet earth. Suddenly she was aware of someone at her side.

"Are you sure... Could I offer you a ride home?"

Ordinarily, Ella liked people who smiled when it rained. But she groaned inwardly when she turned to see Jack's smiling visage. At best, she believed he was patronizing her. At worst... But Ella didn't want to imagine what he might be planning at worst, alone in his car.

With an effort, she responded in a gentle tone, "No thanks, I'm really fine. *Really,*" she emphasized.

Jack's jaw was hard while he watched her walk away into the rain, her small, green umbrella trembling in the wind. He stood, rigid, at the double doors as a rumble of thunder sounded overhead and the forecasted hail began to fall, shooting off the roof in a high arch. In a flash, he was running to the closest stairwell. He took the stairs three at a time as he descended two levels to the underground parking facility. He flicked a button on the ring of keys in his pocket and a nearby engine roared to life.

Outside the gate, Ella almost wished she had accepted a ride home, though she knew he must have an unpleasant reason for the offer. A short distance further she stopped and slipped out of her shoes.

Ella gingerly set one foot then the other onto the wet sidewalk with a gasp. The smooth concrete was like ice. The cold felt surprisingly good under her aching feet. She stepped in a large puddle and cold water splashed up her leg. She shrieked involuntarily and laughed at her own outburst.

With deliberate precision, she hopped into another puddle.

She walked along, whistling a melody and twirling her umbrella, causing the rain and tiny diamond-like hailstones to shoot off in all directions. On the last note, she executed an enthusiastic pirouette, spinning round and round.

As she turned, she saw the sleek, black car idling a few yards behind her. She could not, however, see Jack behind the tinted windows, shaking with suppressed laughter.

She really is fine, Jack thought. *More than fine. Incredible.*

Ella, unaware of Jack's innocent intentions, saw only the faint outline of a man behind the shaded windows of the unfamiliar car edging closer and closer to her. Her body stiffened and she turned, walking with purposeful steps toward home.

In her sudden panic, the wet handle of the umbrella slipped from her hand and fell to the sidewalk a few feet in front of her. She took a step nearer, the heavy drops plastering her hair to her face. The car advanced faster now. She blinked rapidly to keep the sleet out of her eyes and bent down but as she reached for the umbrella, the wind caught it and it was suddenly airborne. Her umbrella flew past the treetops and, in a moment, was out of sight.

Jack, watching this scene, pulled the car sharply to the curb to offer Ella shelter from the rain and hit an enormous pool on the edge of the road, showering Ella with spray from the gutter. Wiping at her eyes and spitting muddy water, Ella dashed the last few steps home.

Jack was too horror stricken to know what to do next. He instinctively stepped on the gas pedal and the car lurched forward. It came to a stop outside Meg's house. He opened the car door and shouted a word of apology but Ella's cell phone rang shrilly as she crossed the porch and slammed the front door.

She stood dripping on the entry rug and looked down at her phone.

"Hi, Lucas," she gasped, trying to catch her breath.

"Hey Ella. You okay?"

"Yeah," she panted, dropping her shoes on the rug, "I sort of ran home."

"Me, too. I hate walking in the rain." He paused. "I was just curious how your first couple days were going."

Her feet squelched up the stairs. "Awful."

"Really?"

"Really. I've tried talking to people in class, but everyone ignores me." She shut her bedroom door. "No, that's not even it. Some of the students seem to go out of their way to avoid me. It's almost like they're afraid to talk to me."

"They're probably just jealous."

Ella scoffed beneath her breath. "Jealous of what?"

She held the phone in the crook of her neck and slowly peeled the clothes from her wet body.

"Seriously?" Lucas exclaimed. "You're Axel Parker's daughter, and you can sing like nobody else on the planet. I bet they're intimidated."

She jumped as Meg called, "Ella, a young man from your school's here to see you."

Ella covered the phone and, poking her head out the door, shouted back, "Can you tell him I'm on the phone?"

She heard Meg speaking to someone below, and walked to the window, resuming her conversation with Lucas.

"That's not it," she said firmly. "No one knows anything about my dad, and they haven't heard me sing. Besides, even if they did, why would a bunch of snobby, rich kids care if my dad used to be famous and I'm a decent singer?"

"Ella, decent doesn't begin to describe it, and your dad was a legend."

Ella took no notice of his objections. "They hate me. That's all there is to it. It doesn't even matter why, they just do."

Lucas was silent and she went on.

"It's the only explanation. The only people who have spoken to me only did it to insult and torment me."

She looked out her rain spattered window to see Jack stepping back into the dark tinted car.

"A boy from class literally just tried to run me down with his car."

"No way," Lucas murmured.

"Maybe my mom would let me transfer to the public school," Ella said with a question in her voice.

"You could ask," Lucas replied slowly, "but I don't think she'd let you. There is no Whitfield High anymore. Kids from around here take the bus over to Ashby."

"Why?"

"When I first moved here, my sophomore year, there was a school shooting at Whitfield."

"No," said Ella, her voice barely a whisper. "Honestly?"

"Two girls were shot, and a boy killed himself," Lucas stated, the last half of his sentence escaping in a heavy breath.

Ella's hand flew to her mouth. "Oh no, I'm so sorry."

They both fell silent. Despite her own experience with death, Ella was unsure what to say. She vaguely remembered hearing something about a shooting in Whitfield a few years ago, and felt stupid for not putting the pieces together before now.

Mom would have the perfect words, Ella thought bitterly. Something helpful without sounding condescending. Something comforting without being trite.

Eventually Lucas spoke. "It happened my first year here, but I hear there used to be a camaraderie between our school and the kids from the Academy before 'the incident' as everybody calls it. Both schools used to host a big summer carnival together in Whitfield. A Ferris wheel and cotton candy. The whole works. But they canceled it that year. It didn't happen last year either. Now those big gates out front are always shut."

Lucas's voice was hard. "You're in good company if they're ignoring you, Ella. They don't want to have anything to do with any of us."

"Well, I do," Ella replied warmly. "You've got one friend at the Academy at least."

"Thanks, Songbird. And don't worry about those trust fund brats. It's their loss. Seriously."

She could hear the smile in his voice.

After hanging up, Ella pulled on a pair of frayed sweatpants and a vintage Wicked Youth t-shirt – made soft by thousands of washings – and joined her aunt at the kitchen table.

"Who was at the door? What did he want?"

"Oh, I didn't get his name. He just said he wanted to be sure you made it home okay." A smile illuminated Meg's face. "He seemed quite concerned. It was very sweet. An admirer, perhaps?" she teased.

Ella stabbed her meatloaf vengefully and mumbled, "Something like that."

The next few days were much like the first, lonely and quiet. The nights that followed were worse – filled with silent tears that left Ella's throat raw from holding back her muffled sobs. But by the end of the first week, Ella felt more at home in her new school. The instructors at the Academy were all Ella had imagined they'd be. Every last one of them had committed her name to memory by the third day of class, a feat her public school teachers had never accomplished. Monsieur Friedman called her "Eleanor" and Dr. Martin even called her "Miss Parker" despite her insistence that they could both call her Ella.

As Ms. Walsh had predicted, she'd learned to navigate around the main building's snaking corridors by certain landmarks, mainly paintings. Ella found her World History class with a little help from a portrait of an elderly woman with sideburns right around the corner from her classroom. The Business Calculus room was only a few steps away from the sailboat painting. The Lincoln Gymnasium was impossible to miss, so Ella was never late for Physical Education. A large glass case, full of glistening trophies and medals, led the way to her French class.

Unfortunately, she still felt like an outsider when it came to the other students, who continued to keep their distance. No one spoke to Ella in class or in the hallways and she always ate alone at an empty table at the end of the Main Hall. It wasn't until the second week of school that two of the other Academy pupils finally approached Ella.

"You're new here, aren't you?" asked Mitch, the boy who'd crossed the Main Hall to offer Ella a seat at their table.

Ella didn't recall seeing him or his mop of wild hair in the crowded Hall before, but that was to be expected. Mitch was short. Ella estimated him to be about five foot two, at least half a foot shorter than herself. He was, in point of fact, only four foot eleven with his hair flat, but every morning he spiked his hair as high as he possibly could to gain the extra inches. Large square-rimmed glasses, balanced precariously on a small pug nose, covered most of his face.

Jayla, the girl beside him at the table, Ella recognized as the dark-skinned girl with ebony hair and velvety black eyes from her French class.

When she sat, Ella beamed with gratitude and laughed almost giddily. "Yeah. It's my second week."

Nodding, Mitch told her that he and Jayla had decided to take pity on her.

Ella glared in sudden disbelief and made a move to leave, but Jayla grabbed her arm.

"I'm sorry," Jayla said quickly. "He didn't mean to offend you."

Slowly, Ella sat back down.

"It's only that Mitch and I were both new here a few years back, and we know what you're going through. You'll discover this on your own soon enough, but the students here," she said with a darting glance around the Main Hall, "they're not like those at the schools you've attended before, am I right?"

"I've noticed!" Ella snorted. "But you guys have been here for years. You fit in now, don't you?"

"We know our place, and we fit in there," Mitch declared, and gave his spiked hair a yank.

Ella lifted an eyebrow. "Your place?"

"We aren't typical students here. We're each here on a merit scholarship, which means we're on a different level than the other students."

"I don't –"

"There are no cliques here, at least not in the usual sense," Mitch said gravely. "There are no 'nerds.' Everyone at the Academy is smart. There are no 'jocks.' Some students choose to play sports and others don't, but they've all had the benefit of the best personal trainers. The social circles aren't defined by race either because practically everyone belongs to the same race."

Ella turned to Jayla. "You're not the only –"

"The only black student? Yeah."

"How is that even possible?"

"I don't know," Jayla replied with a shrug. "I guess all the rich basketball players and pop stars don't have kids," she quipped.

Ella choked.

"Or if they do, they don't attend the Academy," Mitch remarked solemnly, pushing his glasses back up on his nose.

"I was joking," Jayla murmured. "Mitch doesn't have a sense of humor."

"*Actually*," Mitch enunciated, visibly perturbed with the interruption, "looks in general don't mean that much when perfection is just a nip and tuck away."

"And a stack of cash," Ella argued.

"Exactly. Money. Since everyone has an equal footing in nearly every other way, where you fit in here is mainly determined by your wealth and power."

"As I'm sure you can believe," Jayla added, "students here on scholarships don't have a very high social status."

Ella felt a sudden coldness strike at her core. Where did that leave her? She could hardly imagine where the only student too poor to live in the boarding house and too stupid to receive a scholarship would rank.

"The next most vital thing you need to understand are demerits," Mitch continued in a more detached tone.

"A demerit is the basic unit of punishment," Jayla explained.

"Accumulation of twenty demerits results in campusing. Fifty demerits results in expulsion," Mitch recited.

"Campusing?"

"Campusing means the student is, in effect, grounded for a period of time, usually no shorter than a week. He or she may not leave the grounds except for pre-approved reasons. A campused student is also required to turn in the keys to any car registered to them. Communication, verbal and nonverbal, with any campused student is forbidden."

"A mandatory silent treatment? Sounds a little harsh. What exactly do you get demerits for?"

Jayla pulled a crisp student handbook from Ella's stack of textbooks and handed it across the table to her.

"The items listed on pages twenty-six through thirty-three."

Ella flipped to the page and quickly scanned through the list. Seven pages of fine print. She hiccupped.

16. Electronic devices are forbidden during school hours.

17. Pants may not be frayed at the bottom.

18. Shirts must be tucked in at all times.

19. Men may not wear a necklace.

20. Women's skirts must reach the top of the knee when sitting.

21. No tardiness.

22. No chewing gum indoors.

23. No walking on the grass or landscape.

24. No use of profanity or obscene language.

25. No possession or use of alcohol or controlled substances.

26. No squealing of tires in the parking facility.

"So, who gives these demerits?"

"The professors and the class officers."

"And who are the class officers?"

Jayla seemed to shrink and Mitch whispered, "The Crowd."

"The Crowd?"

"The Crowd is a group of the most attractive, intelligent, and wealthiest students here."

"You forgot to mention ambitious, co-conniving, r-ruthless, and bloodthirsty –" Mitch stammered, nervously re-adjusting his glasses.

"Their parents are among the super-rich," Jayla interrupted, "the upper echelon of the top one-percent, and they have a great deal of influence – not only in the business world and political arena, but also here at the Academy. The administration is afraid of offending or upsetting any of them. So the teachers have to cater to those certain students and ensure their happiness, which means they're free to do whatever they please, regardless of the rules."

"They make their own rules!" exclaimed a petrified-looking Mitch.

"Basically," Jayla finished with a sigh, "the Crowd runs the school."

"So who's in this Crowd?"

"The majority of the kids here like to think they're in the Crowd, but the only people who have any real power are –"

She stopped, as if hesitant to say their names out loud. But Ella's gaze followed the direction of Jayla's uneasy glances to the table in the center of the cafeteria, which was round while the surrounding tables were rectangular. At the center table were four students.

The first girl at the table, whom Ella recognized immediately, was a pretty blonde, lazily drumming her long, thin fingers on her empty tray.

"The blonde?" Ella inquired.

"Courtney Harris."

"She's European," Mitch chimed in, nudging his glasses back up on his nose.

"What country is she from?" Ella asked skeptically, recalling her accent.

"Well, actually, she was born in Louisiana and I think she's lived her whole life in the U.S. but since her mother is from France, she tells everyone she's European."

"Unless a certain someone is present," Jayla added, giving Mitch a meaningful look, "then she really plays up the Southern angle."

"She also claims to have posed for British Vogue."

The girl sitting next to the European model had her back to Ella, but Ella knew the hair. It was the redheaded girl from her History and Calculus classes, whom Ella had followed on the first day of school. The girl sat, twirling between her fingers a single strand of the vibrant auburn curls tumbling down her back.

"What's the other girl's name?"

"Diana Taylor."

"She has a fragrance named after her," Jayla said eagerly. "I think it's supposed to smell like apple blossoms."

"I've never heard of it."

After a pause, Mitch murmured, "It is rather high-end."

Ella's cheeks flushed at this comment and she gave a little hiccup. She took a quick sip of water and turned her attention back to the table in the center of the Main Hall.

The blonde boy next to Diana was exceptionally handsome. The sleeves of his dress shirt were rolled up, revealing thick veins protruding from his muscular arms.

"That's Julian Carter. He's captain of the rowing team."

"I could've guessed. And the other one?" Ella asked, nodding to the small, bespectacled boy seated across from Diana.

"That's Caleb Birnbaum. His mother's been ill for the past few years," Jayla said quietly.

"She is a hypochondriac," Mitch interrupted in a whisper.

"Caleb's usually not in school. He misses class for months at a time, but all the teachers still pass him."

"And those are the people who run the school?" Ella asked incredulously.

Jayla shrugged. "More or less."

That night after school, Ella sat perched on the kitchen counter, balancing the phone between her shoulder and her ear, while her aunt shook chicken drumsticks in a bag of breadcrumbs.

"I'm serious!" Ella exclaimed into the phone. "That place is a cult! Being in an all-white school populated with the offspring of millionaires is one thing," she continued, watching Meg arrange the chicken symmetrically on a baking pan and slide it into the oven, "but it's creepy to think a secret society of students is in charge of the school! There are probably animal sacrifices going on in the boarding house this very second."

"I'm certain they were exaggerating," she heard her mother's voice say soothingly. "More than likely, those students were bullied by a group and – in their minds – made this group out to be more than it is in reality. In many cases, victims of bullying imagine the bully has more power than they actually have."

"So you don't think the Crowd exists?" Ella asked, raising an eyebrow her mother couldn't see.

"No, I don't," was her firm reply. "It's possible that there is a group of influential and perhaps malicious students, but I doubt they're a powerful secret society."

"But what if you're wrong? What if there is a Crowd that tells the teachers what to do and torments the other students?"

Ella heard a sigh on the other end of the line.

"Do you remember what Eleanor Roosevelt said?"

"How could I forget, Mom? Every word the woman ever spoke has been used to brainwash me since I was born."

"Well?" her mother insisted.

"'No one can make you feel inferior without your consent,'" Ella quoted, rolling her eyes.

"That's right. Even if there is this omnipotent, omniscient group of individuals at the Academy," she continued, and Ella heard the smile in her voice, "you have nothing to worry about as long as you stand up for yourself. And practice your deep breathing."

Ella groaned, but she had to admit she felt better. Her mother always had a clear, practical answer for every problem. The most complicated issues seemed to make perfect sense when her mother explained them.

Maybe that's what makes her such a good journalist, Ella thought, *or maybe it's just a mom thing.*

On Thursday, while Ella sat with her new friends in the Main Hall, she looked up from her chicken-salad sandwich to see the handsome boy with the lean figure and dark, wavy hair once again surrounded by a large group at the center table.

"Do you see that guy over there?" Ella asked, gesturing to Jack.

"The tall one?"

"Yeah."

"*Hmm*," Jayla mumbled, "that's odd. I didn't think he took meals in here."

"Wait. I thought everyone had to eat in here. No food is allowed outside of a pupil's room and the Main Hall."

Mitch gave a grunt and yanked his hair. "You don't seem to be grasping this concept of 'whatever they want.'"

"Oh, he's one of *them*," Ella said with mock awe. "The Crowd, was it?"

Mitch looked aghast, eyes wide and mouth gaping. "One of them? They say his great-great-grandfather established the Crowd."

"So who is he?"

"That is Jackson Montgomery," Mitch began. He stopped, finished chewing, and after gently dabbing his mouth with a napkin, continued, "He's descended from old Southern aristocracy."

"Three of his ancestors signed the Declaration of Independence," Jayla added without raising her eyes from her plate.

"You guys don't, like, have a crush on him or anything, do you?"

Jayla finally glanced up. "What?"

"Well, you know his vital stats and then some."

"Courtney did a report on him in our public speaking class last year."

Ella laughed. Alone.

"I didn't intend to be humorous."

"But you were joking, weren't you?" Ella giggled.

They both shook their heads.

"You mean you can do a report on a classmate for a class?"

"If it's Jackson Montgomery, you can."

She looked over at the brilliant, white teeth in his crooked grin and soft, dark curls framing his face. Even in his immaculate uniform, his golden skin gave him a slightly rugged appearance.

"Does he have a girlfriend?" The question was out before she could stop herself.

"Multiple, I think."

"No, he doesn't. You don't know what you're talking about."

"I heard he was dating a pair of Danish supermodels."

"No, I'm certain he's single."

"Why? If he's so great and powerful, why is he single?" Ella's gaze went once more to the table where Jack sat, surrounded by gorgeous heiresses. "Apart from being a jerk, what's wrong with him?"

"Wrong with him?" Mitch echoed, alarmed.

"Don't let anyone hear you call him a jerk," Jayla whispered, "or you'll be found in a ditch somewhere."

Rolling her eyes to the ceiling, Ella laughed but felt a hiccup rising uncomfortably in her throat.

Ella slumped beside Lucas on the old wooden bench outside church following the morning service.

"Why don't you sit with the other kids at church?" she asked.

Lucas's lips curved in a wry smile, and he threw a small stone into the street absently. "More like, why don't the other kids sit with me?"

Ella shifted uneasily on the bench and watched the Buick pull away from the church. Meg, who had settled into a quiet acceptance of Ella's friendship with Lucas, had gone to pick up the groceries they would need for the next week, and Ella had asked Lucas to help her with a purchase of her own. But the question had been bothering her since her first week in Whitfield.

"Okay. So why don't they?"

"They're all jealous of my devastatingly good looks."

"I'm serious."

"Me, too. Have you seen this face?"

He flashed her a dazzling grin. Ella scowled but her stomach fluttered. Even clad head to toe in black, he looked vibrant and handsome. The others probably *were* intimidated by his tall frame and broad shoulders, if not his mesmerizing smile.

"Hey, I wish I was as talented and popular as you, Songbird. But some of us have to get by on our good looks. We can't all be Ella's and Axel's."

"Did you know that wasn't my dad's real name?"

62

"What is it?"

"It's actually Alexander."

"Seriously?"

"Yeah. Dad was dyslexic so when he began school, he started going by Axel because he always wrote Alex wrong. He became friends with Blaze Hollander because they each thought the other had a cool name. Apparently ten-year-old boys can build a friendship on a foundation of next to nothing. And the rest is history," Ella chuckled. "Dad always said it was the little things that shape your life."

Lucas looked hard at Ella. "I'd seriously kill to be able to drop names like Axel and Blaze in casual conversation."

"I didn't mean to name drop," Ella replied, flustered.

"I know. It's not really that I want to be famous, or know famous people. I just want to be something bigger, something better than a foster kid dumped in the middle of nowhere." Lucas sighed and changed the subject. "What are we shopping for, Songbird?"

Ella handed him her shredded messenger bag.

"Geez, Ella, what did you do to this thing? It looks like it was attacked by a bear."

"Not a bear," Ella informed him. "A boy."

"A boy attacked your backpack? And I thought my school was rough."

"It's not funny!" Ella cried, biting her bottom lip to hold back a smile. "It was my mom's."

"I'm sorry. What happened?"

"You know how I told you the other students keep their afternoon books in their rooms until after lunch, and then switch out their morning books for the ones they need in their afternoon classes. But I have to carry all of my books with me the whole day – even my Bible, so I can work on my study of Proverbs during the day whenever I get a chance," she explained, swinging her legs back and forth under the bench. "Well, Friday morning, the tiniest little string was loose on the side seam so I cut it off so it wouldn't catch on anything and get worse. I had to borrow my aunt's sewing scissors to cut it, and of course she said I should really re-sew that seam so it wouldn't unravel. But I said it would be fine."

"So you jinxed it?" Lucas teased. "You should have known better. That sort of comment always comes back to haunt you."

Ella fidgeted with the strap of her messenger bag.

"Anyway, we're kind of between texts in History right now, so instead of bringing one textbook or the other, I had to haul both enormous books with me last week because I never know which we'll be reading in class. So my bag's been even heavier than usual. I was struggling with it on my way from Calc to the Main Hall for lunch because the strap was really starting to dig into my shoulder. I was trying to switch it to my other shoulder but fumbling it a little, and all of a sudden this guy is right there and he practically grabs it from me but I was still holding onto it."

"He just took it from you?"

"Yes! He was all, 'Darlin', let me help you with that', and acting so smarmy but I knew he was up to something, so I didn't let go, and then as we were both holding on to the strap – it broke. My books spilled all over the floor and a couple of them got kicked away from me, and one of the covers was torn."

"What did you do?"

"I scrambled around and gathered all of them up, but I almost started crying, and said, 'This is my mother's bag.' You should have seen his face. He was pretending to be so sorry about it but I could tell he did it on purpose. And I had to carry all my books in a huge, awkward stack for the rest of the day. My arms are killing me."

"I thought you looked more buff today."

"You're hilarious." Ella rolled her eyes. "The worst part is now my Aunt Meg is insisting I join her quilting circle so I can learn to sew. She swears she'll make a domesticated woman of me yet."

"Has she followed through on her threat to teach you to cook?"

She nodded. "I've been making dinner twice a week. So far I've done meatloaf, chicken tetrazzini, rotini primavera, and barbeque chicken pizza from scratch," Ella listed with pride. "You'll have to come for dinner sometime."

"Your aunt won't mind?" Lucas asked casually but avoided Ella's eyes, looking instead at the pebble he was tossing from one hand to the other.

"No, of course not," Ella replied quickly. "Why would she?"

"No reason."

Lucas met her gaze with a radiant smile.

Ella grinned back stupidly and said, "Name the day. I'm sure she'd say yes."

"How could she say no to you?" Lucas demanded. "Ella Parker, straight-A student –"

"Hardly," Ella insisted, still swinging her legs back and forth. "I'll be lucky if I pass Business Calculus."

"– and shining star of the church choir," Lucas continued undaunted. "Tell me, when is your single dropping, again? Seriously, I'm pretty sure Sunday morning attendance has doubled since you started singing."

"I doubt that," Ella laughed. Secretly, she agreed that the morning service was feeling more and more like a pageant, but her cheeks glowed with pleasure at Lucas's praise.

She was still aglow an hour later when Aunt Meg's old Buick pulled up to the curb. Ella slowly rose from the bench, slinging her sturdy new backpack across her shoulders.

"Thanks again for your help. I'll see you next Sunday."

"Already looking forward to it."

As she hopped into the passenger seat, Ella's eyes sparkled green.

5. INVISIBLE

During the first two weeks, Ella had become more and more familiar with the complex layout of the campus beyond her four classrooms. She found herself possessed of extra time, especially in the afternoon when her two friends, like most of the students, returned to their rooms to exchange their books and study or sleep. Ella envied their siesta every afternoon but decided a visit to the two hundred fifty thousand volume library was an agreeable alternative.

Some days, Jayla joined her there to work on their French homework together, but mostly, Ella found herself alone. Before being befriended by Jayla and Mitch, Ella would have found the seclusion of the library lonesome, but now appreciated the peaceful solitude.

Ella would pull one of Dickens' novels from the tall shelf at the back of the room, taking a few calming breaths to ease her descent down one of the library's sliding ladders, and curl up on the leather wingback chair in the most distant, silent corner. Soon she would be in another world, comfortably surrounded by supple leather and lost in the London fog.

But the tranquility was short-lived. It didn't take long for the most popular boy in school to find out where the new girl spent all her excess time. The library was generally empty, so it would be the easiest thing in the world to introduce himself to her casually without the risk of frightening her again. Hopefully she would drop something and he could pick it up, or perhaps she would need a book from one of the higher shelves and he – being the gentleman that he was – could fetch it for her.

However, his brilliant plan had one significant, if not obvious, flaw: Jackson Montgomery, whether he liked it or not, always traveled with an entourage. If it didn't take long for Jack to find out where Ella was spending her afternoons, it took even less time for the entire school to find out where Jack was spending his. And, though up to this point the library had enjoyed a life of obscurity, it became the most popular spot on campus almost overnight.

Ms. Bentley, the librarian, could neither account for the sudden epidemic nor handle it. The fact that her once quiet sanctuary was now bustling with students jointly pleased and horrified her. Having books in the hands of the students made her happy. But, at the same time, having those books removed from her orderly shelves and fingered through by unruly teenagers with loud voices was almost too much for her weak heart.

Not to mention the ladders, Ms. Bentley thought. Did they think those ladders were rides? Because that was not their purpose! Ladders were meant –

Well, at least the students were reading, even if a ladder or two had to be sacrificed. After all, nothing could be worse than a generation of illiterates.

Her only concern, apart from the condition of her books and the treatment of the ladders of course, was for the few students who had frequented the library before this sudden population surge. *That pale, thin creature, for example. The one with the big, grey eyes.* She'd been here every day for the past week, always sitting unobtrusively by herself.

But then, the girl didn't appear to be disturbed by the swarms of people. She'd continued to sit off by herself in the corner, as the others bustled and crowded around the large study tables in the center.

Perhaps, thought the librarian, *the dark haired girl hadn't even noticed.*

Ms. Bentley was half right. Ella certainly had noticed the library becoming more packed each afternoon, but she attributed it to the passing weeks. It was, after all, the third week of school. It seemed perfectly logical to Ella that the number of library visits would increase as homework assignments and exams also increased. But Ms. Bentley was correct in thinking Ella wasn't truly aware of her surroundings. Ella had seen more students, but hadn't noticed their behavior. Perhaps if she had observed the guffawing boys, preening girls, and small groups pushing each other around on the ladders, she would have reevaluated her logic.

It was a simple fact that most of the new occupants were no more studying than Jack was. At the center study table, Courtney chattered next to Jack, tapping her fingers on the map of Norway before her. Julian sat on Jack's right side, his blue eyes fixed on Courtney's lips as she spoke. Jack himself was sitting, head resting on his hand, *Animal Farm* open in front of him on the table.

Every few seconds his eyes would stray from his book to the girl at the table in the back corner, attempting to catch a glimpse of what she was studying. He would read another sentence in the book and his eyes would dart back to her. A few times while he gazed, her look of concentration softened and her eyebrows would lift in surprise or a faint smile would play across her face.

Jack dropped his eyes as Ella looked up to say something to Jayla. She pointed out a line in her textbook and Jayla's tinkling laugh resounded through the hushed library.

Jayla turned back to her own book, reading industriously, while Ella found herself watching the occupants of the table across the library.

It was a wonder, she thought, *that Diana's hair didn't get tangled around her finger the way she kept twirling it like that.* Jackson Montgomery sure looked around a lot. And why was Courtney always drumming her fingers on the table? Was it a nervous tic, or was finger-drumming some form of exercise?

"Don't stare!" Mitch hissed nervously, and tugged his hair. "The last person who looked at Jackson Montgomery the wrong way was expelled from the Academy."

"No, I heard Jack bankrupted the boy's dad's company, so he couldn't afford to go to the Academy anymore," Jayla whispered.

Ella tossed her head and groaned. "I really don't see what the big deal is about the Crowd! Apart from a few rude comments my first day, they haven't done anything, and I haven't heard another word about them from anyone else. Frankly, I'm beginning to think –"

"That's because," Jayla interrupted, her voice quiet but urgent, "you're invisible to them."

The comment hurt Ella's pride, and she snapped back, "How can I be invisible? I'm in classes with almost all of them!"

Even as she said it, Ella had to admit Jayla was most likely right. She wasn't the prettiest, or the smartest, or the wealthiest in any of her classes. They had no reason to notice her.

"Don't take it personally, Ella. It's honestly better this way."

Mitch nodded in agreement. Ella looked at her two friends quizzically.

Pushing his glasses up on his nose, Mitch explained, "It's like this: if they notice you – even if it's because you're attractive or brilliant – they'll make your life miserable, simply because you pose a threat."

"And if they notice you because you're ugly or stupid," Jayla added, "they'll make your life miserable simply to amuse themselves."

"If you're lucky, you'll stay invisible forever. Like us," Mitch told her cheerily.

Ella opened her mouth to reply, but only hiccupped. Her eyes fell to the book in front of her. It could do no good to argue, and what did it matter whether a few self-appointed elitists noticed her? Surely it was better to be humble and among the lowly than to be one of the proud anyway. She was almost certain she'd read that in Proverbs chapter sixteen during their Bible study this past week.

Besides, my first big exams at the Academy are more important than wondering what the Crowd is up to, she thought. Opening her book, she turned aside to ask Jayla a question.

It was a quarter to the hour when Ella said a quick goodbye to her friends and gathered her things. Jack also stood and went to return his book, one he'd purposely gotten from the far back shelf. Approaching her corner, he straightened himself to his full height to catch Ella's attention and introduce himself. Ella, however, spotted him coming and – not wanting to be run into or insulted – quickly stepped to the side and dropped her eyes as he passed. She hurried around him en route to the nearest door.

The Physical Education syllabus noted that the third week of school marked the end of tennis drills. Practice was over, and the class would break into pairs and move on to singles matches.

"Benjamin Majors and Charles Morrison," Mrs. Swenson read from her clipboard.

"Jackson Montgomery and Eleanor Parker."

The reading of Jack's name produced sighs of disappointment from several girls, including his partner. Ella was dismayed but Jack couldn't have been more pleased if he had planned it himself. In a way, he had. Although he couldn't reasonably take credit for the curriculum, the coupling was his doing.

Jack knew from years of experience that Mrs. Swenson would pair up the students in sets of two boys or two girls to compete against each other, and if there was an uneven number of boys and girls, she would randomly form one boy-girl pair. Recognizing early the need for one odd pair, Jack had privately volunteered himself and Ella to a relieved Mrs. Swenson.

"Rebecca Mead and Amanda Newsome," Mrs. Swenson continued through the list.

Ella heard no more names, only her steady, focused breathing in and out.

"I am relaxed," she murmured through gritted teeth.

"Next week," she heard Mrs. Swenson announce. "Remember your partner. We'll be pairing up starting next week."

"But, ma'am, the syllabus –" Jack began.

"I know you're eager to start playing, Mr. Montgomery, but a few of you still seem to be struggling with the fundamentals. We'll begin matches next week," Mrs. Swenson repeated.

Ella breathed a deep sigh of relief. She'd hoped to postpone dealing with that discourteous boy as long as possible, and October was worlds away.

Dear God, please let him transfer to another school by then.

Jack swung his tennis racquet through the air with a savage *swoosh*. In the end — at least in the immediate end — his efforts had been in vain. October was worlds away. He would have to find a way to befriend her before then.

Jack was watching as Ella leisurely collected her books and papers in the library. She'd been at a table with Mitch and Jayla, their heads huddled together as they whispered over her French textbook. Mitch was laughing quietly at something Ella had just said, but Jack wasn't sitting near enough to hear the comment.

He suddenly realized someone was saying his name.

"Jack!" Courtney repeated forcefully.

"Sorry," he said a little guiltily. "Yes, ma'am?"

"I've said Jack like ten times now!" She scowled. "Where are you today?"

"Miss Ella — the new girl — do y'all reckon she looks graceful?"

"Excuse me?" Courtney balked. "What in the name of Sam Hill are you talkin' about?"

"We're partnered up in Phy Ed, and we're competin' in a singles match next week."

Diana gaped at him.

Courtney said icily, accentuating each word, "You didn't hear a single thing I told you about my weekend plans because you were wonderin' if the new girl is graceful?"

Jack nodded.

"Well, let's find out, shall we?" Courtney said maliciously and — looking up to see Ella passing their table — she stood, bumping Ella's arm fiercely.

"Oops," she added with mock sympathy as Ella dove after the books that crashed and papers that fluttered in all directions.

With a cruel edge to her voice, Courtney announced to the girl at her feet, "I'm sorry, sweetie, but I'm going to have to give you a demerit for litterin'."

The faintest whisper of a titter echoed through the silent library.

71

Turning to Jack, she said in a loud aside, "No, Jack. I don't reckon she's very graceful at all."

A few people laughed audibly now, and Courtney strode past Ella with the self-confident poise of a model stomping down a catwalk. Ella, quickly seizing her things, fled from the library leaving Jack standing dumbstruck. Jayla and Mitch rushed after her before Jack could say a word of apology.

The story spread through the school body like breaking news. Before the following day was out, everyone had heard about the encounter. Half the Academy, realizing Ella was a marked woman, continued avoiding her entirely. But the other half of the population, wanting to impress the Crowd, had other plans.

Ella returned to school not realizing a change had taken place. When she arrived in Phy Ed after lunch, she found the class beginning dynamic stretches to warm up before breaking into pairs. As Ella lunged forward, focusing on the tight sensation in her thigh muscles, she was knocked from behind and fell hard to her knees.

She knelt for a moment, stunned.

The spot on her back where she'd been hit by a bony elbow was throbbing. She'd skinned her left knee when she dropped to the floor, and a thin stream of blood ran down her leg.

Jack, watching Ella fall from the other side of the gymnasium, sprinted across the room to her. But a boy with a petite, narrow nose standing close to Ella arrived at her side first. The boy reached his hand down to where Ella sat on the floor, and she leaned on it heavily as she rose.

"Thanks," she said to the boy whose hand was still grasped in hers, and Jack was conscious of a fierce rush of envy.

The boy smirked sourly back at her.

She turned to take her place in the line of students still stretching, when the boy said acerbically in a shrill, nasally voice, "Hey, new girl, nice hair."

His nose seemed to be making up in volume what it lacked in size. His remark echoed around the room. Ella shifted uncertainly on her feet, not knowing whether it was meant to be a compliment or an insult. The small crowd around Ella snickered, but the laughter faded as Mrs. Swenson approached the group.

"Eleanor, why don't you come with me and we'll get you a bandage."

"Thanks," Ella replied, and hobbled beside Mrs. Swenson to the girl's locker room.

Her instructor hurried back to the class, leaving Ella behind to wash the blood from her leg with a wet paper towel and apply the large bandage. Ella took her time, plodding slowly back to the gymnasium and discovered that the couples had already begun their matches. Ella grudgingly walked to the court where Jack stood waiting and served the ball to her ill-favored partner. She returned the ball to Jack with a ferocious *whack* at every opportunity, but she was spared having to speak to him.

Ella's French lesson, which usually flew by, dragged on that afternoon. Her back was sore and her knee still stung. She shifted uncomfortably in her chair, first turning so her bruised shoulder blade wouldn't make contact with the chair back, now bending her legs to a less excruciating angle. She fidgeted and squirmed, but no matter how she sat, it was painful.

Finally giving up the struggle, she slumped in her chair. As she flipped her hair over her shoulder, she felt something soft and tacky brush her hand.

Gum? she wondered, feeling it between her fingers. *How?* She couldn't have gotten gum in her hair when she wasn't chewing any.

But there was no denying it. It definitely was gum, and it most certainly was stuck in her hair. As she thought about it, another unsettling truth became clear to her. No one had approached her in any class or the hallway, and Mitch and Jayla had sat across the table from her during lunch, as always. The only person who'd gotten close to her all day was that towheaded boy who had helped her up in the gymnasium.

Ella had a solid two hours that evening to think it over. Meg sat beside her at the polished oak table in the kitchen, determinedly massaging peanut butter into the sticky clump of hair.

"I'm sure it was an accident, Ella."

"Then why did he make that comment about my hair?" Ella argued. "And why did everyone laugh?"

"Who was he? Have you spoken to him before?"

"No." Ella shook her head. "I don't even know his name."

"So what could he possibly have against you?"

"I don't know. But having someone mention your hair, then finding gum in your hair an hour later couldn't be a coincidence."

"That's exactly what I think it was, just an odd mishap. I think all this talk about secret societies has gotten into your head."

By the end of the evening, Meg had finally persuaded her.

With her mind at peace, she slept soundly, believing it was nothing more than a stroke of bad luck until she took her seat in Calculus the following morning and felt something wet. Glancing down, she noticed a crushed pen on the floor below her chair and a puddle of black ink seeping out from under her skirt.

She scanned the room to see if anyone was watching her. But none of her classmates appeared to be paying the slightest attention. She half rose as Dr. Martin entered the room and strode briskly up the aisle. Thinking rapidly, she pulled a tissue from the front pocket of her new backpack and attempted to dab up some of the inky liquid. But after soaking four tissues, a small puddle still remained.

Jack, arriving just in time for class, ambled in and took his seat. He peered over at Ella, fidgeting conspicuously in her chair, and his eyebrows crinkled. With his elbow, he nudged the boy to his left and motioned with his eyes to the row where she sat.

"Why?" he mouthed without a sound.

"Ink," the boy whispered back. His lips barely moved, except to form into a smile.

Jack's brow creased further. Although he generally paid little attention in Calculus, he heard even less than usual in class that day.

It's all my fault, he thought miserably. The situation would only escalate from this point, even though he had spoken to Courtney and squelched the source of the trouble. Jack wasn't certain whether Courtney's remorse was genuine or if she was simply afraid of losing Jack as the foundation of their little circle but she had half-heartedly apologized to Ella in Phy Ed after the scene she'd made in the library. Jack knew that despite the comments they'd continue to make behind Ella's back, neither Diana nor

74

Courtney or Julian would risk bothering her again. Unfortunately, even though the match had been snuffed out, the fire had already spread beyond his control.

When Dr. Martin dismissed the class, Jack collected his books slowly, still absorbed in dark ruminations. He stepped into the hallway and immediately spotted Ella, a handful of students surrounding her. Despite her efforts, she had a large dark stain running up one side of her skirt. She held her backpack awkwardly at her side, attempting to shield the discolored portion of her figure. But both her concealment and her artificial calm were useless. Her distress was shown clearly on her face as the group around her laughed.

A tall girl with vacant, wide-set eyes stepped forward.

"If I were one of the class officers, I'd be forced to give you a demerit for violating the dress code. You're supposed to have a navy blue skirt — not black!" she taunted.

"What do you think, Jack?" one onlooker asked, his dark glance fixed on Ella. "Will you give her a demerit?"

All eyes turned to him, including Ella's frightened ones.

Jack produced his most charismatic grin and announced indifferently, "I hear tell black is the new navy."

The surrounding crowd laughed and snorted. But Jack's objective was achieved. His wit had the effect of bringing him to the forefront and the girl with the stained skirt and tears hanging in her eyes faded safely into the background.

Staring after him, Ella decided Jackson Montgomery was the most conceited, swaggering jerk she'd ever met. Words escaped Ella, her mind spinning with insults. All of her torment and humiliation seemed to center around him and his friends. No one, apart from Mitch and Jayla had said a word to her until that day in the library when Courtney had knocked Ella's books out of her arms. Now she was being pushed in gym class, had gum spit in her hair, and had ink poured over her seat in Calculus — all in a matter of days.

There's no way it's a coincidence. It's all because of the Crowd.

6. THICK SKIN

Ella's feet shuffled through the crisp leaves as she walked slowly to the Academy.

"Mom, please, you don't understand! My cell phone bill for this month was addressed to 'the whore.'"

"I already told you I'd be following up about that. But I doubt it had anything to do with your school. More than likely, the company had an issue with a disgruntled employee, or a bizarre typo occurred when your change of address went through."

Ella bristled at her mother's patronizing tone. "Seriously, Mom?"

"Yes, I am serious, sweetheart. Do you honestly believe someone from your school would do that – or *could* do that?"

"Of course I do! I've had to delete every single one of my social media accounts because of what's been posted, and there's no way you can say that was the work of a disgruntled employee."

"Those sites are all a waste of time anyway."

"Mom!"

"Sweetheart, do you have any idea what a girl your age has to go through to get an education here?"

"I know it's a first world problem, Mom, but that doesn't mean it isn't a problem. I don't know how much longer I can take this. Jayla saw some kids making obscene gestures behind my back and it's even gotten physical. A boy yanked my school bag off me so hard it took the skin off my arms."

"Have you told any of your teachers about it?"

"Ms. Walsh said to talk to the guidance counselor, and she told me to bring it up with the headmaster."

"And?"

"He's not going to do anything about it! No one is! Why can't I transfer to the public school?"

"You know why, Ella." Her mother's voice sounded metallic and distant coming out of the phone. "We've had this discussion."

Ella kicked a pile of dry leaves in her path. "It's not like I'm going to get shot, Mom. Lucas has told me all about their school in Ashby. It's like a maximum security prison. Besides," she said, thinking desperately, "lightning never strikes the same place twice."

"Ella," her mother gasped in an appalled tone, "what an analogy to make! You know that isn't the reason. You are a mature, well-adjusted young woman and I will not have you run away from this problem. I know you can face it and you will be stronger for it. It may be hard to see it now, but I'm doing this for your own good."

"But, Mom, I've tried everything. I've prayed, I've stood up for myself, and I've tried ignoring the other students. It's only getting worse!"

"Do you remember what she said?"

"Mom!" Ella groaned.

There was silence at the other end of the line.

"Yes, rhinoceros skin. Yes," Ella answered grudgingly.

"Develop skin as tough as rhinoceros hide!" her mother quoted Eleanor Roosevelt triumphantly. "Now, I know you were picked on at the last school you transferred to but it didn't last forever. It's common for bullies to gravitate to a new student. I understand it's unpleasant, but you've lived through it before and I'm confident you know how to handle the situation."

"But, Mom, they're not just being rude or mean, I'm talking about persistent, premeditated attacks. And it's not just some bully! It's everyone! People I've never even spoken to! People who aren't in any of my classes, who don't even know me! They've chosen me to entertain the Crowd!"

"Sweetheart, I know it might seem that way, like it's all connected and everyone is out to get you, but really it is simply poor choices from some exceptionally juvenile students. Nothing more. And like every time before, the bullies will get bored and will leave you alone."

"Sure, Mom, whatever you say," Ella said quietly.

She knew defeat when she encountered it. There was no line of reasoning she could use to convince her mother and she was far too frustrated to continue arguing in circles.

"I'm almost to school. I'll call you later."

She looked up at the Academy, still a few blocks away, and quickened her pace. The constant movement somehow made her feel less trapped.

Trapped. Ella repeated the word in her mind as she marched toward the very place she dreaded. *I am trapped.*

She was going to be stuck at that school, relentlessly persecuted, until the day she graduated. It seemed as though everyone had a joke at the expense of the new girl, and rumors about her abounded.

Seven more months, she thought, another twenty-eight weeks before she was free.

Her mother was never going to let her transfer out of the Academy, and only had useless Eleanorisms for comfort. Aunt Meg hardly believed her and listened to her as one might console a small child crying about a dragon under her bed.

Lucas was sympathetic. But all he could do was listen. Mitch and Jayla defended Ella as best they could, but the pair couldn't possibly be everywhere at once. Ella knew it would be easier for them to abandon her and if they did, she would lose more than simply their friendship. She closed her eyes and breathed out a prayer into the chill, autumn air.

Dear God, thank you for my friends. Forgive me for not appreciating them enough.

Mitch and Jayla were her only allies at school now. She felt this keenly that afternoon in the Main Hall as a passing student commented on Ella's meager lunch.

"Did that come from the food shelf, new girl?"

Ella hiccupped, swallowing a mouthful without chewing. Her bite of the complicated German dish which Aunt Meg had helped her to prepare slid painfully down her throat as Mitch shot back a retort that silenced the snickering onlookers.

"Thanks, Mitch," Ella choked out. "It's getting worse. A group of them followed me home from school yesterday. I don't know where they came from but all of a sudden there were these two cars behind me, and the kids inside were shouting the most horrible things out the windows at me. I can't even...I can't even tell you," Ella whimpered. "Some of them were even throwing water balloons. I'm pretty sure...I *think* they might have actually been filled with urine. It was disgusting."

After another hiccup, she said, "All I could think was, 'I can't let them follow me home. I can't let them know where I live.' Who knows what they would do, you know? So I ran past the house and went around the block. I tried to just keep running. But they kept shouting...kept following me. They...they didn't stop, and I couldn't let them see me cry. So I had to run home."

She stifled another hiccup.

"Thank you for listening," Ella told them finally, wiping her nose with a napkin. "I'm sure you're sick of my whining, but it's nice to talk to someone who believes me. I don't feel like anyone else really understands."

"Don't worry about it," Jayla said. "No big deal."

"But, I get it if you guys don't want to sit with me anymore. I won't be offended, I swear." She turned to Mitch, "I heard about the message on your door. Was it really written in blood?"

"No," he replied, shaking his head a little too nonchalantly. "It was only red paint. Jayla's right, don't worry about it."

"But you're not invisible anymore! And it's because of me, isn't it?" Ella asked. Her voice had a wild tremble in it.

"Ella, look, it doesn't matter," Mitch said vehemently. "What they're doing to you is wrong. If I was in your place, I know you would stand up for me. I don't mind."

Jayla smiled weakly. "Who wants to be invisible anyway?"

On Monday during the lunch hour, Ella sat with Jayla at their usual table in the Main Hall. She was in a bright mood. The morning had been uneventful and she was still radiating happy energy from the weekend as Mitch approached the table. The Café was serving chicken cordon bleu, his favorite dish. As he advanced on their table with his plate piled high, the captain of the rowing team repositioned a long, thick leg from under the center table directly into Mitch's path.

Mitch, intent on the delicious smell wafting from his plate, took no notice and tripped over Julian's outstretched leg. He lunged forward acrobatically, but failed to steady himself. Squealing as he fell, Mitch landed with a sickening *squelch* directly on the mound of steaming chicken. There was only the briefest pause before the entire assembly in the Main Hall exploded into loud and delighted laughter.

As Ella listened to the deafening roar, and watched Mitch's glasses slip from his nose and clatter to the floor, a sharp, frenzied pressure filled her chest. *Be kind*, warned the voice in her head. But without thinking, she took the apple she'd been about to bite into, and launched it with her full force at the one round table in the center of the Main Hall. It arched above the gleaming tables, and whistled as it sped through the air. Then it landed, missing Julian entirely but hitting Courtney squarely on the temple. The laughter stopped instantly as she let out a bloodcurdling scream and clutched at her head.

A hushed voice exclaimed in amazement, "Someone threw an apple."

The Main Hall was uncomfortably silent for a long second.

A second voice shouted, "Food fight!"

Before another word could be said, food was flying. Alfredo noodles, fresh peaches, chocolate cupcakes, and California rolls soared overhead.

Ella, having recovered from her momentary rage and horrified at her own action and its result, jumped to her feet, shouting, "Stop! Please stop it! Someone's going to get hurt! It was a mistake!"

But no one could hear her cries over the joy from the other students, freed for a brief moment from their dreary sophistication. Luckily for her, the battle lasted only four minutes and the air finally cleared. Though the students may have wished to continue, there simply wasn't enough food for ammunition. Looking around, Ella saw the paintings were covered in rice, and the long tables and all their occupants were slick with sodas and sauces.

When order had been restored by a dozen agitated administrators, the students were filed out of the Main Hall in a long single line. While the others were taken directly to the boarding house, Ella was escorted to the women's locker room adjacent to the Lincoln Gymnasium to shower. She emerged fresh from the shower but, unlike the other students, didn't have a clean uniform available to change.

She did all she could to scrub the remnants of food from her pleated skirt and navy jacket. Wrapped in a towel, Ella stood at the sink and rubbed an unidentifiable blue slime from her jacket under the hot water.

Her fingers were throbbing and red, and Ella could feel hiccups coming. As the steam clouded around her face, she tried to breathe deeply. But she couldn't seem to breathe at all, let alone deeply.

Dear God, forgive me. Help me. I can't do this anymore.

She attempted to blink away the tears fighting their way out from her eyes, but failed entirely and sank to the floor on her knees, weeping hysterically. When all the tears were gone, she stood again, wiping her eyes on a corner of the large towel. As she looked up to see her blotchy, red face in the mirror, she started crying all over again.

The next few days flew by. Ella's classes were a blur, and she barely remembered a word Meg spoke to her in the evenings during their Bible study. The one good thing that had sprung out of the disaster was that Ella, Mitch, and Jayla were invisible again. So much focus was directed on the food fight, almost a week passed with little more than a sneer in her direction. But she couldn't enjoy it.

Her stomach lurched every day as she walked toward the Main Hall, still thick with the scent of industrial cleaner, and she squirmed in her seat when each of her instructors kicked off their lesson with a plea for the guilty party to come forward. Ella knew what she had to do, but couldn't bring herself to do it. Her mom would be livid – not to mention Aunt Meg. Her teachers would be as well, but that wouldn't matter because she was sure to be expelled.

If Mom won't let me go to the public school, what then?

Perhaps she would have to be homeschooled, or shipped off to military school never to see her family again.

But then the still, small voice inside her would say, *the truth will set you free.* Ella tried to deny it, but eventually, the voice won out over her selfish fears. That, and the voice she overheard whispering in French class.

"I bet it was the new girl."

Her ears pricked up but she kept her head low.

"Probably," replied a boy in the row in front of Ella.

He and the girl next to him both turned to stare at Ella over their shoulders. She dropped her eyes to her textbook.

"What if she gets expelled?"

"So? The school would be a better place without her. Honestly, the world would be a better place without her."

The boy shot a surreptitious glace across the room. "I actually think it was Jayla."

Ella followed their gaze to where Jayla sat, unaware.

"Could be. Everybody knows she and Mitch are a couple," the girl replied, smearing a glob of shiny gloss onto her lips.

"And the apple did come from the direction of their table," he whispered back, nodding earnestly.

The girl smacked her lips. "You should turn her in tomorrow."

"I think I will. First thing."

As Ella leaned back in her chair away from the whispering pair, a cold lump grew in her stomach. Mitch and Jayla had already gotten demerits from the Crowd by standing up for her. Now, if Jayla was blamed for this, she would likely lose her scholarship. She would have to leave the Academy, and she'd never be able to get into a school like this again.

Ella blew out a long breath. She couldn't let that happen. When French was dismissed, she followed Jayla to the library where she spotted Mitch near one of the rear shelves.

Passing a line of tables toward the back of the library, she heard a girl ask, "Is it true her parents are in prison?"

But the comment went unheeded by Ella, intent on her mission.

Courtney, overhearing, said, "I hear tell her parents gave her up for adoption. Bless her heart. She lives with her grandmother down the road, y'know, because she can't afford to board here."

"She *looks* like an orphan," Julian said offhandedly.

Jack growled, "Cut your own weeds, Julian."

"What?"

"Mind your own business!"

Jack's chair screeched against the floor as he rose abruptly from the table. He strode to the long rows of shelves at the other end of the library.

"Nicely done," Diana hissed sarcastically to the other two.

"Sorry." Julian shrugged. "I forgot."

Courtney half stood to go after him.

"Give him a minute," Diana said, glancing over as Jack retreated between two rows of high bookshelves. "You know he's sensitive about that."

Jack was more angry than upset. He was trying to rein in his growing exasperation but failing miserably, when he was distracted from his own struggles by a familiar voice.

"I did it. I'm going to confess."

"I don't understand."

"I threw the apple. I started the food fight. It's all my fault," Ella said in seemingly one breath.

Two muffled voices mumbled words of reassurance.

Jack moved noiselessly closer to the shelf. On the other side, separated by the orderly row of books, stood Ella between Mitch and Jayla, who had a hand resting on Ella's shoulder.

Mitch pressed the tips of his fingers together, and looked up at Ella. "You don't have to do that. It's been days and no one has any idea who is responsible."

"But someone thinks you're responsible," Ella told Jayla anxiously. "He's going to go to the headmaster tomorrow with your name! I overheard the whole thing in French this afternoon."

She lowered her voice and Jack couldn't make out the words.

"Don't do anything rash, Ella!" Mitch interrupted, tugging at his hair. "They don't have any evidence, and it's really the Crowd's fault anyway. Desperate times call for desperate measures!"

Ella opened her mouth to speak, but Jayla was faster.

"He's right," Jayla declared firmly. "Anyone here would let somebody else take the fall. It's not a big deal, Ella. Even if someone does blame me, it won't be that bad. I have a perfect record here up until the last two weeks. Whereas you've been at the Academy only four weeks and have twice as many demerits. Besides, it was just an apple. The rest of the students chose to participate. *They* started the food fight. The administration can't blame the whole thing on one piece of fruit. I'm willing to cover for you."

"It's not only that." Ella hiccupped. "I'm guilty. It's bad enough I brutally attacked someone – even if it was only with an apple – but I feel even worse lying to cover it up."

And yes, said the small voice inside of her, *remaining silent to cover her own guilt was a lie.*

"Please sleep on it, Ella," Jayla insisted.

Ella nodded and left the library, but she had already made up her mind.

Eager for the full confession to be over, Ella hurried home to tell Aunt Meg the truth. She knew her aunt would be furious and was prepared for the worst. Meg sat with a stony face until Ella had finished.

To her surprise, Meg laughed. "Oh, Ella, you remind me so much of your mother."

"What?" Ella asked, wrinkling her brow.

"I bet you think she's always been serious and responsible, but she was such a troublemaker when she was little!"

"Really? My mom?"

"When we were younger, your mom and I used to pluck apples from the tree in the backyard to use for batting practice. One time, I was pitching and she hit a fly ball and shattered the neighbor's window," Meg chuckled. "Applesauce everywhere!"

"What did she do?"

"Well, when your Nana and Papa found out, we were in huge trouble. In the end, they replaced the window. And your mom and I had to wash every window in our house and every window in the neighbor's house once a week for the next year as punishment. She blamed me and I blamed her, and we stopped speaking to each other, we were both so angry." Meg's face softened at the recollection. "We were as close as sisters could be. We never stayed mad long. By the second week, we were best friends again."

Meg sighed a deep, sad sigh and Ella excused herself to go call her mother.

Oddly, her mom hardly sounded upset either. She seemed more interested in Ella's conversation with Aunt Meg. Ella was so thankful her mother didn't mention military school that she retold the tale with gleeful animation. Her mother laughed aloud over the phone and filled in her own particular details of the story.

Her mother ended the phone call with a satisfied sigh. "Ella, I'm so glad you're with your Aunt Meg. You remind me so much of her at your age. She wasn't afraid of anything, and there's nothing she wouldn't do for her friends, especially me. I know she probably seems old and serious to you, but she was just a firecracker when she was young."

"And how am *I* a firecracker?"

"Ella, boring girls don't start food fights."

The next morning, Ella went straight to the headmaster's office. All her courage drained away the moment she stepped into the luxurious waiting room. Everything, from the large picture window framing the main building and grounds to the row of supple leather armchairs lining the side wall, contrived to make her feel insignificant. But the still, small voice reassured her she was doing the right thing.

The headmaster's assistant glanced up from her computer with an expression of pleasant indifference.

"How can I help you, Miss...?"

"Parker," Ella replied. "I'd like to speak to the headmaster as soon as possible. It's important."

Looking back at the computer, the assistant said, "He has a short block of time available this morning. If you'd like to wait, he'll be with you momentarily."

Ella crossed the room to the armchairs where another girl already sat, taking the seat on the end. Her eyes swept gradually around the room again, and Ella hiccupped loudly. As she raised a hand to her mouth, the other girl shifted in her chair, turning her body away from Ella's direction. Ella took a deep breath and folded her hands in her lap.

Dear Lord, please grant me a miracle: don't let me get expelled.

Forcing the rest of her body to remain motionless, she clasped and unclasped her hands quietly until the waiting room door opened. She looked up and groaned.

Of course Jackson Montgomery would be here, Ella thought, to make her nightmare complete. Jack met her eye but gave no sign of recognition. He walked confidently to the assistant's desk where she greeted him by name.

"I'm afraid I didn't make an appointment," Jack apologized, running a hand through his unruly, dark hair. "But I believe Headmaster Tutwiler will understand. I'm hopin' he can see me immediately."

"Certainly," she responded ingratiatingly. "Please have a seat."

Jack took the plush armchair between the two girls and Ella focused on another calming breath. But no sooner had he sat than the inner door opened and Headmaster Tutwiler stepped out. He was a short man, but struck an imposing figure in his well-cut navy suit and black-rimmed spectacles.

"Mr. Montgomery, always a pleasure," the headmaster beamed. "Come right in."

Jack paused in his chair. "Sorry for everythin'," Jack whispered hastily without looking up. "I hope this makes us even."

He stood and shook the headmaster's hand before they stepped into the office.

Ella turned quizzically to the other girl. "Was he talking to you?"

"Excuse me? Do I know you?" she answered, edging away with an expression of disgust.

Ella's gaze dropped to her hands. She picked at her nail polish for what seemed an hour until Jack walked out of the headmaster's office with a light step. He moved to the exit without glancing back.

Ella jumped when the assistant called her name.

"Miss Parker, the headmaster will see you now."

She was ushered into his office. Shelves filled with handsome leather-bound books lined the walls. The headmaster stood to greet her.

Ella had worked out exactly what she would say on the walk to school. She shook his hand hurriedly with a brief, "Good morning, sir," and the moment Headmaster Tutwiler had taken his seat behind the high, glossy desk, she began.

"Excuse me, sir, I'm afraid we haven't met officially, but I'm Ella Parker and I have a confession to make. I, willingly and without accomplice, threw the apple that started the food fight. No one else was involved, and I accept the punishment wholly upon myself alone."

The headmaster raised his hand. Confused, Ella stopped.

He sighed wearily and said, "What you are doing, Miss Parker, is certainly noble but, I must say, misguided."

"Huh?" Ella hiccupped.

"The culprit very maturely confessed this morning. The person responsible –"

"You're wrong," Ella interrupted. "I...I must accept the punishment...wholly upon myself alone..."

She'd lost her place in her meticulously rehearsed speech and didn't know what to say.

"It wasn't Jayla," she mumbled finally. "It was me."

"Jayla?"

"She...she..." Ella stuttered stupidly. "You mean she isn't in trouble?"

Headmaster Tutwiler looked at Ella over the top of his spectacles. "I'm not sure I follow your story, Miss Parker, but was afraid we might have a few students attempt to fall on their swords for this particular pupil. But as I said, the culprit has already confessed and the matter dealt with."

"Then I...I..." Ella stammered. "I'm sorry for taking up your valuable time," she managed.

She stepped out of his office and closed the door gently.

Ella didn't hear a word in her morning classes and when she entered the Main Hall for lunch, her friends rushed at her.

"Did you really do it?" Jayla demanded.

Ella glanced from one face to the other. "What do you mean?"

"Neither of our instructors made the announcement this morning encouraging the perpetrator to come forward," Mitch explained.

"So we thought maybe you'd really confessed," Jayla added. "I couldn't believe it!"

Ella checked to be sure no other ears were listening and whispered, "I did confess."

The other two both spoke at once.

"What?"

"And you're still here?"

Ella nodded. "I went to see the headmaster this morning, but someone else had already confessed. You didn't say anything?"

Jayla and Mitch both shook their heads. "Who would?"

"I wish I knew." Ella shrugged. "It was hard enough for me to confess, and I was the one who actually did it!"

Ella puzzled over it the rest of the day but could make no sense of the turn of events. The strangest thing of all was that the rumors stopped immediately. Since the criminal wasn't made public, she'd expected the students would continue gossiping. But Ella didn't overhear a word about the food fight from anyone. It was eerily as if it had never happened and everything returned to normal.

Ella felt, afterwards, very foolish for believing she was through with the Crowd.

7. A FRIEND

"Miss Parker, would you mind staying after to discuss your test?" Dr. Martin asked as Ella was heading out the door after Business Calculus the following day.

"Of course not," Ella replied cheerily, walking over to stand before his desk.

"I'm a little worried, Miss Parker," he began as her last classmate left the room. "I was under the impression you were a bright student and weren't having any trouble keeping up in the class. But I must have been mistaken, and I fear the consequences of my oversight are severe. You see," Dr. Martin went on, tugging at the sleeve on his purple sweater, "every action has an equal and opposite reaction."

Ella was suddenly having a difficult time following him. "Isn't that physics?"

"Yes, but in this case I think it applies to calculus. For example," Dr. Martin continued, "if a student doesn't understand class material, that student will do poorly on the exam."

Ella nodded in agreement.

"And," he added, handing Ella her test, "if a certain student doesn't get help in this class, that student will fail."

She glanced down at the paper. A small D- was scrawled in the upper right hand corner. Ella hiccupped involuntarily. She'd never gotten anything lower than a B in her entire life and those were when she'd barely opened a book. But Ella had studied for hours before the Business Calculus exam.

"Are you sure this isn't some sort of mistake?" Ella asked softly.

"No mistake. I double checked it. As you no doubt know, Miss Parker, this is a very illustrious school and there are certain standards that must be upheld. I simply can't have a student fail my class. Believe me when I tell you that your failure will hurt me much more than it will hurt you."

Dr. Martin gave Ella what he hoped was a reassuring smile, but it fell flat.

"Due to the fact that both of our futures depend on your success, I plan to do everything in my power to help you. To start with, I am referring you to a student tutor. We can see how things work out with the tutor, and you can be sure that I will be paying particular attention to you in class and will frequently check up on your progress."

Ella gulped back another hiccup and left the room with cheeks burning. Convincing her mother to transfer her to another school would have been one thing, but flunking out was entirely different. Besides, things were finally going smoothly.

She was silent and morose all throughout lunch, but Mitch and Jayla were too preoccupied studying for their upcoming test in Political Science to notice. By the time Ella reached the Lincoln Gymnasium, she had almost entirely composed herself.

Her self-possession was short lived.

"Alright, everyone pair up!" Mrs. Swenson bellowed over the din. "Doubles matches today. You'll all get to spend some time with your partners on the same side of the net."

Ella hiccupped and her stomach dropped to her feet. But, after a hasty sweep of the room, her spirit lightened. Jackson Montgomery was nowhere to be seen.

"Mrs. Swenson!" Ella called out, her arm shooting into the air. "My partner isn't here. Can I sit out?"

Mrs. Swenson scowled and crossed the gym to where Ella was standing.

"Who's your partner, Eleanor?" she asked, flipping through a stack of papers on the clipboard in her hand.

"I was assigned to Jackson Montgomery."

A softly drawling voice close beside her replied, "Present."

Both Ella and her instructor turned to see Jack standing behind them, his hands thrust deeply in his pockets.

Before either could respond, a shrill voice ripped through the air, "Mrs. Swenson! Mrs. Swenson, Rebecca's missing too. Can I partner up with Scott instead?"

The harried instructor scowled again.

"Well, at least one crisis averted," she muttered, walking away and leaving Jack and Ella standing together in silence.

"I believe we've howdied, but not met," Jack drawled, offering her his hand and a smile. "I'm Jack."

She shook his hand perfunctorily. "I know who you are."

"And you're Ella," he said brightly. "Pleasure to meet you."

"My name is Eleanor," she told him icily.

Jack's smile wavered. "But in Calculus you said you prefer to be called Ella?"

"My friends call me Ella. *You*," she said, emphasizing the word, "can call me Eleanor."

She expected this last comment to make her point. But, surprisingly, his face broke out in a charming smirk.

"Not exactly the sweetest cookie in the jar today," he declared with a laugh. "What's the trouble, Miss Eleanor?"

Ella glowered and was about to snarl a response, when she was checked by the *crack* of a shoe hitting the wall on the other side of the gymnasium.

"Rebecca! Amanda! Please!" Mrs. Swenson shouted. "I understand you're upset, but can't we behave like ladies?!"

Distracted by the sudden interruption, Ella paused and took a deep breath. Then she sighed and her shoulders slumped.

I am relaxed.

One brawl in Physical Education was more than enough. Besides, no good could come from blowing up at Jackson Montgomery anyway. He would probably have her fingernails torn off or her kneecaps busted.

"I'm upset," she began slowly, carefully controlling her tone, "because I just found out I'm failing Business Calculus. And Dr. Martin practically said if I don't improve, there is no place for me at this school."

Jack's face fell. "Is that so?"

Ella nodded, and fought to keep the tears from coming to her eyes. Crying in front of Jackson Montgomery was not an option.

"I'm sure he was exaggeratin'," Jack replied soothingly.

"No, I actually think he sugar-coated it a little," said Ella, shaking her head. "He said I would have to have a tutor."

"Really?" Jack's sullen expression lightened. "Well, that may not be so bad. Everybody needs a little help now and again. And maybe you'll make a friend."

"Excuse me?" she snapped. "What's that supposed to mean?"

"Nothin'! It's just –" He stopped. This first real conversation wasn't going exactly as he had imagined. "I only meant that… it doesn't seem as if you… talk to a lot of people, that's all."

"I'm talking to you right now, aren't I?" Ella retorted, her eyes sharp.

Jack cocked his head to the side playfully. "So, we're friends, then?"

"Yes! Fine. We're friends," Ella said and muttered under her breath, "Definitely my most aggravating friend."

Jack laughed loudly. "And you, Miss Eleanor, are by far my most amusin' friend."

"Class dismissed!" Mrs. Swenson barked. "I've had enough! Everyone out – except you two!" she shouted to the two girls who were still bickering in the far corner of the room. "Tomorrow everyone bring the right attitude!"

"Are you sure he knew he was talking to you?" Mitch asked at lunch the next day, ramming his glasses back up on his nose.

"Why?" Ella scoffed. "You think he was talking to someone else? I was the only one there."

"No. That's not what I'm suggesting."

Jayla offered a sympathetic smile. "Maybe he mistook you for someone else."

"I told you. He called me Ella. He remembered it from Calculus."

Mitch shook his head. "I can't understand this."

"What's there to understand?"

Jayla spoke quickly. "We're not trying to upset you. I believe what Mitch is saying is we're not sure exactly why Jackson Montgomery was speaking to you. But I don't think it's because he wants to be your friend. He has enough friends. He doesn't really need you. Unless…"

Jayla trailed off. She and Mitch swapped a look.

"No," Jayla muttered to herself.

"I don't think you'd be his type," Mitch said firmly.

"Unless what? Not whose type? You think Jackson Montgomery is trying to seduce me or something?"

"No, that can't be it. Jackson Montgomery set fire to a nightclub when he was fifteen because they refused to let him in. You're too much of a good girl for him to be interested in you," Mitch replied.

Jayla nodded in agreement.

After a moment, he said in a serious tone, "But still, be careful, Ella. We all know you're not the prettiest girl here, but you're not hideous."

Ella's voice rose. "Is there supposed to be a compliment in there somewhere?"

"I'm only saying Jackson Montgomery is used to getting whatever he wants."

Ella stood up from the table. "I don't know who you've insulted more – him or me."

"I can't talk to you when you are being melodramatic," Mitch said calmly. "Are you menstruating right now?"

Jayla choked and Ella turned a fierce shade of red.

"You two," Ella said loudly. After spotting a few heads turn, she dropped her voice. "You two are the ones who are being melodramatic," she whispered. "There was nothing sexual about the way we were talking, and there is nothing unbelievable about someone wanting to be my friend with no ulterior motive!"

"But –" Mitch cut in.

"Enough!" Ella stormed from the table before Jayla or Mitch could say another word about PMS, and walked briskly to the gymnasium to wait for class.

Unfortunately, Jack had returned to his room for cologne before heading to class, and was tardy again. He stepped into the gymnasium just in time to hear Mrs. Swenson's announcement.

"Recent events have demonstrated that some members of the group need to go back to the basics: proper grip, footwork, ground strokes, volleys, overheads and serves."

A collective groan rose from the class.

Mrs. Swenson raised her voice, "Therefore, we will continue to practice individually, including basic rules and *etiquette*, until I feel that you are all ready. Let's begin."

As they commenced their stretches, Ella hiccupped and glanced quickly over at Jack. Working hard to conceal his disappointment, he turned to the girl nearest him, rewarding her with a dazzling smile and a comment Ella didn't catch. The girl fluttered and blushed and beamed back at him.

Ella grimaced. She hated those guys – the ones who thought they could get any girl. Clearly Jackson Montgomery was one of them.

Watching the scene, Ella wondered if she had looked as foolish yesterday as the other girl appeared today. She was forced to admit she'd been wrong. Jackson Montgomery was simply a flatterer and a flirt, only trying to make her look stupid. He obviously wasn't interested in being her friend after all.

8. METHODS OF INTEGRATION

"This is boring," Julian yawned, and slammed his physics book on the sturdy library table.

Jack jumped guiltily at the sudden noise. He'd been watching the way Ella's dark hair fell gently over her shoulder as she leaned over the book she was so intently reading.

Courtney's voice cut in sharply. "What are you starin' at?" Following his former gaze to where Ella sat a few tables away, she exclaimed, "Bless your heart, Jack, that girl is goin' to think you like her if you don't stop gawkin' at her."

"I didn't realize I was," Jack said glibly. "Dr. Martin wants me to start tutorin' her in Calculus."

"Dr. Martin. What a joke," laughed Diana, tossing her hair.

Jack said nothing.

She scoffed under her breath. "Well, you're not actually considering it, are you?"

"Yes, ma'am. I already agreed."

"When did this happen?"

"This mornin'," Jack replied coolly. "He's goin' to give me extra credit in return."

"Jack," said Courtney, reaching across the table and taking his hand. "Why would you care about extra credit?"

"Especially in Calculus!" Julian cut in.

"Tutorin' will look good on my transcripts," Jack answered, matter-of-factly.

Courtney waved a delicate hand in front of Jack's vacant eyes. "Do you even know who you are right now? Have you completely lost your mind?"

"Maybe I have," Jack replied, getting up from the table.

"Where are you going?"

"To tell her about the tutorin'."

"You can't be serious."

But despite their protests, and Julian's fallen jaw, Jack walked casually over to the table where Ella sat with Mitch and Jayla. He paused a moment when he reached them.

Before Jack could say anything, Jayla said quietly, "You know you'll be grandfathered in to any university you choose, right?"

Jack looked startled. "I suppose I'd prefer to get in on my own merits. How did you —?"

"This is a library," Jayla explained softly, "and you all speak way too loudly."

Jack chuckled. "Point taken."

He glanced over at Ella. She was sitting with her head bowed unnecessarily low over her book, her hair falling over her shoulders and obscuring her face. Still, he could tell her cheeks were red.

"Excuse me, Miss Eleanor, may I speak with you a moment?" he asked gently.

"Yes," she replied in a barely audible whisper, and walked a few paces away from the table to a nearby bookshelf.

"So that explains it..." she heard Mitch say to Jayla in a low voice.

Jack followed Ella and carelessly removed a work of Shakespeare from the shelf where she stood. He paged through it leisurely, saying nothing, hoping to compel her to look at him.

"Dr. Martin must have a vendetta against you," she said, still in a whisper, without raising her face.

His lips tugged up in a crooked grin. "I volunteered, actually."

She glanced up, perplexed. Her eyes were too much for him. Jack forgot the speech he'd painstakingly arranged that morning. Instead, he set his book down.

"Like I said, it'll look good on my transcripts and I reckoned if you got a little help, you could concentrate more on your other classes, and the odds of us winnin' a doubles match together would increase substantially."

"So," Ella said slowly, "it's in your best interest to help me?"

Jack looked amused. "In a way, yes. I suppose you could say it will be equally beneficial. Would you be able to start next week?"

Ella nodded, her face still showing a bewildered expression.

"Monday? After fourth period?"

She nodded again.

"Great." Jack's grin widened. "It's a date."

Ella cringed at his choice of words, but Jack prepared for their first meeting as if it really were a romantic rendezvous. He shaved meticulously on Monday morning, and applied his most expensive Italian cologne. The moment his last class of the day was dismissed, he hurried back to his room in the boarding house to change into a fresh shirt, and back to the Café to pick up two fragrant cups of hot chocolate.

When he reached the library, Ella was already settled at one of the far tables. Her head was bent and her eyes closed, but she fidgeted in the chair.

Dear Lord, please make him forget our meeting. Or let him fall down the stairs on the way. Nothing too serious. A broken collarbone would work.

She opened her eyes, her glance darting from table to table. Although the other students in the library were quietly studying, it was as if she could already feel the piercing eyes that were sure to boggle at Jackson Montgomery sitting with the new girl. Was a passing grade in Calculus class really worth the comments she was sure to face – the ugly rumors that were bound to spring up?

She flinched as she saw Jack standing in the doorway.

It did not escape Jack's notice that although Ella was now leaned back in her chair at the long mahogany table, she looked far from comfortable. He took a deep breath and walked over to greet her.

"I didn't know if you drank coffee, but everyone likes hot chocolate, right?"

As he set the steaming mugs on the table, Ella said apprehensively, "I don't think you can have that in here."

"Don't worry," he said, looking over to Ms. Bentley's desk. He caught the librarian's eye with a smile and a nod, which she returned. "Ms. Bentley's a good sport."

Ella still appeared uncertain.

"Try some," Jack urged, sliding the mug a little nearer. He felt particularly suave as he added, "It has thaumaturgical effects."

Ella wrinkled her nose. "It's what?"

"It's magical... miraculous," Jack explained, his voice soft and low. "I don't know how they do it but it's not like anythin' you've ever tasted before."

Ella lifted the warm mug and sniffed tentatively. The rich, sweet aroma filled her nostrils. She took a sip.

It really is heavenly, she admitted, suddenly feeling relaxed and invigorated. She looked up and, for the first time, Ella smiled at Jack – a genuine, happy smile. That smile did funny things to the rhythm of Jack's heartbeat.

He grinned back idiotically and said, "Let's get started, shall we?"

As he flipped open Ella's textbook, he bumped her cup of hot chocolate with the side of his hand. It toppled and, as if in slow motion, splashed the dark liquid all over Ella's white uniform. Ella gave a loud shriek and jumped up. Jack shot to his feet almost as quickly as Ella. He reached toward her but she recoiled.

"It's hot!" she cried, holding the soaked blouse away from her chest. "It's really, really hot!"

"Go take that off and I'll fetch you another shirt," Jack commanded.

Ella rushed from the library, and Jack ran at full speed to the boarding house.

He dashed to the third floor, and hesitated outside the door of Diana and Courtney's suite. Courtney stood before a floor length mirror, examining her hair pulled up into a complicated twist, and Diana lay on her bed flicking leisurely through the pages of a magazine.

Jack knocked lightly on the open door, and both girls turned.

"Jack!"

He paused to catch his breath and asked, "Either of y'all have a shirt you could lend me?"

Diana giggled.

Courtney fluttered her eyelashes seductively. "Whatever you want, Jack, although I don't reckon mine would fit you."

She unclasped the top button on her blouse, and her fingers moved down to the second button.

"No, ma'am," Jack said quickly. "Please keep the one you're wearin'."

Courtney pouted but her hands dropped to her sides.

"I need a women's sweater or a sweatshirt maybe? And it's not for me. It's for –" He gave a small cough. "– for Ella Parker."

Courtney's face suddenly turned to stone. With a hand on her hip, she said coldly, "In that case, no, I don't think we can help you."

"Miss Courtney! Don't be childish!"

She sighed apathetically. "I agree the girl needs something decent to wear. Have you seen her shoes?" she asked in aside to Diana, then resumed, "But it's really none of my concern. We're not all as tenderhearted and obsessed with charity as you are, Jack darlin'."

"Miss Diana?"

"Sorry, Jack," she said with a fleeting look at her extensive closet, "everything's at the cleaners."

He rolled his eyes, and continued at a trot down the thickly carpeted hallway past gleaming wooden doors. He turned his head side to side, looking at the various room numbers and thinking. *Miranda? Stephanie?* He knew already their responses would be the same. And unlike Courtney, Jack thought with a shudder, a few of them may undress entirely despite his protests.

Ella was beginning to wonder if Jack would ever return when he knocked gently on the door to the ladies room. She'd soaked stacks of paper towels with cool water and applied them like a cold compress to her red, aching chest and stomach. Now she was shivering.

"It's not ideal," Jack said apologetically as Ella opened the door a crack and slid one bare arm out to grab the shirt. "But it is clean."

She pulled the shirt into the bathroom and examined it. It was a bright crimson sweatshirt with a Harvard logo emblazoned on the front, and it was a men's size large.

"Really?" Ella called derisively through the door. "This is all you have?"

"Forgive me for not havin' piles of women's clothes lyin' around in my room," he said with more than a hint of annoyance in his voice.

She slipped it over her head and pulled it down cautiously, avoiding her throbbing skin. The interior fabric was warm and velvety soft, and the sweatshirt gave off the scent of spicy cinnamon.

"Well?" Jack called from the hallway.

"It'll work," Ella replied, stepping out.

Jack surveyed her and couldn't hide a smirk. The pleated skirt of her uniform was barely visible beneath the oversized shirt. She looked like a sweatshirt with legs.

"Sorry I couldn't find somethin' more suitable."

"Actually, this is nice and loose. Thanks," she said timidly.

"You're welcome." He looked at his watch. "It's a little late to be gettin' started. Would you be able to meet Thursday?"

Even though he'd made up for scalding her with boiling cocoa, she still wasn't looking forward to studying with Jack for hours on end and was happy to postpone the misery.

"Can I offer you a ride home?" he asked courteously.

"No, thanks. I enjoy walking by *myself*." She emphasized the word and Jack decided not to press her further.

Ella tried to fall asleep that night but her skin was still uncomfortable and Jackson Montgomery's sweatshirt was annoyingly conspicuous at the top of her laundry hamper. She got up from bed and tossed it into the closet, shutting the door firmly.

On the way from her History class to Calculus the following day, Ella realized Jack's shirt was still crumpled in the bottom of her closet. She paused in the doorway, but decided it would be better to speak to him now before the classroom was completely occupied. Mortified, she approached the desk where he sat.

He looked up and Ella said quickly, "I'm sorry I forgot your sweatshirt. I meant to wash it last night so I could return it today, but I was exhausted. I guess it slipped my mind."

Jack smiled. "Please keep it. It's the least I can do."

Ella had no intention of keeping anything once belonging to Jackson Montgomery, but the other students were beginning to file in and she turned to go to her seat.

"Miss Eleanor," he called in a hushed tone and crooked a finger at her. "Sit here," he said, motioning to the seat in front of him.

She hesitated at her regular chair, and Jack added, "So I can help with questions."

Ella looked down at her chair and back at Jack.

"I suppose that's a good point," she murmured. Slowly, she retraced her steps and slid into the chair directly in front of Jack.

He beamed as Dr. Martin began the lecture. Five minutes into the lesson, a tall girl burst into the classroom, looking abashed. She hurried to where Ella was sitting and stopped.

"I don't appreciate tardiness, Emily," Dr. Martin said dryly. "Please take your seat."

"But, Dr. Martin, she's in my seat."

The entire class craned their necks to stare at Ella. She blushed deeply.

"Oh, I see." Dr. Martin eyed Ella closely through his spectacles.

Jack stood. "It was my idea, sir. I asked her to sit here."

"Oh, of course," Dr. Martin replied, nodding at Jack.

He turned back to the girl hovering over Ella.

"Mr. Montgomery is tutoring Miss Parker, Emily, so it will be necessary for them to sit together. You can take the seat in the back."

The lecture recommenced immediately, but Ella could still feel the inquisitive looks of her fellow students. With cheeks red, she stared hard at

101

the notebook on her desk and fought to control her breathing. Having a fit of hiccups in front of everyone would really be the tipping point of an already humiliating situation.

Dear God, please make me invisible.

It wasn't bad enough to be the new girl. Now she would be the stupid new girl, Ella thought. When Dr. Martin released the class, she jumped up quickly. A petite girl with large glasses tapped Ella lightly on the shoulder as the two were passing out of the room.

"Hey, Ella, don't worry about Dr. Martin. He doesn't really intend to be mean. He's just way too straightforward."

"Yeah," Ella responded and attempted to smile.

"He totally announced it last year when I got a C on the spring midterm and had to be tutored before the final. And I had to meet with Mitch Zagers."

Ella felt a twinge in her chest.

"Mitch is a pretty good guy," she replied loyally.

"Oh, don't get me wrong. Mitch is a sweet kid and I wouldn't have passed without him. But, let's face it, if you've got to spend hours every week going over scores of dull formulas with someone, he should at least be good-looking," she whispered with a wink. Hastily glancing back at the desk where Jack sat, she sighed, "You're so lucky."

Although Ella could not agree with the girl, her meetings with Jack went more smoothly than she'd initially expected. Ella was desperate to improve her grade, and Jack felt fortunate to be assisting her. Though Ella had always thought him blithe and unfocused in class, at their tutoring sessions, he was all business.

Following their disastrous first encounter on Monday, they met briefly on Thursday after lunch. Now that the whole school knew Jack was tutoring her, Ella didn't mind studying beside him in the center of the library, although she didn't relish having Diana and Courtney sit across the table.

"You seem to have a firm grasp on the methods of findin' derivatives and applications of derivatives," Jack observed.

"Yeah, I get the basics. It's the material we just started on that doesn't make sense."

"You're so patient, Jack," Courtney said pointedly, with a sneer toward Ella. "It's so chivalrous of him to try to help you, sweetie. Bless your heart."

I am relaxed.

Ignoring the cutting remark, and flipped through her textbook. "Like this question." She pointed. "I don't even know where to begin."

"That's a good example to work through."

"You're too clever, Jack," Courtney drawled.

"Not to mention rich," Diana added under her breath.

"Be careful you don't get too sugary, ladies," Jack replied as he rewrote the problem on the tablet in front of them in his neat script, "or you'll drown in your own sweet tea."

"Truly, Jack. You're bigger than life and twice as handsome."

Ella thought she would be sick to her stomach if she had to listen to another word.

"It's a pity such a combination is so rare," Courtney complained. "It seems as if they're lettin' anyone into the Academy nowadays. Just the other day in class, a girl actually asked if the Armistice of Mudros was signed in 1918 or 1819. An absolute cretin, and one of the ugliest girls I've ever seen."

"'Great minds discuss ideas. Average minds discuss events —'" quoted Jack glibly, still writing.

"'Small minds discuss people'," Ella recited unconsciously.

"Very good." Jack looked up. "That's attributed to Eleanor Roosevelt, if I'm remembering correctly. You must be mighty familiar with her."

A small smile passed over Ella's face. "You have no idea."

"We all know about Eleanor Roosevelt," Courtney retorted with a scowl.

Jack's pen hovered over the tablet. "But not many know enough to repeat a quote."

"It sounds like you're just congratulating yourself," Ella blurted. She regretted it instantly. The shock on Courtney and Diana's faces was almost worth it, but Jack looked hurt.

Be kind, ordered her father's voice, and Ella reminded herself that he'd volunteered to tutor her. Although she distrusted him, she had to admit he'd been courteous.

"Or w-was that a compliment intended for me?" Ella stammered feebly.

Courtney rolled her eyes but Jack's happy expression was restored.

Ella dropped her voice. "Sorry. I'm having a hard time concentrating with all these interruptions."

"Understandable," Jack murmured. "We'll keep to meetin' after fourth period. Most people will be at dinner." He nodded expressively across the table.

Jack walked Ella slowly through the solution he'd written out, his explanation occasionally interspersed with Courtney's outbursts.

On Friday, they sat at a table alone and Jack declared that they were making good progress.

"Do you reckon I should come over on Saturday and we can get some extra studyin' in?" Jack asked tentatively, as Ella tucked her thick textbook into her backpack.

Although she tolerated Jack's company as absolutely necessary for her academic survival, Ella needed a few days free of him and was glad to have an excuse.

"I'm afraid I can't this weekend," she said, feigning disappointment. "I'm helping a friend from church with a fundraiser for his school."

"What manner of fundraiser?" Jack asked, reaching in the breast pocket of his jacket. He pulled out a thin stack of paper.

Ella watched as he picked up a pen from the table and scribbled on the top sheet, replying, "The public school's hoping to restock the local food shelf before winter. We're collecting nonperishable foods and cash donations door-to-door. The goal is to get five hundred pounds of food, and raise five thousand dollars, so I'm sure it'll take the whole weekend."

Jack tore the top slip of paper from the others and handed it to Ella. The paper was a check, neatly printed, for five thousand dollars.

"Does that help?" he asked calmly.

She stared at him without speaking.

"I left it blank so y'all can make it out to whomever."

Ella bristled. "I still can't meet with you. I promised to help them."

"It's not a bribe, Miss Eleanor." He scowled at her. "It's a donation."

"Thanks, then," she said, meeting his gaze. She made a move to stand, but stopped. "How rich are you?"

Jack stiffened.

"I mean, I know everyone here is rich," she added quickly, "but you must be über rich. I heard you had something like a million bucks."

"Who told you I had a million bucks?"

"Everyone knows that," Ella replied with a shrug.

Coldly, Jack said, "Well, whoever it was, they were mistaken in their facts."

There was a silence and Ella shifted uncomfortably in her chair. With nervous fingers, she curled her navy, cable-knit scarf more tightly around her neck. It was against the dress code but surprisingly, Ella thought, no one had said anything. She gave it another tug, wishing she was at home listening to the quiet *click* of wooden knitting needles.

"So how much are we talking here," Ella inquired conversationally, trying to lighten the mood. "Like, a cool half million? Or do you mean it's a couple million?"

"The latter," he replied curtly.

"So… like ten million, or a hundred million?" she persisted, leaning in.

He crossed his arms over his chest. "Why does it matter?"

Ella shook her head vigorously, and her tone became gentler. "It doesn't matter. I'm just curious. I'm just trying to see this amount," she added, waving the check in front of him, "from your perspective."

"Well, since it doesn't matter," he said pointedly, "my net worth's actually closer to this."

He took her pencil and on the upper corner of a notebook wrote down a number with nine zeros. She stared at him.

"That," he said reluctantly, "times seven or eight."

He erased the figure, but she continued staring.

"What?" he asked finally.

"How is it even possible for someone to have that much money?"

"I don't really have it, y'know. Not until I'm eighteen. It's all tied up in the family business, and savings bonds and trusts."

"But you have enough to throw around five thousand dollars whenever you want?"

"Yes, Miss Eleanor. I receive an annual stipend on my birthday each year, so if I choose to give some money to a good cause, I have the means to do so."

"How – I mean, what –? I can't even wrap my head around the life that you have," she said, tapping her pencil rapidly on the open notebook.

"It's basically the same as yours, except on Tuesdays I have a caviar lunch with Bill Gates."

Her jaw dropped.

"I'm teasin'," he said reassuringly. Ella's expression remained unchanged, and he continued, "My life isn't so very different. I don't have diamonds on my timepiece and I don't buy a new boat every time my old one gets wet. Apart from a few purchases, I try to live simply. I go to school, do my homework, eat, sleep, breathe just like anyone else."

Ella hesitated. "I suppose that's true."

"I'm not one for puttin' on airs," Jack replied, leaning back in his chair. "Even if you are in high cotton, you oughtn't to get above your raisin' and money doesn't define who you are unless you let it, Miss Eleanor. I'd like to think I am more than just my trust fund."

Ella suddenly looked sheepish. "I have a trust fund too," she admitted, squirming uneasily in her seat.

Jack cocked an eyebrow.

"My dad was a musician," Ella explained, "and I suppose our family is comparatively wealthy. Not like Forbes top ten wealthy, but still. I never really thought about it before now."

"Not so very different," Jack repeated.

Ella searched his face for some sign of sarcasm, but detected none.

Talking to Jackson Montgomery was infuriating. She knew he privately despised her as much as she did him, and ached to put him in his place with a clever insult. But, by some superhuman feat, he was persistently polite whenever they spoke and she had no choice but to be civil in return.

9. MASKS

The weather was unusually warm for October, but Meg still bundled Ella up as if a blizzard were in the forecast. Ella shed her unnecessary layers in the garage and set off at a trot towards town.

The rising sun dazzled her eyes, but she spotted Lucas turning round the corner towards the bench outside the church as the clock chimed nine – at five minutes past the hour. As the distance between them decreased, a huge smirk broke across Ella's face seeing Lucas, in his customary black with a harassed expression, reluctantly pulling a little red wagon.

After their eager greeting, they walked from one doorbell to the next, repeating "Would you like to make a tax-deductible donation to the Ashby Happy Hearts food shelf?" as the rusting autumn leaves crunched under their feet.

Between Ella's smiling face and Lucas's imposing figure, nearly every house they stopped at added something to their collection.

"What I want to know," Ella said as they sat on the curb at noon, gobbling pumpkin spice cupcakes, "is why do you have a little red wagon in your garage?"

"It's the old man's, not mine," Lucas replied through the food in his mouth. "I think he's had it since the turn of the century. What *I* want to know is how many cupcakes constitutes a serving?"

"Two?" Ella shrugged.

"Good, so I've only had two servings."

"Save some for me!"

"I'm joking. I've only had three cupcakes." Lucas winked.

"Don't talk with your mouth full," she said, with equally stuffed cheeks. "You're spitting my aunt's secret recipe all over the sidewalk."

"Fine! But it's your turn to pull the wagon!" he replied, playfully slugging her in the arm.

"You're a con artist," Ella protested. "It was practically empty when you pulled it this morning."

He sucked a smear of frosting from his fingertip. "Yeah, but I pulled it the whole morning. You'll only have to pull it for two hours and we'll be done."

Ella's face clouded.

"What's wrong, Songbird?"

"It just hit me that Saturday is half over. Before I know it, the weekend will be gone."

Lucas edged closer to her on the curb. "It's not so bad there still, is it? Why don't you punch one of them in the face? They'd all leave you alone then."

"I don't think I could ever punch someone. I felt awful enough starting that food fight. I know my mom was disappointed. And my dad would want me to be kind." Ella sighed. "'Be strong. Be kind.' It was one of the things he always said when I was a kid."

"You're lucky," Lucas murmured, "to have parents worth disappointing."

Ella glanced at him from the corner of her eye but his head was bent low, his expression hidden. When he didn't go on, she said, "Besides, it's better than it was. At least I'm not getting tortured anymore. But I still have to spend half of my day with *Mr. Montgomery*," Ella said in perfect mimicry of Dr. Martin's monotone voice.

"The one who's been rotten to you?"

"Yeah, he volunteered to tutor me in Calculus. He's spent the last month and a half making my life miserable and now he's suddenly acting nice for some reason. It's suspicious. And that stupid Southern accent of his makes everything he says sound so genteel and good-natured. It's annoying."

"I think I know him," Lucas said unexpectedly.

Ella looked at him accusingly.

"Well, I don't mean I know him personally. But I think I've heard of him from other kids at school. Jack Montgomery, right?"

Ella nodded.

"I thought so. What's he like?"

She frowned. "From what I've heard, he's your typical rich playboy. He sank a yacht off the coast of Spain once."

Lucas choked.

"Well..." Ella rubbed her cheek. "That may have only been a rumor. I also heard he was under house arrest for like eight months a while back, but I think Mitch tends to exaggerate his stories. Jayla said that when Jack was fifteen, it would have been a few years ago, he had this amazing car –"

"What kind of car?"

"Huh?"

"Ferrari? Mercedes? Lamborghini? Lexus? BMW?" Lucas pressed, ticking them off on his fingers.

"How should I know?" Ella waved the question away.

"Porsche?" Lucas continued. "Cadillac? Jaguar? Maserati?"

"Who cares? I didn't ask."

"What color?" he asked eagerly.

She scowled at him. "It was some luxury car. It doesn't make a difference to the story."

"A red Lamborghini Reventón," Lucas nodded, a dreamy look spreading over his features.

"Fine, when he was fifteen he had this red whatever and he would drive it through town on Main Street, revving the motor."

"Engine," Lucas corrected.

"Not important to the story!"

"An engine and a motor are completely different things."

Ella glared. "The point is," she said forcefully, "he was fifteen. Didn't even have his license. But he was driving around, drawing as much attention to himself as possible, because he knew half the cops in town were too scared to cite him, and even if one of them did, he would pay, what? A couple hundred bucks?"

"Why do you ask me, like I'm some kind of convict?"

"If interrupting was against the law..." Ella needled him.

Lucas poked her with his elbow and she dodged out of the way with a giggle.

It felt unbelievably good to laugh with someone. Of course, she had Mitch and Jayla. They'd proved to be faithful friends, but they were impossible to talk to sometimes with their perfect grammar and Vulcan logic. Jayla would crack a joke occasionally, but Mitch was ever subdued and serious. When she recounted her weekend to them on Monday, they wouldn't grasp the humor of Lucas the giant pulling the diminutive wagon, or her nearly burning the first batch of cupcakes to a crisp.

She was jarred back from her thoughts by Lucas tossing a softball-sized apple to her.

"Heads up!"

"Good thing I caught it," she exclaimed, with an unbelieving look at the monstrous fruit in her hand. "You could have bashed my head in with that thing."

"Which brings us back to our original conversation," Lucas replied. "Why is the infamous Jack Montgomery, who has nearly tried to annihilate you on numerous occasions, suddenly being nice to you?"

"Who knows?" Ella shrugged, rising to her feet. "Leading up to some kind of prank, I'm sure."

Lucas also got up and stretched. "I'd be on my guard if I were you, Songbird."

"What are the odds that he's changed? That he's not all that different from you and me?" Ella asked slowly, recalling her conversation with Jack the day before.

Lucas gave her a searching look. "Do you think people can really change?"

"I do. But if he's changed," she added, in a tone that indicated she highly doubted it, "why is he still a notorious bad boy?"

"A reputation like that kind of hangs on you for a while," Lucas mumbled. "You of all people should know that."

Grasping the cool metal handle of the wagon, Ella gave it a tug. She followed Lucas down the sidewalk, thinking, with the wagon wheels squeaking behind her.

Meg met them at the door with two mugs of peppermint tea when they reached her house, the fragrant steam curling into the air.

"I thought you might be ready for a warm drink when you got this far."

"Thanks," Ella murmured, thinking guiltily of the coat and mittens she'd discarded in the garage. "It's not too cold out here, but this is nice."

"Someone sent you dead flowers, Songbird," Lucas announced, lifting a large vase of faded roses from the far corner of the porch. "Another prank?"

Ella handed her mug to her aunt and reached for the vase as they stepped inside. "No, I bet they're for the anniversary of my dad's death."

"I'm so sorry, Ella," Lucas said softly. "When was it? Why didn't you say something?"

"It was last week. It's no big deal." She blinked and looked down at the wilted flowers sadly. "These must have been sent to my old address, and then forwarded here."

"What a shame, Ella," Meg cried. "They look like they were beautiful."

"Who sent them?"

"Pretty sure they're from my Uncle Billy," Ella replied pulling out the card. A few dried petals fluttered to the floor.

"I thought your aunt was your only extended family," Lucas asked, looking between the two of them.

"She is," Ella explained. "Uncle Billy isn't actually my uncle. He's my godfather. He sends me flowers every year on the day my dad died."

"Does he really?" Meg bent slowly, gathering the fallen petals from the floor with her free hand. She stood and looked at them a moment in her palm. "I never knew that."

"Wait a minute," Lucas blurted. "Are we talking about Bill Bancroft here?"

Ella and Meg nodded simultaneously.

"The lead guitarist for Wicked Youth is your 'Uncle Billy'? I shouldn't be surprised, but it's still bizarre." With a dazed expression, Lucas rubbed a hand across his face. His eyes grew wide and bright. "You should get him to come here. We could –"

A sudden crash halted his hurried flow of words.

"How clumsy of me!" Meg exclaimed, looking dumbstruck at the dark puddle and shattered mug on the floor. "It just slipped."

"Don't move," Ella commanded. "I'm closest to the kitchen."

She returned a minute later with the kitchen broom and dustpan.

Kneeling gingerly to pick up the largest sections of glass, Ella told Lucas, "It's not like that. We're not close. My mom and Uncle Billy didn't get along after my dad left the band. Asking Uncle Billy to be my godfather was sort of an olive branch, I guess, because he and my parents hadn't spoken in years. I only met him once when I was really little, but he sends things sometimes, and I have a P.O. box where I send thank you notes. I only –" Ella began but upon standing, exclaimed, "Aunt Meg, you're so pale! Are you feeling okay?"

"Fine, Ella," she replied shakily. "I might sit down."

"I'll stay with you," Ella insisted. "Lucas, you don't mind, do you? We're pretty much done."

"Trying to get out of your turn pulling the wagon, Songbird," Lucas teased gently.

Ella smiled gratefully at him, and followed her aunt into the kitchen.

On Monday afternoon, Ella and Jack sat at a table in the empty library, their heads bent over a notebook filled with sums. Ella's feet – still sore from the weekend's exertion – were propped stealthily on the seat across from her. She wiggled her toes periodically.

It was hard to concentrate today. The usually teeming library was deserted, due in large part to the unseasonably clement weather. The immense skylight in the ceiling above them spilled rays of sunshine that danced upon the table.

112

Jack cupped his chin in his hand and leaned his elbow on the table. Ella echoed his movement. Whenever Jack shifted in his chair, she caught a whiff of the spicy cinnamon scent his sweatshirt had held. It smelled comforting and homey like the kitchen at Christmas.

Her gaze drifted to the orderly bookshelves, looking especially old and somber beneath the dancing light. What difference did calculus make on a day like today? She couldn't concentrate on methods of integration. The warmth and quiet made her feel drowsy. Her eyelids dropped once, twice, and finally for a third time.

Jack glanced up momentarily and couldn't stop his smile as he spotted Ella slumped in her chair. His eyes traced the gentle lines of her face, her peaceful lips and fluttering eyelids. He sighed heavily and raised his eyes to the sparkling light.

In a gruff tone, to compensate for his prior sigh, Jack asked loudly, "Was y'all's fundraiser successful?"

Ella jumped conspicuously.

"Oh, uh, I was thinking," she said, flustered. "What was the question?"

In a softer tone, he repeated, "How did y'all's fundraiser go?"

"Oh, yes," she mumbled, her mind still foggy. "The volunteers collected a total of five hundred seventy pounds of food and raised four thousand three hundred dollars in addition to...to the other amount."

"Glad to hear it," he said good-naturedly. He looked at his watch and, with an exaggerated stretch, added, "Why don't we call it a day? I could use a nap."

Ella nodded and blushed.

"Can you meet a little later tomorrow?" Jack asked.

"No." She shook her head. "I have choir practice. What about Wednesday?"

Jack's lips curved up. "I can't then. I have choir practice on Wednesday nights."

"You're in the Academy choir?"

"No," he chuckled. "I couldn't carry a tune if I had a bucket with a lid on it. I play piano for the chapel choir here on Sundays."

"You do?" she asked skeptically.

113

"Yes," he replied, and detecting the disbelief in her tone, added, "I've played since I was a little boy."

"Oh, I see." Her face cleared, but her eyes remained troubled.

"What?"

"It's nothing," she said quickly, avoiding his eyes. "I just didn't realize...I wouldn't have guessed you went to chapel."

"Oh." His expression changed. "Why not?" he asked, pushing his chair back and stretching out his legs.

"No reason," Ella replied, squirming uneasily in her seat. "I didn't mean to offend you."

"I'm not offended," he responded evenly. "I would just hate to think I've done or said anythin' to give you that impression."

"To be honest, your choice of friends gave me that impression. They don't much care for me," Ella added sarcastically.

"Don't judge me too harshly because I associate with publicans and sinners." He grinned, then looked serious. "You might call them a remnant of a past life, but I hoped I might could be a good influence on them in some way. And I wouldn't be too concerned with what they think. You can't please everyone, Miss Eleanor. Some people are so snooty that if they get to heaven, they're gonna ask to see the upstairs."

Ella smiled but still avoided a direct gaze.

"There's somethin' else?"

"No, it's nothing."

"Tell me." He moved his chair an inch closer to hers.

"Well, I know your money doesn't define you," she said, drawing out the words. The rest of the sentence spilled out in a rush. "But I guess I don't imagine the average churchgoer walking around with a billion dollars in their pocket."

"That's a fair point." He spoke slowly as if choosing his next words carefully. "All I can say is that my family's money was earned honestly, and we've been able to do good work with it, both through jobs as well as charities. I pray often that I'll be able to make godly choices with my wealth when it's finally up to me. Thankfully, I don't have to make those decisions yet. My history with money isn't a good one."

He rubbed a hand across his temple as if the topic were giving him a headache. Ella kindly took the hint.

"We'll meet again on Thursday then?"

Jack nodded and Ella stood, gathering her stray papers.

"You should come sometime," Jack said casually.

Ella hiccupped. "To chapel?"

"Yes. It's specifically for the students, y'know. The messages are directed purposely to people our age."

"That would be nice," Ella replied, faking a disappointed tone, "but I can't. I sing in our church choir on Sunday mornings."

"What time does your service start?"

"Ten o'clock."

"Well, ours is early. Chapel begins at eight on Sundays. It would be finished in time for you to get to church."

"Yeah, I'll think about it," Ella lied.

She hoisted her bulging backpack onto her shoulders and left Jack in the library. The corridors were deserted this late in the afternoon. Devoid of its pupils, the school felt different, more like an elaborate mausoleum. The *click clack, click clack* of her shoes on the marble floor echoed through the empty hallway. She walked quickly to the magnificent double doors and heaved one open.

Stepping from the cold, stone interior of the building onto the sun-bathed lawn was like waking from a bad dream. Her walk slowed. She sucked in a breath of the fresh country air and watched a rainbow of brightly colored leaves swirl across the street in front of her.

Ella's mind was conflicted as she ambled along. Either Jackson Montgomery was genuinely reformed from his playboy days, she thought, or he was working hard to convey that impression. He must be committed to restoring his reputation if he spent his time tutoring hopeless students like her and accompanying the chapel choir. Perhaps he really had changed.

Ella recoiled at the idea. Despite the evidence laid before her, it couldn't be true. The rest of the population seemed to be taken in by his charade, but she wasn't. She had seen the real Jackson Montgomery, who'd humiliated and persecuted her on numerous occasions. He was an enchanting actor, nothing more.

Ella had to admit Jack played his part well. At their final appointment that week, Jack was friendly, almost admiring.

"That necklace," he said, glancing at the small string of pearls encircling her pale throat, "is very becomin' on you, Miss Eleanor."

She'd been absentmindedly playing with it, twisting the necklace around her fingers but, at this comment, her hands dropped to her sides.

"Thank you," she replied meekly. "It was a gift from my dad."

"Are you busy this weekend? Any excitin' plans?" Jack asked. His tone was casual but his eyes were bright. "Apart from studyin', of course," he added with a roguish grin, revealing his dimples.

"I'm planning to eat my weight in candy corn," Ella told him wryly.

"That definitely qualifies as excitin'," Jack laughed.

Whether it was false or not, Ella decided she liked his laugh. He had a hard square jaw, but his face softened when his full lips parted in a laugh.

"I'm also volunteering at our church harvest festival. We're donating apples from the tree at my aunt's house, so I have to pick a couple dozen apples tonight and I'll be supervising the apple-bobbing tub all day Saturday."

"No wonder you're failin' in Calculus," he said with eyebrows raised. "Do you ever have a weekend free?"

"I'm not failing! I'm just not living up to the Whitfield Preparatory Academy standard."

"I was only teasin'," Jack replied quickly.

Ella leaned in and whispered, "So was I."

Jack chuckled again and Ella found herself grinning. A moment passed before she realized that she was actually having a pleasant conversation with Jackson Montgomery.

Jack's smile widened and he looked about to speak, but Ella quickly excused herself.

She berated herself on the walk home for being so foolish over a boy she ought to have an aversion to and forced herself to think of a reason to dislike Jack for every apple she picked from the tree.

As the children bobbed for apples on Saturday afternoon, she repeated those reasons one after another inside her head. Ella had tallied up nearly two dozen objections when Lucas's voice distracted her from her count.

"Hey, Songbird, you coming to our haunted house later?"

Ella turned to see him in a tattered shirt with a mask tucked under his arm, surrounded by a group of boys costumed in varying degrees of gore.

"Songbird?" a gruesome zombie asked, looking her up and down. "Is this the Wicked Youth girl?"

Ella giggled uncomfortably and introduced herself.

A blood-soaked surgeon with a fake knife turned to Lucas and shouted accusingly, "She's hotter than you said."

The others laughed.

"Hey," another zombie rounded on her, "do you think you could get us tickets to the summer tour? They're sold out already."

"Well, I –" Ella stammered.

"No way, her dad's not even in the band anymore."

"But maybe a signed shirt or something?" the zombie persisted.

"Come on, guys," Lucas stepped in, "we've got to get set up."

"I thought you would be working at the festival?" Ella wrinkled her brow.

Lucas's friends snickered.

"I was," he responded quietly, "but we picked the same day for the haunted house."

"We made six hundred bucks last year," a savage looking vampire cut in. "Can't pass that up."

"And it's going to be epic this year." Lucas grinned. "You should come when you're done here."

Ella hesitated. "Yeah, I think I will."

The sky was growing dark when she'd finished cleaning her booth at the harvest festival and made her way through the darkening streets. Ella heard the house before she saw it. Screams echoed inside and a chill ran down her spine.

She crossed the cobwebbed porch and paused with her hand on the doorknob. From the corner of her eye, she saw a shadowy figure crouched on the edge of the porch. It was a large wolf with blood-matted fur around its massive jaws. The wolf uttered a fierce guttural growl and sprang at her. With a scream, Ella turned instinctively to run but tripped. She fell, sprawling across the porch.

The dark figure stood, pulling off his werewolf mask. "Ella? Is that you?"

"Lu-Lucas?!" Ella sputtered. "Are you trying to kill me?"

"Sorry." He frowned. "I didn't think that would scare you. Are you okay?"

Ella tried to stand and winced as pain shot up her leg.

"I think I twisted my ankle. Guess I'm not the best candidate for a haunted house," she said with a weak smile.

"Sorry, Songbird," Lucas mumbled again, hanging his mask over the porch railing and pulling off his ragged over-shirt to kneel beside her. "I really didn't mean it."

"It's getting puffy." Ella ran her fingers lightly over her swollen ankle. "I think... I think maybe it's sprained."

"Here, I'll help you home," Lucas replied, offering her his hand.

He lifted her gently. She draped her arm across his broad shoulders, leaning on him for support. With Lucas's arm curled around her waist, Ella took a few hobbling steps. They walked slowly together as the rising moon bathed the houses and yards in a soft blue hue.

In the dim light, Ella glanced over at Lucas but he was staring intently at the sidewalk. She'd seen the tattoo on his bicep up close for the first time when he'd knelt beside her on the porch. Three white roses, intertwined, and three names. She had a suspicion about it, and was nearly overcome with curiosity.

"Lucas?" Ella said quietly, adjusting her grip on his massive shoulder.

He murmured absently, "*Hmm.*"

"Will you tell me about your tattoo? It's for the kids from your school, isn't it? Shawn, Tiffany, and Claire," she said softly.

"Claire," Lucas said, his voice slightly husky. He sighed. "Claire wasn't like anyone else in the world. Claire was so smart. She could seriously read any book and solve any problem she came across. And she was beautiful. She had the brightest eyes I've ever seen."

"Were you guys....together?" Ella interrupted.

"Something like that. It was complicated. I was crazy about her and she liked me too. We were close, but her family didn't approve. She was way too good for me."

"Lucas!" Ella reproached him.

"What? It's true. I'm nothing but some fatherless kid whose mom is a crack whore. I've got no talents and no future. I'm not being modest, Songbird. She really was way too good for me. But she never treated me that way." He paused and cleared his throat. "Tiffany was exactly like Claire. Smart and pretty. She would have had an amazing life. Tiffany was Claire's best friend, and Shawn was mine."

A look of acute anguish passed over his face.

"I haven't really talked about this…" He trailed off. In the moonlight, his pained features appeared somehow ghoulish and Ella shivered involuntarily.

"I shouldn't have asked. You don't have to tell me, Lucas."

"I don't mind telling you," he said firmly. "You might actually understand. Shawn was my best friend and he was bullied relentlessly from the day I first met him when I transferred here to the day he brought a gun to school."

Ella felt suddenly numb. She heard herself saying, "So he did it? He shot them? Your best friend?"

Lucas stopped walking.

"I could never defend what he did, but you can't even imagine some of the things he went through. The things they did to him. It would make you sick to your stomach. I know you had a hard time at your school, Songbird," Lucas said slowly, his tone controlled, "but his was worse."

Ella shook her head, unable to find the proper words. She looked up at Lucas with pleading eyes. "What happened?"

"I wasn't in the class where it happened, but the story goes that they were halfway through taking attendance in first period when Shawn walked to the front of the room and pointed a gun at the class. I guess Claire thought she could calm him down. She was always kind to him. But when she got close, to try to reason with him, he thrust the gun in her face." Lucas's words came out faster now, more frantically. "Tiffany rushed up to defend Claire and he shot them both before anyone could make a move.

Standing over them, they say he started bawling, and turned the gun on himself. Shawn put the gun in his mouth and blew his brains out before the police were even called."

Ella shuddered.

"Tiffany died in a pool of his blood on the classroom floor. Claire was in a coma for four weeks before she woke up."

"Wait. Claire's still alive? Where is she?"

"She lives in Washington now. I never got to say goodbye. Her parents were so upset, and insisted she was traumatized. They moved a month after she was released from the hospital."

"You mean they wouldn't let you see her? But they couldn't possibly blame you, Lucas. You didn't have anything to do with it."

"I guess they thought if there had been nothing between us, she wouldn't have approached Shawn. Claire would have just been a bystander, not a victim," he said hoarsely. "Besides, I doubt she wanted anything to do with me."

"So now you're friends with those guys?"

Lucas gave her a mocking smile. "I don't get to be too picky in my choice of friends nowadays. Not many people want to sit by a murderer in the lunchroom at school."

"But you're not, Lucas. You weren't responsible."

"Guilty by association, Songbird. Besides, I knew the bullying had gotten worse. I should have done more. I should have seen it coming or…" Lucas faltered. "Or something," he whispered.

They started walking again. Ella leaned more heavily on Lucas's arm, but it didn't seem to bother him.

"I can't imagine," she murmured finally, "losing someone in such a brutal way – it must have been horrible."

Lucas nodded. "I'm sure it was heartbreaking for Claire."

"I meant you, Lucas. In one day practically, you lost your best friend, your girlfriend, and suddenly became an outcast. How did you survive?"

"I'm pretty tough, Songbird. I can take care of myself."

Lucas was quiet for a few paces.

"Actually, the old man was there when I needed him. He made me keep going to church, even when I didn't want to, but he didn't pressure me to talk. He just gave me a journal and I started writing lyrics in it. Somehow it helped."

"I didn't know you'd written songs. Do you ever perform?"

"Not much. My guitar isn't great and my voice is nothing like yours. But the guys and I have something of a band." He caught Ella's eye. "They're really not so bad. Maybe a little rough around the edges."

"I'd love to hear you play sometime."

"I'd like that too," Lucas replied, his mouth curving up slightly.

Slowly, they walked together in silence through the dark streets, listening to the leaves rustling in the branches overhead.

Ella lay in bed and prayed for Lucas long into the night. She'd prayed for him in the past, trying to tell herself with sisterly indifference. But tonight, for the first time, she could not deny she cared for him. His story and his suffering had touched her heart, and a person cannot wrench your heart unless they occupy a place in it.

10. BREAKING AND ENTERING

"Should I even bother inquirin' if you're available this weekend?" Jack asked as they were dismissed from their Calculus class the following Friday.

"Afraid not," Ella chirped, slipping her textbook into her backpack. Dr. Martin had announced at the end of the period that Monday's midterm exam would be rescheduled and Ella was aglow with relief. "We're having a quilting bee on Saturday."

Jack chuckled as he stepped to the door.

"I'm serious," Ella told him.

She paused outside the classroom to let the crowd pressing behind her pass on their way to the Main Hall.

"Oh no, I believe you." Jack lingered beside her in the hallway. "I'm just impressed. Fundraisers, festivals, choir practice and quiltin' bees. You're so busy, you'd think you were twins. How do you get involved in so much?"

"The church does a lot of community projects, and my aunt is teaching me to cook and sew."

"So the quiltin' bee was her idea?"

Ella nodded. "I'm hosting the event at our house with coffee and treats and in return, she's helping me make a dress for the Holiday Ball in December. She's kind of old-fashioned. She says a young lady is not truly educated if she cannot clothe herself and the people she loves, and have guests look forward to coming over for dinner."

"She sounds like my grandmother," Jack replied. "'A Southern gentleman,'" he quoted in a heavily drawling falsetto voice, "'is always available to lend a hand or a word of encouragement.'"

Ella burst out laughing.

"What?"

"Is there any way you could repeat that and I could get it on video?"

One corner of Jack's mouth pulled up in a crooked grin. "Not a chance."

Ella bit her lip in an attempt to suppress another laugh.

Jack could be so charming when it suited him, she thought, and he made it nearly impossible to hate him. With a determined sigh, Ella turned to follow the others to lunch.

Jack took a step after her, half reaching for her arm. "Miss Eleanor, will you... Would you like to sit with us?"

"Oh." Her mind raced for an excuse. "Actually, I was going to skip lunch today. I need to finish some French homework before fourth period."

Ella's stomach rumbled as she walked regretfully to the library.

A simple 'no, thanks' probably would have satisfied him, she thought, or an explanation about needing to speak to another student. But of course, her first idea had to involve abstaining from lunch entirely.

She flung her bag into the first empty chair she saw, still angry over her mental lapse, and absently scanned the shelves for an agreeable book to fill the time.

Suddenly, in the stillness, Ella heard a girl's voice echo aloud exactly what was in her mind.

"I'm so glad I don't have to study calculus all day tomorrow."

Ella stopped to listen to the conversation on the other side of the bookcase.

"But do you know why?" a masculine voice urged.

"Who cares? All I know is it's the last good weekend for sailing in Newport, and now I can go."

The boy continued resolutely, but in a lower key, "The exam key is missing. I overheard Dr. Martin telling Dr. Chamberlain that he thinks one of his pupils took it, so now he has to rewrite the whole midterm because someone has the answers."

"Who?" the girl whispered back. "And how?"

"It was Jack Montgomery." The name was scarcely louder than a breath. "Think about it," he insisted in a hushed tone. "He never has to study and he's at the top of the honor roll. Nobody's that smart. He either stole it or bribed someone to get it."

"Are you going to tell Dr. Martin?"

"Rat out Jack? Are you kidding me?"

"I wasn't saying you *should* tell him. I was just asking," she muttered defensively.

"No, I value my life too much. Jack can keep the answers with my good wishes."

Ella returned to her chair without a book. Instead, she had a scheme to contemplate. She'd always known Jack was a liar and a cheat, and what's more, she was brave enough to do something about it. The room assignments were in the student directory at the back of her handbook. After classes were out for the day and the other students went for dinner, she would sneak up to the boarding house to unmask Jackson Montgomery once and for all.

Ella paid little attention to her classes the remainder of the day, her mind too preoccupied with her plan to focus on anything else. She was so absorbed in thought, it was almost a shock to find herself on the second floor of the boarding house.

She was nearly there. 236...237...and...238.

Ella tapped softly on the door and prayed no one would answer. She'd decided that if Jack was in his room, it would be easier to come up with a reason for knocking at his door than to invent an excuse for sneaking in. Thankfully no one answered.

Grateful that the school hadn't yet converted to a more modern form of security, Ella examined the keyhole in the door handle and hiccupped. *How did you open a locked door? With a credit card? A hair pin?* She sighed, disappointed in her own lack of criminal prowess. Not that it mattered, as she clearly wasn't cut out for a life of crime.

Ella jiggled the handle and, to her surprise, the door popped open an inch. Poised to swing the door fully ajar, she hesitated. It had seemed like a reasonable idea that afternoon. But it had all happened so quickly and now – standing at the threshold – the full weight of what she was doing finally hit her. There would be consequences if she was caught. No doubt she would face disciplinary action from the Academy...not to mention retribution from Jackson Montgomery himself. An uncomfortable shiver went down her spine. Then she pulled her shoulders back.

This is about the truth, and the truth will set you free.

Ella darted inside.

Her first impression was of the smell. Memories of Malcolm's old room had prepared her for the stench of two teenage boys, but the aroma that hit her as she entered the room caught her by surprise. The prevailing scent was the familiar spicy cinnamon. Underneath that, she detected a lingering smell of fresh, clean laundry and crisp autumn air.

Ella stood motionless for a moment, breathing deeply, taking it all in.

She'd expected the room to be large, but it was more elegant than she had imagined. A wall-sized window, draped with thick olive-tone curtains, looked out over the edge of a small lake and the grounds at the rear of the school. Even with the two queen beds on opposite ends of the room, arranged with opulent olive bedspreads, the space didn't appear crowded.

The room was immaculate. There were no mounds of dirty clothes littering the floor. Giving into temptation, she went over to one of the dressers and peeked in. Socks were folded compactly and arranged by color. She examined the walls. Not a single mark. Leather-bound books were neatly straightened on the shelves and papers were stacked in tidy piles on each desk.

"Papers!" Ella whispered to herself.

She stepped to the mahogany desk on the left side of the room and recognized Jack's neat script on a draft of a Political Science essay. She shuffled through the remainder of the pile and moved to the next, checking the calculus pages with particular attention. She found nothing but old homework assignments, and frowned.

A row of pictures caught her attention. A younger version of Jack and a smiling man with Jack's jetty blue eyes and a woman with Jack's dark, curly hair stood in the desert with pyramids in the background. The next two photos displayed the same faces at the Eiffel Tower and again standing at what looked like a section of the Great Wall of China.

Spotting a few loose pages sticking out from between the row of textbooks along the desk, she grabbed them greedily. It took little more than a glance for her to realize, with disappointment, they were not the test key.

These were letters, written in a graceful hand. Ella reached to put them back between the row of textbooks and paused. If he was hiding the key, perhaps he would have disguised it as something else. She flipped to the back page in the stack and read,

> *My dearest Jackson,*
> *What a delight to read of the growth of your Bible study! You can be sure I will continue to pray for it. I believe it's a credit to your parents' upbringing that you have a love of God, respect for others, and appreciate the finer things in life. Regrettably, the Southern gentleman is a dying breed. Good values are judged passé in our ever more discourteous and vulgar society. However, I can still recollect the days when I knew many young gentlemen such as yourself, and what a pleasure it was to be in their company...*

Intrigued, Ella skipped ahead to the middle of the pile, and scanned the page. She read hastily.

> *My dearest Jackson,*
> *How your last letter made me laugh! It brought me back to a day when I was very young, and my brother and I were allowed out to the garden to pick strawberries for a treat. He caught me sneaking one into my mouth and smashed a ripe berry into my lovely hair. I was not such a lady at that age, and by the time the two of us returned to the house, we were both red from head to toe with strawberry juice. I do hope your uniform wasn't too badly stained...*

126

Although, by this point, Ella was aware these weren't the object of her search, she was too engrossed to break away. She turned to the first page, on the top of the stack. Leaning comfortably against the desk, she continued.

> *My dearest Jackson,*
>
> *I'm pleased to hear your lessons are going so well. Remember, my dear, that a gentleman will never be caught boasting about his achievements. On the contrary, he is at all times attentive to other people's endeavors; making others feel at ease and happy in his presence. That being said, I brag about my gifted grandson to the other ladies as if your accomplishments were my own. I am especially proud that you've chosen to use your remarkable intellect to help another, and that you kindly offered your services without being asked. The young lady sounds...*

Ella lifted her head as she heard a key slip into the lock. Dropping the letters in her hand, she looked around the room and scuttled to the closet.

When safely behind the door, she noted that it was more like an extra room than a closet. It was wide, extending back nearly six feet, with clothes hung neatly along the two side walls, and ended in a leather upholstered bench under a small window.

Very cautiously, she peeked out the narrow crack of the door and saw Diana and Julian slip in through the bedroom door before she ducked back into the closet. Ella heard a giggle and a light *click* as the lock was turned in the door.

She crouched to a seated position and peeked out again to see the two of them tumble onto the bed.

Gross, she thought, as an uncomfortable foreboding crept over her.

The giggling turned to restrained shrieks and the shrieking subsided into soft, low moans.

Way beyond gross.

She drew her knees to her chest, scrunched her eyes tightly and covered her ears. As the noise grew quiet, Ella let her hands fall from her ears and heard what sounded worryingly like breathing coming from the tidy row of suits hanging behind her.

She froze. Though soft, there was definitely steady breathing.

127

Ella's heart seemed to stop and she couldn't draw a breath. She was about to jump up and run, when a strong arm caught her about her middle.

She found enough breath to utter a screech when another hand closed over her mouth. A vague thought of the worthlessness of tennis and the benefits of mixed martial arts formed in Ella's mind the moment following her capture.

But this reflection was interrupted when a familiar drawling voice, close to her ear, whispered, "What were you readin' on my desk?"

It was Jack.

Ella's fear instantly turned to anger, and she spat back, "Why are you spying on me?"

"What are you doin' in my room?" was his quiet reply.

This reality hadn't yet occurred to her. It did look pretty bad. Going to his room. Rifling through his property. Hiding in his closet.

"I thought you were the one who stole the key to the Calculus midterm," Ella admitted sheepishly.

Even in the dim light, she could see he was giving her a look.

With a teasing sharpness to his voice, Jack asked, "If I can explain the material to you, why would I need the answers to the test?"

He had a point there. In fact, he had probably written the Calculus test for Dr. Martin. Ella was about to reply when the rhythmic moaning began again and she had to suppress a gag.

When the sounds had died down once more, she whispered, "So if you didn't steal the key, who did?"

"No idea," Jack replied. "But you don't know me if you believed I'd steal it. I reckon if you did know me, we could actually be friends."

"But if you're innocent, why were you hiding in your own closet?" she continued. "What are you up to?"

"I heard a knock, so I checked the peep-hole and saw you trying the handle."

Stupid peep-hole.

"You could have just answered the door!"

"That would have been far less entertainin' than this."

"See," Ella exclaimed, pointing a finger at him, "it's that kind of behavior that makes me not want to be your friend."

"Whereas I have no issue bein' your friend, despite your tendency for breakin' and enterin'. What does that say about me?"

"You have lower standards than I do," Ella shot back.

Jack snorted. Ella remained serious.

Finally he whispered, "Clearly you dislike me. I know we got off on the wrong foot, Miss Eleanor, but I hoped after four weeks of studyin' and talkin' together, you'd managed to forgive me."

"Forgive you?"

"For splashin' you with that puddle on the second day, wreckin' your bag, and pourin' boilin' chocolate on you. Would you believe me if I told you it's all been accidents? Stupid mistakes. And that I'm sorry? You have no idea how sorry."

"I might if it was only the things you've done to me personally. But I've heard stories about you, Jack, and I've even looked you up myself. I appreciate you tutoring me but I have no reason to trust you and definitely no reason to be your friend."

"So nothin' I could say or do could persuade you?"

Appalled, Ella exclaimed under her breath, "You've clearly already won the popularity contest at this school. Why do you even want to be my friend? Why do you care what I think?"

"Why not?"

By her expression, Jack could tell his simple answer would not suffice.

"I can't explain it." He shrugged. "You're interestin'. You're like the opposite of everybody else at the Academy. Present situation excluded, you seem principled. You may not be perfect, but you're not fake either. You strike me as authentic, when everyone here seems to be puttin' on a show. You're industrious and altruistic."

Jack was thankful for the dim light as he felt his cheeks flushing.

"I'm curious to know you and figure out what makes you so...different."

Ignoring what she deemed to be his empty flattery, Ella asked, cringing, "Figure me out? Like an alien autopsy?"

Jack didn't laugh audibly, but he was still sitting near enough that Ella felt his chest vibrate with laughter.

After a deep breath, he replied, "That's your analogy? You reckon bein' friends with me would be that bad?"

Ella didn't answer.

"Honestly?" Jack asked, his expression pained. "Okay," he sighed, "so clearly I have not yet proved myself to you in spite of my apology. Tell me what I have to do to convince you I'm not such a bad fella."

"How about an act of faith? You want to know what makes me so different?" she whispered scornfully. "You go first. Tell me why, if you're such a nice guy, your reputation is the exact opposite."

His expression changed instantly, and he held her eye solemnly for a moment before replying.

"I'm waiting," Ella taunted.

"It's a long story."

"Fine, don't tell me. You'd probably lie anyway."

Jack's heavy brow creased. "You may not believe me, but I was a decent kid before my parents died."

Ella gasped, and her hostile façade collapsed.

"I-I'm so sorry. I had no idea. You really don't have to tell me about it. It's not any of my business. I'm sorry," she said again.

"It's okay," he replied nonchalantly. "I wasn't able to talk about it for the longest time, but it was years ago now. When I turned thirteen, my parents were killed together in a car crash, and I had nothin' left in the world but the inheritance. Everyone said I grew up overnight, but the truth is I was just a kid without a lick of sense." He paused. "I felt totally alone and all at once had more money than a kid should ever have, with no one to keep me in check. I completely lost control. If it was illegal, immoral, or insane, you could count me in. At the age of fourteen, I was either drunk or high, or both," he added bitterly, "every single night. I reckon you saw a few newspaper headlines from that year."

Jack was quiet for some minutes, his mind sifting through memories he had long hoped to forget.

Ella sat staring at him in silence. It was as if a secret, unspeakable bond between them had suddenly become visible, and even if he continued to be her enemy at the Academy, nothing could change the fact that they were members of this horrible private club together.

She cleared her throat and steadied her voice to reply when finally, Jack continued, "My grandmother became my legal guardian after I lost my parents. I couldn't have asked for a better woman to raise me. But she has such a gentle heart and I was so wild. The year I turned sixteen, she sold half her estate and left for Europe."

"She abandoned you?" Ella cut in. "How awful."

"Not really abandoned," Jack corrected. "I reckon she felt there was nothin' she could do anymore. For years, she'd tried to get me into counseling and I'd blow off appointments. She checked me into rehab and I'd pay my way out. She poured herself into helpin' me for three long years, with no result. And watching me become what I was then…. It must have been devastatin' for her."

Ella mulled over Jack's words for a minute, pulling a strand of dark hair over her shoulder. "I suppose she was grieving in her own way as well. Your grandmother lost a piece of her heart when your parents died, just like you did. She missed them, too."

Jack stared at her.

Softly, she whispered, "My dad had cancer. He died when I was eight and it was like the world went black and white for a time. But having my mom and my brother made it easier. It must have been awful for you both, going through that season of grief alone."

He paused, waiting for her to say more. But Ella, twisting the strand of hair between her fingers, remained mute.

"A few months after that, I got my first Ferrari." Jack raised his eyebrows and grinned.

Ella laughed unexpectedly into her hands, remembering how mesmerized Lucas had been when speculating about Jack's vehicles.

"I bought it in the afternoon," Jack went on, "and went out immediately to break bad. At the end of the night, all I had to show for it was a black eye and an empty fifth of gin on the passenger seat. The sun was just beginnin' to come up and I was racin' down a windin' country road in southern Vermont when I blacked out and lost control of the car. It flipped into a ditch and rolled three times, finally landin' in a field. When I opened my eyes, I was somehow in the back seat, and the whole front seat was completely flat. I managed to kick out the back window because it was already broken from the crash."

Jack's eyes were distant.

"I was bleedin', disoriented, and couldn't find my phone, in the middle of nowhere with no way of getting help. I collapsed in the grass and reckoned I was going to pass out and die right there, all alone. Suddenly, floatin' over the field, I heard music. I dragged myself to my feet and saw a car stopped on the road and a man in a suit walkin' towards me. I can't imagine what I looked like, standin' there drippin' blood and caked in mud, but he just said, 'Can I give you a hand, son?' as if I'd only pulled over with a flat tire."

Jack shook his head at the memory.

"He was a pastor headed to a tiny neighborhood church up the road a pace from the field where I crashed, up at the crack of dawn to put the finishin' touches on his sermon. He skipped his own service that mornin' to drive me to the hospital. I had a mild concussion, a hairline fracture in my arm, two cracked ribs, a dislocated shoulder and a broken nose."

"Really?" Ella squinted at him in the dark closet. "You'd never know."

Jack dropped his eyes under her scrutiny.

"Actually, my injuries from the crash weren't the worst part. I had a concoction of drugs in my system when I got to the hospital and I started goin' through withdrawal less than a day after I got there. As soon as I was patched up from the accident, they stuck me in rehab. I spent three weeks in the hospital and six months in rehab. In that whole time, I got a few perfunctory get well cards from some of my parents' old business associates, and not one visit from any of my strawberry friends."

"What does that mean?" Ella wrinkled her brow. "Strawberry friends?"

"Someone who only shows up when you have somethin' to share. I even gave a girl a car once. Nothin'. Not even a phone call when I was in the hospital." Jack sighed. "But that pastor came back and saw me once a week like clockwork. I –" He stopped. After a moment, he said quietly, "If it hadn't been for him and those conversations we had, I don't think I'd be alive today."

He paused again, and once more Ella waited. There was a change in his voice when he finally spoke.

"I was barely able to move in the beginnin', so on his first visit, he brought a little leather bound Bible. Just somethin' to pass the time, he said. I set it on the desk beside my bed after he left and forgot about it. As the weeks drew on, I grew more miserable and depressed. I started to realize how revoltin' I'd become – that literally no one in the world cared about me. When you're alone, all the money in the world is no comfort. A few months in, I bribed one of my nurses for a bottle of pills. She must have reckoned I needed a fix, but I'd planned to commit suicide."

Ella gasped in spite of herself. "So, what happened?"

Jack quirked a heavy eyebrow. "Well, I didn't go through with it if that's what you're wonderin'."

Ella snorted. "Seriously."

"Well, I'd planned to wait until the shift change to do it, right after my evenin' nurse did her rounds. So I stuck the pills inside the desk next to my bed, and when I shut the drawer, I knocked down that Bible that had been sittin' there for months, untouched. It fell and lay open on the floor. Without really thinkin', I just picked it up and started readin'."

"Was it the prodigal son?" Ella asked, breathless.

"No," Jack chuckled, "but that would be poetic. It opened at the middle, at Psalm sixty-nine, which was perfect. The funny thing is, my parents were Christians and I'd grown up goin' to church and attendin' Christian schools before they died. I'd read my Bible before, but it finally opened up to me that day."

His eyes grew distant.

"*I am the favorite topic of town gossip, and all the drunks sing about me.* I was a joke. I was nothing." He paused. "I came to realize I had nothin' left except God, but somehow God was more than enough." Slowly, he repeated, "God was enough."

"So now y'know my tale of woe and debauchery," he finished grandly. "I'll spare you the details of my physical and spiritual recovery, but I returned to the Academy with my notoriety cemented in every mind. Mendin' my reputation has been a gradual process."

Jack looked at her intently.

133

"Which brings us back to you and me. Now that you've heard my side of the story and how sorry I am for everythin' that happened between us, can we start over? Will you forgive me, Miss Eleanor?"

"Of course." She spoke without hesitation, but although her lips smiled, her eyes did not, and Jack still looked a little doubtful.

"Truly? No hard feelin's?" he coaxed.

Ella paused, and this time her smile was sincere. "Never between friends."

Hearing another faint *click*, she turned, peeking out from behind the closet door, and completely missed the dazzling grin that flashed across Jack's face at her words.

"I think they're gone," she said, still in a whisper, and slowly pushed the closet door open by a few more inches. But neither she nor Jack rose to go.

"What about your grandmother?" Ella asked at a normal volume. "Did you reconcile? Did she move back?"

"She did forgive me but she hasn't moved back. She has a villa in the south of France. We rarely see each other but we write."

"What do you write about?"

"Nothin' too thrillin'. Whatever fills our days and our thoughts. I write about school mostly." Jack shrugged. "Chapel. Tutorin'."

Ella hiccupped and said haltingly, "I think...I may have read a...*few* letters when I was looking for the test key."

Jack looked suddenly serious. "What did they say?"

"*Um.*" Ella hiccupped again. "There was something about a Bible study, and how well you're doing in your classes. A lot about gentlemen —"

Jack's face relaxed. "Yes, that's a bit of a recurrin' theme with my grandmother," he laughed, and Ella noticed his dimples with a smile of her own.

"Oh, and a funny story about strawberries," she said eagerly. "Did you tell her about the food fight here?"

Jack nodded.

With an unnecessary glance around at the empty closet, Ella whispered conspiratorially, "Do you want to know a secret about that food fight?"

Jack bit hard on his bottom lip and nodded again.

"I started it," Ella announced.

His mouth twisted up into a crooked grin.

"I'm serious," Ella insisted. "I never got in trouble because someone else admitted to it before I told the headmaster."

Jack looked long at her, as if trying to make up his mind about something. "Do *you* want to know a secret?"

Ella leaned in as Jack whispered his confession, and neither noticed the growing darkness around them.

Ella's growling stomach awoke her, and a shaft of sunlight from the window blinded her as she opened her eyes. She pulled a section of dark hair over her face but the glare was still unbearable. Ella shifted her body and rolled over into a wall. No, not a wall. It was too soft for a wall, too firm for a pillow.

She jabbed it with her elbow.

It grunted.

"*Ugh*. Good mornin' to you, too."

Ella scampered to her feet, entangling her torso in the hanging shirts. "Morning? Where am I? What happened?"

Jack stretched his arms above his head and mumbled groggily, "I reckon we fell asleep."

"Oh, do you?" Ella snapped sarcastically, flailing her arms in an attempt to free herself. "You *reckon?*"

"You're grouchy in the mornin', Miss Eleanor."

Jack frowned and attempted to roll over. Ella prodded him with her foot.

"Jack, I didn't go home last night," she whispered, ducking down under the clothes and nudging him again. "My aunt probably has the police out looking for me."

Jack sat up with a start. "I'll drive you home, and I can explain to your aunt."

"Good luck." Ella scoffed, tossing her head.

Jack moved swiftly to the closet door, glanced out, and beckoned Ella to follow him. Tiptoeing through the room, Ella was thankful to see Julian was the only occupant of the bed, and that he was snoring. She moved behind Jack like a shadow to the underground parking facility. He held the door as she slid into the passenger seat of a glaringly white sports car.

Looks fast, Ella thought approvingly.

She sat beside him in the flashy roadster, listening to the engine purr, and silently counted the minutes that passed as Jack drove the short distance to Aunt Meg's house.

Relaxed. I am relaxed. I am relaxed.

When they pulled into the driveway, Jack raced to open Ella's door. But she jumped out before he rounded the car, and dashed across the porch as if arriving home a millisecond earlier would save her.

Meg opened the door just as Ella reached the handle.

"Eleanor Grace Parker, where on earth have you been?" Her voice and face were stern, but she clasped Ella in a crushing hug.

When she'd been released, Ella took a step back. "I was at the Academy. I'm so sorry, Aunt Meg. I fell asleep. This is Jack," she added, with a gesture to him. "He's the one I've been meeting with."

Meg gave Jack a withering look. "You're Ella's tutor?"

"Yes, ma'am."

Her lethal eye fell on Ella. "I called you at least a dozen times."

"I'm so sorry, Aunt Meg. My phone must have died. I was... well..." Ella fell silent, remembering the mission that brought her to Jack's door.

He came to her rescue. "We got to talkin' and just lost track of time."

"Where?" Meg asked suddenly.

A lie formed in Ella's mind but she hesitated, and Jack spoke first.

"We were in my room, ma'am."

Ella winced and said quickly, "But his roommate, Julian, was there almost the whole time, Aunt Meg."

It was essentially true.

Meg looked hard at Ella, and back at Jack. Her face softened and she confessed, "I'm glad you said that." Turning back to Ella, she said, "I called the headmaster after dinner when I still hadn't heard back from you. The faculty searched the campus. I thought it was possible you'd be in the library or a classroom. But I don't suppose they went door to door in the boarding house."

136

"If they did, we didn't hear them," Jack insisted.

Ella nodded her head in agreement and Meg appeared satisfied.

"I am so sorry, Aunt Meg!"

"I can assure you it won't happen again, ma'am."

"I'm confident it won't," she retorted. "You'll be doing your tutoring here in the future where I can keep an eye on you both and make sure you don't lose track of time."

"Yes, ma'am. I'd be only too happy to come whenever it's most convenient for y'all. And I hope you'll allow me to take y'all to breakfast to make up for all the bother."

Meg brushed his suggestion aside but Jack stood firm.

"I insist, ma'am. After causin' you a sleepless night, it's the least I can do."

A few plates of waffles and bacon worked wonders. Seeing how much Ella wolfed down ravenously, Meg was happily convinced nothing amorous had occurred between the tutor and her niece. It was her firmly held belief that a girl would never eat so enthusiastically in front of a boy she liked.

With a simple meal and a phone call to the headmaster, Jack smoothed everything over with surprising ease.

Ella thanked him shyly on Monday morning in their Calculus class.

"I'm still in pretty big trouble," said Ella, slipping into the seat in front of him. "Pretty sure my aunt will keep me under lock and key for the next few weeks, but I think it would have been a lot worse without you."

"I hardly did a thing," Jack protested, "and it was my pleasure to help."

Ella studied his face. "You're very diplomatic. Not many people would have been candid with my aunt and still left her presence alive, let alone in her good graces. I'm still not sure how you pulled it off. I think you'll be an excellent business tycoon."

"Business tycoon." Jack laughed aloud. "I like that. I'll have to get my cards reprinted."

"CEO. Whatever. I think you'll make a very good CEO."

"Much obliged." He grinned and shook his head.

"What?"

"I never reckoned I'd hear a compliment from you, Miss Eleanor."

"I thought we were supposed to be friends now," Ella retorted. "Friends can give compliments."

Jack's eyes danced with tiny flames as he raised an eyebrow. "Is that so? What else do friends do?"

Ella blinked. "I don't know. We'll find out...I guess."

Jack reclined in his chair, lacing his fingers behind his head, and answered with a dimpled smile, "I look forward to the discovery."

Dr. Martin began his lecture and Ella was spared a reply. She opened her notebook but her pencil hovered above the page as Ella tried her best to ignore the unbidden warm glow Jack's comment had given her.

"Just friends," Ella mumbled to herself.

Only friends because he feels bad about accidents in the past. Barely more than acquaintances.

Ella blew out a deep breath and began writing her notes.

11. MORE THE MERRIER

Ella was near the door at church on Sunday when Lucas caught her.

"Hey Songbird, the guys and I are meeting this afternoon to practice. You wanna come listen? Maybe sing a few with me?"

"Oh." Ella groaned. "I can't. I really wish I could, Lucas. I'm still sort of grounded."

"Yeah, you never told me what you did. I seriously thought you were perfect."

"I broke curfew," Ella told him. "It was just a weird situation."

"I'm disappointed in you, Songbird." Lucas shook his head mockingly.

"You've never broken curfew?"

"I don't get caught!" Lucas grinned. "Now I'm never going to see you again, huh?"

"Not unless you want to volunteer at the soup kitchen on Thanksgiving. That's the next time my aunt's letting me out of the house."

"If that's what it takes."

"Really?" Ella exclaimed. "Would you really volunteer with me?"

"Sure." Lucas shrugged. "How bad can it be?"

"No, it'll be great!" Ella cried eagerly. "Then you could come have Thanksgiving with us on Friday. You and Mr. Sherman. You don't have other plans, do you?"

"You kidding? Can you imagine me and the old man trying to cook a turkey?"

"I'll ask my aunt, but I'm sure she'll say yes," she said with a glance over at Meg, chatting quietly in her pew.

Meg waited at a respectful distance until Ella and Lucas had said their goodbyes. As they walked to the Buick, she searched Ella's face for a blush or secret smile, but her expression was calm, ordinary. Still, Meg felt certain she'd seen something as the pair stood together in the doorway. But it was difficult to say whether the attraction was mutual or one-sided.

She was also growing less and less certain about the platonic nature of Ella and Jack's relationship as the new friendship blossomed.

The following evening, Meg watched them from the corner of her eye as she kneaded bread on the kitchen counter.

"B- is nothin' to be ashamed of, Miss Eleanor," Jack remarked. He was sitting across the table from Ella, looking over the midterm they'd gotten back that day. "You should take pride in your improvement."

"It probably would have been a C- if I hadn't gotten an extra week to study."

"I appreciate your confidence in all my hard work," Jack chided.

Ella scowled at him but her eyes glittered green.

"Why did you get an extra week?" Meg asked over her shoulder.

"Our teacher misplaced the exam key, but there were rumors it had been stolen." Jack gave Ella a mischievous wink. "Some people will believe anythin' they hear."

Ella kicked him under the table.

Stifling a laugh, he said quietly, "Some people also can't take a joke."

Ella kicked harder, but missed Jack's leg and instead kicked the leg of his chair. She yelped and Meg turned to look at them both.

With a wide grin, Jack asked, "What's in the oven, Ms. Keller? It smells gooder'n snuff."

"Chicken Parmesan and apple-gingerbread cobbler for dessert. Would you like to stay for dinner?"

"I'm afraid not tonight, ma'am. I'll have to hurry back for Bible study."

"Well, that's a wonderful reason to decline," Meg replied, dusting her floury hands on a kitchen towel. "Ella and I started working on a Bible study together a few months ago. Proverbs."

"We just began the book of John," Jack responded. "But I hope I can join y'all some other night. I do miss home cookin', especially around Thanksgiving time."

"I would have thought a place like the Academy would have a big Thanksgiving dinner for all the students boarding there."

"Oh, yes, ma'am. They do a right good meal every year but it isn't quite the same as my momma used to make."

"You could come here," Ella offered impulsively.

Jack's inky blue eyes met her green ones searchingly. When he spoke, his voice held real regret.

"I wish I could have Thanksgiving with y'all. I have to be in New York all day on business. I won't be back until quite late Thursday."

"You're in luck," Meg replied. "We're serving at the soup kitchen in Ashby. They do a big meal of turkey and mashed potatoes on Thanksgiving, so our Thanksgiving dinner will be on Friday."

"In that case, it would be a pleasure to join you. Would you like me to bring anythin'?" Jack asked Meg.

"Ella is doing Thanksgiving herself." Meg smiled proudly. "I'll just be helping in the kitchen if she needs me."

Jack beamed at Ella. "Anythin', Miss Eleanor?"

"Pie maybe? I'm still figuring out the menu."

"I'll check with you next week then."

Jack excused himself when the kitchen timer rang, and Meg and Ella sat down to dinner. It was a quiet meal.

As Ella stacked the dirty dishes into a pile, Meg remarked, "You certainly don't shy away from awkward situations."

"Why?" Ella's eyes were wide. "What do you mean?"

"You haven't forgotten that Mr. Sherman and Lucas are coming too, have you?"

"You mean Thanksgiving? I just thought the more, the merrier." Ella paused. "And I felt sad thinking about Jack missing his parents and having Thanksgiving in that huge, empty room. Thanksgiving dinner shouldn't be prepared en masse in some industrial kitchen. It should be made in a real home and served at a crowded table, don't you think?"

Meg nodded slowly and made a move to leave the kitchen. Ella jumped up after her.

"Aunt Meg, is it going to be awkward?"

"At least it will be interesting," Meg said with a wry face. "It isn't every day you get to introduce the two corners of your love triangle."

Ella scrunched up her nose in disgust.

"Love triangle? We're just friends. Barely friends," Ella added. "Jack feels responsible for me being bullied when I first started at the Academy, so he's trying to be nice now to make up for it."

"And Lucas?"

Ella's cheeks reddened. "We're friends too."

"Just friends?" Meg pressed.

Ella nodded matter-of-factly but didn't meet her aunt's eyes.

"Lucas has really grown on me."

Ella looked up, surprised. Her aunt's expression was free from any sign of sarcasm.

"He certainly doesn't have Jack's intellect or social graces, but he's not what I once thought him either. You two seem like you get along well together."

Ella was silent, and Meg added gently, "I'm not trying to be the Spanish Inquisition, Ella. It's only a conversation."

Ella blew out a deep breath. *I am relaxed*, she told herself.

"Lucas is a Christian, and he's handsome and funny and he probably loves my dad as much as I do."

"But?"

"I don't know. I suppose I like him and I think he likes me, but it's not really that simple."

"It never is," Meg said with a half-smile.

"I get the feeling he's holding back. Sometimes I wish he would just make a move and other times, I'm glad he hasn't."

"So just friends for now?"

"Just friends."

After spending the weekend brooding, Ella hit on the idea to include Mitch and Jayla in her ever-growing Thanksgiving feast, and wasted no time on Monday.

"You'll be around for Thanksgiving, right?" Ella asked Jayla over a bowl of steaming clam chowder.

"No," Jayla's eyes glittered as she replied, "Mitch and I both got a stipend to visit our families over the long weekend."

"That's great!" Ella exclaimed, but inwardly her heart sank.

She secretly hoped some mortification could be avoided if all of her friends were present instead of a select few.

"So you're both going home? Even to California?"

Mitch nodded. "Yes, I'll only have about a day and a half there before I have to turn around and fly back, but it's worth it."

"Sure," Ella mumbled, still lost in her own disappointment. "I'd do the same."

Her mind was recalled to the Main Hall when Jack paused beside their table, tray in hand.

"Pie, right, Miss Eleanor?"

"Yes. I'm making a pumpkin pie but you can bring any kind you like."

"Perfect."

Jack rapped the table with his knuckles and nodded to Mitch and Jayla before walking away.

"Is that –? Did he –?" Mitch faltered. "Jackson Montgomery is going to your house for Thanksgiving? How did that happen?"

"I invited him."

"You mean, you just...*invited* him?" Mitch asked in a horrified tone.

Ella nodded, and slurped her chowder. "Yep. Just like I invited you."

He blanched and looked like he was about to be sick.

"I can't tell if you're upset because he's coming or because I asked him?"

"Both. Equally," Mitch managed. "I hope you're having it catered."

"No, I'm making everything myself."

"I wish I could be there," Jayla admitted.

"I wish you could too."

"Maybe I could get a refund on my airplane ticket..." Mitch mused, giving his hair a yank.

"Don't be ridiculous!" Ella snorted and scraped her bowl. "It's only Jack."

Mitch went from white to red. "Only Jack! Are you insane?"

"No, but I'm starting to worry about *you*," Ella laughed. "A long weekend away will be good for you. Try to forget about the Academy and the Crowd for a few days."

"I'll try," Mitch replied dubiously. "But I won't be able to eat any pie without thinking about Jackson Montgomery."

"I'll let him know you said that."

Ella rose from the table, enjoying the sudden purple hue that colored Mitch's face.

The soup kitchen was crowded on Thursday. Hot steam from the ovens clouded the windows and a cacophony of voices filled the air. Nearly every inch of the building was filled, either with warm bodies or piles upon piles of food.

Potato peelings scattered across the linoleum floor as Ella and Lucas collided in the kitchen. She hugged a cherry pie to her chest, saving the pie but bespattering her apron with ruby spots of cherry juice.

"I can't believe you talked me into this, Songbird," Lucas groaned, scooping a handful of dirty peelings into the trash can. "You know there's a football game going on right now? And normal people are taking food-induced naps."

"You're not having fun?" she asked earnestly, kneeling beside him to collect the peelings.

For a moment, Lucas looked scornfully at Ella, on her knees next to him. He paused. Ella's sleeves were rolled to her elbows and her hands worked gracefully and diligently on the floor. Her cheeks were pink from the warm glow of the ovens and her exertion in the kitchen. Sweaty

144

ringlets curled about her face and she met his glance with bright, sincere eyes.

Lucas swallowed his intended reply and said, "You have a strange definition of fun."

"Aunt Meg told me it's not usually this crazy. They don't always make stuffing, vegetables, rolls and dessert. The director mentioned that someone anonymously donated the works for a full Thanksgiving meal, instead of just turkey and mashed potatoes. I wish I knew who it was," Ella wondered aloud.

"I wish I could give them a piece of my mind," Lucas growled, shaking his fist.

"I promise you won't have to cook a thing tomorrow. All you have to do is show up, stuff your face, and fall asleep."

"I'll hold you to that!"

They each went back to their assignments, Lucas quietly fuming as he peeled potatoes and Ella humming to herself as she slid yet another pie into the blazing oven.

Ella felt less energetic and much less charitable when her alarm rang at 5:30 the next morning. After snoozing her alarm once, she rolled out of bed. Throwing on yesterday's jeans and a crumpled sweatshirt from her closet floor, she plodded down the stairs, berating herself for choosing such a large turkey and for announcing that the meal would be served at noon.

Through bleary eyes, Ella read the handwritten note on the refrigerator.

Don't forget to turn the wings back to hold the neck skin in place.

Gross. Why did raw poultry have to be so slimy and disgusting? Maybe there was something in veganism after all.

Beneath that note was a second.

Make sure you stick the meat thermometer into the lower part of the thigh without touching the bone.

Aunt Meg obviously thought Thanksgiving was going to be a disaster.

145

As she violently stuffed the turkey, Ella grumbled at her aunt for coercing her into preparing the meal, selectively forgetting that she'd insisted on doing it herself. She managed to fit the behemoth of a turkey inside the oven and slammed the oven door.

For a few hours, she worked sluggishly. With two pies waiting on the counter, a green bean casserole in the refrigerator, potatoes peeled and ready, and rolls left to rise, Ella decided to set her alarm and go back to sleep.

She shuffled upstairs, growing increasingly angrier and angrier at Jack, Lucas, and even Mr. Sherman for accepting their invitations. Ella collapsed into bed fully clothed and was unconscious almost instantly.

When her alarm rang, she smacked it. There was a pause and it rang again. It took her a moment to realize that the doorbell, and not her alarm clock, was chiming musically.

"Ella! Can you get the door?" Meg called. "I think your guests are here."

Ella raced down the stairs, missing the last step in her haste and tumbling to the floor. A curse rose to her lips, but she collected herself, and opened the door to see Jack, pie in hand.

"You're early," she said with a frosty edge to her voice.

He glanced at his watch. "Well, two minutes early. Yes, ma'am."

"You're early," Ella repeated, and taking in the rest of him, added in dismay, "and you're wearing a suit."

She'd seen him nearly every day in his trim Academy uniform, but it was somehow a shock to see him standing on her porch attired in a crisp blue dress shirt under a dark, single breasted suit. Both his silk tie and his pocket square were the same shade of cerulean, and his leather shoes appeared newly polished below his cuffed pants.

"I prefer to find myself overdressed than underdressed," he replied nonchalantly. He slanted her a sidelong look. "You probably don't want to know about the flowers."

From behind his back, he produced a bouquet of mini sunflowers arranged with vibrant circus roses, burnt orange calla lilies, and red tulips.

"Thank you." Ella blushed. "These are beautiful. I feel like you're a better guest than I am a hostess. I'm a mess."

"Nonsense. That sweatshirt looks better on you than it ever did on me." Jack beamed.

Ella looked down at her ensemble. Bare feet, jeans spattered with day old food, and Jack's crimson Harvard sweatshirt.

And my messy ponytail is the icing on the cake, she thought.

"Oh," Ella stammered, "I hadn't realized. I just threw it on and started cooking. I could go change."

"Don't. You look prettier than a glob of butter meltin' on a stack of pancakes."

Ella found herself at a lack for words.

"The food is a little behind schedule," she managed. "Have you ever made mashed potatoes and gravy?"

"I'm afraid not, Miss Eleanor. In the kitchen, I'm about as handy as a back pocket on a shirt."

"My Southern gentleman can't cook?" Ella gaped at him in mock horror.

She had never seen Jack blush. He flushed red to his ears. Though she'd meant nothing significant, her possessive wording caught him off guard.

For the first time in their acquaintance, Jack's quiet self-assurance failed him and he stuttered, "M-much to my grandmother's chagrin. She would agree it's my biggest flaw as a gentleman."

Thinking she'd insulted him, Ella quickly said, "I nearly burned the house down the first time my aunt left me in charge of the kitchen. I think there's hope for you."

Jack followed Ella to the kitchen, set the pecan pie on the counter, and slipped off his jacket.

"Well, if you don't mind keeping an eye on the potatoes, I'll start working on the gravy. They're already boiling so as soon as you can poke them with a fork and they feel soft, I'll have you drain the water and mash the potatoes with the hand masher," Ella instructed. "Then just add milk and butter – right there on the counter – and mash some more."

"Sounds foolproof enough. I reckon I can manage." Rolling his sleeves past his wrists, Jack asked, "How was the Thanksgiving dinner yesterday, Miss Eleanor?"

Ella blew out a breath. "Busy. Very busy. But good. I was running around the kitchen all morning, making mountains of food, and on my feet all afternoon serving. It really was a good day though. But I do wish I could have slept in this morning."

She glanced at Jack.

"Still, I probably won't get much sympathy from you."

Jack started, and asked, "Why not?"

"Well, flying in and out of New York in one day. It must have been a nightmare. All those long lines and crowded terminals and people putting their seat back into your lap."

"I did get back rather late, but my flight was pleasant. I have a private jet actually," Jack replied without looking up from the bowl of steaming potatoes.

"Of course you do." Feeling foolish, Ella shook her head. "I keep forgetting."

"I like that you forget," he murmured. "Most people don't."

"It doesn't define you, right?"

Jack met her eye and grinned. "Exactly. Is this enough milk?"

Ella inspected the measuring cup. "Probably. Start with less and add more if you need it till it seems right."

She heard voices in the hall, and Lucas walked into the kitchen unannounced.

"Whose Mustang is that?"

He stopped short. Lucas looked from the jacket, neatly folded over a kitchen chair, to Jack with sleeves rolled back, hovering over the stove beside Ella. Jack crossed the kitchen with agile grace and introduced himself, extending a hand.

"Lucas," was the swift reply.

"I almost forgot, I brought some CDs," Lucas said to Ella. "I'll go grab them while I'm thinking of it."

Jack inquired curiously, "What CDs?"

"Some classic Wicked Youth and Axel Parker acoustic albums," Ella explained.

"*Hmm,*" Jack murmured.

"What?"

"Oh, nothin'. I wouldn't have pegged you as a Wicked Youth enthusiast, Miss Eleanor."

Lucas returned with a stack of CDs nearly a foot tall before Ella could reply.

"Wow." Jack cocked an eyebrow. "Are you the president of the fan club?"

Lucas and Ella exchanged a look.

"These are actually mine," Ella answered. "They're originals from in the studio. Lucas was borrowing them."

Lucas chuckled. "I think Ella can safely be named fan club president."

"Why?" Jack's eyes traveled from one face to the other. "What am I missin' here?"

Ella looked amused but explained kindly, "Axel Parker's my dad."

Jack had barely had time to process this new information when Lucas asked, "You have a '67 Shelby GT 500?"

"It's a recent acquisition but yes, sir, it's mine."

"I'm jealous. That's got to be the perfect blend of sports car and muscle car. Fun to drive?"

"I reckon it's the best car I've ever driven."

"Does she really do zero to sixty in six point two seconds?"

Jack nodded.

Lucas turned to Ella. "Speaking of which, sorry we're so late. I was seriously beat after yesterday, and I slept through my alarm this morning. The old man finally came and woke me up."

"Don't worry about it. Your timing is perfect. The turkey is resting and the green bean casserole is in the oven. Everything should be ready in about ten minutes."

"Ten minutes..." Lucas deliberated, running a hand over his short hair.

He addressed Jack, "Do you mind if I take it for a spin?"

"Not at all."

"Do you want to come with, Songbird?"

There was a momentary chill.

Ella's brow furrowed as she said, "No, I would feel bad leaving Jack behind."

149

Jack dug his hands into his pockets. "Don't fret about me. Someone has to mind the food."

"Then yes," Ella beamed, trying to hide her excitement, "I'll go for a spin."

Lucas smirked at her. "Do you want to change first?"

Ella hiccupped and glared at Jack. "I was planning on changing, but I was assured I looked fine."

"I stand by my words."

"You always look fine," Lucas said quickly. "I just wouldn't want you to get cranberry sauce on the upholstery."

Lucas delivered the CDs to her bedroom as she slipped into the bathroom. She exchanged her jeans and sweatshirt for a belted grey dress under a slouchy burgundy sweater, hoping it was a comfortable medium between Jack's suit and Lucas's jeans and black polo. Ella wished she could do something nice with her hair, but it was hopeless without a shower and a straightener. So she combed her hair into a slightly less messy ponytail, and ran downstairs.

Lucas was waiting by the door, jingling a ring of keys in his hand.

"Thanks again, Jack. We'll try to keep it under a hundred."

Jack leaned against the kitchen doorway, his arms crossed casually before his chest. Though his posture was loose, his jaw clenched as he watched them go.

As they peeled out of the driveway, Lucas turned to Ella. "I look good in this car, right?"

She rolled her eyes at him. "Stop fishing for compliments. You know you're attractive no matter what."

"You really think so?" Lucas grinned.

Ella nodded and quickly pulled a section of her ponytail over her shoulder to conceal her suddenly burning cheeks.

Lucas sighed. "What do you say we just take this car and run away together, Songbird?"

Ella knew it was a joke, but her heart beat a fraction of a second faster. "I think Jack would notice if we didn't come back with his car."

"What is he doing there anyway?"

"I invited him. I meant to tell you yesterday, but it slipped my mind in all the chaos."

"But I thought you hated that guy?"

Ella shook her head slowly. "He's not so bad. I told you things had gotten better."

"Yeah, I thought you meant that they weren't torturing you at school anymore, not that you'd be inviting one of them to your Thanksgiving dinner."

Lucas shifted and the car accelerated.

"Jack's not just 'one of them,' Lucas. He's really nice, and he's helped me a lot."

"He seems like a showoff. Why's he dressed like he's getting married?"

"I doubt he's trying to show off. I think being well dressed is just his way of being polite. Besides, I'm pretty sure I'd be flunking Calculus right now without him, and he even took the fall for the food fight."

"*He* says," Lucas cut in.

Ignoring him, Ella continued, "He's known you two seconds and he let you take his favorite car. Even Aunt Meg likes him."

"And he's a gazillionaire," Lucas added pointedly.

"So?"

"Maybe you wouldn't think he was so great and wonderful if he wasn't so rich."

Ella went white. "I'm going to pretend you didn't just say that. I don't pick my friends by their bank account balance."

"No," Lucas admitted, "I know you're not that shallow, Ella, but you are naive if you blindly believe he suddenly wants to be your friend with no ulterior motive."

She sucked in her breath as Lucas rounded a curve at full speed, the momentum pushing her against the passenger door.

"That's ridiculous. What could he possibly have to gain by befriending me? Did you have an ulterior motive for becoming my friend?"

Lucas glanced over at her.

"No," he murmured.

"No," Ella echoed. "So is it so hard to believe he would just want to be friends with me? Like you?" she insisted.

"Forget it. You're right, Songbird. I'm tired from yesterday. I wasn't expecting anybody else, and I was guaranteed a relaxing day."

He flashed her a beguiling smile.

"It'll still be relaxing. You guys can just talk about cars the whole time. I think you'd actually like him."

"We'll see," Lucas replied darkly. "Just...don't be too trusting, Songbird. Not everyone out there is as good as you. Believe me."

He pulled into the driveway and Jack met them at the front door.

"You like it?"

"I think I need one."

Lucas frowned suddenly. "Did it always have that big scratch on the passenger side?"

Jack hesitated, his face stony.

"I'm just yanking your chain," Lucas laughed. "It's fine. Ella, I'm starving. Let's eat."

"Seconds, anyone?" Ella asked over the empty plates.

Lucas and Mr. Sherman shook their heads.

"No, thanks," Meg replied.

"Jack, can I tempt you?"

"No, thank you, Miss Eleanor, I've had more than a plenty."

Passing out generous slices of pie, Ella asked, "What are you most thankful for, Mr. Sherman?"

"Well, now, I'd have to say my health. Good health is a miracle at my age, dolly. And of course, Lucas. I'm not sure what I'd do without Lucas," Mr. Sherman acknowledged warmly.

"Lucas?"

"Ditto. I'm also thankful for my friends. And this pie, Ella. It's delicious."

"Aunt Meg?"

"Well, I'm afraid I have to repeat what's already been said. For health and friends, and this wonderful meal. It was all very well done, Ella. Excellent job."

152

Ella beamed, pleased at her praise. She'd worried that every dish was lacking, but if Aunt Meg had enjoyed it, that was enough.

"I'm especially thankful," her aunt went on, "that you came to stay with me, Ella. My home wouldn't feel the same without you."

"I think we're all thankful for Miss Eleanor," Jack whispered.

She looked around the table with rosy cheeks. Surrounded by good food and good friends, it was difficult to tell which was more full, her stomach or her heart. For an impossibly long minute, time remained still, a glow seeming to hover over them.

But like all perfect moments, it slipped away, as Meg said, "Jack, that doesn't count. What are you really thankful for?"

"I'm honestly grateful for the struggles I've been through over the past few years. I found that fightin' through those bad days taught me strength and to find joy in the ordinary. I'm thankful for everythin', because I've been blessed beyond what I deserve."

"You can say that again," Lucas muttered under his breath.

Ella hiccupped and froze, a bite of apple pie halfway to her mouth.

"I beg your pardon?" Jack's voice was quiet but icy.

Lucas scoffed under his breath. "No offense, but it's easy to say that you're thankful for everything when you have everything you could ever want."

An uncomfortable silence fell over the table.

"I'm sure in your eyes, I have never been other than rich, but my parents brought me up simply," Jack replied calmly enough but met Lucas's eyes with a fierce glare. "It's a fact that my momma's family had money, but it may surprise you to know that my daddy was poor as gully-dirt when they met. My parents took what would be considered a very modest net worth and turned it into a frankly embarrassin' fortune within my lifetime."

"How did he do it? Your dad?" Ella asked gently.

"Pardon?"

"How did he sweep her off her feet when he was so poor?"

Jack's face softened into a crooked grin and the chill was broken.

"He may have grown up on firebread and soppin' gravy while she grew up on ham and eggs, but my momma always said raisin' trumps money every time. She could tell he had a good heart and a good head on his shoulders."

"That reminds me of my parents," Ella replied eagerly. "My mom was a rookie journalist at this insignificant little newspaper when she got assigned to interview my dad. He was rich and famous and handsome, but they fell in love at first sight, like a fairy tale."

Meg choked on her water. All eyes turned to her.

She coughed and asked, "Where did you hear that story?"

Ella shrugged. "Mom told me once before Dad died, when I was six or seven."

"Well, love at first sight is not *quite* accurate, Ella. Your dad had to win her over, slowly and painfully. And it wasn't easy. Your mom despised him."

"What?"

"Maybe I shouldn't say." Meg glanced swiftly at the other faces around the table. "If your mom didn't tell you –"

"No, I want to know," Ella insisted. "I'm sure Mom wants me to know the truth. She just never talks about Dad."

"Well," Meg began slowly, "did you ever hear the tape of their first interview together?"

"No, but I've read the original transcript."

Meg shook her head. "The interview questions and responses themselves were conventional. But if you hear it, you can tell your mom wished herself a million miles away. Her voice just *drips* with disdain. She thought that talking to Axel Parker, even for an interview, was a waste of her time."

"But she said that interview was a huge opportunity? She called it her first big break."

"And after the fact, it was. But she never wanted to interview a rock star. She considered herself too serious a journalist, even then. She only did the interview because her job was on the line. When her editor found out she had a connection to the band, he forced Kate to pursue the story."

"I don't understand. How did Mom have a connection? I thought they'd never met."

"No, they hadn't. Her connection was me." Meg flushed. Her cheeks grew redder with every word. "I was, well, you'd probably call me a groupie. I was actually with your Uncle Billy back then."

Ella gasped in spite of herself, and Lucas whispered, "Seriously? Like, with him?"

"Yes, in every sense of the word."

"Seriously? Bill Bancroft....and you?" Lucas's mouth fell open.

"Hard to believe, I know."

Ella nudged Lucas and he closed his gaping jaw.

"Billy and I were engaged when your mom and dad first met for that interview," Meg continued. "When our engagement was announced, Kate's editor put the pieces together and insisted she try for a personal interview with the band. Axel didn't do interviews, but I convinced him to meet with her."

She smiled softly.

"You could say it was one-sided love at first sight. Your dad was head over heels for your mom from that first day he met her."

Dazed, Ella asked, "But why didn't she like Dad?"

"Like you said, he was rich and famous and handsome, but he was also an arrogant, selfish drunk back then."

Meg looked up to see the shock and hurt in Ella's eyes, and she whispered, "I'm sorry, Ella. That was a bit harsh. Your dad was a good man. A wonderful husband, and a great father. But he and the rest of those boys became rock stars practically overnight and they were just a bunch of stupid, small-town teenagers who struck gold with Axel's voice. It's no wonder they lost their heads. By the time he met your mom, your dad had been a living legend for a half-dozen years, and living a lifestyle to fit his status. He had everything he could have wished for until he met Kate."

Meg suddenly smirked. "It was like a joke in a way. I'm sure you can picture your mom – quick, good with words – grilling an intoxicated, licentious narcissist. She put him in his place, very gracefully and politely, I might add."

"So what happened?"

"After the interview, he pursued her every way possible. But she made it clear she wouldn't have any part of him or his habits. He lost interest in other women, in drinking, partying, and eventually in the band. When he left the band, I think Kate finally took him seriously for the first time."

"Wait," Lucas interrupted. "You mean Axel Parker left before he even got the girl? I can't imagine walking away from Wicked Youth in their heyday. I'd kill to be in the band now! Your mom must be incredible, Songbird."

"Ella reminds me a lot of her actually," Meg said thoughtfully. "I really thought it was crazy, too, at the time, but looking back, it was the best thing that ever happened to either of them. Kate found a passionate, adventurous artist who brought color to what had been a very ordered, ordinary life. Axel got away from his destructive, selfish way of life, and as low as he had been in his early days, that's how high he rose."

Lucas frowned. "I thought he wasn't as successful on his own?"

"No, from a commercial perspective he was never as successful. But he found a joy he'd never had before. It was visible, tangible when he was with Kate, and later with Malcolm and Ella."

Ella brushed a tear from her cheek. After a pause, she asked, "What about you and Uncle Billy?"

"When your dad left the band, Billy called off the engagement."

"Oh, Aunt Meg, how horrible! Why didn't you ever mention it before?"

"Well, we were all so angry for the longest time. Blaze, Troy, and Billy were angry at Axel for leaving, and they all hated your mom for stealing him away. I was angry at Axel and Kate for breaking up my engagement, and they were angry at me and Billy because we wouldn't try to understand or forgive. Eventually, our family came around to polite visits at Easter and Christmas, but your parents and I never talked about the past. I believe your dad tried to reconcile with Billy and the others a number of times, including asking Billy to be your godfather, but didn't make much progress. Billy can be very stubborn." She sighed. "We have that in common. It took me years to realize that I'd been a foolish teenager too. But I never told Kate. I'm sure she saved my life. I would have probably died of a drug overdose or some other nonsense if I had stayed with Billy."

"Why didn't anyone ever tell me the truth?"

"You were so young, Ella. And then, after your dad died... You didn't need to know the details. Your parents served God, they adored each other, and they loved you and your brother. That's all that really matters. Don't get too caught up in the past."

"We've all made mistakes," Jack breathed.

"And we'll make plenty more, I daresay," Mr. Sherman added, rising unsteadily from the table. "It's getting late. I hope we haven't outstayed our welcome."

"Of course not," Meg insisted. "You don't have to go. Are you sure you don't want another slice of pie?"

"No, we should be leaving. Lucas."

Lucas stood. "Thanks again for dinner, Songbird. It was great. Thanks for having us, Ms. Keller." He paused. "Jack."

Jack stood and extended a hand. "Lucas."

They exchanged a firm handshake over the table.

"I'll walk you out," Meg offered.

"See you Sunday," Ella called after them.

"Would y'all like some help with the dishes?"

"No, don't worry about it," Ella replied. "I'm going to let them soak."

"Then I should probably go as well."

"Sorry for the...unpleasantness." Ella winced. "Lucas really is a good guy. I'm not sure what got into him."

Jack frowned. "Honestly, Miss Eleanor, he seems like trouble lookin' for a place to happen. I know it's probably none of my business but, as a friend, I wouldn't trust him too much."

Ella dismissed the comment offhand, but his words came back to her later as she scrubbed the dinner dishes in the sink. How absurd that they had both felt the need to caution her about the other, as if she had anything to worry about from either of them. She chuckled at their machismo. Boys could be so ridiculous sometimes.

Protective.

The word flashed into her mind, and instantly she thought of Malcolm.

He could meet them both over Christmas break. She sighed happily. A few more weeks and he would be here.

12. COOKIE DOUGH

"Hey, are you coming?" Ella asked into the phone, looking out the window at the soft, powdery snow that blanketed the ground and was still continuing to fall.

"Hey Songbird," Lucas's voice answered into her ear. "I'm sorry. The flu is raging through our school and I think my time has come. I should have called last night but I was hoping I'd feel better this morning."

"No big deal," Ella replied lightly. "I'll bring some to church tomorrow."

"I'm really sorry, Ella. I know you were looking forward to it."

"Don't worry about it. Get some rest. Let visions of sugar cookies dance in your head."

"Thanks," Lucas laughed. "Hopefully I'll see you tomorrow."

Ella hung up the phone and slumped into a chair at the table. She exhaled a heavy sigh and peered at the kitchen counter. Flour, sugar, milk, and eggs were arranged in a tidy row. Behind those ingredients stood bowls of sprinkles and sugar crystals along with royal icing prepared in a rainbow of colors.

She looked down at her phone.

"Couldn't hurt to ask," she murmured to herself.

Ella dug her student handbook out of her backpack in the hallway and flipped to the directory in the back. She plodded slowly into the kitchen and resumed her seat at the table. Taking a deep breath, she dialed the extension.

It rang twice and a male voice answered boisterously.

"Is J-Jack there?" Ella stuttered.

"Jack. Some girl," Julian bellowed in a bored tone.

"Hello, this is Jack."

"Hi, Jack. It's —" She hesitated.

Ella Parker? Miss Eleanor?

"This is Ella," she blurted finally.

"Oh." He sounded shocked. "Hello."

"Hi," she repeated, and started to babble. "So, this is really last minute and probably rude, and I'm sure you have more exciting plans, but I was going to bake Christmas cookies today, and I was wondering if… if…" Ella faltered. "If you wanted to help," she said finally.

"Now?"

"Yes."

There was a pause and Ella held her breath, waiting for his reply. Seconds passed and she planted her face on the table. This was humiliating. She'd obviously gone too far. Thanksgiving was one thing but what was she thinking asking Jackson Montgomery to hang out and bake cookies? Mitch would have an aneurysm if he knew.

"I'll be there directly."

"Okay." Ella exhaled. "See you soon."

After a few minutes, Ella heard tires crunching in the snow outside the house and raced to the door to greet Jack.

Stepping inside, Jack stomped the snow off his shoes and unzipped his jacket. Ella started. It was somehow a greater shock to see him in jeans and a dark sweater than when she'd found him on her porch in a suit.

"Wow," she said. "I almost don't recognize you with clothes on."

Jack flashed her a crooked grin.

159

"I mean..." She hiccupped and went red. "I mean, I don't recognize you with *normal* clothes...without your uniform..."

"I gathered that, Miss Eleanor." Snowflakes still clung to Jack's hair and he shivered. "My Southern blood doesn't like this cold."

"Come into the kitchen. It's warm."

Ella handed him a pale purple and white gingham apron.

"It's the only one without lace," she explained apologetically.

With a playfully persecuted expression, Jack slipped it over his head. "What can I do?"

"Turn the oven up to three hundred and seventy-five degrees, please."

Tying her own apron, Ella watched Jack fiddle with the dials. She giggled.

"What? Is it the apron?"

"No," Ella reassured him, suppressing another giggle. "You just remind me of me! I thought you were being modest when you said you couldn't cook." She smirked. "Have you ever used an oven before?"

"Of course I have! This one's just...different." With a sheepish smile, Jack asked, "Do you regret invitin' me?"

"No, it's great. I'll finally get to teach *you* something."

Ella measured and Jack mixed the ingredients. While the dough chilled in the refrigerator, they sat at the table talking and eating lumps of sweet cookie dough.

"So what are you askin' Santa for this year?"

Ella glanced out the window at the glittering snow. "We're already going to have a white Christmas. What more could I want?"

Jack shook his head. "No, that doesn't help me. What do you really want for Christmas?"

Ella choked on a bite of dough. "From you?"

Jack nodded. "Yes. I know you're partial to readin'. A signed copy of *To Kill a Mockingbird*?"

Ella tilted her head quizzically.

"It's the book you were readin' your first day at the Academy."

"I can't believe you remember that."

"I was readin' it too." Jack grinned. "I've seen you carryin' Tolkien, too. A first edition, maybe?"

Ella hiccupped. "Don't you dare. I'd be afraid to breathe near it. You shouldn't get me anything."

"That's out of the question." He crossed his arms over his chest and leaned back in his chair, studying her. "I know I'm gettin' you somethin', I just haven't settled on the item yet."

"Honestly, Jack, I don't need a thing."

The timer rang and together they rolled out the dough and cut shapes of trees, stockings, and stars. By the time the first batch emerged from the oven, the whole house was toasty and filled with the scent of sugared vanilla.

"Those cookies smell delicious," Meg called down the stairs. "You two got an early start!"

She stepped into the kitchen and exclaimed, "Jack!"

Meg looked surprised, but recovered quickly.

"I hope Ella's letting you sneak a taste here and there."

"Yes, ma'am."

"Ella, I'll just be wrapping presents in the other room if you need me."

"Okay, Aunt Meg."

"No peeking!" She winked and left the kitchen.

Jack deftly slid a cookie snowflake from the baking sheet to the cooling rack and asked, "Where is Lucas today?"

"What?"

"Your aunt knew there were two of us but she wasn't expectin' to see me."

Ella flushed. "Lucas has the flu."

Jack nodded knowingly. "That explains the short notice."

"I'm sorry."

"Don't apologize. Whatever the circumstances, I'm as happy as a calf in clover. I get to have cookies with you and Lucas gets to have the flu at home. Everythin's perfect."

He grinned wickedly.

"Meanness doesn't suit you," Ella said, scowling at him. "I've never heard you crack a joke at anyone else's expense. The tongue can bring death or life, you know."

"That sounds scriptural. Your Bible study with your aunt?" Jack asked, looking abashed.

"Proverbs eighteen," Ella replied and, noticing his expression, added quickly, "I usually decorate cookies with my brother, Malcolm. I couldn't bear the thought of doing it alone."

"Where's your brother?"

"Mal's at Michigan State. He's a sophomore. He was supposed to come here for a few days over break, but now he says he can't."

"Why not?"

Ella shrugged. "I don't know. Something to do with the Great Lakes Invitational. It's this big ice hockey tournament the Spartans are in, and he can't miss it."

She sighed heavily.

"This will be my first Christmas without any of them. I miss my mom and my brother so much." She dropped her voice. "My aunt is working so hard to make it special, but it won't really be the same. I mean, it's never been the same without my dad. Do you know I still feel my heart aching in my chest whenever I hear his voice? Every single time I hear one of his songs on the radio." Her breath hitched and she paused. "What was your first Christmas without your parents like?"

"I don't remember it much. That was at the beginnin' of my reckless phase. Some parts are a blur. Probably a good thing."

"Do you ever stop thinking about them?" Ella asked softly. "Sometimes I feel like I should have gotten over losing my dad by now."

"No, you never stop loving them so I don't reckon grievin' ever really ends, Miss Eleanor, and anyone who tells you otherwise has probably never lost someone. But I do believe you strike a balance, in time, between tryin' to forget how much you miss them and still holdin' on to the good memories."

Ella smiled. "We used to snuggle up on the couch together and he'd read from *A Christmas Carol*. My dad always did voices for the different characters. Fezziwig was the best."

Ella piped a stream of blue icing onto a star cookie. Jack sprinkled sugar crystals on top.

"We would get the biggest tree that could possibly fit in the house," Jack recounted. "We'd spend hours stringin' lights and puttin' on ornaments. My momma sang carols the entire time. I remember bein' mighty impressed as a boy that she knew so many."

A strand of Ella's hair fell into her eyes as she bent over the table. She blew it away but it fell back across her face.

"Can you help me? My hands are all sticky."

Jack brushed the offending strand behind her ear. She couldn't tell if his fingers or only the sensation lingered on her cheek.

"Thanks."

Ella looked at him over the table.

"A headband for Christmas?" she joked, but his eyes remained serious.

"I've thought of somethin' better."

Ella jumped as the kitchen door swung open.

"Do I get to try one of these cookies?"

"Yes, of course, Aunt Meg."

"*Mmm*, how can I pick? They're almost too pretty to eat." She surveyed the table, full to the corners with brightly decorated confections. "You must have done a triple batch."

Ella shook her head. "Only double, but it made a lot. Don't worry. Jack's taking half."

"No, ma'am," Jack protested. "I won't take more than a few. I never could resist any sweet thing."

His gaze fell on Ella's face, but she'd begun gently stacking the cookies in festive tins.

Meg caught the look.

"Nonsense. You'll have to share them with your friends. Ella can pack them up and I'll help you carry them to your car."

A biting wind was swirling the snow outside but Meg halted on the porch, blocking the door.

"Can I ask you a personal question?"

"Ma'am?"

Meg asked bluntly, "What are your intentions with my niece? I know as far as Ella's concerned, you're just friends."

163

Jack reddened. "I do aim to be more than friends," he responded frankly, "but my intentions are entirely honorable, ma'am."

The wind whistled through the bare trees but Meg remained motionless.

"I can assure you, if my intentions were anythin' less, I would have quit a long time ago. You've no reason to fret," he added, "I don't want to come on too strong and I'm takin' things slow."

"You seem like a very nice young man, Jack." Meg's eyes were kind. "But you should know I've been expecting something to develop between Ella and her friend, Lucas. I've no desire to sway her one way or the other. All the same, if you're serious, I wouldn't be too subtle."

"I have an idea about that. I'm fixin' to get Miss Eleanor a gift for Christmas, but I'm not certain the dog will hunt. I could use some help."

Meg pulled her coat more tightly around her. "I'm listening."

The front door opened, wafting a cloud of warm air out onto the porch.

"What are you doing freezing out here?" Ella rebuked them. "I was sure one of you slipped. These are the last two tins."

She handed them to Jack.

"Much obliged. I'll see y'all soon."

Jack gave Meg an expressive glance, and Ella a dimpled smile before turning away, cookies in hand.

"Thanks for the cookies, Songbird," Lucas said, bounding up to her at the church on Sunday evening. "I ate them in one sitting."

"I hope Mr. Sherman got a few!" Ella laughed.

"Just barely. He had to fight me off."

"I'm glad you're feeling better."

"Me, too." Lucas shifted his guitar case in his hand. "What are we waiting for?"

"I heard Mark wants to see how many carolers show up before splitting us into groups," Ella replied with a glance around the steadily filling sanctuary.

The choir director stepped up to the pulpit and addressed the room. "Ella? Where's Ella?"

She hiccupped and raised her hand.

"Excellent." Mark beamed. "We couldn't start without our virtuoso, could we? To make things simple, why don't we have everyone on my right side," he said, gesturing with his arm, "go to the east part of town, all you on the left go to the west, and the rest of you here by me will head to the hospital. We'll meet back here at the church in about two hours and share some coffee and treats."

Ella quietly groaned.

Lucas quirked an eyebrow. "You're the one who wanted to spread holiday cheer. I thought you loved singing?"

"I do. But I hate hospitals."

"Because of your dad?"

Ella nodded.

"A hospital at Christmas can't be that bad." Lucas shrugged. "They probably have it all decked out with trees and lights and stuff."

"Are you kidding? A hospital at Christmas is the saddest place in the world! It's full of people separated from their families at the one time of year when everyone should be together."

"You'll be fine. You'll make all their faces light up, so it won't be that depressing, and then you get to come back here and eat cookies."

"More like come back here and try to keep you from eating all of my cookies."

"Well, yeah."

He grinned and she smiled back at him as they stepped out into the frigid parking lot and marched briskly behind the rest of their group to the van.

Ella choked on the familiar antiseptic scent that met her nostrils as she walked through the sliding glass doors of the hospital. The air felt a degree too cool and there was an unpleasant hum of machinery and squeak of rubber soles against the floor.

"One, two, three," Mark chirped and the choir burst into song.

Ella was mute, trying simultaneously to focus on her breathing and ignore the overpowering hospital smell. An orderly bustled passed them in the hallway, and Ella jumped at the sound of food trays chattering on a metal cart.

165

Lucas strummed his guitar beside her and whispered, "You okay? Seriously?"

"Fine," she murmured, pressing her temples. "Just sing."

He watched her a moment longer, and lifted up a rich baritone voice. Ella drew back, her slow smile building as the surprise sunk in.

"I seem to recall you saying you weren't a good singer."

"No," he replied in a low tone, "I said my voice was nothing compared to yours, which is true."

"You have an amazing voice. Why aren't you in the choir?"

Lucas grimaced. "It's not really my thing."

"Well, you're in it now."

Lucas deliberated. "Tell you what, I'll be in the church choir with you if you come and sing with my band some time."

"Deal," she whispered back.

Ella began to sing as they walked through one of many waiting rooms, past a table full of torn magazines and stiff, discolored chairs. As people heard the voices approaching, patients stood and wheelchairs crowded the halls.

A young girl caught Ella's eye. A sheen of sweat covered the girl's forehead above a pair of glassy bright eyes. She flashed Ella a brief, trembling smile and Ella sang a little louder. Security guards and nurses paused to listen.

A man near her leaned forward and filled the hallway with harsh, hacking coughs, and Ella clenched her fists. Lucas dropped the guitar to his side and reached for Ella's hand, giving it a gentle squeeze. She exhaled slowly through pursed lips.

"Look how happy everyone is," Lucas murmured close to her ear. "They're all captivated."

Ella's gaze swiveled over the hallway to the patients in hospital gowns bouncing on their toes and clapping their hands to the steady beat. She started looking beyond the sallow faces as they made their rounds through the hospital and into their eyes. Gradually, Ella's gait slowed and her expression softened.

All at once, a door slid open and they heard a siren blaring in the distance. The snap of a gurney being raised echoed through the hallway and the choir hugged the wall as medical personnel dashed past, calling for assistance.

Ella hiccupped and breathed and hiccupped again. Her palms flattened against the cool, smooth wallpaper as her back hit the wall. Ella let her head sag and closed her eyes.

I am relaxed.

Lucas was staring at her, a grim twist to his mouth, when she opened them.

He looped a muscular arm around her neck as they walked gingerly through the icy parking lot. "You survived, Songbird."

Ella nodded weakly.

"I think you need a cookie, stat," he teased.

She had more than one back at the church, and a cup of burnt decaf to wash them down.

"You made all these?" Lucas asked, his gaze cascading from one tray of glossy, sugared cookies to the next. "Seriously? Were you up all night?"

"No, actually," she replied, her cheeks feeling suddenly hot, "Jack helped."

"Oh, that's good." His face was expressionless, but his rough fingers worked rapidly, tearing a paper napkin to shreds. "I'm glad you didn't have to do it all yourself."

Ella examined his outstretched hands, sinewy and tan, twisting at the napkin pieces.

"Thanks for that, at the hospital," she whispered.

"I just held your hand, Songbird. It wasn't anything."

"Regardless, it helped. I owe you one."

Lucas grinned. "You could always send Bill Bancroft a demo of my band."

"You're hilarious." Ella rolled her eyes.

"Seriously." Lucas scratched behind his ear. "Why not?"

"Well," Ella faltered, pressing a finger against the plate to gather her last few crumbs, "we're not close like that. We've barely even spoken, and it would be awkward to contact him after all these years, especially to ask a favor. Besides, after finding out about Uncle Billy and my Aunt Meg.... I don't know, it would just be weird."

Lucas gave a half-hearted shrug. "No big deal." He dropped his eyes. "You'll still come sing with us some time, though, won't you?"

"Gladly. Will you still be in the choir with me?"

"Of course, Songbird. Anything for you. Speaking of which, I have something to give you. I know it's a little early for Christmas presents but I wanted to be sure you wouldn't make other plans."

He leaned to the side and reached into his back pocket, handing Ella a crisp concert ticket.

"We've got a gig at the Ashby Community Center on New Year's Eve."

"Wow! That's awesome. Congratulations."

Lucas beamed. "Only a couple of bands are playing. It's the real deal. Advance ticket sales and an emcee and everything. Your aunt will let you come, right?"

"I wouldn't miss it," Ella promised.

13. A PRESENT

"No tutoring today?" Meg asked from the stove. "I thought Jack was going to stay for dinner."

"You and me both," Ella replied, glowering. "He wasn't in class today and no one seems to know where he is."

Meg rose to his defense. "Well, it's not like Jack to neglect an appointment. I'm sure he has a reasonable explanation."

"He'd better. We're supposed to be studying for the final." Ella lay her head in her hands and groaned. "What am I going to do without Jack?"

Meg turned away to hide a smirk.

"Well, there's nothing you can do about it now," Meg answered. "Why don't you go change and we'll have a cup of tea?"

Ella smiled weakly and dragged herself upstairs. She tossed her backpack onto her desk chair and fell into bed. *Friends*. Jack was the one who'd said they were friends. Ella hiccupped and hugged her pillow to her chest. She had finally come around to the idea of Jack as an actual friend and now he'd disappeared without a word, blowing off their meeting and even dinner.

As she lay there, still, her ears detected a faint shuffling sound. Ella sat up in bed. She heard the shuffling again and a floorboard squeaked inside her closet. Rising slowly to her feet, she crept quietly to the door.

Dear Lord, please don't let it be a mouse.

She opened her closet and a pair of piercing blue-green eyes stared back at her. Ella screamed and stumbled backward, nearly tumbling over the bed.

The shadowy figure laughed and exclaimed, "Do you have any idea how long I've been standing in here?"

"Mal?" she sputtered, a hand over her racing heart and the other clenched in a tight fist. "What are you doing here?"

"Take a deep breath, Ella," he insisted, placing a firm hand on each of her shoulders.

She inhaled and exhaled shakily, and Malcolm replied, "I'm a present. Jack brought me."

The color came back into her cheeks. "You mean he sent a private jet...just for you?"

"No, I mean he brought me in his jet."

"Jack went and got you himself?"

"Yeah. Didn't you know he had his pilot's license?"

Ella shook her head, feeling slightly numb. "I knew he had a plane. I didn't realize he flew it himself."

"Yeah, I guess he tried to get Mom too, but there was too much red tape with her visa."

"I can't believe you're really here."

"Me neither. That's quite a guy you've got. Are you going to invite him over for breakfast tomorrow?"

"So you can embarrass me by telling him about the time I tried to flush the cat down the toilet? I don't think so. Besides, Jack's only a friend, Mal."

Malcolm laughed. "Someone should probably tell *him* that. But wait until after he brings me back to Michigan, okay?"

"I can't believe you're here," she repeated, still bewildered.

"It's good to see you, Ella." Malcolm hugged her close.

The bedroom door swung open slowly.

"I see you found Malcolm." Meg grinned. "What took so long?"

"You knew?"

"Obviously! You'll find some cookie dough in the fridge and there's icing and sprinkles on the counter."

"You're kidding."

"Nope," she replied. "I don't know what we're going to do with another four dozen cookies."

"I'm taking them all!" Malcolm announced.

"How long are you staying?" asked Ella.

"I have to go home in the morning."

"Then we'd better get started."

They baked a great deal, and talked a great deal more. The clock on the mantel was striking ten when they hung up their aprons, their faces still dusted with sugar and flour. Malcolm collapsed onto the couch and propped his feet on the coffee table. Ella sank down beside him with a satisfied sigh.

A book lay spread open on the coffee table next to Mal's outstretched feet. Ella picked it up, tracing a finger over the gold lettering on the cover. It was a red, leather-bound copy of *A Christmas Carol*, turned to Ebenezer's visit to Fezziwig's with the first spirit. Tears came to her eyes. She held the book out to Malcolm and he took it with a smile.

"Do you remember Dad reading this?"

Malcolm nodded.

"Will you read some, Mal?" she pleaded.

"We probably don't have time for the whole book."

"Just start there."

"Okay," Malcolm agreed. "I can't promise any crazy voices though."

Ella laid her head on his shoulder and followed along as he pored over the pages. Malcolm had not read far before his words slurred and his chin slowly dropped to his chest. Ella lifted her head and studied his face. If she wasn't touching him and listening to his steady breathing, it would be hard to believe he was really here.

A present. A perfect present.

Being friends with a billionaire wasn't fair. Finding presents for Malcolm was hard enough.

"What can I possibly buy for Jack?" she murmured aloud, gently pulling *A Christmas Carol* from Malcolm's hands and setting it on the coffee table.

Her mind echoed the question back, unanswered.

Ella couldn't decide if it would be more embarrassing to give Jack nothing or to present him with an insignificant trinket. There wasn't time to make him something. Clothing or cologne seemed too personal; electronics too impersonal.

Jack read extensively, but after his comment about a first edition, a book was out of the question. She knew he liked cars and traveling, but he had a collection of rare automobiles and could fly anywhere he wanted. Even if she had the funds to splurge on an extravagant gift, chances are he already had it.

A guttural snore erupted from Malcolm. Ella's eyelids flickered and a smile crept across her features. Mal would be on the plane with Jack for hours in the morning. Certainly he could steer the conversation in that direction. What else did they have to talk about anyway?

School. Hockey. Cars.

Ella hiccupped.

Her. Forget about them discussing childhood anecdotes over breakfast. She had probably already been their main topic of conversation on the flight in. Ella glanced at Malcolm again, a half-formed idea in her mind to wake him. He'd said something earlier. Something about Jack not being just a friend.

That was nonsense, of course. Only the words of a brother teasing his baby sister. They both knew Jack was too rich. *Too smart. Too handsome.* The list ran through her head in Courtney's sugary drawl, making Ella shudder. But for the briefest second she wondered if Jack ever thought about her as she was thinking about him. The idea of it gave her a warm glow.

She hiccupped and buried her face in a pillow. It was only a daydream. Nothing more than make believe.

"You're delusional, Ella Parker," she whispered into the fabric. "Don't get carried away."

Ella refused to make any special effort in her appearance bright and early on a Saturday morning. She answered the door in her pajamas, but had awoken with the sun to brush her teeth and comb her hair before the doorbell rang.

"Tell him I'll be right down," Malcolm hollered from the second floor.

She held the door open as a burst of frigid air blew Jack over the threshold.

"Good morning, Jack."

"Miss Eleanor. I'm sorry I missed our appointment yesterday. I was out of town." His mouth curved in a smug smile.

"You're ridiculous." A smile illuminated her face. "I don't even know what to say."

"I'm fixin' to come on Sunday afternoon if that's alright. I reckon you want to study for the final exam."

"I do. I'm dreading the final. Plus, we've restocked our supply of cookies."

Jack looked about to say something but stopped as Malcolm plunged down the stairs.

"Sorry, Montgomery. I'm running late. My aunt made breakfast and I couldn't tear myself away from the table. I've had about all the cafeteria food I can take."

Malcolm slung his backpack across his shoulders and Jack waited a pace away while Malcolm pulled Ella in for a hug and whispered close to her ear, "I'll miss you, Ella. Merry Christmas."

"Bye, Mal. Thank you, Jack." Ella's voice was thick and she was glad they left quickly.

After watching the car pull away, she shuffled to the couch and picked up *A Christmas Carol*, turning to where they had left off the night before. She flipped through it absently, scanning the pages.

Realizing she'd read the same sentence for the fourth time, Ella closed the book.

"Not in the mood for Dickens?"

Ella jumped, a hand flying to her chest. "Aunt Meg, I didn't hear you come downstairs."

"I was in the kitchen." She raised a cup of steaming tea to her lips. After a sip, she sighed. "What a treat to see Malcolm. It was quite a kind gesture on Jack's part. Thoughtful. And to go himself —"

"Jack can afford to be generous. He probably gets really extravagant gifts for all of his friends."

Ella didn't even want to imagine what he was giving Courtney.

"Still just friends then?"

Although she felt warm, Ella shivered and pulled a knit blanket over her knees.

"Of course. Jack dates underfed Brazilian supermodels and actresses, not girls from his Calculus class. But I'm happy we're just friends," she said, her voice bordering on shrill. "Anything more than friendship with Jack would be a nightmare anyway."

Meg's eyes widened. "How so?"

"Think about it. The more money and power a person has, the more complicated their life is. Jack is constantly busy. Constantly traveling. Constantly the center of attention. Who would willingly sign up for that lack of privacy? Your relationship and personal life always on display. Having your clothes, body, hair criticized on the cover of a magazine. I could never hold up under that judgement."

"You know, your mother would have a quote for this occasion."

"Eleanor Roosevelt says, 'We are afraid to care too much, for fear that the other person does not care at all.'"

"Actually, I was thinking of what she said about life in the public eye: 'While it may be most difficult to keep the world from knowing where you dine and what you eat and what you wear, so much interest is focused on these somewhat unimportant things, that you are really left completely free to live your own inner life as you wish.'"

"Oh..." Ella stammered. "Oh, of course. Right."

Meg took a seat beside Ella and set down her tea, saying, "That may not be much consolation if you're inside the goldfish bowl, though. Not to mention, in the case of Jack, that at any given moment there would be thousands of other girls vying for him."

"Exactly." Ella grimaced. "Exactly. No, thank you."

"You're right. A boy would have to be pretty extraordinary to be worth all that. Good thing you're just friends."

Meg picked up her knitting needles. Ella sighed and tried to put that final barb from her mind, reaching once again for the book. She read slowly, trying to focus on the words in front of her as other thoughts quietly gnawed at her concentration.

It was dark on Sunday night and only two cookies remained when Ella and Jack finally closed their textbooks. He stood to go.

"I'm sorry I couldn't get your mother. I truly did have a plan in place, but it just didn't come together."

"Sorry? That was the nicest...." Ella trailed off, shaking her head in disbelief. "It was perfect. I'm sorry I didn't get anything for you."

"Don't carry on about me. I'm pleased I could give you a tiny bit of your old family Christmases."

A sudden inspiration flashed in Ella's mind, and she asked, "What's your favorite Christmas carol?"

Jack squinted at her.

"Can I...sing you a song? A carol, like your mom used to sing."

His face lit up. "'O Holy Night.'"

"Okay." Ella nodded. "You have to play though."

Perched on the piano bench, Ella reached for the faded hymnal and flipped through the thin pages. She gently bent the songbook open to the proper page and placed it on the music rest.

Sliding onto the bench beside her, Jack stretched his fingers and played the introduction. His hands danced elegantly across the keys but as Jack reached the melody, Ella remained silent. He glanced over at her and she reddened.

"I'm sorry. This is weird." Ella made a face. "I've never sung for just one person before. Somehow I feel more flustered singing for you than a crowd."

She hiccupped nervously.

"Go again. I'll sing this time."

175

He began his accompaniment a second time and Ella closed her eyes. *I am relaxed.* She pulled in a deep breath and drew out a hauntingly pure aria, her rich voice flowing through the song.

Jack's fingers froze above the keys.

Opening her eyes, Ella nudged him with her shoulder. "You have to keep playing."

"I'm not sure I can. You're like an angel, Miss Eleanor. How come you never told me you sing like that?"

"I told you I was in the church choir."

"But you ought to have said, 'I sing in the church choir *like an angel*.'"

Ella laughed and blushingly finished the carol. Jack sat in awe.

"Are you singin' for the Holiday Ball?"

"Of course." Ella shrugged. "I signed up a few weeks ago. Do you want to see my dress?"

Jack nodded and Ella led him upstairs, thankful she'd remembered to make her bed. The room looked suddenly smaller and shabbier with Jack standing beside her.

"It's tiny, I know," she mumbled apologetically.

"It's cozy. I like it." Jack lingered in the doorway. He pointed to the maps. "Places you've been?"

"No, someday hopefully. I'd love to travel."

He moved slowly to the desk, lifting a picture frame. Ella looked over his shoulder.

"That's me and my dad," she pointed out. "It was our last family vacation before he got sick."

"Where are y'all?"

"We were in the Hall of Gems at the Museum of Natural History," Ella replied, opening her narrow closet. "Our family went everywhere growing up. I remember my mother making me wear a floppy sun bonnet in Colonial Williamsburg, and watching baby sea turtles hatch on a beach in Georgia. We even did a road trip on Route 66 one summer. I think after touring across the United States and Europe all those years, my dad couldn't stop traveling." Ella turned back to the closet, blinking, and said, "It's one of the things I miss most."

176

The fabric rustled as she pulled the dress gently from the hanger. Jack touched the silky material.

"You made this?"

"Actually, my aunt sewed most of the dress, but she taught me this stitch, so I've embroidered the detail," Ella explained, tracing it with a finger. "I have a little left to do, but I think it will look nice, with my hair done up," she said, twisting it at the base of her neck, "and a flower there."

An image of Ella materialized in Jack's mind, the pale blue satin against her ivory skin and a white rose at the nape of her neck. He inhaled sharply at the thought.

Ella didn't seem to hear, and went on, "I'm hoping it will look vintage and not frumpy. Still, I'd rather look old-fashioned than disappoint my Aunt Meg. She's so proud of this dress."

She held it out in front of her a moment, examining her needlework, before carefully hanging it back in the closet.

Jack rocked back and forth on his heels. "I reckon I ought to go before your aunt catches me in your room and tans my hide."

"Oh, it's fine. She knows we're just friends."

A muscle twitched in Jack's jaw but he smiled. "Do you feel prepared for Wednesday?"

"I think so. I'll be so glad when Calculus is done. I can't seem to stop thinking about it."

"Worryin' gives small things big shadows, Miss Eleanor. We can meet again Tuesday evenin' if you'd like," Jack offered.

"No." Ella shook her head firmly. "You're right. I'll just drive myself crazy. I'm going to take good notes when we do the review in class and then on Wednesday —"

"You'll ace it."

"I'll pass it, *hopefully*," Ella corrected.

"That makes this our last meetin' then."

Ella's face fell. "I guess so. What classes do you have for the spring semester?"

"Molecular Biology and Mandarin Chinese at the Academy, and two courses at Harvard through the post-secondary program again this next semester."

177

"Wow." Ella gulped. "That's very –"

"Ambitious?"

"Masochistic, is what I was thinking."

Jack grinned. "I was fixin' to do more, but I play lacrosse in the spring."

"You'll be very busy." She'd intended it to be an observation but it left her lips as a complaint. Ella reminded herself that she had no right to feel disappointed.

"Not *that* busy, Miss Eleanor. There's always time for the important things."

What those important things were, Jack didn't have the opportunity to disclose. Meg rapped on the open door and stuck her head in.

"It's getting late, you two."

"We wouldn't want to lose track of time talking," Ella agreed facetiously.

Jack's lips twitched. "No, ma'am."

14. BACKSTAGE AND ONSTAGE

The vision in Jack's mind didn't do Ella justice. As she walked into the concert hall a week later, Jack wondered how he ever thought her anything less than breathtaking. She spotted him in the crowd and made her way to his side.

"I didn't realize this was such a formal event." Ella blushed, glancing around at the other girls in their glittering designer gowns, with artificially bronze skin on full display. "They look like models."

"They look like mannequins. Stiff. Manufactured." Jack took a step back to admire her. "You look fresh and real."

"Like I just plumb skipped out of a spring garden," Ella mocked, mimicking his accent, "with a kiss of sun on my cheeks."

"Exactly," he replied still more seriously. "Brimmin' with the sweetness of youth."

Ella laughed. She saw Mitch and Jayla seated together, and waved.

"Looks like they have a seat for me."

"Miss Eleanor," Jack called after her, "will you promise me somethin'?"

She turned. "Sure."

"Remember that we were friends before you went out on that stage."

"Okay?" She looked at him quizzically.

"Just trust me. You're goin' to have a lot more friends after tonight."

Feet shuffled in the crowd, and programs crinkled. Ella was listed second to last in the program and the audience were all anxious for the final act, a Christmas rap, written and performed by a select group of Academy instructors. Watching their somber educators spitting rhymes onstage was always the highlight of the year.

She peeked from behind the velvet curtain at the glamorous dresses and crisp tuxedos, and breathed a silent prayer.

Dear God, let this bring you glory. And don't let me hiccup.

Ella was given no introduction, and few were even aware she'd stepped onto the platform until she began. She started softly, her voice building. At once, the concert hall was silent. Even the sounds of breathing were muffled as many held their breath.

With the heavenly singing from the angel before them, the audience that moments ago had raucously applauded a sexy snowman dance routine was brought back to the hushed town of Bethlehem over two thousand years ago. A star, high in the heavens, sparkled brilliantly in the midnight sky. A tiny baby blinked up from a bed of straw. The air was filled with song as the new mother sang a lullaby to the Lord, and the angel chorus echoed over the hills.

Students who had been mentally reviewing bank statements and travel itineraries now could think of nothing but the manger. Tears filled teachers' normally dry eyes. There was an unusual moment of silence as she finished. The audience didn't know whether to applaud, shout, or cry.

Finally the stillness was broken by a call of, "Encore! Encore!"

Jack was waiting offstage when Ella finished her second song.

"*Brava!*" he congratulated her. "That was extraordinary."

She beamed, the electricity of the performance still pulsing through her veins. It took her a moment to notice his coat.

"You're leaving before the dance?"

"Regretfully, Miss Eleanor. I was fixin' to stay at the boardin' house over the break, but my grandmother isn't doing well. I just discovered this evenin' that she's in the hospital, so I'm headin' there directly."

"Where?" asked Ella. Her hand flew up, lightly clasping her throat. "To France? Right now?"

Jack nodded. "I wanted to hear you sing first, and to say goodbye."

Ella could hear the beatbox from the stage behind her and the audience's peals of laughter but felt a sudden heaviness in her stomach. She extended an open palm.

"Have a safe flight."

Jack's grasp was steady and his long fingers curled around hers firmly.

"I'll miss you." She'd spoken the words as they formed in her mind.

He took a step closer, her hand still wrapped in his. "Will you?"

"Of course," Ella breathed. Avoiding his eyes, she focused on the slight dip along the bridge of Jack's nose – only visible if you knew to look for it. "I don't know what I would have done without you this semester. A few months ago, I thought coming here was a mistake, but I'm starting to think I'm exactly where I'm supposed to be. You've had a lot to do with that."

Ella met his gaze and wished she hadn't. The heavy knot in her abdomen turned to a flutter. Ella's eyes shifted from Jack's face to his fingertips twined around her hand.

"Miss Eleanor," Jack said, his voice soft and low, "I reckon y'know what I'm fixin' to say. You *must* know."

A thunderous applause interrupted him and the voices of the faculty were suddenly close. Ella dropped Jack's hand and sprang back a step as Headmaster Tutwiler approached at a brisk clip.

Jack tilted his head to the ceiling and let out a heavy sigh.

"Miss Parker, we had no idea you were so musically gifted. We must get you involved in our choral program. Were you aware we have a recording studio here on campus?"

"I – Yes," Ella stuttered. "Yes, I did know that, and I'd be very interested in the choir."

"Mr. Montgomery, I hope you're not leaving us early?"

Jack rubbed his brow as if to ward off a headache.

"I'm afraid so, sir." His tone was uncharacteristically sharp and held a note of annoyance. "I'd best be goin'."

Jack gave Ella a tight nod. "Merry Christmas, Miss Eleanor."

"Goodbye, Jack."

Her farewell was drowned out in a rush of footsteps from the concert hall. A swarm of people wedged backstage. The petite girl with glasses from Ella's Calculus class pushed her way forward.

"Ella, you have to talk to my dad," she said breathlessly, pressing a business card into her hand. "He's a producer. Broadway. You'll call him over break, won't you?"

Ella gave a quick bark of laughter but recovered herself. "Thanks. I'll think about that."

Mitch and Jayla emerged from the mob.

"Ella! What was *that*?" Jayla bubbled, embracing her.

Before she could respond, Mitch said through a hard, obvious swallow, "I'll understand if you don't want to dance after all."

He gave his hair a yank, and shuffled his feet as if poised to run.

"Mitch, it's me."

"I know, but you're... It's different now."

"You've sat next to me at lunch every day for the past four months. We're friends," Ella said, grabbing his upper arm and shaking him. His posture relaxed. "Please don't get all weird. I'd rather dance with you than any of those other guys."

Ella's hand tingled as she released his wiry bicep and her mind leapt unbidden to Jack. She made a fist, mentally willing the prickling sensation to cease.

Mitch's palms were sweaty in hers as they fumbled their way across the dance floor.

"Honestly, Mitch, I can deke an opponent on the ice as well as my big brother, but this Foxtrot is impossible."

"Wait for the Quickstep," Mitch panted.

"How do they know all the steps?" she asked, whipping her head around to marvel at the elegant pairs swaying on either side of them.

"Private schools," he gasped, "featuring dance."

"Can we sit?"

Mitch gulped and nodded.

Ella had scarcely caught her breath when a boy from her Phy Ed class with a petite, narrow nose approached them.

"May I have this dance?" he asked in a shrill, nasally voice.

Ella's mouth pulled into a straight line and she answered unwillingly, "I suppose so. You're not chewing gum, are you?"

The boy coughed. "I...er... Sorry about that. It was an accident, obviously."

"Obviously."

Ella tilted her chin at him and he dropped his eyes.

"I think it will be a short dance," she whispered to Jayla, rising from her seat.

Ella was right, though not in the way she imagined.

"Do you mind if I cut in?" A stocky boy with bright, eager eyes held out a stubby hand.

Ella was disappointed but tried not to look it. Though she would have much rather joined Mitch and Jayla back at their table, she slid her hand into his. He was surprisingly graceful despite his square frame and thick limbs.

"You're an excellent dancer," Ella remarked when she could spare a breath.

"And you're —"

"Not." Ella chewed her bottom lip.

"You're really not," he chuckled, trying to keep a straight face but failing.

Ella threw her head back in a burst of laughter.

"It's okay." He cleared his throat. "You can't be good at everything."

"Right now, I wish I was a little worse at everything else and a little better at dancing."

He smiled at her. "You seem really nice, Ella. Especially after we've all been so awful. I'm glad I finally get to talk to you."

"Finally?"

"Yes, I couldn't before," he said matter-of-factly, "because of the Crowd."

"What?" Ella stumbled over her own high heels but her sturdy partner supported her.

"You haven't heard about the Crowd?"

"No. I have. I just didn't realize that *everyone* was afraid of them. At first, I thought it was made up, or at least exaggerated."

"It's very real," he assured her.

"So, what would have happened if you had spoken to me before now?"

"Something bad."

"Like what?"

"I don't know," he admitted. "Just something bad."

Ella narrowed her eyes. "'It is not so much the powerful leaders that determine our destiny as the much more powerful influence of the combined voices of the people themselves.'"

The boy's feet faltered in their rhythm. "That's very well put. Did you come up with that just now?"

"No," she informed him with a small smile. "Eleanor Roosevelt said that a long time ago. But have you ever thought that the Crowd is more powerful than you because you all treat them that way?"

His lips parted but he hesitated. A well-manicured hand tapped his shoulder.

A tall boy with sleek, black hair stood at her side. "May I cut in?"

Ella and her partner stopped.

"Thank you for the dance...?"

"Josiah."

"I'm glad I finally got to talk to you too, Josiah."

When Ella finally plopped down at the table, she'd lost count of her dance partners.

"I'm jealous, Ella," Jayla cried. "You didn't have to sit out a single song."

"I'm a little jealous you got to sit! I think my feet are permanently fused to these shoes," Ella replied, wiggling her toes under the tablecloth. "Besides, you and Mitch looked like you were having fun."

"We did have fun." Jayla's eyes brightened. "But it would have been exciting to dance with every boy in school."

Not every boy, Ella thought.

Jack was probably a superb dancer. It seemed like something a gentleman ought to be good at. A pleasant shiver raced up from her spine as she imagined standing inches from him, his firm hand on her waist and another clasped in hers.

She sucked in a sharp breath at the idea, but exhaled slowly. He was only a friend, she admonished herself for what seemed the dozenth time in as many days. Jack had emphasized that fact just before she'd sung. Ella thought there had been a moment backstage of something more than genteel politeness when he held her hand. But his farewell had been cold and brief.

Ella hiccupped. Jack would be somewhere over the Atlantic right now. Far away and doubtless not thinking of her.

The old Buick skidded across a patch of black ice under the freshly fallen snow as Ella drove to the community center on New Year's Eve. Ella gripped the wheel and made a slight correction, narrowly missing a truck stopped on the side of the road. She slid into one of the few empty spaces in the parking lot and closed her eyes.

Dear God, please let him understand.

Ella hiccupped and hugged her cold arms tightly around herself. It seemed presumptuous to think that Lucas liked her, but after praying for months that he would care for her, she was afraid he finally did.

She had to tell him about Jack. He was untouchable, out of reach for so many reasons but she couldn't stop herself. However insignificant she may be to Jack, his sudden absence the past week forced Ella to admit that Jack meant something to her.

Ella rested her head on the steering wheel. Lucas would say it was because Jack was rich. Because he could buy her an ocean worth of pearls or sweep her off to Italy on a whim.

Ella thumped her forehead on the steering wheel and the horn blasted. The truth was his fortune only complicated things. If Jack had simply been a boy in her Calculus class, they could easily have been friends from the first day. Instead, he'd been someone with status. Someone to be feared. Avoided. It had been as easy to hate Jack in the beginning as it was to fall for Lucas.

Dear God, were hormones really necessary?

Her initial infatuation with the handsome boy at the church had faded, leaving only an affectionate friendship. But she feared the attachment had only bloomed on his side.

Knuckles rapped on her window and her eyes flashed open.

"You okay?" Lucas's face was concerned and Ella's stomach rolled.

She forced a smile and opened the door. "Yeah, just a rough drive."

"I was starting to think you weren't coming. We're about to go on."

With quick steps, he led her inside. Ella could feel the beat of the music pulsating from speakers before she reached the door. She surveyed the room from the outer edge, allowing her eyes to adjust to the dim light. Strobe lights above the stage lit the space with sudden, choppy beams of color. Backstage, it was darker still.

"You remember Ben, Tyler, Paul." They nodded one after another. Lucas turned to Ella. "We'd better get set up. See you in the audience?"

"I'll be in the front row." Ella made a move to go, but stopped. "Can I talk to you after?"

"Sure."

Lucas's face was bright, full of energy. Ella's stomach twisted inside her.

She snaked her way around dancing couples and pressed past the densely packed supporters nearest the stage. The boy beside her leaned close and shouted something. Ella felt his warm breath against her neck as he spoke directly into her ear but she couldn't make out the words.

The people around her applauded as the band on stage took their bow but the applause fell away rather quickly.

Lucas and his friends bounded onto the platform. Girls, dressed to draw attention, pointed and hooted amongst themselves. Lucas's gaze shifted over the crowd until he met Ella's eye and winked.

As they performed their set, Ella critiqued them without meaning to. Paul's bassline was subtle and solid. Their keyboard was noticeably old, but Tyler's fingers moved across the keys with a casual grace. Ella could almost admire Ben's intensity on the drums if he didn't lack a sense of time. She was disappointed to see that Lucas hadn't just been self-deprecating about his rough guitar-work. But his vocals made any other shortcomings meaningless.

A sweet sadness filled his eyes as he sang and there was something haunting – a mingled pain and strength – in the rich baritone of his voice. Lucas's face contorted with the lyrics and a passion that totally enraptured and silenced the crowd at one point.

Ella was drawn out of the spell as familiar chords reverberated from the guitar. Lucas knelt directly in front of her, and held out a hand.

"Come on, Songbird," he shouted. "You know this one."

Confused, she braced her knee against the platform and he hoisted her up in one smooth pull. Lucas grinned at her – the brilliant, hypnotizing grin she'd seen the day they first met – and tilted the microphone down.

"This is Ella. Her dad wrote this song. Maybe if you all cheer loud enough, she'll sing it for us."

The mob in front of her writhed and jumped and whistled beneath the chaotic strobe lights. Ella blushed red and waved the microphone away. Her hands were shaking but Lucas plucked his guitar with a calm, steady rhythm.

"Looks like you're not loud enough," Lucas shouted and the audience erupted.

He reached for Ella's arm and pulled her beside him, wrapping a muscular forearm around her waist.

Lucas swept a strand of hair behind her ear with one callused finger and whispered, "You promised you'd sing with us sometime."

His lips lightly brushed her skin near her ear as he spoke and Ella hiccupped. She was going to break his heart tonight. She had to do this. Besides, it was Dad's song. One of her favorites.

I am relaxed, she told herself.

Ella lifted a trembling hand to the microphone and the clamor fell several decibels. She began and, a few lines in, Lucas's voice joined hers. Their lips were inches from the microphone, inches from each other.

Her voice caught suddenly as she envisioned Lucas trying to kiss her. Would she have to push him away here in front of everyone? She refused to humiliate him, but she couldn't kiss him either.

With an effort, Ella summoned her voice, her eyes darting to Lucas's face. But he didn't seem to have heard her uncharacteristic error.

On the final note, Ella took a quick bow, said 'thanks,' and trotted offstage. As the concert ended, Lucas rushed after her and caught her in his arms.

"That was seriously amazing, Songbird." He spun her around in the air. "Thank you for singing."

"You're welcome," she replied and stabilized herself on her feet. "A little warning next time?"

"Would you have still showed up?"

"I probably would have come down with something at the last minute," Ella admitted. "That was at the edge of my comfort zone."

She glanced at his friends packing up their instruments. "You guys were good. And I had fun."

Lucas ran a hand over his short hair and Ella studied his face while his eyes were turned away. It was hard to tell how he felt. She only hoped they could still be friends after tonight, because Lucas truly was a good friend. Like the other boys, he was a little rough around the edges. But he had a golden heart for someone who had been hurt by his parents and lost nearly everyone he loved. Impulsively, she embraced him.

"You can wrap me in those arms," Ben called out. "Or legs."

Lucas took a step and shoved him.

"What?" he chuckled. "I was just joking around."

"Well, don't," Lucas replied, his voice stern.

Ben's eyebrows came together. "What's your problem?"

"You're about to be my problem."

"Come on, Lucas." He sneered. "You're going to fight me over the Wicked Youth girl? We both know she's not worth it."

"You don't know anything," Lucas growled with another vicious push.

Ben fell back into the wall. Chairs screeched as other musicians behind the curtain jumped back and some rushed forward.

Ben steadied himself and rubbed his shoulder. "You've wasted all this time and she's never going to do it."

Lucas clenched his fist and there was a sickening crunch as it met Ben's face. Ben hit the floor with a thud. Standing a few feet away, Ella could see his nose and lip were both bleeding but it was difficult to tell where one injury ended and the other began.

He struggled to sit and spat on the ground.

"Stay down if you're smart," Lucas said through his teeth. "And shut your jaw if you don't want me to break it off."

Ella's eyes were burning as she elbowed her way to the door. She turned away from the blowing snow as she stepped outside, swiping at something wet on her cheek. Ella told herself it was a snowflake melting against her skin and not a tear.

Reaching the Buick, she scraped the windshield as quickly as possible, her fingers growing numb. Ella wanted to get away but knew she couldn't navigate the slippery roads with tears still hanging in her eyes.

She slumped in the driver's seat and blew a warm breath into her hands. The passenger door opened and Lucas slid into the car.

"Those guys really grow on you, huh?" Ella said shakily.

"I'm sorry, Ella. What Ben said in there...about wasting my time with you..." Lucas swiped a hand over his face. "There's something I need to tell you."

At his words, Ella's stomach tightened. There was no flutter of butterflies. Only a hard knot.

Please, Lord, not now. Of all the times for Lucas to tell me, not now.

Lucas faltered, "When he said you were never going to do it —"

"I know what he meant, Lucas. I'm not a nun," Ella cut in. "I know you're not like that. You're better than that."

"I'm not," Lucas murmured into his hands. "You don't know."

He lowered his hands and looked at her.

"You're seriously the best person I've ever met. You honestly believe everyone is good and kind at heart, don't you?"

Ella shivered. "Except maybe Ben."

They sat in silence, their breath fogging the windows around them. Ella watched as a new layer of snow blanketed the windshield she'd just cleared.

"Do you want to come back in?" Lucas asked softly. "They should be doing the countdown soon."

"No, I think I'm going to go. Do you need a ride home?"

"I have the old man's truck." He reached for the door handle then leaned back in his seat. "Was there something you wanted to talk to me about?"

Ella hiccupped. "Another time."

15. A CELEBRATION

Whumph. Ella's book slipped from her hand as a snowball hit her bedroom window. Icy crystals on the glass bore evidence of the white explosion.

She pulled back the curtain to see the driveway. *Whumph.* Another snowball hit the glass in front of her face. Swirls of frost coated the window but she could just make him out. A warm glow spread from her abdomen to her cheeks.

Jack was back.

He crooked a finger at her, beckoning Ella outside. She tugged on her boots and mittens downstairs, and wound a scarf around her neck. A shock of cold made her gasp as the frigid air outside found a patch of bare skin between her mitten and sleeve.

"I thought you hated the cold?" Ella called from the porch to Jack, still in the driveway.

"I do, Miss Eleanor. But I love a good snowball fight." He assumed a pitching stance. "Fair warnin'."

Ella's lip twisted up in a half-smile. "You wouldn't —"

She ducked.

Jack launched another, narrowly missing her chest. Ella shrieked, dashing from the porch to the other side of Jack's car for cover. Ella lobbed a snowball in Jack's direction but it fell wide. Her second was closer but he dodged it. An answering volley made Ella dive.

Kneeling to form more ammunition from the snow bank, a snowball hit the back of her neck. The chunk of ice slipped under her collar and down her spine.

"I surrender!" Ella laughed. "Mercy!"

She toppled into the snow bank and Jack collapsed beside her. Feeling light snowflakes land in her hair, Ella brushed them away. "How's your grandmother?"

Jack pulled the stocking cap from his head and placed it gently on hers. "Finer than a frog's hair split four ways and sanded twice, thank you for askin'. Did y'all have a pleasant New Year's?"

Ella nodded and pulled the hat down to cover her ears. "Lucas talked me into going to this big party in Ashby."

"A party? I pictured you and your aunt havin' a quiet New Year's at home," said Jack. His tone was light and conversational as he tossed a snowball from hand to hand. "Did you kiss anyone at midnight?"

"No. I left early," Ella responded, suddenly glad she had. The possibility of a midnight kiss hadn't crossed her mind before.

"Y'know, they say that if you don't share a midnight kiss with someone you love, you're guaranteed a bad year. Sorry." He made a wry face.

"Well, the past year hasn't exactly been painless either. Moving across the country. Bullies at school. Almost flunking out," she replied, ticking off the list on her fingers.

"You're missin' the part where a brilliant tutor," Jack said, giving a theatrical bow, "turned everythin' around."

Ella fought for a deadpan expression and raised another finger. "Grounded for a month."

"But you passed Calculus."

"Yes. But you shouldn't be so smug. You're in for the same rotten year as me."

"No, ma'am. I'm lookin' forward to happiness and fortune in the comin' year."

His words hung in the air like the fog from his warm breath.

"You...kissed someone?"

"I gave my sweet grandmother a peck on the cheek."

Ella exhaled a shaky laugh. She squeezed her hands together and asked, "You want to go in? My mittens are soaked through."

After shedding their ice-encrusted coats and gloves in the entry, Jack fetched a kitchen towel to sop up the puddles of melting snow and Ella carried two mugs of steaming hot chocolate to the living room.

"Careful now!" Ella warned as Jack reached for his.

His eyes crinkled. "You'd better move back, just in case."

Jack took a quick sip and returned his cup to the coffee table. "I meant to ask, how was the Holiday Ball, Miss Eleanor?"

"My feet have yet to recover."

Jack's face dimpled as he reclined on the couch but Ella sat stiffly beside him, her cup warming her hands.

"Jack, tell me about the Crowd."

"The Crowd? It's like an Academy urban legend. This group of powerful students that used to run the school."

"Used to?

"Well, there's obviously no such thing now."

"So you're not a part of it? You and Courtney and Diana and Julian. You're not all secretly...in cahoots." It sounded ridiculous as she was saying it.

"Would I tell you if I was?"

He held her gaze for a moment, then slyly raised one eyebrow. Ella snorted.

"Do you want to know a real secret about me?"

"Sure."

He took a slow sip. "Today is my birthday."

Ella choked and sputtered, "It's what?"

"My birthday. My eighteenth birthday."

"And you're just telling me now?" Ella glanced at the clock on the mantle. "I'll make something special for dinner. I might need to run to the store..."

Jack was silent and Ella blushed. His eighteenth birthday meant more than cake. Today, he was head of a major company, responsible for billions of dollars in investments, and was most likely meeting an NFL cheerleader for sushi later.

Ella dropped her eyes. "I mean, unless you have other plans."

His lips formed a twisted smile. "You always think I'll have other plans."

"Well, you're...important. You must have more influential people to meet with, more interesting places to be than here."

"If I'm so *terribly* important," Jack said, his tone suddenly biting, "don't you reckon I'm in control of my own schedule?"

"I suppose."

"And I'm here with you because...?"

"Everyone at the Academy is home for break." Ella's shoulders drooped. "I'm the only one around."

Jack narrowed his eyes. "I don't have other plans."

"So what would you like? Beef Wellington, duck à l'orange, braised pork loin with caramelized pears?"

"You're gettin' good. Your aunt must be gratified. If it's my choice, buttermilk biscuits and sausage gravy."

"Are you sure?" Ella asked, wrinkling her nose. "I could make something fancier."

"I don't need anythin' fancy. I know what I want. Biscuits and gravy, please. May I help?"

"With your own birthday dinner?" Ella shook her head. "No. But I'll let you keep me company in the kitchen."

"I'd likely burn it anyway," Jack admitted.

Ella slid the baking sheet of pale biscuits into the oven and asked, "So are you officially the richest person in the world now?"

"No," Jack mumbled, leaning his back against the floury counter. "Fourth."

194

"I can't tell if you're joking or serious."

Ella, crumbling sausage into a saucepan, swiveled her eyes to his face but it was distant. Jack rolled up his sleeves, walked to the table, and paced back.

He crossed his arms, cleared his throat, and asked, "Do you ever think about goin' out, Miss Eleanor?"

Ella hoped he didn't notice her sudden intake of breath.

"Like dating in general?"

She tried to reply calmly but her hand shook, knocking a measuring cup to the floor. Jack bent to retrieve it.

"No..." he replied slowly, rinsing the cup in the sink and holding it out to her.

Ella grasped the handle but Jack didn't let go. She lifted her chin reluctantly to face him. Jack's jaw was a hard line, but his eyes were warm, amused.

"I meant datin' me."

"Oh." Ella dropped her face and let her hair fall over her shoulder.

He relaxed his grip on the measuring cup and said softly, "Forgive my lack of subtlety, but you seem immune to any hints."

He paused and Ella held her breath.

"Have you ever thought about it?" Jack repeated.

"I suppose it's crossed my mind before, once or twice."

"It has." Ella detected the smile in his voice, but didn't look up.

Yes. The word stuck to her suddenly dry tongue. All of the reasons she'd repeated to herself over the past weeks came rushing back to her.

Her stomach wrenched in a hard knot. Not only would it break Lucas's heart, she was wrong for Jack. She would never be the beautiful, brilliant socialite to hang on his arm while he ruled an empire. His declaration, miraculous as it was, could not change that.

Ella wet her lips. "I think it would be a bad idea."

"What? Why?" asked Jack, his voice holding undisguised shock. "You don't reckon I could make you happy?"

Ella almost laughed. She bit hard on her bottom lip. "That's not it."

"What then?"

"Well, we're both graduating in four months," Ella said. Her voice was now calm but her hand still trembled as she measured a cup of flour into the saucepan. "What's the point of starting something that's just going to end then?"

Jack's carefully controlled tone matched hers. "You say it like I'll be droppin' off the face of the earth."

"You'll be going to another school —"

"I have a jet. It's not as if you won't be able to see me."

"There are other reasons."

"Enlighten me."

The golden brown mixture on the stove bubbled. Ella kept her eyes low and stirred as if the fate of the world rested on the smoothness of her gravy. "You won't understand."

"Try me."

"It's hard enough just being friends with *Jackson Montgomery*." Ella said his name like a carnival barker. "I can't imagine being your girlfriend."

Girlfriend really is a lovely word, Ella thought. A tender, silly, happy word. Another giddy laugh nearly bubbled up from inside her, but she covered it with a cough.

"You don't just go out with the fourth richest person in the world."

"Someone ought to," Jack replied sardonically.

Ella poured the milk, sloshing a large white puddle on the counter. "Yeah, but she should be a debutante or a Southern belle or something."

Jack's eyes went to the ceiling and he chuckled, "A *belle?* Really? You reckon I should keep to my own kind?"

"I'm serious," she said softly, her cheeks burning. "I'm wrong for you, Jack. You've been groomed for a life of prestige and I'm a nobody. I'll never fit in like those other girls."

"You shouldn't *want* to fit in with them. I'll let you in on a secret: those other girls may have wealth or beauty or other trappings of happiness but they're not happy. Most of them are shallow and hollow and they're miserable to be around. I'm not interested in a high falutin' society darlin'. I would rather be with you."

"But why? I'm not —"

A shrill beep interrupted her.

196

"The biscuits," Ella cried, rushing across the kitchen and wishing she could flee further.

A cloud of steam burst from the oven as she opened the door. She turned her head away from the searing heat and saw Jack. His shoulders sagged as he picked at an imperceptible spot of lint on his sleeve. His face was drawn, his lips tight.

Ella hung her head. She'd worried before about hurting Lucas. It hadn't occurred to her that she could hurt Jack.

She reached for the pan and yelped. Three crusty biscuits rolled to the floor as Ella stared stupidly at the growing red welt on her hand.

"I don't know what I was doing," she mumbled.

Jack grabbed her arm and pulled her to the sink. A cascade of ice cold water numbed the throbbing pain. Jack stood behind her, his chin above her shoulder, his two hands holding her aching one open under the stream.

"Did I distract you?" he asked, his slippery fingers gliding over hers.

"Just clumsiness," Ella croaked. She cleared her throat. "It was my own fault."

Ella felt his warm breath tickle her neck and closed her eyes. *I am relaxed.* She inhaled, but the sweet, spicy scent of him didn't help to clear her head.

"Better?" Jack asked, reaching for a towel, and Ella missed the pressure of his hands.

She nodded, not trusting her voice.

He rested a palm gently on the small of her back and a tingle raced up her spine. She shivered and Jack pulled his hand away.

"I'm sorry," Jack murmured hastily. "I know it took some time for you to come around to being friends but I reckoned... It seemed like you felt..." he stammered. "I shouldn't have assumed you liked me in that way."

Ella grinned and bit her lip. "You're actually standing there, asking me in that aggravating drawl if I *like* like you?"

"Do you?"

A strangled laugh broke through and she cupped a hand over her mouth.

"Yes, Jack. I like you." Her words came out in a rush. "You're smart, and you're kind, and I never get tired of talking to you. I wake up happier on the days I know I'll get to see you."

Ella stopped. She had said more than she had intended to, but it was too late now.

Jack's eyes gleamed. "Then why not give it a chance? I'm not askin' you to sign a prenup, Miss Eleanor. Just have dinner with me once."

"We're about to have dinner now," Ella pointed out.

"Y'know what I mean."

Ella sighed. It wasn't funny anymore.

"If you were just a boy I played tennis with or sat by in class, then maybe. But, as it stands, the situation is way too complicated."

"As it stands? You reckon you'd like me better if I was the sixteenth wealthiest instead of fourth?"

"It would be easier if you weren't on the list at all, Jack. But I'd never wish any misfortune on you."

"There are worse things than financial loss, Miss Eleanor."

Ella avoided Jack's eye and looked around the kitchen. All but three biscuits were ready, buttery and golden, and the sausage gravy was warm on the stove.

She wasn't sure she could swallow a mouthful.

"Can we talk about this later?" she asked softly. "For tonight, can it just be enough that we're friends celebrating your birthday?"

"For tonight, yes. I'm goin' to be in New York for the next few days. Promise you'll think on it?"

Ella made the promise needlessly. It was impossible to avoid thinking of Jack whether he was there or away, and the first week back at the Academy would be strange without him.

She took special care in plating their food, garnishing Jack's with a striped candle. Snowflakes swirled and fell like confetti outside the kitchen window, erasing all traces of their snowball fight in the yard as wax dripped onto Jack's biscuit and Ella serenaded him.

He stared at her intently before blowing out the flickering candle. Although he didn't share it, Ella could have guessed his wish.

16. FITTING IN

Ella hugged her book to her chest as she stepped out of Statistics into the teeming hallway. A hard, square shoulder nudged hers and she turned, expecting an angry glare, but met a grin.

"Hi, Josiah," Ella greeted him. "How was your break?"

"Two weeks in Aspen. It was great. How was yours?"

"Fine," Ella replied. "I just stayed here. Not exactly Aspen, but I recuperated from all that dancing."

Josiah chuckled, "That sounds peaceful actually. Hey, do you know my girlfriend, Beth?"

A curvy girl beside him smiled shyly at her. She had a white, cable-knit scarf looped around her neck, resembling Ella's own navy scarf. She'd spotted a few other girls with similar knitwear since returning to the Academy.

Ella nodded. "Beth, yes. We were in the same World History class last semester."

"Yes, we were. I'm sorry I didn't introduce myself before."

Ella stopped. "The Crowd?"

"Yeah, I'm so glad you understand." Beth's hand flew to her heart and a curl fell into her face. "I remember when I got in here six years ago, my first semester was so bad, I thought I was going to kill myself."

"What did you do?"

"There isn't anything you can do. A really chubby girl, bigger than me, transferred second semester and we all started in on her. I've never been so thankful," Beth said. Her arms went limp at her sides momentarily. "She doesn't go here anymore."

The three stood in silence, students filing past them noisily, until Ella gestured to the classroom behind them.

"This is me."

The cloud lifted from Beth's face and she pushed her hair back from her forehead with a graceful hand.

"Okay. See you around."

"Can we sit by you at lunch?" asked Josiah.

"Sure," Ella agreed.

She shuffled into Environmental Science and spread open her book on the desk. Her eyes flitted over the words as if she were reading, but her thoughts were elsewhere.

She'd memorized the Academy motto on her first day. *Knowledge crowns those who seek her.* It was a lovely sentiment, but *Dog Eat Dog* seemed a more appropriate expression.

The more they opened up to her, the more Ella felt her fellow students were generally nice people. Even a few who had persecuted her had come forward with apologies. How could seemingly warm and friendly people be so horrible to each other?

"Anybody seen Jack?" Julian asked as he lumbered into the room. "I thought he was in Molecular Biology but he wasn't there this morning or yesterday."

"I haven't seen him since I got back," answered a thin, bespectacled boy.

Courtney swiveled in her chair and said, "Why don't y'all ask Ella?"

Ella looked up from *Lord of the Flies*. "Why me?"

"You're our own little Academy starlet, after all. Aren't you two a thing now?"

Ella's breath caught in her chest. Jack had told Courtney. *What exactly had he said, and who else knew?* She couldn't fathom why he would confide in Courtney, but the second answer was obvious. This was the Academy. *Everyone* knew. No wonder they were all speaking to her, dressing like her, and going out of their way to be nice to her. Not only did she have the Crowd's stamp of approval, they all knew she had Jack's.

Ella hiccupped. "Who told you that?"

"I'm sorry." Courtney's lashes fluttered over wide, innocent eyes. "I just assumed after the Holiday Ball, he'd want to snatch you up. Did he not?"

Ella exhaled. *What did it matter if they knew, after all?* Jack hadn't said a word, that was what mattered. That, and wiping the flowery smirk off Courtney's face.

Ella lifted her eyes to the ceiling and blinked. "Now that you mention it, Jack did say something about going to New York when we had dinner on his birthday."

Courtney's smug pout flattened into a sneer. "Enjoy your time in the spotlight while it lasts, sweetie. Fifteen minutes passes right quick and he'll find a new and better plaything."

Ella smiled through gritted teeth and replied, "Thanks for the heads up."

She bent over her book, her hair a dark curtain around her face. Her cheeks were red and her breath unsteady, but no tears came to her eyes. Ella wasn't upset or embarrassed, she was mad.

Courtney may be rich and beautiful but she's nothing more than a petty, grasping little snake, spitting venom at anyone in her path. Diana and Julian were just like her. Their poison rippled out from them, infecting anyone it touched.

The others seemed to think the only defense against them was attacking the weak. Focus attention on someone else and you're invisible on the sidelines. Gang up on an easy target, and you're safe yourself. It was a defense of sorts, but not the best. The best defense is a good offense.

That's all well and good, Ella thought with a hiccup, but no one would ever fight back. As she swallowed a gulp of air, her mother's voice came to her with a familiar quotation, "Light a candle instead of cursing the darkness." It was one of her favorite Eleanorisms.

201

Ella flinched as Mitch flicked a wad of paper at her and whispered, "Are you really going out with Jackson Montgomery?"

She leaned over and whispered back, "No, I'm definitely not... At least, not yet. I don't know... It's complicated."

Mitch stared at her, slack jawed.

"What?" she hissed.

"Nothing. I mean, Courtney's right. After the concert, it makes sense. But I can't quite wrap my head around it."

Ella rolled her eyes. "Jack would be appalled if he knew about this hero worship. If you would actually try talking to him, you'd see he's just a normal person."

Mitch considered a moment and said, "No, I couldn't do that."

"So help me, Mitchell Zagers, this school is going to get over the Crowd and it's going to start with you. Jack says the Crowd doesn't even exist!"

"Of course he would tell you that." Mitch shook his head. "Sorry, Ella. There's nothing you can do to me that would be worse than talking to Jackson Montgomery."

Ella narrowed her eyes. "If you don't say something to him the very next time you see him, I'll tell Jack I can't go out with him because I'm madly in love with you."

"You wouldn't... You can't do that. He would... I'd be dead," Mitch sputtered.

"Your choice." Ella shrugged. "Talk to him, or die."

17. BILLIONS

Ella's phone rang. She reached for it groggily, knocking a picture frame to the floor. The crash startled her awake and she sat up in bed in her still dark room.

"Hello?"

"Are you aware of what your boyfriend's done now?" demanded a loud voice.

"Not my boyfriend, Mal," Ella croaked. She cleared her throat and said, "Do you have any idea what time it is? Why are you awake?"

"I'm at the gym. Have you heard, Ella?"

"Go back to sleep!" Ella groaned. "You're a psycho! Or maybe a sadist," she mumbled, rubbing at her eyes. "Why are you calling me at the crack of dawn?"

"I'm trying to tell you!" Malcolm shouted into her ear. "I'm on the treadmill at the gym and they just said on TV that Jackson Montgomery of Montgomery Enterprises donated half his fortune yesterday to a laundry list of charities across the country. They're estimating the total combined amount to be in the billions. Billions with a B, Ella."

"What?"

"Turn on the news. It's practically on every channel."

"How do they know? Is Jack on TV?"

"No, supposedly Jack was unavailable for comment. It's some disgruntled financial manager who left the company. Sounds like he didn't approve of the decision when Jack informed the board of directors."

"Was it company money then?"

"No, I guess it's all personal wealth, but Jack is the face of the company, and it's a pretty crazy move. Their expert is saying if investors are smart, they'll pull their money out of Montgomery Enterprises right now. Did you know about any of this, Ella?" Malcolm asked accusingly.

"Not exactly," Ella replied slowly.

"Not exactly? What does that mean? Have you seen Jack?"

"He hasn't been at the Academy. He went to New York last week."

Ella's phone chirped in her ear and she glanced at the screen.

"Mal, I have to go. I'll call you back."

Malcolm protested on the other end of the line but she ended the call.

"Hello?"

"Hello, Miss Eleanor." Jack's voice was tight. "You haven't seen the news this mornin', have you?"

"No," Ella said hesitantly, "but Mal called me."

She heard Jack exhale.

"Did he tell you what they're advisin'?"

Ella hiccupped. "Sell."

"Sell," Jack echoed. "My parents spent almost two decades buildin' the company and I manage to tank it in under a week."

She heard a muffled groan.

"How bad is it?"

"Well, our stock price has no effect on the bottom line of the company but it impacts the shareholders a great deal."

"Aren't you the majority shareholder?"

"My grandmother and I, but we'll survive. That's life. One day you're the peacock, the next day you're the feather duster. I'm more concerned about the other executives and employees. We offer a portion of their compensation in the form of stock options and employee purchase plans. So if the stock drops —"

"They're in trouble."

"It could be devastatin' for some folks. I could be responsible for the hardship of thousands..." His voice trailed off, ending in a moan.

"Jack?"

"It was all supposed to be anonymous," he barked. "Just once, I'd like a situation to go as planned! There should have been nothin' to trace it back to me or Montgomery Enterprises, but then that stupid, son of a —"

Ella heard a crash of shattering glass and gripped her sheet.

"Jack!" she shouted into the phone.

"I hope he was paid well for his story because he's going to need a good lawyer after violatin' my non-disclosure."

Ella rolled her eyes, thankful he couldn't see her. "Because what you really need right now is to jump into a lawsuit."

Jack uttered a strained laugh.

"Would you really have grounds for legal action?" Ella asked.

"Probably. He ought to have been legally gagged when he signed his contract but it's possible he found some loophole. Provin' financial harm is always difficult, but I believe there will be a sizable impact, if only from the bad press."

"How?" Ella asked, twisting her sheet in a knot. "If the stock doesn't really impact the bottom line, how can there be financial harm?"

"Morale is sure to take a big hit. I'm lookin' at a loss of talent, as well as difficulty in hirin'. It's hard to attract good people when there's no confidence in senior leadership. That can be pretty disastrous over the long haul." Jack's voice shook. "My biggest fear is that if the stock drops low enough, Montgomery Enterprises could become an acquisition target."

"What do you mean? Like a hostile takeover?"

"Exactly. If the stock drops low enough, someone could try to come in and grab a bunch of that stock just so they can raid the cash, physical property, intellectual property — really anythin' the company has of value — and dismantle Montgomery Enterprises in the process. Everythin' my parents worked for. Their whole legacy, gone."

He breathed deeply, noisily.

"Jack, you didn't..." Ella hiccupped. "It wasn't because of me, was it?"

There was a change in his voice. It was warm, teasing, as he said, "Don't be so vain, Miss Eleanor. I started makin' that list over a year ago... It did seem like a convenient time, though."

There's my Jack, Ella thought, relaxing her grip on the sheet. She leaned back in bed.

"Would you take it back?"

"I'm not sure now. But I was excited yesterday. I reckon my parents would have been right proud. I doubled all of the bequests they left in the will, and chose some endowments of my own." Jack paused. "No, I don't reckon I would do it differently if I could. I may still be able to minimize the fallout personally if necessary."

"You'll tell me about the charities you picked when you're back?"

Jack didn't miss a beat. "Over dinner?"

Ella hiccupped.

"Okay. Over dinner. You realize this is the most costly first date in history?"

"That's not exactly how I see it, but still..." He gave a satisfied sigh. "Worth it."

Jack met Ella at the massive double doors on Monday morning. The warmth of the crowded hallway beckoned, but Ella hesitated in the entryway, suddenly conscious of the change in their relationship. *Would he be expecting more than a hello?* A kiss so soon was out of the question. A hug seemed more reasonable but Ella's palms felt sweaty despite her numbing walk, and she thrust them deeper into her coat pockets.

I am relaxed, Ella told herself.

Jack didn't seem to notice her weak smile as she said, "Good morning," though the greeting sounded cold in her own ears.

His phone buzzed and he silenced it without looking.

"Do you need to get that?"

Jack shook his head stiffly. "It's only one of my financial managers. He keeps callin' to update me, but I'd rather not know at this point."

"It probably doesn't seem like it at the moment, but I'm pretty sure you did the right thing," Ella whispered. "It's going to be okay."

"Right," Jack mumbled. He rolled his neck from side to side but his posture remained rigid. "Right," he repeated.

Ella's eyes swiveled first to Jack's tight lips, and around to the others in the hallway, currently giving the two of them a wide berth. She took a step closer and slid her hand surreptitiously into Jack's.

In a soothing tone, Ella said, "So, tell me about this date on Friday."

"That didn't take long." He lifted her hand to look at their interlaced fingers and his shuffling steps quickened. "I expected to have to dance around that subject for the next week."

"Well?"

"It's a surprise," Jack replied, his eyes gleaming. "Dress comfortably and bring a penny."

"That's awfully enigmatic." She squinted up at him. "Just one? What am I buying with one penny?"

Jack responded with a half-shrug and a grin. "You'll find out Friday."

She knew if she pressed him, he couldn't resist revealing more, but Mitch and Jayla were waiting outside her Statistics class.

"Hi, Ella," Mitch said, turning red. "Jack, how are you? You look surprisingly zen. I'd be freaking out if I were in your position."

"I'm mostly tryin' not to dwell on it."

"That's mental discipline," Mitch commended him, flushing still more crimson. "It's not even my money and I can't stop thinking about it. If I were in your shoes, with that kind of burden on my shoulders, I'd replay my choices over and over and over again. Analyze. Reanalyze." Mitch caught Ella's eye. "But that's just me."

"I'm sure it will all work out. Don't y'all fret about it."

"Thanks, Jack."

"Any time." He flexed his grip on Ella's hand. "I'd best get to class. I'll see you at lunch, Miss Eleanor?"

When Jack turned the corner, she spun around to Mitch.

"Feel better?"

"I do. He really has a way of putting you at ease."

"Are you kidding me?" Ella punched his arm. "Could you have been more awkward? Don't ever try to talk someone down from a ledge, okay?"

"I'm sorry. It's just fascinating. We're all wondering when he's going to snap."

"Were you trying to speed up the process?" Ella asked sharply. "When I encouraged you to talk to Jack, I had no idea you were so socially impaired!"

Mitch was silent and Jayla gaped at her.

"I...I'm sorry, Mitch," Ella stammered. "That wasn't... I didn't mean that."

"It's okay. I knew it was inappropriate as I was saying it. I just couldn't stop my mouth." Mitch tugged his hair. "I was more shocked at you defending him. Did you see their faces?"

Mitch shifted his gaze to the now empty hallway.

"I didn't notice."

"He's hemorrhaging money by the second and you're still with him." Jayla scoffed. "You're a rising star. He's a sinking ship. Nobody knows what to make of it."

"I don't like him for his money any more than he likes me for my voice."

"You're honestly not in it for the money? Not even the status here at the Academy?"

Ella's 'no' was emphatic.

"Then why do you like him?"

"I don't know," Ella said, blushing, but lifted her chin defiantly. "Lots of reasons. I like the way he says 'yes, ma'am' and 'no, sir' without sounding painfully awkward or insincere like anyone else. He can explain a math problem or a business scenario without making me feel like a complete idiot. I like the way he calls me 'Miss Eleanor' in that ridiculous accent, and his dimples make me smile whenever he smiles. Is that enough for you?"

"Wow, Ella!" Mitch cried.

"What?"

"You've got it bad!"

"No, I don't." Ella scowled at him. "Shut up."

"Ella and Jack sitting in a tree, K-I-S..." Jayla chanted.

"What's your I.Q., again?"

Jayla beamed. "Off the charts."

"Try to act like it. And don't tell anyone," Ella pleaded.

"So you like my dimples, Miss Eleanor?"

Ella slammed her lunch tray down on the table. "This school is the worst. Is there some hidden speaker system nobody's told me about?"

"We all just love gossip."

"You don't."

"Not usually, no. But that was worth listenin' to."

Jack's phone buzzed. He fumbled in his pocket to silence it and said, "You have to admire his persistence."

Ella wrinkled her nose. "Do you, though?"

"No, Miss Eleanor, I suppose not."

Jack pressed a hand to his face and rubbed his eyes.

Ella sighed and said, "Tell me how I can distract you."

Jack looked up. "You don't have to try. I could watch you for one minute and discover a hundred different things to captivate me. Just tell me what you're thinkin' about."

"Excluding worrying about you?" She glanced around their empty table, asking, "Do you know why no one is sitting with us?"

Jack took a bite and shook his head. "I hadn't noticed."

"It's because they're afraid that Jackson Montgomery is now out of the good graces of the powers that be. Or that as an emerging prima donna, I'm now part of the Crowd."

Jack set down his fork. "I thought we talked about this already."

"I know you don't think the Crowd exists at the Academy, but it does. At least in people's heads. It dictates who they talk to and how they treat each other." Ella crossed her arms over her chest. "It has to stop."

A smile tugged at one corner of Jack's mouth. "You're plottin' a revolution. That *is* mighty interestin'."

"The way I see it, when you're the victim, there's not much you can do. Passive protest doesn't work. I tried ignoring it at the beginning and nothing happened. One bully might get bored if they don't get a reaction, but an entire school of bullies could go on forever. Aggression doesn't really work either. The food fight didn't accomplish anything –"

"Apart from gettin' me in trouble."

"Thank you again," Ella said, reaching for his arm across the table.

He caught her hand and held it. "So if the victim is helpless, what's your plan?"

"Step one: weaken the image of the enemy. Change has to come from the masses. They have to realize that you and Julian, Diana and Courtney don't have power over them."

"I'm the enemy in this scenario?"

"Well...you aren't an enemy... exactly," Ella said slowly.

Jack quirked an eyebrow. "This is makin' me feel a lot better."

"But you are larger than life to almost everyone here. Or were," she mumbled.

Jack laughed unexpectedly. "Nothin' humanizes a fella quite like insolvency."

"Exactly. You're already making great strides on that front. The mighty can fall just like that," she said with a snap of her fingers.

"So step one of your plan is well underway, thanks to me. And step two in your plan is?"

Ella hesitated. "That's on a need to know basis."

"You'll keep me apprised as we go along," Jack replied, his eyes twinkling. "Smart."

He was making fun of her, but she didn't care. At least he was smiling.

"Actually, I could still use your help with step one. I need you to...talk to people."

"Talk?"

"Yes. You're just not very," Ella said with an uncomfortable swallow, "approachable."

"Other students speak to me all the time. I feel like I'm constantly the center of attention."

"They do their best to entertain you. It's not the same thing as actual human connection."

Jack's smile disappeared.

"Don't get me wrong. You're wonderful," she said quickly. "But nobody knows that because you don't reach out of your little circle. That's why they all still think you go around dating Russian gymnasts and burning nightclubs to the ground."

"None of that is true."

"It doesn't have to be true to be believed. I heard both of those rumors within the last four months. Most of the school is terrified of you. I had to threaten Mitch with certain death just to get him to speak to you."

"So you reckon I should talk more? About what?"

"About anything." She shrugged. "About you. Pick a random person in class and ask if they play an instrument. Tell them you play piano."

"I also play trumpet, guitar and drums."

"Oh, is that all?" Ella asked, feigning disappointment. "Someone as well-rounded as you should be able to find a common point of interest with almost anyone. Prove that you're just a person like they are. Prove that you're not all that different."

Jack's eyebrows creased as he studied her face. "You really aim to do this, don't you?"

"I do."

"Well, I don't reckon much will change, Miss Eleanor. But I'm game to try."

Ella's eyes glittered. "That's why I like you, Jack."

He grinned wickedly. "What about my Southern drawl and – what was it? – my sincere respect for others?"

Ella closed her eyes and groaned. "I'm leaving now."

"No, you can't yet," Jack declared, holding fast to her hand. "What was the last thing? Somethin' about math. I'm good at math?"

Ella wriggled her hand free and tried to scowl but couldn't with his stupid, dimpled face in front of her. She bit her lip. "I'm not telling."

"Never mind, Miss Eleanor. I reckon I can ask anyone."

She snorted and stood up from the table.

Jack called after her, "It'll give me somethin' to talk about."

The morning sky was grey as Ella trudged through drifts of snow the following day. She turned her face against the wind, hair whipping into her eyes, and pressed on. Ella trusted the old Buick to make it to the Academy, but she didn't trust herself behind the wheel at the moment. Both her heart and her mind were racing and it seemed the walk to school had never taken so long.

Reaching the boarding house, she took the steps two at a time, snow still clinging to her boots and a newspaper clutched in her numb fingers. Ella pounded on Jack's door unceremoniously and pushed her matted hair out of her face. The door swung slowly open. Jack leaned an arm on the door frame, clad only in loose, navy pajama pants.

"Miss Eleanor?" He covered a yawn. "An unexpected pleasure."

Jack stretched his back. Any other time, Ella's eyes might have gotten lost in the contours of his chest, but instead she snapped, "You didn't answer your phone."

"I'm sorry." Jack frowned. "Come in. Is somethin' wrong or are you just here to seduce me...because if you are, it's workin'."

He tilted his head as she tugged off her coat.

"What do you call this hairstyle?"

"I'm being serious."

"So am I. You look prettier than a store-bought doll. Bed head suits you."

Ella was too irritated to blush, but ran a hand through her hair. Her fingers caught on a tangle.

"It's windy, okay? Just listen. Aunt Meg saw this in the business section this morning."

Jack gave a drowsy chuckle. "Your aunt has to be the last person in the world to still get a newspaper."

Ella stamped her foot, propelling slush across the floor.

"That's not the point. Will you just listen, please? Honestly, there are some times when it pays to answer your calls. It's no wonder he was trying so hard to reach you."

"Miss Eleanor, you are lovely but it's awful early, and I have no idea what you're talkin' about."

Ella held up a finger.

"Listen to this." She read, "*In a stunning turn of events, after a widely predicted opening sell off, Montgomery Enterprises stock has erased losses and was up over ninety-three percent at its highest point during the one day of trading. Like his parents before him, Jackson Montgomery seems to have a knack for creatively impacting*

212

and influencing the marketplace." She looked up. "Jack, they're calling you the whiz kid of Wall Street."

"They're what?" Jack choked, snatching the paper.

He fell back unsteadily into a chair as his eyes swept the page. Ella waited patiently until he dropped the newspaper onto the desk and reached for her hands. His palms were burning against her icy ones. Jack briefly bowed his head then turned his eyes up, looking heavenward.

His voice was shaky when he finally spoke. "Does this change anythin'?"

Ella laughed out loud, "You tell me. You're the math expert."

"No, does this change us?" Jack's grasp on her hands tightened momentarily and his eyes flashed up to hers.

Ella's lips parted. *It changed everything.* Her eyes flickered away from his to the desk and fell on his name in newsprint. She looked down at her feet. All the old complications remained, and Jack's name in the media meant renewed scrutiny inside the Academy walls and without.

As she hesitated, there was a bump at the door and Julian reeled into the room.

"Jack, you missed out last night. You know that wild –"

Julian stopped short when he saw them. He looked from Jack's bare chest to Ella's rumpled hair.

He slurred, "You two been celebrating?"

"Word travels fast," Ella mumbled.

Jack's face was stern. "We're talkin'."

Julian careened across the room to the desk and grinned at Ella.

"How did you know?" Julian slung an arm over her shoulders. Her knees half buckled under his weight. "How did you know this *wunderkind* would turn it around?"

"I didn't."

"*Hmm.*" His breath was sharp and sour in her face. She leaned away but his muscled arm held her secure.

Jack stood. His voice was soft but menacing as he said, "Julian, keep it up and I'll cancel your birth certificate."

Julian raised both hands. "Didn't mean to intrude. I'm sure I can find a more companionable shower around here anyway."

He winked and lurched his way to the door, leaving the room unnaturally still. Ella hoped for an instant the interruption had distracted Jack, but he tugged her hands, pulling her a step closer.

"Please tell me you didn't only like me when I was the underdog, Miss Eleanor," he coaxed, "because I have Friday circled on my calendar already."

Ella hiccupped. "In pencil or pen?"

"Pen. And I got a new penny in case you didn't have one."

"I forgot about that part."

Jack released her hands and slid open the top desk drawer. The penny shined in his long fingers as he placed it in her palm.

"You'll hold on to this until then?"

Ella wrapped her hand around it firmly. Her stomach fluttered unsettlingly as she whispered, "I will."

18. PENNY DATE

"I wish you'd tell me where we're going. Are you sure this is okay?" Ella asked, turning in a circle. She'd changed her outfit three times after school, but was second guessing her choice again.

"You look exquisite," Jack insisted, helping Ella into her coat, "and it's a surprise."

Meg poked her head out of the kitchen door. "You both look nice. Should I take your picture?"

Ella rolled her eyes discreetly. "It's not prom, Aunt Meg."

"You'll remember curfew?"

"Yes, ma'am."

"And you both have your phones charged?"

"Yes," Ella exclaimed. "Stop worrying!"

"I'll bring her back safe and sound," Jack promised.

He walked Ella to the car and opened her door. She slid back into the warm seat and pressed her hands together in her lap to keep them from shaking. Jack slipped into the driver's seat.

The engine purred powerfully and Jack said, "Pick a number between ten and twenty."

"Why?"

"Just humor me."

Ella squinted at him. "Eleven."

"Alright." He cleared his throat. "Flip the penny. Heads, we go right and tails, we go left."

Ella flipped the penny in the air, caught it, and turned it on the back of her hand.

"Heads. Go right."

"That's one," Jack explained as they pulled out of the driveway. "Every time we come to an intersection, flip the penny, and the eleventh time, we stop and make a date wherever we are."

"And this whole time I thought you were just being coy. It's actually a surprise for you too." She peered down at the penny. "I like it."

"I reckoned you might," Jack said, his chest swelling.

Ella's brows drew together. "You're pretty pleased with yourself, aren't you?"

"I ought to be. Livin' in high cotton and goin' on a date with my best girl. If times get any better, I'll have to hire somebody to help me enjoy 'em."

She shook her head. "Pride goeth before a fall, Jackson Montgomery."

He beamed.

"What?"

"It sounds like music when you say it. There is no sweeter sound than you sayin' my name."

Ella unclasped her hands to flip the penny and point in the assigned direction as they came to each intersection. She shifted in her seat, aware that Jack's eyes followed the movement of her legs as she crossed her ankles.

"Go on." Her foot bounced. "You like the way it sounds when I say your name. How else do I *enchant* you?"

A spot of color appeared on Jack's cheeks and he coughed. "Haven't we been over this already?"

216

Ella caught her lower lip between her teeth to hold back a laugh. Jack was always so annoyingly poised and confident. It was refreshing to watch him squirm.

"I'm pretty sure you owe me. The whole Academy knows why I like you."

Jack tightened his grip on the steering wheel and was suddenly riveted by the road before them. His words came slowly. "I feel...at home with you. I know you'll tell me what you're actually thinkin'...instead of what you reckon I want to hear. And I live for your quirks."

"My quirks?"

He glanced over. "Like how you hiccup when you're nervous, or embarrassed, or hungry maybe? It happens a lot. And then your cheeks and your ears get pink...kind of like right now."

"That's from the cold."

He smirked and pressed a button. Hot air blasted Ella's warm cheeks.

"I find myself readin' or listenin' to a song and – instead of thinkin' how much I enjoy it – I think about how happy it would make you."

"Speaking of," Ella interrupted, "I was considering making grits. But Aunt Meg said she's never made them or eaten them, so you'd have to tell me if they taste right."

"Make me grits and I'm liable to propose."

Ella laughed.

"You think I'm teasin' but you don't know how long it's been since I've had grits," Jack said with a grin. "I reckon I'll make a Southern belle of you yet."

Ella's mouth turned down. "I only know one Southern belle and I don't much care for her."

"Miss Courtney may be Southern, but she's not a belle. It's less to do with a twang in a girl's voice and more to do with manners and makin' others feel at ease. In that respect, you're more the belle. A true Southern gentleman knows a thing or two about belles."

Ella scoffed. "Men don't know a thing about women, no matter where they come from."

"Perhaps, but a gentleman does his best to learn."

"That's eleven," Ella announced. "Turn left here."

"And," Jack said, glancing back and forth, "we're in the middle of nowhere. *Wonderful*."

The narrow road stretched in front of them, a jungle of bare trees the only visible landmarks.

A slow smile crept over Ella's face. "When was the last time you climbed a tree?"

"It's been a while." Jack glanced over at her and pointed out the window. "But that one is callin' to me."

Halfway up the gnarled trunk, Ella began breathing hard, her breath forming a cloud in the crisp air. She gripped a knot in the bark and closed her eyes.

"Do you need a break?" Jack called from above.

"I should probably tell you," Ella gulped, "I'm just a tiny bit afraid of heights."

Jack shimmied down the tree and sat on the branch nearest her. "Why did you suggest climbin'?"

"Eleanor Roosevelt said, 'You must do the thing you think you cannot do'."

"Do you always do as Mrs. Roosevelt says?"

Ella's mouth was dry and she swallowed. "My mom is a big fan of the First Lady of the World. She was my namesake and I was brought up to believe Eleanor Roosevelt was always the ideal to aspire to, just like you were brought up to be a Southern gentleman."

Jack chuckled and dropped to a foothold below her. He eased her stiff fingers from the knot and guided them to the limb where he'd sat. With a hand on her waist, he boosted her to a seated position and scrambled up beside her.

Jack straddled the branch. "It's a shame you didn't have the good fortune to be raised in the South, Miss Eleanor. What a belle you'd make!"

Wind swayed the tree and Ella clung desperately to the branch.

"You're not far from the mark," Jack went on. "You already joined a quiltin' circle and do needlepoint. You have pearls for everyday wear. Y'know how to cook. You'd just have to embrace fryin'."

"I've made fried chicken before," Ella contended.

"Yes, but we fry *everythin'*." Jack swung a leg back and forth. "Fried okra, fried corn, fried green tomatoes, fried catfish, fried pies and pickles."

"What else?" Ella asked, motionless. Every muscle tensed as she watched him move with carefree grace.

"What else do we fry? Literally everythin'."

"No. What else do I need to know to be a Southern belle?"

His face was suddenly serious. "I don't really want you to be anythin' other than you, Miss Eleanor."

"I know, but now I'm curious." Ella gasped for air. Her head spun from the height, but she felt a manic compulsion to speak. "It's not like you're really going to change me. It would just be a supplement to my education. Like learning French."

"In that case, I suppose lesson two would be to accept gossip. Southern girls don't exchange salutations. They greet each other with bits of gossip."

"I don't think that's exclusive to Southern girls," Ella argued, "but continue."

"Do you have anythin' monogrammed?"

"Yes," Ella cried. Her voice sounded shaky and she exhaled. "I have a monogrammed blanket."

"We're makin' some headway. Ever been muddin'?"

Ella shook her head.

"Tailgatin'?"

"Nope."

"SEC football team of choice?"

Ella wrinkled her nose. "None of the above."

"That's nearly a deal breaker," Jack replied, cringing. "We'll work on that one."

"Lesson three: root for football."

"It's a little more specific than that, but we can start there."

"Lesson four?"

"Lesson four..." Jack thought aloud, readjusting his position on the branch.

He edged a few inches closer to Ella on the limb. The bough beneath them creaked and she grabbed ahold of his arm.

Jack grinned at her. "You're not still scared, are you?"

"Of course not," she lied. "Just chilly."

He shifted to unzip his coat and the branch gave way. A scream stuck in Ella's throat as Jack pulled her to his chest, and twisted to impact the ground first.

Ella landed on top of him, with arms outstretched to break the fall. Her fingers sunk through the layer of snow and she heard a *pop* as her hand hit the frozen turf. A surge of pain rippled out from her wrist up her arm and to the tips of her fingers.

Ella cried out and rolled off of Jack into the snow. She exhaled a few shuddering breaths, her arm cradled against her ribcage.

Jack knelt over her. "Are you okay? Are you hurt?"

"My wrist." She winced, and blinked hard.

"Let me see."

He extended her arm gently and examined it. Ella's wrist was a sickening purple hue and appeared to be growing thicker.

"I reckon we'd best be goin' to the emergency room, Miss Eleanor."

Jack pulled Ella to her feet and brushed the wet snow from her clothes. Distracted momentarily from the pain, Ella tried to breathe normally as Jack's hand skimmed the back of her legs.

He reached for her bulky, knit scarf. "May I?"

Ella nodded silently and Jack stooped to pack snow across half the length of it. He folded the scarf over on top of itself and wrapped it tenderly around her wrist.

"This'll have to do for now."

"It's going to melt," Ella said reluctantly.

"I aim to be at the hospital before then." Jack retraced their footsteps ponderously through the heavy snow. He jerked open Ella's door. "In any event, I can pull over and get more."

Ella hung back. "Your leather seats will get all wet."

Jack rolled his eyes and pulled her forward.

"Ella darlin'," he said, sounding exasperated. "Don't carry on about the seats. Please just get in the car."

Ella sat and allowed herself to be buckled into the seat. Jack was silent next to her, but she smiled. He'd said it sharply, but 'Ella darling' still rang musically in her ears.

The paper on the exam room table crinkled against Ella's damp clothes as she dialed her phone.

"Hi, Aunt Meg."

"Ella?" There was a clatter in the background. "Is everything okay?"

"Everything's fine now. I just wanted to check in. So don't panic...but we're at the hospital."

"Which of you is hurt?"

"I broke my wrist," Ella replied quietly.

"My goodness, Ella, what happened?"

"It's kind of a funny story actually." Ella laughed weakly. "We fell out of a tree."

"What on earth were you doing in a tree? I thought you were at dinner."

"Well, we had this penny and we were going left or right with heads or tails, and we ended up by this big tree, so we climbed it."

Meg's voice was incredulous. "You climbed a tree at the end of January because a penny told you to? You two have given me more grey hair in last four months..." She trailed off. "Are you in Ashby?"

"Yes."

"I'll be right there."

"No, please don't, Aunt Meg," Ella pleaded. "There's no reason for you to drive over here. I have my insurance card, although Jack thinks he's paying for everything, and we're just waiting for the cast to set. I'm sure they'll send us on our way soon."

"Alright," Meg agreed hesitantly. "Let me talk to Jack, please."

Jack stopped pacing long enough for Ella to pass him the phone.

"Ma'am?"

"Keep her on terra firma for the rest of the night, please. No more trees."

"No, ma'am."

"Thank you."

There was a sigh, then silence on the other end of the line.

Jack sank into a chair and dropped his head, his hands making fists in his hair.

"Are you mad at me?" Ella whispered.

Jack straightened. "Of course not."

"You've barely said three words to me since we got in the car."

"I'm not upset with you. It's just this disaster of a date."

"It doesn't *feel* like a disaster. I was having fun up until the —" Ella paused to look at the doctor's pad on the desk. "— distal radius fracture."

"You're on painkillers. Trust me, it's a disaster," Jack said through his teeth with forced restraint.

"You shouldn't argue with a lady," Ella teased, hoping to lighten the mood. "I'll tell your grandmother."

Jack replied seriously, "We'll have to agree to disagree."

He leaned back, his limbs rigid. Ella watched him slowly shake his head, and frowned. This was one of those moments; the kind her mother always handled so well, but left her at a loss for words. A few familiar phrases bounced around her head in her mother's reassuring tones but as the words of comfort formed on Ella's own tongue, they somehow felt wrong in her mouth and she swallowed them.

Instead, she heaved a loud, bored sigh and said, "I suppose you're right. I'm not sure why I ever said yes in the first place."

Lifting his head, Jack met her sparkling eyes.

"I mean," she went on with another exaggerated sigh, "you're not really *that* cute."

The corners of his mouth tugged up reluctantly. "Yes, I am."

"So-so intelligence."

He raised his eyes to the ceiling with a snort.

"Not remarkably courteous."

"Alright," he murmured.

Pushing himself out of his chair, Jack crossed the room to stand at her knees. He placed a hand on either side of her and leaned in until his forehead met hers.

"Terrible taste in cars."

"Easy now." He pulled back with a scowl. "Don't be ugly."

"Luckily, there's still time to redeem yourself, Jackson Montgomery," Ella said, drawing out his name.

His dark eyes focused on her. "I await your commands."

Ella turned her head, resting it on Jack's shoulder. She felt the quickness of his breath in her hair. "I'm starving."

He brushed a loose tendril off her cheek and his gaze drifted downward to her lips. His eyes lingered there a moment as if in a silent struggle, before he whispered, "I'll find somethin'."

Ella stared at the white walls as the minutes passed, trying to block out the murmur of activity in the hallway. She closed her eyes and inhaled but the air was too cold, too sterile. Her chest felt tight, almost brittle.

Dear God, please help me relax. Please just help me breathe until he gets back.

When Jack returned a short time later, a perceptible warmth entered with him.

"The cafeteria is closed, but —" He held out two pudding cups. "Ladies choice. Chocolate or vanilla?"

"Swirl, please."

"My pleasure."

Jack scooped a spoonful from each cup and exchanged them.

Ella took a bite and moaned. "Who did you have to bribe to get this?"

"Lesson four: Never bribe someone for somethin' you can charm them into doin'."

Ella licked her spoon. "I somehow feel even hungrier than I did before."

"I was fixin' to run out and get somethin', but I'd rather not leave you alone."

"I'm seventeen years old, Jack. I think I can handle the hospital by myself."

She'd been pale since they'd pulled up to the hospital, but Ella blanched further as she spoke, and Jack's face tensed.

"You reckon they'd deliver a pizza here?"

The question was scarcely out of his mouth when there was a tap at the door and the doctor stepped in. He examined Ella's forearm and nodded.

"Looks good," he announced. "Be especially careful with it for the next day or so. Your cast can easily crack or break while it's drying and hardening."

Ella thanked him, and slipped her free hand into Jack's. Her palms tingled as he laced his fingers with hers firmly.

The doctor paused in the hallway outside the exam room.

"You were fortunate your bone was in a good position. Most of the time, it's necessary to re-align the broken bone fragments. You should consider yourself lucky."

Ella's eyes flickered up to Jack's face for an instant as he stroked a long finger down her palm. She felt giddy and lightheaded. Maybe the pain pills were kicking in.

"I do," she almost laughed. *Very lucky.*

The porch light illuminated the front door with a hazy glow as they lingered on the steps.

"Broken bones aside, thank you for the most creative," Ella said, fighting to keep from smiling, "and memorable first date I've ever had."

Jack groaned and pressed a hand to his face. He peered at her through his fingers with a crooked grin. "You reckon we've finally hit rock bottom and our interactions will only get better from here?"

"I certainly hope so," Ella said, tugging his arm down. "I don't know how much more my aunt can take."

Jack's amused expression faded into seriousness and his eyes hovered over her lips.

"I realize I'm returnin' you wet, injured, and past curfew." Jack took a step closer. "It may be askin' too much, but may I kiss you?"

"You're asking?"

"A gentleman," Jack replied with a half-smile, "ought to let the lady initiate a social kiss. But I am itchin' to kiss you, Miss Eleanor."

"Are we back to 'Miss Eleanor' again?"

Jack's brows lifted.

"You called me 'Ella darling' back at the tree."

"Did I?" He shifted his weight between his feet. "I reckon it just slipped out."

"If you're going to be kissing me, something less formal than Miss Eleanor is probably appropriate."

"Then, Ella darlin', may I kiss you?" Jack's hand grazed Ella's cheek as his long fingers slipped through her hair.

Ella lifted her face to his and waited, her heart throbbing in her chest. Jack pressed his lips to her forehead, just between her eyebrows. She closed her eyes.

His lips were warm against her cold skin and she shivered in anticipation. As he pulled away, Ella was sure her insides would melt from the heat in his eyes.

"Good night." Jack turned and walked away.

She shuffled to the door in a daze, and turned back. Jack was nearly to his car.

"That was it?" she yelled after him.

Ella instantly regretted the outburst. Jack spun around with a blank look, his brows drawn together.

"I mean," she called out, her cheeks burning, "all that talk about kissing and then… and then…that's it?"

Jack sprinted from the car and crossed the porch in a single step. His gaze was soft on Ella's flushed face. He pressed a palm to her cheek, his fingers curling around her jawbone, and pulled her mouth to his.

Jack's lips touched Ella's gently and every muscle in her body loosed. She was relaxed, and needed no reminder. Ella felt his arm wrap around her and flex until there was no space between them. She couldn't breathe, and didn't want to. No matter what happened after tonight, she'd keep that kiss on her lips forever.

"Was that better?" Jack mumbled against Ella's lips, sending goosebumps racing across her skin.

Ella gasped and murmured incoherently, "*Mhmm.*"

He grinned and with a final, soft brush of his lips, stepped back.

"Good night, again, Ella darlin'."

19. A CONFESSION

As Ella sat down in Environmental Science, Courtney flinched away, her lip curled in disgust.

"What is *that*?"

"It's a cast." Ella gave an exaggerated sigh. It had been a morning of questions. "The medical community uses them for treating broken bones."

"Oh sweetie, it's so conspicuous," Courtney said with a sneer, sliding her books between Ella and herself like a shield.

"How long do you have it on?" Mitch whispered.

"Six weeks."

"Too bad. It *is* really noticeable."

Ella crossed her good arm over the cast. "I'm fine, by the way. Thanks for asking."

Mitch was immune to sarcasm. "You'll still have it for the concert."

"What concert?"

"The Valentine's Day concert." Mitch squinted at her behind his glasses. "I'm surprised no one told you. I heard you were performing half an opera."

Ella threw up her hands. "How am I always the last one to know anything?"

"Maybe the choir director forgot you were new this year. We have one every spring, but this time they're inviting all the alumni and donors and it's going to be a big benefit."

"For what?"

"For us, I guess. All the proceeds go to the Academy."

Ella sat with her hands folded, seemingly docile, as the lecture began. But inside, she was fuming.

My voice is a gift, she reminded herself. A gift to be shared. She'd heard that repeated again and again.

But just once, she wished she could sing for something where the outcome would make a difference. Something that would really glorify God. The faces at the hospital flashed into her mind, their careworn expressions lifting as she sang carols. As uncomfortable as that evening had been, at least it had impacted people who needed it.

Even the church choir had become a spectacle. Hymns that had been worship felt more like a recital. And now this. As if the Academy needed any additional funding.

When class was dismissed, Ella stalked to the library where Jack was studying and flung herself onto the arm of his chair.

"Did you know I'm headlining a concert in two weeks?"

"Of course. *La Bohème*, I believe." He stretched to plant a kiss on her temple. "I reckon it's a little morbid for Valentine's Day, but some folks think it's passionate."

Closing his book, Jack propped his head in his hand and frowned, his fingers running lightly along her cast.

"Not the most romantic token of a first date. What did your friend, Lucas, say?" he asked, his eyes still fixed on her arm.

Ella swallowed hard. "I haven't told him about it."

"Wasn't he at your church yesterday?"

"He was..." Ella replied slowly.

Lucas had seemed preoccupied, almost sad, as he'd taken his place next to Ella in the choir and she didn't have the heart to tell him.

"I mean, I haven't purposely *not* told him we went on a date. It just hasn't happened."

"It's funny how that works." Jack kissed her briefly, and whispered, "It won't happen unless you do it."

"But I know he likes me and I feel like I'm abandoning him. What am I supposed to say?"

"Don't over-complicate it, Ella darlin'. Tell him you had a date on Friday and see what he says. He might not even be upset, and if he is, explain that you can still be friends."

"That line is the worst." Ella made a wry face at Jack but he wasn't smiling. He looked suddenly serious and embarrassed and...nervous. More than anything else, he looked nervous.

"Do you want more than friendship?"

"No."

"Then be honest with him. I'd want to know right away if it was me. Would it help if I came with?"

"No." She grimaced. "I'd like to avoid a fight if possible."

After school, Ella drove directly to Mr. Sherman's house. Even over the roar of the old Buick, she could hear music emanating from the closed garage. She walked gingerly along the icy driveway, tugging her coat sleeve down over her cast.

Lucas hadn't seen her arm – the billowy choir robes covered it at church – and she didn't want to start off with questions. Ella hoped a piece of good news would help to soften the blow.

She was met by a discord of haphazard notes as she pushed the garage door open and each instrument stopped in turn. Ella froze, suspended in the doorway. The familiar faces of Ben, Tyler, and Paul stared back at her. Lucas was the only one who didn't seem bound by the silence.

"Hey, Songbird."

He jumped nimbly over the network of extension cords running between space heaters and amps that crisscrossed the concrete floor. Lucas reached her and his mouth drew into a straight line.

"Is everything okay?"

"Yes. Sorry." Ella shook her head. "I just didn't expect to see any of them here."

"Oh, yeah," Lucas said, his voice low. "Well, I sort of figured forgive and forget."

Ella noticed his eyes bounce around the room, thankful she didn't have to meet a direct gaze.

"I know they're not a bunch of winners, but neither am I." Lucas sighed. "I don't really have anyone else."

A cold lump formed in Ella's throat. She choked and gulped it down, saying, "You'll always have me for a friend, Lucas."

Lucas's scattered glance darted to Ella. "Songbird, I have to tell you something."

She held up a hand. "Please let me say something first. I'm going to be in a concert on Valentine's Day. A bunch of bigwigs and fancy donors from the Academy will be there. Anyway, I asked the director if a friend could sing a duet with me and he said yes."

"You mean me?"

"Yeah, I thought it would be good publicity for you. One guy is a Broadway producer, and I think a couple recruiters from Juilliard will be there."

"That's...that's seriously thoughtful."

"The concert is going to be a bit formal, mostly opera, but it might be cool if you and I did something fun and edgy at the end. I figured maybe we could do the same song we did at New Year's. I was afraid we'd have to find some accompaniment, but I guess that's not a problem."

Her eyes went to Ben and the others, openly watching her and Lucas by the door.

I am relaxed, she said to herself.

Ella dropped her voice and plunged ahead. "That's not the only thing I needed to tell you. I went out with Jack last week on a date. I think we're..." She shuffled her feet. "I really like him, Lucas."

"That's great, Ella."

Ella opened her mouth, and closed it. "Really?" she squeaked.

"Seriously. I'm glad."

He looked it. There was no trace of anger or jealousy on his face, but Ella was almost certain she caught a flicker of discomfort in his eyes.

"I was worried," she confessed. "When you said you had something to tell me, I thought maybe –"

"I understand." Lucas rubbed the back of his neck and looked away. "It's actually about New Year's."

He blew out a breath.

"There was a recording of us singing together that I sent to Bill Bancroft."

Ella blinked. "You what?"

"I needed someone to hear us play and I knew Bill Bancroft wouldn't pass over a demo if it came from you. I know you didn't want to, Ella, but it seemed like such a good idea. Now I can't stop thinking about it. It's been haunting me for the last month. It was seriously stupid and I'm sorry. Will you forgive me?"

Ella had been prepared for a stormy reaction about Jack, but this fevered apology left her stunned. It took her a moment to sift through his words.

"What do you mean, 'came from me'?" she asked slowly. "You mean you wrote a note as *me*?"

Lucas nodded. "Will you forgive me?"

"You pretended to be me after I specifically said I didn't want to contact him." Her limbs were suddenly heavy, numb. This wasn't real. "How did you even send it to Billy?"

"I got the address off your computer."

Ella's head jerked up sharply. "My computer? But you've never been in my room."

"It was at Thanksgiving. I brought a stack of CDs up there when you were in the bathroom."

"Thanksgiving? You've been *plotting*," Ella spat the word out, "this whole thing since November?"

"It wasn't like that."

She gave a snort of rage and tossed her head. "Oh yeah, I forgot. Uncle Billy's P.O. Box is my desktop background."

Lucas started to reply, but she cut him off with a snarl. "You searched my computer!"

"It just sort of happened."

Be kind, the voice warned. But the words were faint and Ella pushed them aside.

"So you didn't mean to violate my privacy or lie to me for months, it just sort of happened? Exactly how long have you been planning this?"

"Not that long."

Ella shouted, "How long?"

"It's been at the back of my mind since you told me you were Axel Parker's daughter, okay? I figured you'd have some connections."

"You... That..." Ella stammered. "I told you that the day we met."

Ella's skin prickled and went cold. He'd been planning this since the day they'd met. Everything from the past six months suddenly shifted in her mind. She had only ever been Axel Parker's daughter. All those times they'd talked about her family, her memories, he'd only been pumping her for information.

"Axel Parker was my *dad,* Lucas," Ella whispered. "Do you understand that? You may think of him as your ticket to fame, but he was my dad. I miss him." Her lip trembled. "I miss him so much it feels like I've been walking around with all my ribs broken for the last eight years. And I see his picture in a magazine or I hear his voice on the radio and it hurts to breathe."

The other boys were staring at her but Ella didn't care.

"Axel Parker's daughter," she echoed. "Is that the only reason you were friends with me?"

"At first," Lucas admitted quietly. "That was the reason at first. But you were so easy to be friends with – so easy to talk to – I forgot for a while. Then out of the blue, you told me about Bill, and later when I found myself alone in your room, I couldn't resist. I felt awful about going behind your back, but the opportunity was too good to pass up. All the pieces just seemed to come together." He ran a rough hand over his face. "I made a stupid mistake, Songbird."

"Don't! Don't you dare call me that."

"Ella, I wish I hadn't sent it. I wish I didn't do any of it. Please believe me," Lucas implored, extending a hand.

Ella stepped back beyond his reach and stumbled over a power cord. He caught and steadied her, but she recoiled at his touch.

"You are a liar," she breathed.

Ella turned and fled out the door. As she rounded the corner of the garage, her foot slipped from under her and she fell to her knees. Voices followed her through the still, frigid air.

"Wow." There was a cold snicker. "Lucas, you know what the definition of a chump is? You had everything –"

"Enough!" Lucas boomed.

"Look on the bright side," came a crooning reply. "At least you don't have to pretend you want to bang her anymore."

Ella turned on her heel, skidding across the ice, and charged through the open door.

"You are scum," she shouted at Ben.

Ella shifted her weight to her back foot and, twisting her hips, exploded forward with her heavy, shrouded arm. It sunk into his gut. Ben dropped to all fours, clutching his stomach.

"Ella." Lucas stepped forward and she shoved him.

"You're worse, Lucas." She glared at him, tears brimming her eyes. "I hate you."

Ben was rising to his feet and Ella raced outside, slamming the door behind her. She heard a scuffle and a *crash* on the other side of the door but didn't look back.

Ella pulled up to the curb at the Academy and adjusted the rear-view mirror to assess her face. She turned away quickly. It was worse than she'd imagined. Her pale skin was still splotchy from crying, her nose red, her eyes and lips puffy.

She took a deep breath but it caught in her lungs, an aftershock of the angry tears that had convulsed her in the car.

"I am relaxed," she whispered as she crossed the school grounds.

Momentarily, she was. Though it hadn't gone as planned, she'd talked to Lucas. Jack would be pleased. And after weeks of guilt and anxiety, Ella knew she hadn't broken Lucas's heart. Everything was simple now.

It's for the best.

Jack opened his door and Ella's face crumpled. She crashed into him and he wrapped an arm around her.

"What happened? What's wrong?"

Ella buried her face in Jack's shoulder. A sob rocked her chest, and she whimpered, "I went to tell Lucas."

A muscle twitched in Jack's jaw and his body went rigid against her. His voice was steady, but dangerously low. "What did he do?"

"Nothing."

She pulled back to sweep the tears from her face with the edge of her finger. His grip around her waist relaxed but, looking up, Ella saw his heavy brows still lowered in a hard line. Something a little frightening, almost predatory, glinted in his eyes. For the first time, it was easy to believe some of the stories of his past life.

"Nothing," Ella repeated. "He's just not who I thought he was."

Jack waited silently.

"Lucas was only using me – my dad and my influence – to get his big break. He's nothing but a liar." Ella scrunched her eyes tight. "How is it possible to hurt so much?"

"It hurts every time you lose someone, no matter how it happens."

Jack touched her cheek and she opened her eyes to see his, dark and serious.

"If you say 'I told you so,' Jackson Montgomery, I'm never speaking to you again."

Jack traced a finger down her jawline and sighed. "I'm relieved. For a minute, I thought either he'd touched you," Jack paused, clearing his throat, "or else you'd changed your mind."

"Changed my mind about what?"

"About me. I've been worried you'll tell me you're choosin' him."

"Jack," she scolded. "Honestly? I'm not heartbroken because I was in love with him. I'm heartbroken because I thought he was my friend. Lucas said he'd been after my connections since the day we met."

As she spoke, Ella's mind went back, not to the moment when Lucas had heard her singing in the church, but to her first day at the Academy when a boy with unruly dark hair had approached her in Calculus. Ella studied Jack's face. She remembered his angular jaw, but how did she overlook his dimples or dark eyes that day? It was incredible to think she'd once shrunk under the shadow of the tall, lean frame that now held her secure.

"What made you first notice me?" she whispered.

Jack cradled her head in his hand and Ella felt a thrill in her stomach.

"We were readin' the same book." His lips brushed hers. "And you have very pretty eyes."

Ella suddenly felt close to tears again and leaned against him, pressing the side of her face to Jack's chest. His heart beat steadily against her cheek.

Jack rested his chin on her head. "I do still have a few shady contacts in my acquaintance, Ella darlin'. Do you want me to make him disappear?" He bent and kissed the tip of her nose. "Feed him to the fishes?"

"No," Ella's swollen eyes crinkled in a smile. "But it helps to know you could."

20. SILENCE

The muscles in Ella's neck were tight and a dull pain was beginning to throb behind her eyes as she walked to the Main Hall for lunch. A harsh vibration shook the phone in her pocket and Ella gritted her teeth.

Dear God, please make him stop calling. Fire and brimstone if necessary.

Although Lucas seemed a permanent occupant of her mind, Ella had successfully avoided his presence the past week. Her incoming calls were another matter. She silenced her phone and, almost immediately, it buzzed again.

Wrenching the phone from her pocket, Ella barked, "Stop calling me!"

There was a startled pause before Lucas spoke, his voice brittle. "I seriously need to talk to you, Ella. I don't know what to do. I don't have anyone –"

"You should have thought of that before you lied to me."

"Ella, you can be angry with me. I know I deserve it. You can say anything you want to me – call me the worst names you can think of – but please don't shut me out. I can't take your silence."

Tears sprang to Ella's eyes. She remembered silence. Lucas had been the one she'd turned to in those early days at the Academy when the silence from her fellow students had been nearly as bad as the harassment to come.

Ella's tone softened as she gave a clipped reply. "Goodbye, Lucas."

I'm sorry.

She'd wanted to say the words but couldn't get them past the lump in her throat. *I'm sorry we can't be friends. I'm sorry I can never trust you. I'm sorry we ever met.*

Ella blinked the tears away.

In a moment, all painful thoughts of Lucas were driven from Ella's mind as she heard chanting in the hallway ahead.

"O-L-I-V-I-A, Olivia makes the straight boys gay."

Rounding a corner, Ella saw a slim girl with fine blonde hair standing opposite a semicircle of students. Courtney stood at the center of the group, her smooth drawl clearly audible amid the call. Glaring at Courtney, Ella felt her face grow warm. Courtney was beautiful, rich, and popular. There was so much she could do, and *this* is what she chose.

Ella looked at Olivia, wondering what fault Courtney found to merit terrorizing her. Jealousy perhaps. Though Olivia lacked Courtney's complexion and starry eyes, with their equally slender frames and pale hair, the two girls could have been sisters. Yet one stood tall while the other shrank away.

"O-L-I-V-I-A, Olivia makes the straight boys gay," a few voices continued.

They grew quiet as Ella approached.

"Can someone explain to me why that's funny?" Ella sighed wearily.

"Because it rhymes," one boy replied.

There was a general snicker.

"Really?" Ella scrunched up her face involuntarily, and released it, trying to regain a sense of calm.

The ugliness with Lucas on top of hours of choir practice every week at the church, and now hours every night at the Academy were taking a toll. It was all too much, and this wasn't her fight. What did it matter if the

Academy continued on as it always had? If they wanted to tear each other to shreds, let them.

Besides, she could probably earn some credibility with the other students if she joined and justified them. But the look on Olivia's face sent a twinge through Ella's chest.

Ella sighed again, exhaling a hasty prayer. She fixed eyes with Courtney but addressed the whole of the hallway as she said loudly, "'Will people ever be wise enough to refuse to follow bad leaders or to take away the freedom of other people?'"

"Lord love you, sweetie. Somebody's got to." Courtney's lip curled up, visibly shifting her hostility from the thin, blonde girl to Ella. "What fool said that?"

"Eleanor Roosevelt," a silvery voice whispered.

Ella turned a delighted face to Olivia.

"Exactly. We all know about Eleanor Roosevelt if I remember correctly, Courtney, though not many know enough to repeat a quote."

Courtney opened her mouth as if to say something, then closed her lips in an acerbic sneer. An uncomfortable stillness filled the air in the hallway.

Reluctantly, the group around them dispersed, half hoping to see an altercation between Courtney and Ella, and half fearing to be caught in a crossfire. But Courtney simply shrugged her golden hair over her shoulder and spun on her heel as her companions disintegrated. Soon, only Olivia and Ella remained.

"Thank you," Olivia murmured in the same musical tone. "No one has ever stood up for me before."

"No one?" Ella's eyes widened. "I'm sure I've seen you with friends before."

"Oh, of course, I have friends," Olivia said quietly, wiping her nose. "But I'd never expect them to take my side against the Crowd."

"I doubt it would even occur to them to defend you," Ella mumbled.

They were all too afraid and, in a culture of cruelty, brutality was starting to come too easily to many of them. Although Ella no longer found herself persecuted, she still felt trapped there. For all the glitter and prestige the Academy held, it was a disgusting place inside the vaulted walls.

"No," Olivia agreed. "I can hardly believe *you* did. Thanks."

"Don't worry about it." Ella shrugged, avoiding Olivia's pink-tinged eyes. "No big deal."

"No, it is, Ella," Olivia said earnestly, her sweet voice rising. "It is a big deal. Thank you."

"You're welcome."

Ella wished she could tell Olivia that she understood, that things would get better. But she knew it was an empty platitude. So Ella did the next best thing she could think of. She smiled.

Olivia returned the smile and in that moment something happened. It was tiny, perhaps insignificant, but a tangible ripple of hope passed between them. Ella felt it as clearly as she had heard the chanting moments before. It was a far cry from reforming the whole Academy, but still, even one smile was something.

"Are you going to lunch?" Ella asked.

Olivia sniffed and nodded.

"Come on."

Ella parted from her at the door to the Main Hall, almost bouncing on her feet, feeling light and giddy. Beaming, she spotted Jack, his back turned to her, and crossed the room with newly energized steps.

A plan was forming in her mind. She may not be the prettiest, or the smartest, or the wealthiest at the Academy, but she could be kind. Anyone could be kind.

Ella trailed a hand across Jack's shoulders as she passed and took her place next to him. She closed her eyes and lifted her lips for a kiss. Jack's mouth covered hers and her mind went fuzzy.

It took a few seconds to collect her thoughts before she said, "I have a request about Valentine's Day."

Jack's face dimpled. "Anythin'."

"Promise you won't get me any roses."

He swallowed hard and picked at his food.

"You already ordered them, didn't you?" Ella smirked. "How many?"

He grinned sheepishly. "You don't want to know."

"Then I want you to amend your order," Ella said, stealing a French fry from his plate.

"You'd like somethin' other than roses?"

"I want you to get flowers for every girl at school," Ella announced.

He laughed uncertainly. "Like a secret admirer?"

"No." She reached for another fry. "From you."

Jack slid his plate closer to her and quirked an eyebrow. "Fixin' to stir up trouble, Ella darlin'?"

"Not at all. It would get around that they're all from you anyway."

"I'm not sure I know every girl at the Academy," Jack replied, his tone skeptical. "What am I going to write for all those cards? Happy Valentine's Day?"

"You can say, 'You have a beautiful smile'."

His brows rose. "For all of them?"

"Yes. Have you ever met anyone who *didn't* have a beautiful smile?"

Jack narrowed his eyes. "Is this part of your revolution?"

"Maybe."

She took a bite and dropped her eyes.

"What is it?" Jack wheedled.

"I want to transition the Academy from a culture of cruelty to a culture of kindness."

"Kindness?" Jack slowly drawled the word.

"Yes. Not just common civility and everyday politeness but purposeful, widespread generosity and kindness."

Ella pressed her hands together to keep them from trembling. It had seemed such a brilliant plan inside her head as she walked to the Main Hall with Olivia, but sounded so stupid out loud now with Jack. She glanced at his face. A trace of amusement danced in his eyes but otherwise he seemed to be listening attentively.

Ella continued, "Imagine if we were able to replace aggression with empathy. They're all so used to tearing each other down that it's become the default. Just think how much would change if more students would stand up for one another. I honestly believe that if a few key people –"

"Namely me and you, Ella darlin'?" Jack grinned.

"Yes. I think we can get the others to think differently and act differently toward each other. I think it will catch on."

"So we're enterin' phase two: an attack campaign of kindness."

Ella focused on the plate in front of her, but could hear the levity in his voice.

"And you reckon flowers are the best way to accomplish social change?"

"All I'm saying is that kindness is contagious. Acts of kindness have a way of multiplying themselves. Even if all we do is make sure every student at the Academy gets a flower or a card for Valentine's Day, we'll have set something positive in motion. It's a starting place."

She lifted her face. Jack looked pleasantly entertained, a half-smile playing at his lips, and Ella cringed.

"Do you think it's stupid?"

"Of course not." He still smiled but his dark eyes grew serious. "You're right, sayin' somethin' nice makes the old feel young and the poor feel rich, and doin' somethin' nice is twice as good. I'm honored to help, Ella darlin'."

"Thank you, Jack." She pecked his cheek. "I can always count on you."

"Y'know I love —"

Jack paused to clear his throat and Ella froze, mouth agape, a fry halfway between her parted lips.

"— your ideas."

Ella blushed furiously.

Jack tilted his head. "Are you alright?"

"Yes. Fine." She hiccupped. "I'm going to get some food."

Ella got up quickly from the table and a frightening realization struck her. She'd been perfectly ready to echo the three little words that didn't come. *I love you.* Exquisite, terrifying words. It was the truth, but better left unsaid, for now.

Kindness may come easily, but love... Ella shivered, thinking of her father, of Lucas.

Love is dangerous. Love leaves scars.

Lucas spoke stiffly through a split lip when he slid into the choir stall next to Ella on Sunday. "What happened to your arm?"

Ella wished she could slap him. But here, on stage in front of the whole church, all she could do was grit her teeth and edge away.

"None of your business."

She lifted glowering eyes to his face. A purple bruise spread over the side of his cheek and blackened one eye. Clearly the brawl hadn't gone in his favor. Then again, she hadn't seen Ben. He may be missing teeth. Or a limb.

The pastor began the opening prayer. Lucas lowered his head and whispered, "Ella, I'm never talking to those guys again, and I'm sorry."

"As if I'd believe you!" she snapped under her breath. "What else have you lied about?"

"Nothing. It wasn't like that, Ella, I swear."

She peeked at him through the corner of her eye. "Did you ever care about me?"

Lucas's face went slack.

"And don't lie," she hissed.

"You are seriously the nicest person I've ever met."

"That's not what I asked."

Lucas dropped his eyes and murmured, "I thought you might be more willing to help your boyfriend than your friend."

"So, no. You never cared."

Ella felt a wave of heat burn her cheeks, remembering the nights she'd spent praying for Lucas, worrying about him.

"I thought you and Jack were –"

"We are, but that's not the point. How long were you going to let me think you were interested in me?"

"I figured maybe after a while, there would be a spark." He sighed. "Honestly, I haven't felt that way about anyone since Claire."

"Oh good, well, at least it's not just me." Ella rolled her eyes contemptuously.

"Ella, you're smart and you're funny and you seriously are the best person…the best friend…"

Her eyes stung. "I'm not your friend, Lucas. You are nothing to me."

"Ella, please. Without you…"

Lucas grimaced as if in pain. He reached for her hand and she sprang up, tramping the foot of the girl beside her. The sopranos in her row kept their heads bowed, but shifted and whispered as Ella pushed her way past their knees to the end of the choir stall.

The choir director looked up and caught her eye, but she dashed by him and escaped the sanctuary before the congregation opened their eyes. Safely in the ladies bathroom, Ella gave in to tears, her sniffles echoing noisily off the tiled walls.

She leaned her weight against the counter, suddenly weak, and covered her face with her shaking hands. But even as she closed her eyes, Lucas's anguished expression materialized in her mind.

Ella's stomach wrenched.

Why did she feel guilty? Lucas was the one who'd betrayed her, the one who ought to be running away. She pounded her fist, splashing a puddle of standing water on the counter. The spray made a pattern of dark circles on her choir robe, matching the dark patches of mascara under her eyes.

Lucas doesn't matter, Ella told herself. She only had to see him at church, and even here, she didn't have to speak to him. The problem, Ella realized, was that she wanted to. It hadn't even been a week, and she already missed him. Somehow, losing Lucas as a friend and confidant cut more deeply than a thousand breakups.

Although they had never discussed anything very philosophical or particularly deep in the grand scheme of things, in the end, they had talked about the things that mattered most to each of them, and Lucas was the first person she'd genuinely opened up to since her father died. Jack had her heart, but she never could have given her heart to him if Lucas hadn't unlocked it.

Ella looked hard at her own face in the mirror. It was blotchy and streaked with running makeup. As she focused on the grey eyes that stared back at her, Ella could almost hear her mother's voice in her ear.

"Do you remember what Eleanor Roosevelt said?"

"'If someone betrays you once, it's their fault,'" she recited to her reflection, "'if they betray you twice, it's your fault.'"

Lucas was a liar. He had lied before and would do it a second time if she let him. He was *not* her friend and never would be again.

Her eyes were dry, her face composed, when Ella heard the final notes of the organ and left the bathroom to find Aunt Meg.

In the parking lot, Ella spotted the choir director and hiccupped as he advanced on her.

"What happened this morning?" Mark asked. "The nervous stomach?"

She nodded.

"I'll schedule an extra practice for this week."

"No, please don't," Ella cried hastily. "It would be better if I just practiced some more on my own. I'll carve out some time, I promise."

Mark seemed appeased and turned to go.

"Also," Ella added, "could you move Lucas Morales somewhere else? His baritone is throwing me off."

He looked at her through narrowed eyes and Ella shifted uneasily. Finally, Mark replied, "I'll make some adjustments."

21. FLOWERS

Ella was finishing her last spoonful of cereal when a black SUV parked in the driveway. As she rinsed her dishes in the sink, Jack ambled into the kitchen. He wrapped a cold arm around her waist, hugging her from behind.

"Happy Valentine's Day." His lips brushed her neck and Ella held her breath. "These were on your porch."

Jack placed a bouquet of three yellow roses on the counter.

"There wasn't a card. You reckon they're for your Aunt Meg?" he asked, his eyes twinkling mischievously.

"No." Her stomach tightened into a heavy knot. "I know who they're from."

Ella exhaled a heavy sigh. Jack spun her to face him, capturing her mouth in a kiss. Her stomach lightened.

"There will be no frownin' today," Jack ordered. "Are you ready?"

"I am, but you didn't have to come get me," Ella protested, shrugging on her coat and tugging it over her cast. "I like walking."

Jack held the front door ajar and frigid air invaded the entry. "In this windchill?"

"I could have taken the Buick."

"And it would have been warm right about the time you got to the Academy. I ought to have started drivin' you long before now."

"No, you shouldn't. You don't have to treat me like a damsel in distress. I like walking," Ella repeated as Jack ushered her into the car.

She hated to admit he was right. Her cheeks were already ice cold from the biting wind, and she lifted both palms to her face for warmth.

Jack dropped into the driver's seat and his eyebrows creased in a playful scowl. "I know you're capable of walkin'. Let me be a gentleman, please? Maybe I want to spend a few extra minutes with you."

Ella's lips curved in an expression of pleasure and her eyes fell to the full cup holder in the console between them. "Should a gentleman have old paper coffee cups in his automobile?"

"That's hot chocolate. I brought it for you. But it's hotter than a billy goat in a pepper patch, so be careful."

Ella snuggled into her heated leather seat and sniffed her steaming cup.

"*You* be careful," she warned Jack. "I could get used to this."

Jack leaned over and pressed his mouth to hers softly but with a firm determination that made her stomach flutter. "Me, too."

Ella's palms tingled as she lifted them to her face again, this time to cool her now flushed cheeks.

They were nearly to the Academy when Ella's phone vibrated in her pocket. Jack adjusted his grip on the steering wheel.

"Is he still tryin' to call you?"

"Yes. I need to just block him. I know it's silly, but his was the first number I added in Whitfield."

Jack laced his fingers through hers, stroking her palm. His hand was still in Ella's when they passed Beth and Josiah in the hallway. With a smile, Ella noticed Beth's vibrant pink scarf as Beth shifted her books in her arms, giving Ella a timid wave.

Squeezing Jack's hand, Ella said, "I'm going to talk to Beth for a minute."

"Alright. I have to run back to my room before Biology. I'll see you at lunch, darlin'."

Beth's greeting burst from her as Ella approached. "You must be excited for the concert. I can hardly wait for classes to be over."

"I'm either excited or I have food poisoning." Ella grimaced. "I have kind of a nervous stomach."

"With your voice, I can't imagine being nervous," Beth replied as they mounted the stairs to the second level.

Josiah parted from them and the two girls continued on together.

Ella explained, "It's gotten better. I used to get a fit of hiccups every time I got up on stage, but I've been singing in my church choir once a week since August and it doesn't phase me as much anymore."

"Well, I'm glad. It's incredible to hear you sing."

They passed a cluster of students in the hallway and Courtney stepped out of the group.

"Trouble in paradise, sweetie?" Courtney linked her arm through Ella's, her fingernails grazing Ella's sleeve like talons. "Your boyfriend sent me roses."

Ella returned her saccharine smirk. "He's sweet like that."

"I got flowers from Jack, too," Beth giggled timorously, pushing her curly hair behind her ear.

"Imagine that." Ella beamed.

"It was a nice surprise. Although, I have to be honest, I'd take chocolate over flowers any day."

"It shows," Courtney said with a sneer.

The animation drained from Beth's face, her hair falling back over her shoulder, and Ella felt her own cheeks growing hot.

"Beth, I would kill to have your curves," Ella insisted.

"I suppose *you* would," Courtney drawled. "You really are all edges, bless your heart."

"Courtney —" Ella hissed through gritted teeth, and stopped. Proverbs chapter twenty-one said to watch your tongue and keep your mouth shut, and she would, no matter how impossible it might seem.

Relaxed. I am relaxed. It wasn't enough to empathize with the oppressed while cheering for the downfall of the oppressors. She was going to do something more. She was going to be kind, not only to Beth but to Courtney as well. *Kind-ish*, at least. She exhaled and smiled.

"–I hope your Valentine's Day is as pleasant as you are."

There was a momentary pause and Courtney's eyelids flickered. She opened and shut her mouth twice, releasing Ella's arm, before sauntering away to another group.

Beth's expression brightened as she watched Courtney's retreating back and pushed a stubborn curl away from her face again. "Did you put Jack up to it? The flowers?"

"Why would you say that?"

"I don't know." She shrugged. "It just seems like something nice you'd do. Honestly, after the torture you went through this fall, I figured you'd go psychokinetic on all of us or burn the school to the ground."

"Maybe I'm saving that for the spring formal." Ella widened her eyes and gave her a hollow stare.

Beth guffawed and clapped a hand over her mouth. "Consider me warned."

They grinned to each other as the courtyard bell clanged and Beth turned hurriedly to reach her own class down the hall.

"Hey, Ella," she called over her shoulder, "I hope your day is as pleasant as you are."

Jayla accosted Ella in the hallway outside her Statistics classroom. "You'll never guess who sent me flowers," she said breathlessly, bouncing on her heels.

Ella bit her lip, holding back a knowing smile. "Tell me."

"Mitch," Jayla whispered.

"What?" Ella sputtered. "Our Mitch?"

"Yeah," Jayla squeaked. "At first I was shocked too. I mean it's *Mitch*. I never would have thought of Mitch like that. But he wrote the sweetest note in the card. He said when we danced at the Holiday Ball it was like he saw me for the first time and I was the most perfect thing he'd ever seen."

"Mitch...our Mitch wrote that?"

"Yeah, I know! Who would have thought he could be poetic? He usually sounds like a technical manual. Anyway, I kissed him."

"What?"

"Yes! I was sort of on the fence up until then because, you know, it's *Mitch*, and we've been just friends for two years. But it was amazing!" She grabbed Ella's arm for support. "Like weak-in-the-knees, died-and-gone-to-heaven amazing. I'm telling you, he has a gift."

Ella shook her head, dazed. "I can't believe it. I'm so excited for both of you. I just...I never would have seen it."

"I know. I'm sure we look like an odd fit. But I don't care. He may be shorter than me but he's really big where it counts."

"*Gah.*" Ella made a sound at the back of her throat and squeezed her eyes shut. "Jayla, I definitely don't need to know that."

"Eww, Ella. I meant his brain. I like smart guys."

Ella snorted as they stopped in the doorway of her Environmental Science room, where Mitch was already seated. He blushed and tugged his hair when he noticed them whispering intently.

"He's taking me out to lunch," Jayla announced proudly. "I figured you'd have plans with Jack today anyway. In case I don't see you later, break a leg tonight."

As she walked to her desk, Ella noticed with wicked pleasure that the back of Mitch's neck glowed pink.

"Happy Valentine's Day, Casanova. I hear you've been sweeping Jayla off her feet."

His cheeks flushed a deeper shade of red. "I found out she got flowers from Jack today, too. I know he's taken, obviously, but still... She's pretty and brilliant and she gets flowers from someone like Jackson Montgomery, and she still wants to go out with me. Can you believe it?"

Mitch's eyes shone behind his glasses. Ella felt a tug in her chest.

"You are a catch, Mitch. Never believe anything less." She paused. "That being said, she's a catch too, and you'd better not hurt her."

"Don't worry, Ella. She's my best friend."

"Good. Remember," she whispered menacingly, her eyes gleaming green, "the Crowd will be watching."

22. A NOTE

Ella swept down the stairs from her bedroom in a delicate, taffeta gown with a white satin sash. The lace bodice of organza apple blossoms hugged her upper body and spilled into a full skirt of dreamy gossamer tulle.

She smoothed the material and admitted, "I wish we'd had enough warning to make a dress for tonight instead of buying this thing. I feel like a stuffed goose in this getup."

"You look more like a swan," her aunt replied. "A very downy swan."

Meg glanced at her watch and back at Ella, stepping carefully into pearly high heels. She opened her mouth to hurry Ella along, but paused. It was strange to think that less than a year ago, her life had felt complete without Ella. Could this elegant young lady really be the girl who'd shown up on her porch so unexpectedly? No miraculous transformation had occurred, but she was different somehow. She stood taller, smiled more freely.

"We'd better go," Meg said with a sigh. "I'm sure Jack would like to see you and wish you luck before the concert."

Meg stopped the Buick in front of the main building and Ella extricated herself along with her bountiful folds of fabric. Jack was indeed waiting, pacing restlessly just inside the entrance. He watched her approach with a smile.

Ella appeared to be dancing to the gentle melody composed by the *click clack* of her shoes and the rustle of her gown as she sashayed toward him.

"What do you think? Aunt Meg said if I hold my wrap just so, you can't see my arm."

"I doubt anyone will notice a cast while you're in that dress. You could be a fairytale princess."

"Is that a roundabout way of saying you're Prince Charming?"

"You tell me." Jack grinned. "I have somethin' for you."

Ella furrowed her eyebrows. "You promised you wouldn't get me anything."

"I only promised no roses. And I reckon I've kept my word admirably in spite of temptation."

Jack refused to say anything more but led her by the hand, fingers interlaced, through the darkened corridors of the main building. He stopped in a hallway Ella hadn't encountered before and held open a door. It was as if the door in the brick wall had exposed a secret garden. Tables of lush vegetation filled the glass chamber and exotic looking plants cascaded from hanging baskets.

He drew her inside quickly. The air was heavy and warm within the greenhouse. She sucked in a breath of the sweet floral perfume, and caught a whiff of pungent mint leaves as Jack guided her deeper into the room.

Her shoes, which had echoed loudly on the marble floors, made no sound against the damp concrete under her feet. Ella ran a hand over felty leaves and her fingers caressed the satin petals until Jack stopped before a pot with a single stem protruding from a bed of pebbles.

Ella looked at it uncertainly. "You got me a stick? I know I said no flowers, but –"

"This is a Nightingale orchid." Jack's eyes creased in a smile as he pulled her closer. "They're very rare. This particular specimen comes from the Royal Conservatory in London."

"Jack." His name escaped on a sigh. "What if I kill it?"

"You won't. Trust me. If I can make it grow, you can keep it alive."

"Wait." Ella looked up at him with wide eyes and a small, delighted smile. "You planted this yourself?"

"No, botany has never been my specialty and these are right difficult to propagate. I've only been tendin' to it."

"Tending to it? Since when?"

"A few months ago, when I learned you liked to sing."

Ella's lips parted in a gasp of wonder. "But we weren't even friends then."

"I know." Jack lowered his eyes. "But I hoped we might be."

She fingered the delicate stem. "I love it."

I love you. Ella was thankful the phrase caught in her throat. Without saying the words out loud, Ella did her best to show him. She took a step toward Jack, a hand on his arm, and he met her halfway.

Reaching up, he cupped her face in his hands and tenderly, sweetly, claimed her lips with his own. Ella pressed her mouth to his, first lightly, then with a growing firmness.

She rested a hand on his chest and something crinkled under her fingers.

Jack pulled back and groaned. "This is literally our first interaction that hasn't encountered disaster," Jack said, his voice husky, and cleared his throat, "and I'm about to ruin it."

Ella laughed shakily. "How?"

Jack reached into his breast pocket and withdrew a wrinkled sheet of paper. He unfolded it and handed it to her. Ella's eyes skimmed the page of words and chords scrawled in faded pencil.

She glanced at him with a quizzical expression. "You wrote me a song?"

"It's not from me." He pinched the bridge of his nose. "It's from Lucas."

Ella held it out to him. "No, thank you."

"You ought to read it," Jack said, squaring his shoulders. "It was on your porch this mornin' with the roses, and I tucked it away because I knew it would upset you. But then I read it. It's...it's really somethin'. He's broken, Ella."

"I don't care." She gave a hard shake of the head. "I'm not interested in what Lucas has to say."

"I know you'd rather not speak to him again. The rational side of me would prefer for you to avoid him as well. But I reckon you ought to forgive him."

"He betrayed me, Jack." She glowered at him. "Eleanor Roosevelt said —"

Jack tossed his head. "I reckon there's an Authority higher than Eleanor Roosevelt on this one."

Ella planted her hands on her hips. "You're telling me to turn the other cheek?"

"Ella darlin', he's sorry." Jack lifted the paper to her face. "What about your campaign of kindness? We all make mistakes. Believe me, I've done far worse. Think of your father. He had to receive a measure of forgiveness in his time." He pressed it into her hand. "Please just read it."

Ella snatched the page from him grudgingly and glared at it. She perused Lucas's words quickly and was about to roll her eyes when she stopped. Her grip on the paper tightened.

Slowly, Ella's face softened and her pointed chin dropped. The air was suddenly too thick, too sweet to breathe and she choked. She raised a hand to her mouth to check a sob as a tear fell to the paper, obscuring the lyrics. The words on the page danced in front of her bleary eyes and she folded it in half, nearly crumpling the sheet in her hand.

Ella leaned heavily against Jack, feeling limp. "Can I borrow your car?"

"Let me drive you."

"No, I need to go by myself," she whispered. "I have to talk to him alone. Do you think you can stall the concert?"

Jack nodded. "Take all the time you need, Ella darlin'."

Mr. Sherman's windows were dark and the house was silent, but as she edged up the driveway, Ella heard movement in the garage. She took a steadying breath and pushed open the door.

"Lucas?" she asked, peering into the dim room.

The tall silhouette turned and Ella took a step back.

"Ben." Her voice was shaky. "Where's Lucas?"

"He's not here."

Ben leered, and the direction of his roaming eyes sent a cold shiver through her. Ella wondered how far her voice would carry if she screamed.

She curled her hands into fists to stop them from trembling and Ben's expression changed. Whether because she struck an imposing figure in her ballooning ivory gown, or because she'd attacked him at their last meeting, Ella didn't know, but he kept his distance.

Beware the stuffed goose with fists of steel, she thought with a grin that nearly burst in a frenzied laugh.

Ben gave her a black look. "I haven't seen that kid in weeks. I just came to get my stuff."

He lifted a plastic tote.

"What?" Ella asked, her voice shrill.

"This equipment is mine, and I'm taking it."

"I don't care about your stuff." She held up an arm, blocking his path. "What do mean you haven't seen him?"

"He's not at school, and he's not returning any calls."

"I know," Ella agreed quietly. "I tried his phone."

"If you find him, tell him he still has my amp and I want it back."

Ben pushed past her to the door.

Ella hiccupped and felt her chest tighten as a new fear gripped her. *What if Lucas ran away? What if I never see him, never speak to him again?* No. That was ridiculous. Air eased back into her lungs. He could bail on school without Mr. Sherman or anyone else knowing for some time, but this was Whitfield. Lucas couldn't have skipped town completely without some rumor reaching her ears. Besides, Jack said the note was on her porch this morning. Lucas had to be somewhere.

It's possible he decided to go to the concert after all, she thought, keeping a watchful eye as she made the journey through town. Ella bowed her head in a prayer of thanks when she spotted Mr. Sherman's pickup parked at the curb outside the church.

Bong. Bong. Bong. Bong. Four chimes. Six. Eight. Ella stepped out of the car and glanced up at the old clock above the familiar wooden bench. The concert was beginning. *No, it would have already started.* She was five minutes late.

Pulling her wrap around her, Ella tugged open the heavy front door. The sanctuary was dim, nearly as dark as the fading evening light outside. It was difficult to make anything out clearly but she heard labored breathing.

Ella squinted and finally saw him, hunched in a pew a few rows from the back. Something in the slump of his shoulders and his raspy intake of breath made Ella stop in the aisle.

"Lucas?" Her voice trembled.

"Ella?"

A beam of half-light from the stained glass window in the wall above illuminated his face as he stood, turning. Lucas stared at her a moment and Ella caught a glimpse of something shiny in his hand.

"Why are you here? Don't you have a concert?"

"I wanted to talk to you. I got your song."

Ella took a step closer, the paper clutched in her hand, and froze. In the twilight, she distinguished a pistol glinting in Lucas's hand, hanging limp at his side. A few seconds of thick silence passed before Ella's heart began beating again and a few seconds more before she was able to speak.

"Lucas, what's going on?"

"I tried to contact my mom in rehab and she's not there." His voice sounded hollow.

"What do you mean?"

"She's just gone. She left rehab. She left me." Lucas raised a hand to his face and Ella winced at his sudden movement. "I'm basically an orphan."

Ella licked her lips. "Why don't you put that...that..."

Gun. Her mouth couldn't seem to form the word. Her tongue was heavy and dry and she licked her lips again. Lucas with a gun.

"Put *it* down and talk to me. I know about losing someone."

"You do, but this is worse, Ella. Your dad left you because he died. My parents left me on purpose." He laughed a cold, almost hysterical laugh

254

and Ella felt a sudden urge to flee. "How worthless am I if two parasites like them don't even want me? Nobody wants me."

"What about Mr. Sherman? What would he do without you?"

"I'm just a burden to the old man. The truth is, I'm not worth caring about."

"That's not true. I care about you."

Lucas sneered. "You hate me."

"I don't." Ella shook her head wildly. "I really don't, Lucas. I was hurt and angry but I don't hate you. I forgive you."

"I've been playing you from the very first moment we met." He readjusted his grip on the pistol and wiped his nose on the heel of his hand. "You *should* hate me, Songbird."

"I don't care how or why you became my friend —" Ella's voice broke. He'd called her Songbird.

Ella breathed a silent prayer. This was Lucas. Smiling, joking Lucas. It didn't look much like him at the moment, but it was still him.

"You were still the first friend I had here. Honestly, you were the first real friend I had in a really long time. That's got to count for something. I know you. I know you don't want to do this."

Ella took a hesitant step closer but Lucas recoiled. Both of his hands wrapped around the pistol and he raised it, the barrel pointed at her chest.

"Stop. This is the only way, Ella. I'm trapped." His voice was hoarse. "I'm always going to be trapped."

Ella swallowed a scream and tried not to stare at the gun a few inches away.

"It may seem like you're trapped right now, but you're not. You have a future. I know it. You're not going to be stuck in Whitfield forever."

She held out her hands. One more step and he'd be within reach.

"I'm so sorry for the things I said. I'm sorry I wasn't there for you when you found out about your mom. I know you don't see it, but you're talented, Lucas, and you're loved."

"I wish I could believe you."

"You can. I'm telling the truth. You're my friend, Lucas. I'm not going to lose you. Not like this."

Ella shuffled one foot nearer. She felt certain that if she could just touch him, she could calm him.

Dear God, please help me reach him. If I could just rest a hand on his trembling arm...

Those arms that had pulled her up on stage to sing, had comforted her at the hospital, had supported her weight on Halloween night. Those arms were almost as familiar as her own. She knew every tendon and every shade of his tattoo.

"Lucas," she cried, "think of Tiffany and Claire. You wouldn't do that to me. I couldn't live through that."

"Then you'd better close your eyes."

He bent his arm to turn the pistol on himself and Ella sprang forward. "Lucas, don't!"

A blast echoed in her ears, and Ella staggered as a flaming stake pierced her chest. The impact flattened her lungs and she wheezed out a fine, red mist. Ella gasped for air while her legs gave way under her. She slumped to the floor.

Rough hands pressed on her rib cage. Ella looked up at the face hanging over her. *Lucas is safe. Thank God, Lucas is safe.*

Something warm and wet plastered her white, gossamer gown to her skin, and somewhere far, far away she could hear Lucas shouting, "Please, God, no! Oh please! Not Ella!"

His voice was too wretched, too pitiful to listen. She tried to reach up to cover her still ringing ears but her arms and legs were shaking too violently to control them.

Time passed and Lucas's words died away but the ringing grew hard and metallic, finally morphing into an earsplitting wail. Suddenly she was surrounded by many voices, many hands touching her. Lifting her.

I should speak to one of them, she decided. But something hard and thick filled her throat and an oppressive weight crushed her chest. *I should open my eyes.* But it was so quiet, almost peaceful. The ringing in her ears faded to one continuous note, blurring every other background noise. Her eyelids were too heavy to open and it felt so good to rest. Jack would say she wasn't sleeping. She was just checking her eyelids for holes.

Where was Jack? She had a vague idea he was waiting for her somewhere. Jack, so calm. So patient. He would understand she needed to sleep. He'd waited so long already, what was another few minutes. Yes, he would wait.

Perhaps she should have told him she loved him. No, that could wait too. He'd mentioned something about taking her time. *Take all the time you need.* There was no rush. She had all the time in the world.

Ella hovered on the edge of a medicated sleep but never felt rested. Instead, she was tired. Tired in every joint and ligament, down to her very bones.

Lifting an eyelid, she saw a room full of people and heard a single word in the hubbub. She blinked and now only one face was suspended in front of hers.

A voice she didn't recognize whispered, "Hang in there, kiddo." Ella opened her lips to reply but her throat was thick and her chest tight.

Grating voices, repeating the same, single word, pierced her disordered dreams and a harsh beeping was constantly in her ear.

She caught fragments of conversation, always hearing the same word. The same word spoken and whispered. The same word repeated again and again amidst the noise of a fan and the ever-present beeping.

Terminal.

That meant she was going to die.

Hearing the word once more in an exchange, Ella opened her eyes. Her vision was blurred. Two Aunt Meg's sat beside her somehow carrying on a conversation. Ella felt dizzy, confused. She closed her eyes and drifted back into a deep, empty sleep.

23. AN AWAKENING

Ella opened her eyes in a garden. All around her were colorful flowers and the scent of roses perfumed the air. She was warm and drowsy. Golden sunshine fell upon her face and, silhouetted against the light, her father's face smiled down at her.

This must be heaven, she thought dreamily. Ella forced her drooping eyelids open to take in the glory of it all. The blurry figure came into focus. She blinked.

Not Dad.

"Mal?"

She hiccupped and the motion sent a wave of dizzying pain through her chest. Other faces shifted into focus. Aunt Meg and...

"Mom?"

"Hi, sweetheart. Don't sit so quickly," she urged as Ella rose in bed.

A sharp spasm checked her.

"Careful, Ella. You just had a chest tube removed."

"Mom," Ella whispered again. "You're *here*..." The words stuck in her dry throat and her voice cracked. "Why? When?"

"Hush, sweetheart. It's alright. Mal flew in a few days ago, and I got here yesterday."

"Days?" Ella croaked.

Her eyes moved from one face to the other and she took in the sterile, white room. It was surprisingly cheery and bright. Light streamed in from a wide window, slatted with narrow blinds, and crystal vases brimming with flowers covered nearly every surface. But no amount of flowers could cover that overpowering hospital smell. Ella leaned back in bed with a shudder.

"What happened?"

Her mother and Malcolm exchanged a look, both equally unsure where to begin.

Meg laid a hand over Ella's. "Do you remember anything?"

"I remember..."

A flurry of images slipped through her mind as she struggled to recall her last coherent memories. A white dress. An orchid. The clock chiming eight. Lucas sitting in the twilight.

"I remember Lucas was upset. His mom left. He had a gun," Ella whispered, "and it went off."

"Yes," Meg replied. "You were shot, Ella."

"It was an accident," Ella said, her voice hoarse, but urgent.

"We know." Meg nodded gently. "We know. At least, we hoped so. Lucas called 911 right away and the paramedics said it looked like he attempted to stop the bleeding. Based on the angle of the bullet, the police guessed it was accidental. But they would like a statement from you for confirmation."

"That can wait," her mother cut in. "You can answer questions later. Right now, you need to rest, and focus on getting better. It's going to take some time."

She kissed Ella's forehead lightly and Ella closed her eyes, her mother's last word echoing in her mind. *Time. Taking my time.* Something in it struck Ella and she glanced around the room.

"Where's Jack?"

Meg smiled. "Jack's here too, along with a few of your friends from school. Mal, will you tell them she's awake?"

259

Malcolm complied with a nod, and Ella's hospital bed creaked as both her mother and Aunt Meg stood. A flash of panic jolted through her as they approached the door. They were all with her. Mom. Malcolm. After months of distant conversations over the phone, they were all here. Her entire family, together. It was impossible to watch them go.

"Will you stay with me?" Ella cried, propping herself up in bed on an unsteady arm.

"Sure, sweetheart."

Ella turned gingerly to the sound of footfalls. A legion burst through the door. Jayla and Mitch entered hand in hand, followed by Josiah, Beth, and others from church and the Academy whom Ella's fuzzy brain worked furiously to match with names.

A man in a white coat and two women in purple scrubs came in with Ella's friends and crossed the room to speak to her mother and aunt, perched on a long, narrow bench under the window. Malcolm joined them.

"Hi, Ella!" Jayla raced to her side. "I can't believe you're finally up. How are you feeling?"

"Okay," Ella laughed. It sounded more like a cackle in her ears. She cleared her throat.

"You look...better," Mitch gulped. "You were pretty grisly there for a while."

Trust Mitch to be blunt, Ella thought. Blunt, but honest.

Ella raised a hand to her matted hair. At least a week's worth of tossing and turning was evident under her fingers. No doubt her face was sporting similar proof of her restless sleep, with no makeup to cover the dark circles under her eyes. If she had been grisly previously, she must look like an absolute zombie by now. Maybe that was why Jack was hanging back.

While the others clustered close to her, he'd hardly come beyond the doorway. She caught his eye over Josiah's shoulder and smiled, silently praying her teeth were not as disgusting as her hair. Jack didn't seem to notice anything revolting, though he didn't return her smile. He moved lifelessly to the bed, and sat stiffly on the edge of the mattress.

"Ella, I'm sorry," he said. His voice was tight, his normally smooth drawl stilted. "I hope you can forgive me."

Ella's brows creased. "For what?"

"When I gave you that note, I never reckoned... I never would have dreamed..." Jack gripped the cold metal bed railing, his dark eyes hard. "I right near got you killed."

Her mouth fell open. "Don't be ridiculous. You have nothing to be sorry for."

"I told you to speak to him. It's my fault."

"That's nonsense. I chose to go. And I'm glad I went," Ella insisted. "If I hadn't gone –" She didn't want to think about what would have happened if she hadn't gone to see Lucas.

With a start, Ella noticed Lucas's absence from the crowd for the first time.

He must be in some kind of trouble over the gun. Aunt Meg had mentioned the police, but surely all that could be sorted out in time. The important thing was Lucas was alive.

But she couldn't think about him right now. Not with the expression on Jack's drawn face. It hurt Ella more than her scratchy throat and the aching pain in her chest to see him sitting at her right hand, a million miles away.

He just didn't understand.

If he would just look at me, Ella thought, *he'd see I'm fine.* Granted, a little bruised and tender, but far from dead. Lucas was alive and she was here, surrounded by everyone she loved. How could she blame Jack for anything? He'd had nothing to do with the accident, beyond encouraging her to do the right thing. It was so simple, so clear. But she couldn't explain it to him. Her brain felt jammed. And Jack's eyes were downcast, avoiding hers.

"You're right." Ella gave an exaggerated sigh. "I've had nothing but trouble since I met you. Getting splashed with mud and losing my favorite messenger bag was one thing, but I've been scalded with chocolate, cracked my wrist, and gotten shot. You'll be the death of me."

Her voice was mildly biting but Jack still would not meet her eye.

"I'd be a lot better off with someone else, someone who doesn't have it out for me."

261

He finally looked up. His dazed expression was almost too much for Ella. She swallowed the lump of broken glass that had formed in her throat and forced a small smile.

"Somebody who doesn't offer to give me a ride in the rain, or try to carry my book bag, or bring me hot chocolate, or plan a spontaneous date, or make me reconcile a friendship."

His heavy brows lifted over eyes that shone with a juxtaposition of pain and joy.

Encouraged, Ella went on, "I've been in the hospital, my least favorite place in the entire world, for a week. My chest is killing me. I can't sleep and I don't feel awake either. But do you know what the worst part is?"

Jack shook his head silently.

"I missed you, Jackson Montgomery," she told him, drawing out his name in the most musical tone she could manage with her raw throat.

"Ella darlin'."

The whisper had barely reached her ears before Jack snaked an arm under her waist, his hand clutching at her back. He cradled her head, his free hand brushing her cheek and sliding to make a fist in her messy hair. Their mouths collided, too hard, and Ella winced. He made a move to pull away, but Ella pressed herself into him, as her racing heart throbbed against the ache in her lungs. Jack kissed her again and again, firmly, deeply, leaving her lightheaded and breathless.

A recollection of the crowded room inserted itself into her clouded mind. Ella's lips left Jack's but he continued to hold her close. His fingers traced her cheekbone, shifted to her jawline, and down the nape of her neck.

He leaned in and whispered thickly, "You are the most exasperatin' thing. You could start an argument in an empty house. I don't know why I put up with you."

"You know you love me," Ella teased in a raspy voice.

She felt his lips curve into a smile close to her ear. "Heaven help me, I do."

Ella hiccupped. "I didn't mean it like that."

"I did." He looked down at her as if memorizing her face. "I love you, Ella."

262

He said it, just like that. As if it were the easiest, most natural thing in the world to say. Right in front of Mal. In front of Mom. In front of Aunt Meg. In a room packed full of unknown medicos, her entire family, and a company of friends.

Thank goodness we're in a hospital, Ella thought, because Mitch looked like he may need immediate medical attention.

"I have for a while. I reckon I ought to have said it before. When you went in for surgery, they told us there was a chance that you..." Jack trailed off. "And then the cancer."

The rosy glow faded from Ella's vision as everything narrowed down to a pinpoint.

"The what?"

Jack's jaw went rigid and everyone spoke at once.

"You don't need to worry."

"It's gone now, Ella."

"She looks like she's going to hyperventilate."

Ella strained for air but only felt a pang in her chest.

Terminal.

She heard the word vaguely in Aunt Meg's voice. In Malcolm's. In her mother's. In Jack's. Spoken again and again while she slept. She had cancer. *Terminal* cancer. She was going to die.

"Let the doctor explain, sweetheart."

Ella's mother moved to the bedside and clasped her hand. It felt suddenly clammy in her grasp.

"Dr. Carter, can you give her the short version? I'm afraid she may pass out."

The man in the white coat was immediately next to her.

"Try to stay calm. Breathe with me," her doctor commanded.

Ella fought to control the catch in her lungs and managed a few shallow breaths.

"Much better. Now, Ella, I need you to try to remain calm. Can you do that for me?"

Ella nodded and exhaled. *I am relaxed.* It had never been less true.

He began slowly, in a soothing voice, "When you were shot, Ella, the bullet nicked your right lung. Thankfully for you, your —"

He glanced at the small circle of people around her hesitantly and back at Ella.

"– your friend was using a small caliber bullet and there was a relatively minor degree of nearby tissue disruption. The trauma surgeon removed the bullet and repaired your injured lung. However, we saw something unusual during surgery and did a biopsy of your lung tissue."

Dr. Carter paused, and continued gently, "Lamprecht's disease is extremely rare, and very little is known about this particular form of cancer. It's nearly always discovered post mortem as a cause of death. I've been doing some research and yours may be the earliest documented case of Lamprecht's. It's quite exciting, in fact."

Ella felt the muscles in her neck slacken and her head drooped.

"Ella. Take a breath now, sweetheart," she heard her mother order as spots of black clouded her sight once more.

Her eyes fluttered open and she breathed.

Dr. Carter explained, "Ella, I can only say it's exciting because it's not in you anymore. After the diagnosis of Lamprecht's was confirmed, we were able to remove the affected section of your lung."

"You took out my lung?" Ella gasped.

"No." Dr. Carter shook his head. "We did what's called a segmentectomy or wedge resection. That means only part of a lobe was removed in surgery. I'd like to do more extensive testing now that you're feeling recovered and a bit more alert. But all of our imaging tests to date indicate that single lobe was the primary site and the cancer hadn't metastasized any further."

"I know this is a great deal to take in all at once, sweetheart," her mother murmured, "but you should consider yourself very lucky."

Ella felt tears in her eyes. "Lucky?"

"Yes," her doctor agreed. "Very lucky, in fact. I'm hesitant to use the term under these unfortunate circumstances, but it is basically... Well, basically a *miracle*, medically speaking."

"You're saying it's a miracle I was shot? A miracle I'm missing a chunk of my lung?"

"Sweetheart, it's a miracle because it would have been years before you had symptoms. And by then, it could have been too late."

Dr. Carter nodded emphatically. "You still have two functioning lungs, you should have little to no long term damage from your gunshot wound, and the odds of discovering an occurrence of Lamprecht's disease this early are otherwise astronomical."

Meg spoke gently in the silence that followed, "I think we should give her a minute."

"That's probably wise," Dr. Carter agreed. "You should rest, Ella. Would you like something to help you sleep?"

"No, I'd rather just close my eyes. I'll see you all later?" Ella asked beseechingly.

"Of course," Jayla promised. "We'll visit tomorrow."

Jack bent low to kiss her.

"You don't have to go," Ella whispered to him.

He brushed his thumb across her cheek. "I won't go far, but your doctor's right. You'd best get some sleep. You've been through a lot."

"Jack." Ella caught his hand as he stood. "I love you, too."

Before Jack could reply, Mitch said flatly, "We know. You said it at least four times a day in your sleep. The whole school is buzzing about it. Just wait till they hear about Jack."

His eyes lit up. Then he saw Ella's flaming cheeks.

"I mean... That is..." Mitch stuttered, tugging his hair. "Obviously, I wouldn't..."

Ella sighed. "Knock yourself out."

Jack squeezed her fingers and raised an eyebrow.

"What can I say?" She leaned back in bed, grinning at him. "I'm embracing gossip."

He beamed and planted a kiss on her temple. "That's my belle."

24. VISITING HOURS

Later that day, Meg entered Ella's hospital room quietly and solemnly.

"There's someone here to visit." A queer expression flitted over her face as she said hesitantly, "I wasn't sure if you'd want to talk to him. But I think so."

"Yes, please," Ella replied eagerly. Up until now, she hadn't seen or heard mention of Lucas. It was finally time. "Please let him come in."

Meg went softly from the room again. Ella shut her book and focused her breathing. She knew exactly what she wanted to say to Lucas, and she repeated the words over again in her mind so she would not lose them. Minutes ticked by on the clock on the wall before the door swung open.

At first, with her heart pounding wildly in her chest and her breath coming in shallow gasps, Ella thought her eyes must be playing tricks on her. In the doorway, where she'd expected to see Lucas's massive frame, stood a slender, middle-aged man. An almost imperceptible grey colored the hair at his temples, and a shadow of stubble darkened the leathery skin of his jaw.

He saw Ella and his eyes went wide. "Wow. I haven't seen you in person since you were a little chubby, round thing. Do you know who I am?"

If she hadn't recognized him before, his voice gave him away.

"You're famous, Uncle Billy. Of course I recognize you."

His eyebrows shot up. "*Uncle* Billy?"

"That's what Dad always called you," Ella murmured, her cheeks suddenly warm. "Should I not?"

"No, it's fine. Uncle Billy has a nice ring to it. I'm just surprised your dad would call me that." Bill shook his head with a jerk of nervous energy. "I'm honestly surprised Axel ever mentioned me."

"My dad talked about the band all the time, and you most of all," Ella replied, straightening the hem of her crisp white sheet.

Bill's eyes flashed and his voice grew hard. "And what did he say?"

Ella met his eye. "He said you were his best friend."

The hostility drained from Bill's face.

"You have no idea what it means to hear you say that," he said with a sigh, and uncrossed his arms in a swift movement. "After your dad left the band, we never really reconciled."

As he spoke, Ella watched him tap a hand against his leg, realizing she'd seen the motion somewhere before. His wide stance, his constantly fidgeting fingers, his expressive voice were like a shadow of her father. Although years and death had separated the two men, Ella could still see a trace of their old friendship.

"It's funny how you can go for years without talking to someone and still think about them every day. I know Wicked Youth has been going all this time, but it's never been the same without him."

"I know what you mean," Ella whispered. It was almost painful to hear the familiar tones of Billy's voice unmingled with her father's.

"Your dad was a great man. You know that, right? Some people have that spark and some don't. Your dad had it and then some. It was an honor to perform next to him." Bill squinted intently at Ella. "I suppose you're wondering why I'm here."

Ella twisted the admittance band on her wrist and replied, "I'm guessing it's because you got a note in the mail."

Bill went white. "How —?"

"You should probably know I didn't send that demo," Ella went on hurriedly. "It was a misunderstanding. It's my friend Lucas's band and they're not a band anymore."

The color returned to Bill's cheeks. "I *did* get that demo, but that's not really why I came."

Bill crossed the room, pulling a chair to her bedside.

"About nine years ago, Axel wrote to me and asked if I'd consider a reunion tour. All the original guys, me and Troy and Blaze, back together for a final summer tour."

Bill frowned and rubbed his stubbled chin.

"He never mentioned the cancer. I suppose he didn't want my pity. Didn't want me to feel obligated. I wrote a letter back to him, but for some reason I couldn't put it in the mail."

He glanced at Ella with a wry face and said, "We sent letters by mail back in those days, kiddo."

"You're not that old, Uncle Billy."

Bill's smile slowly faded as he picked at the thin padding on his chair.

"My letter was still sitting on my desk when your dad died five months later. I never got to say goodbye. The stupid part is, I agreed to the reunion tour. I've always regretted not sending that letter and having the opportunity to sing with your dad again. Not a day goes by that I don't regret it. When I heard about your accident, and saw your picture on the news..." He studied Ella's face. "You look so much like him. Same smile. Same intense eyes. It was almost like losing Axel all over again. I just...I just couldn't make the same stupid mistake again."

He paused and Ella heard the squeaky wheel of a stretcher or food cart pass in the hallway outside her room.

"You know, I've been thinking about that demo. The guitar was a little rough, but the vocals were top notch."

Ella nodded in agreement. "Lucas has an incredible voice."

"Your friend is good, but I'm talking about you, Ella. I haven't heard anything like that in twenty years. You looked like you were having fun up there, too. Do you like singing?"

"I do," Ella answered quietly. It *had* been fun – that last perfect night onstage with Lucas before everything went wrong.

Bill pressed his hands together tightly, suddenly still, and said, "I've got a proposition for you."

"Okay?"

Bill shifted in his chair, and the metal legs scraped the floor. "This might sound unusual, but would you consider taking your dad's place for a reunion tour?"

"What?" Ella hiccupped. "You mean me? Sing for Wicked Youth?"

"Exactly." Bill edged closer. "What do you think?"

"I...I don't know..." Ella faltered. "I don't know what to say. It's very...sudden."

Impractical. Crazy.

"I know it's out of the blue. We'd obviously wait until you're feeling up to it. There'd be a number of details to sort out."

Ella narrowed her eyes. "Is this some kind of publicity thing?"

He gave a hard shake of the head. "Absolutely not. This isn't about the money. It's just something I have to do. We can even make it free if you don't want to charge for tickets. And I'll let you pick the songs and cities."

Ella lifted an eyebrow. "What if I pick hymns?"

He paused and repeated, "I'll let you pick the songs and cities."

Ella still looked skeptical. "I'm not sure what my mom would say. I mean...it's Wicked Youth. You have a bit of a reputation."

"I'll talk to Kate. I'm sure I can put some of her worries to rest. We're pretty tame compared to what she might remember. Blaze and Troy both have families of their own, and I gave up that life a long time ago. If it makes her nervous, she could come along. Your whole family could come along."

Ella's breath caught in her chest. A cross-country road trip with Mom and Mal. Singing Dad's songs, *any* of Dad's songs. Maybe this was heaven, after all.

Bill noticed her hesitation.

"You just let me worry about your mom. I'm having dinner with her and your aunt tonight."

269

Her eyes gleamed savagely as she said, "Don't tell me Aunt Meg's making you a home cooked meal while I'm stuck here picking at hospital food."

No doubt her dinner would consist of bland chicken, mashed potatoes, a dry bun and lime gelatin...if she was lucky.

"Megs can cook?"

Megs, Ella thought with a secret pleasure.

"My Aunt Meg? She's the best cook I know."

"Impossible." Bill tapped a finger on the arm of his chair. "When I saw her, I couldn't believe it. Almost twenty years and she hadn't changed at all. I guess she has."

"I have a hard time picturing an Aunt Meg who isn't a culinary genius," Ella admitted.

"She's that good, huh? Tell you what, why don't we move dinner here? That way you can help me convince Kate."

Bill pushed himself out of his chair, and extended a hand to Ella.

"Okay." She shook his hand. "But it will take a miracle to convince my mom. And I hear I've already had one of those."

"What's one more?" Bill grinned.

Ella wondered how many concerts had sold out on the merits of that grin. Maybe it wasn't such an impossible plan after all.

"Sorry to invade you, sweetheart," Ella's mom said hurriedly, with a kiss on her forehead. "It was supposed to be a quiet dinner. I'm not quite sure how it turned into this."

"Invade away."

Ella beamed at the figures crowded into her room, paper plates precariously balanced on their laps. Her eyes fell on Meg and Bill huddled together on the bench under the window.

"Did Uncle Billy tell you his idea, Mom?"

"We'll talk about that later, sweetheart."

"But it's an interesting idea, right, Mom? Wouldn't it have made Dad happy, to share God with so many people through his music? Especially people not being reached by churches," Ella coaxed.

"I imagine it would," her mother murmured. "I'll think about it."

Ella was thankful it wasn't a flat 'no'. Her mother stepped to the bedside table to dish up another serving of lasagna.

Jack, seated at her knee, whispered, "I can hardly believe you're fixin' to become a rock star yourself, darlin'."

"I have to do something this summer to keep myself occupied while you're running the business world." Ella slipped her hand into his. "You don't mind, do you?"

"Not so long as you don't take up with a handsome groupie on the road," Jack replied with a wink. "I reckon it was only a matter of time before you were on an album cover. Still, I'd be right nervous singin' in front of heaps of people every week."

"What do you know about being nervous?"

His mouth twisted into a crooked grin. "I was plenty nervous when I asked you out, and when I kissed you for the first time after that awful date."

Jack fit his lips to hers. For a moment, all she could feel was his warmth against her and the accompanying glow at her core.

Ella heard a creak at the door and opened her eyes.

"Hi, dolly. Can I come in?"

"Mr. Sherman," Ella cried. "It's so good to see you! Is Lucas..." Her voice died away. "Is Lucas with you?"

Slowly, Mr. Sherman shook his head and the room fell uncomfortably still.

"I'm ready to see him, you know," she whispered with a glance around the room.

No one met her eye.

"Can he come here? Is he...in jail?"

"He's gone, Ella," Meg said gently.

Gone. The word seemed to hang in the air. He couldn't be gone. The earth would go silent if Lucas was dead, and it wasn't. There was the *bing* of an elevator reaching her floor. *He isn't gone.* A high-volumed radio or TV was audible from another room and, in the hallway, people spoke in low voices. *He can't be gone.* A phone rang somewhere.

Lucas couldn't be dead.

A drinking straw was pressed to her lips. Ella's mouth formed words but no sound came out.

Her dry tongue loosened and she managed, "He can't be! He can't be dead."

She fumbled for Jack's hand as a tear ran down her cheek. He reached to wipe it away.

"Not dead, Ella darlin', just gone."

"What?" Ella sat up sharply and winced.

"Lucas stayed with you to stop the bleeding but he ran when the paramedics arrived," Meg explained. "The police tracked him as far as New York, but they aren't sure what happened to him after that."

"But how?" Ella asked haltingly. "How could he just disappear? It doesn't make sense."

Meg sighed. "It was all so chaotic, Ella, and saving you was the main concern at the time. You didn't have your purse, so at first the paramedics and police didn't even know who you were, and only Jack knew you'd gone to see Lucas and taken his car."

Jack took her hand in both of his, running a finger over her palm. "I reckoned somethin' must have happened when you were nearly an hour late for the concert, but by the time I told your aunt and she reported you missin', you were already at the hospital."

"Lucas must have slipped away when he heard the sirens," Meg went on, "and taken Jack's car from the church parking lot. But it took some time to piece together the type of vehicle they should be looking for and who was driving it. The car was found in New York City but by then, he'd gotten a massive head start. They're still looking, but the police said the trail is pretty cold."

Jack's face darkened. "I've been tryin' to find him, Ella darlin'. Private detectives, the whole lot."

Ella shot him a look.

"I'm not fixin' to kill him, Ella. But I've a mind to deck him. Two wrongs don't make a right, but they sure do make it even, and I reckon one solid punch would do both of us a world of good."

"Get in line," Malcolm cut in.

Ella replied angrily, "You don't know him, Mal."

272

"You wouldn't like him much better if you did," murmured Jack.

"We thought –" Meg inserted, her voice soothing yet authoritative. Ella and the boys quieted. "We thought he should know you're alive. That's why we encouraged the publicity, why it's been on the news, and how Billy heard about you."

With a trembling hand, Ella reached for her cup of ice water. Jack handed it to her.

"Lucas was obviously in a rough place," he acknowledged. "And then if he reckoned he'd killed you.... I knew you'd be devastated if he...if he did anythin' stupid."

Ella's throat felt scratchy and her eyelids stiff. "So that's it? He's just gone? What if..."

What if he dies all alone somewhere? What if he never knows he's forgiven?

"What if I never see him again?" she asked softly.

"I'm sure we'll find him, sweetheart," her mother murmured reassuringly.

Bill spoke for the first time. "I don't know much about your situation. But I do know that friends have a way of making it back to each other."

"I'm not done searchin', Ella darlin'. I don't mean to give up."

She smiled into Jack's inky blue eyes through her own tear filled ones. Perhaps it was for the best if her mother didn't let her do the concert tour. She would miss Jack. *So much. Too much.*

Ella glanced at her mother but she was staring at Bill. It looked like she had made up her mind.

Ella was just finishing a seemingly unnecessary series of coughing techniques and deep-breathing exercises with her physical therapist to help facilitate lung re-expansion when her mother poked her head into Ella's hospital room.

"Ella, there's someone from school here to see you." She held the door ajar for a willowy blonde and excused herself, saying, "I'm just going to run down to the cafeteria for a cup of coffee."

With an effort, Ella straightened up in bed. "Hi, Olivia."

"Hi," she giggled nervously. "I didn't know if you'd remember me."

"Of course I do. How are you?"

273

"I'm fine. I came to see how *you* were doing," she laughed. "I hope we'll see you back at the Academy soon."

"I hope so, too," Ella sighed, pushing a hand through her hair. "I'm already behind and it will be hard to catch up if I'm stuck here much longer."

"You haven't missed that much in your classes, have you?"

"Not too much. My instructors have been coming by for private lessons the last few days and I have a couple of friends who've agreed to study with me as well. It's not so bad. But I'd rather be there than here."

Ella looked grudgingly around at her hospital room. Even with Jack's constant stream of flowers, it wasn't exactly cozy. Still, the sight of it no longer turned her stomach and she hardly noticed the antiseptic scent anymore.

"That's understandable," Olivia agreed in a silvery voice. "Hospitals always give me the creeps."

"Me, too."

They fell silent and Ella wiggled her toes under the blanket, trying to think of something to say.

"Well...it was good to see you," Ella said tentatively.

Olivia shifted on her feet as if turning to go. "Actually, there was something I wanted to tell you about. Some students at the Academy were teasing me again. You know," Olivia said and cringed, "the rhyme."

"I'm so sorry," Ella groaned sympathetically, searching for words. "That's just unbelievable. It's so immature."

"Oh, it's not like that!" Olivia cried. She stopped and shook her head. "I mean, it *is* immature, but that's not why I wanted to tell you. I was in the hallway after my first class yesterday when a couple of kids started."

Olivia twisted her hands together and Ella squirmed in indignation for her.

Olivia's eyes softened and she went on, "Usually everyone laughs and then they all join in. But yesterday, no one – I mean absolutely no one – laughed. That's never happened before. It was so eerie. Everyone just stood there, like they were waiting for lightning to strike or something. It was honestly kind of awkward," said Olivia, scrunching up her nose. "Just three little voices chanting in the hallway. And then there were two, and then one, and then there were none. So I just smiled at them and walked away to class."

Ella stared at her quietly, unsure what to say and unable to speak through the lump in her throat. It was a small victory, probably inconsequential to anyone beyond the two of them in the room, but it somehow felt like the first shifting of snow as an avalanche begins.

Looking intently at her feet, Olivia murmured, "I just wanted to thank you."

"Thank me for what?" Ella's forehead wrinkled. "I wasn't even there."

"I know." Her eyes flashed up to Ella's. "But it felt like you were."

There was a long pause before Olivia cleared her throat. "Anyway, I'm sure you have homework to do or you need some rest. Take care, Ella. I'll see you at the Academy."

"Soon," Ella called after her, as Olivia turned to leave. "I can't wait to get back."

Alone in the room, Ella's parting words echoed in her mind and it came as a shock to realize she'd spoken the truth. The Academy was changing, and there was nowhere else she'd rather be than there.

EPILOGUE

The June sun was beginning to dip in the sky as Ella ambled down the familiar path to the Academy. She'd walked the same quiet road hundreds of times in the past year, and could number every rut and crack in the sidewalk. But today was different.

A hum of activity floated in the humid air, and a line of tail lights stretched far into the distance. Cars inched by, searching for open parking spots on the already crowded street. A few beeped and waved, and Ella returned their wordless greetings with a smile.

Leaves shimmered overhead as she stopped at the high iron gate to look at the school in the hazy twilight. A shrill horn tooted behind her and Ella turned.

Mr. Sherman leaned his head out of the open pickup window and called in a trembling voice, "You're not going to be late for your own concert, are you, doll?"

"Don't worry," she replied, skipping over to stand at the driver side door. "I was nearly about to head up there, Mr. Sherman. I just wanted see the Academy again before tonight."

Ella glanced up the hill again. The long line of windows reflected the sunset colors, and she sighed.

"It's beautiful, isn't it?"

He nodded in agreement. "You sure you want to leave?"

"I'll be home soon," she assured him. "It's only a few months."

"I heard you're going to Juilliard in the fall."

"Yes, the Marcus Institute for Vocal Arts. But I'm driving home to Aunt Meg's as many weekends as I can manage."

"It'll be awful lonesome around here without you, dolly."

Mr. Sherman's eyes clouded and she felt her own fill with tears.

"I know," she whispered. "I miss him too."

She pressed a finger to the spot on her chest where a rugged scar lay beneath the carefully selected blouse.

"Losing Lucas was the most painful thing that happened that day," she said in the same low tone.

Mr. Sherman blinked and coughed softly. "I know you've had a hard time, but I'm awful glad you came to stay with your aunt when you did, Ellie. You don't know the change I saw in him –"

"No one could be gladder I came than me."

She reached through the window and pressed her hand over his on the steering wheel.

He swallowed hard and said shakily, "Well, now, I'll see you at the concert, doll."

"In the front row, I hope."

Mr. Sherman drove away, the old pickup rattling loudly, and Ella walked back to the iron gate. She leaned her forehead against the warm metal and closed her eyes.

Dear Lord, please be with Lucas and keep him safe.

Ella lifted glittering eyes to the ivy-covered main building and murmured the words etched above the towering double doors. *Suos Cultores Scientia Coronat.* Knowledge crowns those who seek her. Apt words.

It hadn't always been the perfect school she'd always imagined, but it had been worth it – *absolutely worth it* – in more ways than she'd ever dreamed. Closing her eyes once more, Ella whispered a quiet prayer of thanks for Jack, for each of the friends she'd made, and for the remarkable school that had brought them all together.

She heard the sound of footfalls close behind her and, like an answer to prayer, Jack was there. His dimpled grin met hers and suddenly she was in his arms.

"When did you get back?"

"Just now," he replied, holding her tightly. "I parked at your aunt's house, but your mother said you'd already left."

"I'm sorry," Ella apologized as, hand in hand, they followed the tinkling carnival music beyond the main building, onto the sprawling Academy grounds. "I couldn't wait any longer. I thought you might not make it in time."

"I hit some turbulence. But I'd miss my own funeral before I'd miss this."

Strangers and friends brushed against them while they made their way through the maze of rides and vendor's carts. Passing a ring toss booth and a flock of plastic ducks floating on a small pond, Jack led Ella toward the Ferris wheel in the distance.

As their carriage rose in the air, the clamor of the carnival dimmed. Ella bit into a mouthful of pink cotton candy, the stringy fluff melting on her tongue. Children shrieked and hollered in the bouncy castle and ball pit below and Ella hazarded a glance down. Her mouth went dry and she edged closer to Jack on the bench seat.

"You alright, darlin'? I can signal them to let us off if this is too much."

"I think I can face it with you next to me," Ella said with another hesitant look at the crowd beneath them. "There's a lot more people than I thought there'd be. You used to do this every year?"

"Not exactly. This is extraordinary, Ella darlin'. I don't know how you managed it."

The Ferris wheel lurched to a stop to exchange passengers in the car at the ground, setting their carriage swinging at the pinnacle of the rotation. Ella laced her fingers with Jack's tightly and took a few calming breaths, focusing on the feel of his strong hand in hers.

"I had a lot of help," she admitted. "Uncle Billy honestly set up the concert and I was amazed at all the students who pulled together to arrange the carnival. Courtney certainly won't be winning a peace prize any time soon, but Diana actually helped organize the food vendors."

The smell of corn dogs wafted up to them. A pirate ship ride swung back and forth through the air. Beside it, on the carousel, colorful horses spun round and round.

Ella smiled. "Don't you think it's funny?"

"What?" Jack pinched off a cloud of cotton candy.

"It's funny how a shooting could divide everyone in Whitfield the way it did, and another shooting could bring everyone back together."

Jack's lips twitched as if unsure whether to smile or frown. "Funny is not the word I would choose."

As he spoke, a thousand brightly colored bulbs burst into light, covering the carnival rides and Ferris wheel, setting the evening sky ablaze.

Ella looked up at his face, silhouetted against a brilliant orange light. "It's all because of you, you know. If you hadn't given me that song, Jack...if you hadn't urged me to go –"

"I will forever be sorry, Ella darlin'."

"I'm not blaming you. I'm trying to give you credit. If you hadn't urged me to go, I wouldn't have ended up in the hospital, and I doubt I would have ever reconnected with my Uncle Billy, who made this whole concert possible. And Lucas would probably be dead."

"We don't know he's not, darlin'," Jack said gently.

"*I* know he's not," Ella replied with a conviction that Jack thought best not to argue with. "Not only that, but if I hadn't gotten hurt and needed surgery, I would have been slowly dying right now." Ella paused. "Don't you see? You saved us both, Jack. In a way, I suppose I owe you my life."

"I'll settle for your heart."

He reached up and cupped her face with his hands. Ella felt the warmth of his fingers against her cheeks and the heat inside her when his lips touched hers.

Time seemed suspended as they hung swinging in the air, with a rainbow of lights glittering around them. His lips were still on hers when the wheel shuddered to life, propelling their carriage forward and down. As they sank toward the ground, Jack pulled something from his pocket.

"Here. You left this at your aunt's house." He pressed a folded paper into her hand. "In case you get nervous. I don't want you to forget the words. And Ella darlin', don't break a leg out there."

"I think the expression is –"

"I know," Jack interrupted. "Please, just don't."

On the ground, he bowed his head with hers and prayed, then kissed her for good luck.

Ella snaked her way past funhouse mirrors and around the bumper cars course to the performance stage. Bill was waiting backstage. He looked relaxed and refreshed, youthful in a black v-neck shirt, his dark hair rumpled and his chin rough with stubble.

"Sorry," Ella apologized sheepishly. "I got caught up."

"No sweat. Your dad liked to cut it close, too. Are you ready?" He grinned. "What am I saying? You're Axel's daughter. You were born ready."

The teeming audience shouted their love as the band took the stage. Whether it was adrenaline hitting her bloodstream or simply Bill's characteristic electricity rubbing off on her, she didn't know. But Ella felt aglow as she stepped out in front of the packed crowd.

Spotting a cluster of her friends and family near the foot of the platform, Ella smiled humbly and waved. The group danced and cheered with extra enthusiasm.

Ella laughed out loud as minutes passed and the applause only grew. Young and old screamed and jumped – an incandescent energy fusing them all together. Bill strummed casually on his guitar and the speakers swelled with the sound. Gradually, the din lessened.

Bill straddled the microphone stand and shouted, "Welcome to the Axel Parker Memorial tour!"

The crowd erupted again, and he lifted a hand.

"This beautiful young lady right here is Ella Parker, and she's got a voice like you wouldn't believe."

Ella grinned nervously as Bill tilted the microphone toward her. But she couldn't seem to raise her arm to reach for it.

Dear God, what was I thinking?

They had practiced and practiced, perfecting songs she'd already known by heart as a child. She was ready. But nothing had prepared her for the mob of people staring expectantly at her. She could hear her heartbeat thumping loudly in her ears.

Bill spotted the panic in her eyes and continued the introduction with a charismatic grin.

"We're so pumped to be kicking off this summer concert tour in Whitfield, surrounded by so many of Ella's amazing friends. Many of you already know, one hundred percent of the proceeds from our entire cross-country tour go directly to cancer research. But tonight, all of the funds raised from the carnival and concert will go toward refurbishing and reopening the Whitfield High School."

The audience roared in approval. Ella's stomach fluttered and she slipped a hand into her pocket to conceal its trembling. Inside, she felt the edge of a crumpled piece of paper, the lyrics dotted with tear stains and one corner marked with dry, brown blood. She folded her fingers around it and looked down at Jack. His dark blue eyes were warm and calm.

In that moment, she was relaxed. Ella stepped up to the microphone stand next to Bill and the crowd grew still.

"Hey, everyone."

A buzz of feedback crept into the speakers. She wet her lips. The air held the scent of fresh popcorn and hot mini donuts. Ella pulled in a deep, sweet breath.

"Tonight, in addition to performing a few of the more popular songs my dad wrote when he was with Wicked Youth, we'll also be singing some songs you might not be as familiar with. Songs written at the end of his life, the songs he loved best, the songs about God."

Ella saw her mother wipe both cheeks with a hand.

"But first," she went on, "I want to sing something written by a very talented, very dear friend of mine." Despite the tears that shone in her own eyes, her voice remained strong and clear. "I only hope he's out there listening. This one's called *Songbird.*"

Ella lifted the microphone from the stand, and sang.

Here's a sneak peek at

THE JOURNEY

the irresistible sequel to THE CROWD.

PROLOGUE

It was mid-afternoon when a car pulled up to the curb where a figure was sleeping. He lay half-reclined against the red, brick building, a guitar case cradled against his outstretched body and his black baseball cap pulled low over his face, leaving only a firm, square chin visible.

The driver side window edged down, filling the still, humid street with a blaring anthem from the radio as the driver shouted to a friend through an open window in the brick building. The figure on the sidewalk stirred, tugging at the shirt sleeve stretched across his muscular bicep in an almost anxious movement. He lifted the cap to run a rough hand through his shaggy hair and over his tanned face, muttering a curse when the brilliant sunlight met his eyes.

The word died on his lips as he heard a name on the radio. He straightened, straining to catch the exchange.

"...just tell me another artist that can do that."

"I think you're forgetting some of the greats that have come before her," a second announcer responded.

"No. No, I'm not saying she's better. All I mean is, she's unique. I said it when we had her in the studio with us last year to talk about their summer tour, and I'll say it again," the DJ continued. "Sweet little thing. Not at all what you might picture if you've only ever heard her sing."

"And if you haven't seen her perform live, there are still tickets available for the final three shows of the tour, but you'd better move fast."

"What I want to know," the first DJ cut in, "is when are we going to see an album from her?"

"Lots of rumors floating around, but the band hasn't confirmed anything. Until they do, we'll all have to be content with her single. Topping the charts for the second summer in a row...here's *Songbird*."

The listener's mouth twitched, neither in a smile or frown, but rather a twisted combination of the two as he sat motionless and waited for the familiar voice. Hearing it, he closed his eyes.

A group of young men emerged noisily from the building behind him, the tallest stumbling over the other boy's outstretched legs and half-turning to swing a motorcycle helmet in his direction.

"Sorry," the boy murmured, pulling his legs to his chest.

His penetrating brown eyes followed the laughing group as the car and two motorcycles pulled away from the curb and disappeared into the distance, leaving the song hanging in the air, unfinished.

1. SYMPTOMS

Pulling wide the set of heavy drapes, Ella Parker slid her window open a crack. Sounds from the road construction below drifted up to her hotel room on the eleventh floor, but the fresh breeze was worth it.

Get ready, she ordered herself, but remained where she was, leaning her forehead against the windowpane, warm with sunshine. She closed her eyes. The height was unnerving but the sun felt so good – too good to move away.

Her phone chimed inside her pocket and she brought it to her ear without looking.

"Hello?" she mumbled through a yawn.

"Hey darlin'."

Ella straightened. Even just the sound of Jackson Montgomery's voice – his rumbling drawl accentuated over the phone – made her heart skip a beat.

"I didn't think you'd call this afternoon," Ella said, rubbing her bleary eyes. "I thought you had classes?"

"Well, I wanted to wish you luck before tonight. Are y'all still at the hotel or are you practicin' already?"

"Hotel," she said as another yawn broke free.

Ella could hear the smile in his voice as Jack asked, "Am I borin' you, darlin'?"

"No, I was just waking up from a nap. I'm still in kind of a stupor."

He was suddenly all seriousness. "I hope I didn't wake you."

"No, I was up. I ought to be getting ready."

"Well, I won't keep you. I only wanted to wish you luck."

"Thanks." Ella turned away from the window but remained in the beam of sunshine, still reluctant to get dressed for the concert. "Is there any chance you can make the last show next week?"

"I'm afraid not."

Ella groaned. "I wish I could see you."

"Trust me, darlin', I'm equally disappointed. There is nothin' more beautiful than your eyes when you sing for a crowd," Jack said, his voice warm, "excepting your eyes when you're lookin' at me."

Ella hiccupped.

Dear God, why did he have to say things like that?

It was like dating Wordsworth. And why did she always have to hiccup like an idiot? Jack knew she got hiccups when she was nervous and seemed to take some diabolical pleasure in causing them. It was beyond embarrassing.

Jack already knew she loved him. He didn't need to know how much, didn't need to have her admiration stroking his ego when he was already rich and powerful and handsome. Because the truth was she loved him too much. *Way too much.* It was frightening – as dangerous as an open wound or exposed nerve.

There was a light tap at the door and Ella's eyebrows creased together. What was the point of hanging a 'do not disturb' sign if people were just going to disturb you anyway? At least they hadn't knocked when she was sleeping.

Then again, Ella thought as she stalked to the door – her bare feet shuffling against the carpet – *perhaps a wake-up call would have been a good thing.* She really *was* going to be late…

Balancing the phone between her ear and shoulder, she asked, "Jack, can you hold on a minute?"

She opened the door and stared stupidly at the tall, lean young man for a few seconds longer than was necessary to take him in, but felt like she must still be dreaming.

"You are a sight for sore eyes, darlin'," he sighed. "Pretty enough to make a hound dog smile."

Before Ella could speak, Jack slipped his arm around her waist and tugged her against his chest. His lips covered hers in a firm kiss that left her mind fuzzy.

She was supposed to be doing something. *What was it again?* she wondered as her phone dropped to the floor.

"What are you doing here?" Ella breathed as Jack bent to retrieve it. "What about classes?"

He ran long fingers over his unruly hair as he stood, leaving it nearly as untidy as her own after tossing and turning in the bed all afternoon.

"I was in the shower this mornin'," Jack drawled, "and I decided I couldn't wait to see you."

Ella smirked at him mischievously. "How often do you think about me in the shower?"

He closed his eyes and pressed a hand to his reddening face. "It wasn't like that."

"I know." Ella tugged his hand down, wrapping her own around it. "You're just so cute when you're embarrassed. It doesn't happen often, so I have to savor it."

Jack's dimpled grin widened and under a pair of heavy eyebrows, his dark blue eyes sparkled. "You should know I think about you all the time. I fall asleep thinkin' about you."

Ella hiccupped. It was her turn to blush.

"I'm glad you're here," she whispered, pulling him into the room. "How long can you stay?"

"Only a few hours," he replied, sitting at the end of the bed, with a light bounce as if to test its softness. "I have to fly to New York tonight and back to Harvard tomorrow afternoon."

Ella shook her head as she sat next to him. "You're spreading yourself too thin. Running a company —"

"I'm only involved in high level decisions at this point," Jack interjected.

"— and summer courses at the same time."

Reaching around her, Jack gathered Ella gently onto his lap. She rested her head on his shoulder.

"Gardens aren't made by sittin' in the shade, darlin'," he mumbled, burying his fingers in her hair.

"But all work and no play makes Jack a dull boy," she replied, looking up at him.

A slow smile curved his lips. "So you reckon...I'm...a...*dull*...boy?" Jack asked, punctuating his words with kisses. Ella's breath hitched as his mouth brushed her cheek, her brow, her nose, her jaw and found their way back to her lips.

"No," she managed feebly after the overwhelming flood of affection. If she wasn't so late, Ella would have been tempted to keep kissing him.

Too tempted.

She swallowed and slid off his lap to sit beside him, sinking into the plush bedding.

Jack looked over at her almost apologetically. The intensity with which he focused on her eyes gave her the distinct impression he very much wanted to focus on the rest of her body, but his controlled gaze never fell below her face.

"No," she said again, slightly more coherently, lacing her fingers with his, "but I've missed you."

"You survived without me last summer."

"Barely," Ella replied, fighting desperately to suppress the flutter in her chest, "and you weren't taking nearly as many classes then. It's been lonelier this summer...and I blame you for Mal missing the tour."

Jack started to protest.

"I know it's a good internship for him," she admitted, "but it's not the same without him, especially with my mom deep in this Department of Education scandal."

"Is it all true?"

Ella shrugged. "You know my mom. She's pretty tight lipped until a story officially breaks. But I think so. She wouldn't be plowing through mounds of government documents if there wasn't —"

A hard, rhythmic rap interrupted her. Ella raised herself from the bed and opened the door to a thin man in the hallway.

She started and said quietly, "Oh. Hi, Peter."

"Hey, I got your message. I imagine you're getting ready, but I wanted to check in."

"Yeah, I'm running pretty late..." Ella dropped her voice and subtly shifted to block Jack's view beyond the door frame. "Do you mind if I catch up with you later? After the show, maybe?"

"Sure. Just stop by."

Ella shut the door gently and crossed back to the bed, but didn't sit. She could feel Jack looking at her but didn't make eye contact. Instead, she reached for her empty suitcase and dropped it on the bed. With shaking fingers, she struggled to draw the zipper past a snag, opening it with a quick jerk.

"Who was that? I don't mind steppin' out if you need to talk to someone."

"That was just Peter. Our...medic," she said hesitantly. "I can talk to him later."

"Your medic? You'd best talk to him directly, darlin', if you're feelin' under the weather. I'll run after him, if you'd like."

"No, I only had a question for him." Ella shook her head nonchalantly. "Not anything important. It can wait."

"What manner of question, darlin'?" Jack pressed.

Ella, avoiding his eyes, slid a stack of roughly folded clothing into her suitcase. "I just wanted to know if he could recommend a vitamin or some kind of supplement I could take. It's not a big deal."

With a creased brow, Jack opened his mouth to speak, but Ella cut him off.

"Speaking of magic elixirs," she said, looking around hopefully, "did you bring some?"

"Sorry, Ella darlin', I'm afraid I can't moonshine sweet tea every time I go home." Jack paused and Ella's face clouded. "But I did this time. I left it in my car."

She made a move towards the door but Jack grabbed her hand, pulling her back to the bed, beside him.

"Why are you askin' about vitamins? What's wrong?"

"It's nothing, really. I've just felt a little tired since we started the tour and..." Ella trailed off, wishing she hadn't tacked on that final conjunction.

Jack seized on the word. "And what?"

"It's nothing. It's just...I've been dizzy a couple times this past month. I had trouble catching my breath." With a small cough, Ella rose abruptly from the bed again and began recovering her books and various odds and ends from the large bureau across the room. "I'm sure it's nothing. I read online it could be low iron, or low blood sugar."

"Dizzy?" Jack drawled the word slowly. "What did Dr. Carter have to say? Have you seen him?"

"No." Ella scoffed under her breath, hastily stuffing the items in her suitcase. "Of course not. We're on the road."

He gave her a black look. "Excuses are like backsides, darlin', everybody's got one. And that's not much of one."

"Are you talking about my reason or my backside?" She grinned flirtatiously as she bent to check under the bed for any lost items.

"Darlin', the view from here is exquisite and you know it. Don't change the subject," Jack replied. His inky blue eyes remained uncharacteristically serious and Ella rolled hers at him.

"I'm not going to bother a specialist over something so small. Dr. Carter is busy. I was going to talk to Peter first."

Jack stood, frowning. "I'm surprised at your Uncle Billy. I would have thought he'd postpone the show if you're not feelin' well."

Ella shrugged, and Jack crossed his arms in front of his chest.

"I may have been born at night, but not last night, darlin'. Billy doesn't know, does he?" Jack asked, his voice dangerously casual. "Your mother?"

She remained silent but her cheeks went pink.

"Have you told anyone? When were you fixin' to tell me?"

"There's nothing to tell, Jack," Ella replied flippantly. "I got lightheaded the last time I sang and I've been a little short of breath. It's probably the blood sugar thing or I caught a bug. My nose is a little stuffy. I'm sure it's nothing."

"That's *not* nothin', Ella. You know it's not nothin'."

"Don't worry about me. I thought most problems were," she said, smiling triumphantly as she mimicked his accent, "no bigger than the little end of nothin' whittled down to a fine point."

"That only applies to needless worry. I'm *allowed* to worry about your health."

Ella tried to keep her voice light but felt alarmingly close to crying. "This is why I didn't want to tell anyone. I knew you'd get all worked up. Besides, my last scan was only six months ago and I had another report of NED –"

"Y'know that only means there was no *evidence* of disease. Dr. Carter was right clear that even if you're considered to be in complete remission, you may still have cancer cells in your body. And he specifically said to contact him if you had any shortness of breath. Those were his exact words."

"It's been over a year, Jack. I'm fine. It's just a cold, honestly."

It wasn't a persuasive argument and she knew it. Jack was always so confident and sure of himself. In the face of his certainty, hers was slipping.

She stood on her toes and stretched to kiss his lips. "Do you know how much I love you?"

Jack glowered but gave her a light kiss.

"How much?" he replied reluctantly, unable to resist. The exchange had never altered, from the first occurrence over a year ago.

"I love you all the way," Ella said. She drew herself up to her highest possible stature, and raised a hand to her forehead as if in a salute. "I love you up to here."

"Well, I also love you all the way." Jack gestured to his forehead – without stretching, a good nine inches taller than Ella's. "So I'll always love you more… and you're going to call Dr. Carter."

"I will," Ella promised, "but not now."

She glanced at the clock next to the bed.

"I'm going to be so late."

The bathroom tile was frigid against her bare feet but Ella paused to examine herself in the mirror. When Jack was with her, she felt beautiful, irresistible. But, alone with her reflection, Ella wondered what it was he saw in her.

The girl she saw was thin – thinner perhaps than the last time she'd stopped to really study her likeness – and pale, too. *Paler*, she thought. The only color on her white skin came from a spattering of freckles across her cheeks. Her dark hair was plain and stick-straight.

Ella knew Jack admired her eyes and she was beginning to take pride in them as well. There were times, in candid photos with Jack or videos of her singing onstage, when her eyes looked impossibly green, just like her father's. But they looked grey now, staring back at her, dull and lifeless. She looked... She hated to admit it, but she looked...sick.

She spun away from the mirror. Stripping quickly, Ella tossed the messy lump of clothes on the floor beneath where her concert outfit hung. She turned on the shower, tested the water with her hand, and adjusted the cold water tap. It was still hot – probably too hot – but she jumped in anyway.

Definitely too hot, she realized, plastering her body against the cold tile wall of the shower. She gritted her teeth and stepped back under the burning stream. The fiery pinpricks hitting her skin made it easier to ignore the hollow sensation in her chest.

Gradually, her skin grew accustomed to the searing heat though her jaw remained rigid. She had to find a way around calling Dr. Carter. But Jack would make certain she did.

Dear Lord, why did he have to come?

The impulsive prayer made the empty feeling inside her sharpen and twist. She had been anxious to see Jack for two and a half weeks. Now he was here and Ella wished he wasn't.

Lather slid down her back and sides, and she scowled. *Why couldn't he just let it go? Why did he have to start an argument over nothing?* The answer echoed back in her mind.

Because he loved her. Because he was right. Because it wasn't nothing.

Ella pushed the thought away, rinsing off hastily and wrapping a fluffy, white towel around herself.

She scrubbed her skin with unnecessary vigor until it glowed pink and dried her hair, hoping the rush of the blow dryer in her ears would drown out the unwelcome thoughts that kept resurfacing. If it wasn't nothing, that meant it was terminal cancer. And if she had terminal cancer, she didn't want to know.

"You're late, kiddo," Bill called from the waiting car, his tone rising and falling in a sing-song voice.

"Sorry, Uncle Billy," Ella mumbled, jogging to the passenger door. Her ankle turned underneath her and she slowed. The concert would really be delayed if she had to go back to her room because she broke a heel. Or an ankle.

Besides, Jack was waiting upstairs and she needed time to think before she spoke to him again.

"No big deal." Bill drummed his fingers along the steering wheel. "Jack called earlier to get your room number. I figured you might get caught up."

Ella buckled herself in, and replied, "He's here, but he'll come later."

"You didn't want to ride with him?"

She shook her head.

Bill glanced at her out of the corner of his eye, rubbing his rough chin. "You lovebirds aren't fighting, are you?"

"No," Ella replied, more sharply than she'd intended.

He raised both hands momentarily. "Sorry I asked."

"We're not fighting." Her voice was calmer but her knee bounced up and down, up and down, as if of its own volition. "It's just...why does he have to be so...so...*apprehensive* about my health? He wants me to call Dr. Carter about the stupidest little thing. It just seems so...*controlling* and..." Ella waved her hand, compelling her mind to summon the right description.

"Protective? Caring? Either of those the word you're looking for?" Bill said wryly.

"No." Ella scowled.

"Too bad all the good ones are taken. You know, all the inattentive, unconcerned guys who don't really care whether you live or die. We should try to find you one of them."

The car stopped at a red light, but Bill kept his gleaming eyes on the windshield. Ella glared at him anyway. How was it possible all the people she loved could be so aggravating?

"There's such a thing as *over*protective. It's annoying. He's worrying about the past just when I feel like things are finally getting back to normal."

"As normal as a rock star dating a multibillionaire can be."

"Well," Ella said with a shrug, "normal for our family, I guess."

She looked over to see Bill's eyes creased in the same smile he always got when Ella grouped him with her family.

He *was* family, she thought. Or would be any day now. Examining her own ring finger unconsciously, Ella's mind slipped wistfully to Aunt Meg. This time of day, she'd be sitting on the front porch of her beautiful, little house in Whitfield, Vermont – the only place that had actually felt like home to Ella since her father died – with knitting needles flying in her hands.

Ella believed Meg was waiting for the proposal more patiently than any of the rest of them, especially after waiting two decades for them to reconcile. Maybe Aunt Meg and Uncle Billy were waiting for things to settle down...if that would ever happen now that Meg's shoestring operation had taken off.

It was hard to say whether Ella was featured more often in the media due to her promising musical career or her association with the young head of Montgomery Enterprises. But one thing was certain. The world had taken notice of Ella's unique knitwear. Metal heads and punk rockers alike were sporting chunky scarves similar to the one Ella wore onstage during chilly evening concerts, fashionable young businesswomen adored her professional and feminine cable-knit boot cuffs, and chic college students in Ella's classes at Juilliard and around the country were wearing dainty, fingerless gloves.

What for many years had been inventory on the shelves of Whitfield's countless antique stores or an occasional online order was growing into a thriving business. So much so that even in these warm summer months, Meg was working tirelessly to fill the orders that kept flooding in. The thought alone made Ella feel tired.

She sighed, and suddenly realized that the car had stopped moving. Glancing up from her hands, Ella found that they had parked and Bill was looking at her through squinted eyes.

"What did Jack want you to call Dr. Carter about?"

"Nothing." Her mouth went dry and she swallowed. "I'm just getting a cold. It's nothing."

He eyed her narrowly and she looked away.

"Jack may be right."

"I'm fine," Ella insisted.

"You've got to take care of those lungs, kiddo. Call Dr. Carter after, okay?"

As she finished her vocal warm-up backstage, Ella's legs wobbled and she leaned against the wall.

I really have to be more careful. I must have twisted my ankle harder than I thought in that run to the car.

High heels were the worst, but their fashion consultant would probably quit if Ella went on stage barefoot. Still, she considered it.

Ella pushed her palms down the front of her pants, but her legs still felt weak and her hands still felt clammy. So did the skin on the back of her neck. She blew out a shallow breath.

I am relaxed.

Ella hiccupped.

When was the last time I had to say that?

Weeks, maybe? Months? How strange to feel this anxious now, after performing so often. But the cold sweat and tight sensation in her chest were unmistakable.

Ella frowned. Jack and Uncle Billy's ridiculous unease must have crept into her head. As if conjured by her thought, Ella turned to see Bill staring at her, his mouth drawn in a narrow line.

"You sure you're feeling up to this? You really do seem like you're coming down with something."

She rolled her eyes. How nice to know she looked like death right before she stepped onstage.

"I'm fine, Uncle Billy."

Even if it had been a convincing lie, she knew Bill would have seen through it. His lips pressed more firmly together.

"It's just…" Ella paused.

She wasn't going to let Uncle Billy worry, even if she didn't feel like herself. It was bad enough having Jack worry about her. But Bill, though reformed, was a practiced liar – his early life in the public eye had sharpened the skill – and he would recognize a lie.

"It's just the song," Ella said, dropping her face. "*Songbird* breaks my heart every time I sing it, no matter how many times I have."

It was honest enough to have the ring of truth, and when Ella glanced up, Bill's gaze had softened.

"He'll hear it, Ella. You'll see Lucas again."

Although she'd only said it to put Bill off, all at once Ella found it impossible to breathe. Lucas had been gone so long. Her name had been in the newspaper, her face on television, her voice on the radio so many times in the last year that he had to know she was alive – that is, if he was still alive himself. The police hadn't been able to trace where he'd ended up and if Lucas was desperate enough to commit suicide before she'd walked in on him with a gun, there was no knowing what he might do after he accidentally shot her.

There was no body, she reminded herself, clinging to that one small hope. If he had killed himself, they would have found his body. So he must be out there somewhere. But what kind of life could he be living?

Penniless, out on the street. Struggling to survive. All alone.

Her eyes smarted and she rubbed them hard. Bill reached for her, squeezing her shoulder in a one-armed hug, the stubble on his chin grazing her temple.

"He'll hear it, kiddo," he whispered again.

They stood for a long time in silence, his arm over her shoulder, before Bill asked gently, "Ready?"

Nodding weakly, Ella blinked away the tears.

The audience cheered as the band took the stage, Bill bounding onto the platform with his usual energy and Troy and Blaze following a few paces back. Ella stepped out behind the others and the applause peaked when she came into sight.

Her gaze shifted over the crowd until she saw Jack's face near the front row. Touching her fingertips to her forehead, she winked at him. He echoed her gesture with a silent salute of his own, but his eyes were serious. Uncle Billy may have been pacified but Jack would not be so easy.

He's not going to stop worrying until I call Dr. Carter.

Ella's stomach churned at the thought. It would mean tests. Scans and needle pricks. Scratchy hospital gowns and cold exam rooms and looming, beeping machines. All because of a lousy cold.

Her thoughts broke off as loud chords reverberated from the guitar. Ella blushed. She was supposed to be singing. She moved quickly to the microphone stand though her legs felt like jelly under her.

"I hope you'll all sing this one with me, if you know the words," she said, her own voice sounding unfamiliar in her ears.

A sheen of perspiration beaded on Ella's forehead as the guitar began again. She wiped it away with the back of her hand.

If only we were outside... There was something exhilarating about performing in a wide open space. Here, the concert hall felt tight, packed with bodies jumping and writhing in front of her.

She was warm. *Too warm.*

It must be the stage lights. They were brighter here. Certainly the brightest of any stop on the tour.

Almost blinding, she thought, squinting up at them.

But somehow in spite of the light, the room appeared to be fading into darkness. The faces before her blurred together. They were here to hear her sing, she remembered.

Ella blinked and bent her knees – it had helped last time – but the darkness grew, speckling her vision like raindrops on a window.

She *had* to sing. Ella pulled in a deep breath but nothing happened. There was no oxygen in the room. No oxygen in her lungs.

She opened her mouth and gulped for breath. None came. The floor seemed to sway beneath her and she extended an arm to steady herself but her hand met only open air.

Reeling, she fell from the platform into the crowd below as everything went black.

ABOUT THE AUTHOR

Alleece Balts is an American YA fiction author best known for her debut novel, *The Crowd*, the first in a trilogy she is currently penning. When she's not writing, you can find her studying the Bible, reading a novel with a strong heroine, or drinking (another) chia tea. Alleece lives in Minneapolis with her cheesehead husband, three sticky children, a spoiled cat, and a shamelessly flatulent dog. Visit her on the Web at www.alleecebalts.wordpress.com.

Made in the USA
Charleston, SC
09 November 2016